EILEEN FUMBLED AT THE ROPE THAT HELD HIS RIGHT WRIST...

"I can't untie this." She pulled out a dagger and sawed at the knots.

"Why are you doing this?" he asked. He watched as she concentrated on the rope. When she severed it, he freed his hand, and taking the knife from her, he cut through the bond on his left wrist.

"Hurry," she whispered, giving him his bag and pointing up the stairs. "Go!"

"Eileen, come with me," he said. "I cannot leave you here to face him alone."

"I cannot. I don't know who, or what, you are. I wish you well, but I cannot go with you. Now, please, go before we are discovered. Go! Adieu."

He leaned forward and slid his hand along her neck, pulling her mouth to meet his. It was a short kiss, but sweet nonetheless, his lips softer than she could have imagined, his touch gentle and somehow wistful. He lingered for a moment before pulling away from her, his fingers tracing where his lips had been.

"Not adieu, Eileen Ronley," he said. "I will see you again."

ALSO BY KATHLEEN GIVENS

The Legend

The Destiny

KATHLEEN GIVENS

WARNER BOOKS

An AOL Time Warner Company

WARNER BOOKS EDITION

Cover design by Diane Luger
Cover illustration by Steve Assel
Hand lettering by David Gatti

Warner Books, Inc.
1271 Avenue of the Americas
New York, NY 10020

Visit our Web site at www.twbookmark.com

An AOL Time Warner Company

Printed in the United States of America

First Printing: April 2003

10 9 8 7 6 5 4 3 2 1

This book is dedicated to

Russ, Patty and Mike, and Kerry, John and Gavin, who make my life rich with laughter and love

Acknowledgments

I'd like to thank Karen Kosztolnyik, for her enthusiasm and perfect suggestions; Beth de Guzman for her encouragement; and Maggie Crawford for inspiring this book. It was a pleasure to work with all of you.

I received invaluable information from The Clan MacKenzie Society in the Americas, especially from Stephen McKenzie, President and Lieutenant to Caberfeidh, and Alan McKenzie, the head of Clan MacKenzie of Canada, and am very grateful to both for their help.

For his precise editing, endless plotting sessions, and unflagging support, I thank Russ; and for critiquing and suggestions, thanks go to Patty Collins, Kerry Trevino, Cheryl Becker and Debra Holland. Thanks also go to my family; to my cousins, who have been staunch allies all my life; and to the gang at the office for filling in so often and never complaining.

One does not choose one's destiny;
one may only choose
whether to embrace it or resist it.

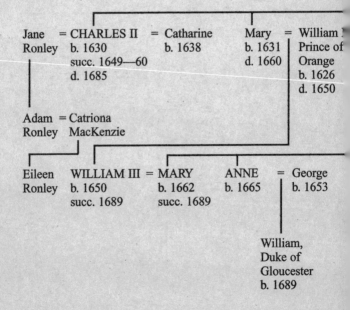

Jane = CHARLES II = Catharine   Mary = William
Ronley b. 1630   b. 1638   b. 1631   Prince of
        succ. 1649—60   d. 1660   Orange
        d. 1685   b. 1626
                                             d. 1650

Adam = Catriona
Ronley MacKenzie

Eileen   WILLIAM III = MARY   ANNE   = George
Ronley   b. 1650   b. 1662   b. 1665   b. 1653
         succ. 1689   succ. 1689

                                          William,
                                          Duke of
                                          Gloucester
                                          b. 1689

House of Stuart

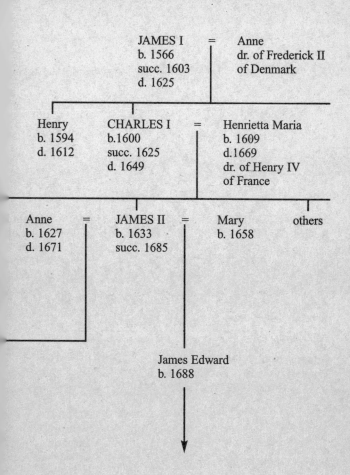

JAMES I
b. 1566
succ. 1603
d. 1625

= Anne
dr. of Frederick II
of Denmark

Henry
b. 1594
d. 1612

CHARLES I
b.1600
succ. 1625
d. 1649

= Henrietta Maria
b. 1609
d.1669
dr. of Henry IV
of France

Anne
b. 1627
d. 1671

= JAMES II
b. 1633
succ. 1685

= Mary
b. 1658

others

James Edward
b. 1688

Chapter One

December, 1691. Warwickshire, England

"Is he dead?"

They were just wee lads, the two who spoke over him, their voices hushed and excited as they discussed whether he was still alive.

Neil MacCurrie wasn't sure himself. He should open his eyes, should say something to the lads, get them to tell him on whose lands this small stone cottage in which he'd slept was. And in a moment, when he was sure his body still worked, he would.

He'd not frozen last night, which for a while had been a distinct possibility; nor had he been set upon on his way north from London, another good thing. But overall the trip had been a disaster from the moment his cousin Duncan had rowed him ashore on the coast of France.

It was supposed to have been a simple—and short—trip. He'd visit James Stuart, find out what, if anything, the deposed king planned, and head home. But nothing had gone as he'd hoped. Instead of staying for days, he'd been in France for weeks, waiting with myriad others for a five-minute conversation with the king. When at last it came, the conversation was as illuminating as it was cheerless. But it helped him decide what he would do next.

The first thing was to get home, a task that proved as elusive as securing the royal interview. The delays at court meant he missed the ship that he planned to take on his return, and instead had to take one heading for London, which meant he had to make his way overland, through an England that would not welcome him.

And now this, getting lost in a snowstorm. He should have stayed in Warwick yesterday when the storm hit, but he'd been watched too closely at the inn and thought it wise to head north. It seemed that no matter what he did, something unexpected changed his course, as though he were struggling against a force that was playing with him, challenging him to find a way out of the latest maze. It was not a feeling he enjoyed.

"I think he's dead," one of the boys whispered. "Touch him."

"No! You touch him!"

Neil opened his eyes. The boys scurried across the room and watched him with terrified expressions. Speak French, he reminded himself. The disguise was tedious, but necessary.

"Bonjour," he said.

The boys exchanged a look.

"Hello," he tried, careful of his accent. He was rewarded with a tempering of their fear. One of the boys swallowed, then echoed his greeting. Neil waved his hand to indicate the filthy cottage they were in. "Where . . . ?"

"Ronley Hall, sir," the boy said.

Neil smiled. He'd found it, despite the deep snows and the wild winds that had driven him to find shelter where he could. In good weather he would have reached Ronley Hall in two hours, but the blizzard had almost stopped his progress, leaving him facing a night outside. He had breathed a prayer of thanks when the cottage appeared through the waves of ice that pummeled him, then stumbled into the empty house and ate a hasty meal before rolling himself in his topcoat and letting sleep find him.

He began to relax. He'd been told in London that this house, between Warwick and Coventry, was safe, that Sir Adam Ronley welcomed those who shared his politics. His luck, it seemed, was turning at last.

"Sir Adam?"

The boys shared another look, then gestured for him to follow. They led him outside into the daylight, where he paused, taking a moment to look around. He'd spent the night in an old gatekeeper's cottage, at the edge of the manor house's property, only a few minutes from the main house. In the snowstorm he had not seen the new cottage built nearby, nor the small cluster of outbuildings, nor the long sweeping drive to the elegant country home. Sir Adam, it seemed, was a wealthy man.

The boys left him in the yard, where footmen greeted him with curious questions, but no hostility. Neil spoke French to them, or very broken English with a heavy accent, asking how far it was to Coventry. They didn't understand him, nor know what to do with him, that much was obvious. They watched with wide eyes and told each other that someone should fetch Milford, then led him into the hall, where he was shown a seat by the fire.

Milford would be here soon, said the girl who brought him a plate of steaming food. When he smiled at her, she darted away like a mouse. He ate the meal without haste, ignoring the curious glances thrown him by the bustling servants. Most likely this Milford was the factor or steward here, who would be sent to inspect the new arrival, then report to his overlord. Neil would be polite, but would speak to Sir Adam himself.

The wait was long, but he was content to stand before the huge fireplace in the comfortable hall, well furnished with the long table at which he'd eaten his meal, chairs before the fire and couches set below the glazed windows. There were pictures on the wall, a Chinese vase on a table. Adam had done well for himself.

Neil tossed his topcoat onto a nearby bench and opened his coat, thinking as he did that no matter how long he wore these French clothes, they still did not feel like his own. It wouldn't be much longer. For now, he was full, he was warm, and soon he'd be able to speak English again. His ruse had been successful thus far, and would be needed to get him home, but he was weary of it.

The man who joined him after more than an hour's wait was tall and fleshy, but fit, several years older than Neil, with dark hair still wet with snow. And a guarded expression. He stood in the doorway for a moment, then came into the hall followed by several armed men, who filed into a line along the wall. He stopped before Neil, looking into his eyes.

Neil nodded. "Monsieur."

Eileen Ronley looked up from her embroidery as Sim burst into the room, skidding to a stop in front of her. The scrawny boy was breathless, his face scrunched with worry, but since Sim had spent most of his ten years in that condition, she was not particularly alarmed. Still, his agitation was contagious and she gave him all her attention.

"You're wanted in the hall, miss," Sim gasped. "Milford said to tell you to hurry, he needs you at once."

Eileen sighed and looked over the boy's head. Milford always said to tell her to hurry. He thought of no one's needs but his own; everything must be done on his schedule. She knew what he wanted—she'd hurry to the hall, smile and sit while the latest of Milford's marriage prospects assessed her.

What would he see? A woman with thick blond hair that defied the pins she kept in it, whose freckles showed no matter how much she stayed out of the sun. This one wouldn't want her either, but at least she had the comfort of knowing it was not just her person that he would reject. A woman without connections or dowry was not welcome in the marriage market, especially one whose family had chosen the wrong side to back in the war between King James and King William.

As usual, Milford had not warned her, would not want her to take time to change her clothes or comb her hair. She sighed again, looking down at the gown she wore, one of her oldest. Black, despite the fact that she was now out of mourning. It had been two years—two long years—since her parents' deaths, but there had been no money for new clothes and she'd not had the luxury of putting it aside. It would have to do yet again.

"Hurry, miss, please." Sim shifted his weight, his brows furrowed.

She smiled to calm him. "Don't worry, Sim. Tell Milford I'll be there shortly."

The boy started away, but she called him back.

"What does this one look like?" she asked.

Sim's expression shifted from worry to confusion.

"Is there a man Milford wants me to meet?"

The boy nodded.

"Who is he?"

"I've never seen him before, miss."

"What does he look like?"

Sim shrugged. "Big. Fearsome, miss. Looks through you. Milford brought his guards with him."

"Splendid," she murmured. This, then, would be the one man with standards so low that he would agree to marry her.

When she entered the hall, Milford was sitting at the end of the long table, the stranger facing him with his back to her. Sim was right; the visitor was big. And heavily armed. A sword hung from his hip, a long dagger from his waist, two pistols were tucked into the sides of his belt.

In the past, when Milford was introducing her to a possible husband, he'd been falsely jovial, loudly welcoming, treating her as though she were a treasured relative that he would hate to lose. Now he gave her only the briefest of glances and grunted for her to join them. Milford's guards, standing behind him and near the fireplace, looked relieved to see her.

Eileen walked toward them and stood next to the stranger, but did not look at his face. What little she'd seen on her approach had been daunting. He wore no wig, his dark hair instead drawn back neatly and tied behind his neck. His clothes were fashionably cut. He wore a black fitted brocade coat that stretched across his wide shoulders and hugged a lean torso; a topcoat of fine black wool trimmed with braid lay on the bench next to him. His linen shirt was white, his gathered breeches buff, his neck cloth silk. Simple black leather gloves rested in his long fingers. A man of obvious means.

She looked down at her clothes, seeing the many places

she'd mended the muslin, the tear in her hem. He would think her a pauper.

"He's French," Milford said. "Or at least that's what he speaks."

The stranger rose to his feet and faced her. He was very tall; she stepped back as he bowed to her, then straightened to meet her gaze. He was extraordinarily handsome and somehow she knew he knew that. His eyes were deep blue, framed by dark lashes and straight brows, his cheeks dark with several days' growth of beard, his nose straight, his mouth wide. It was difficult to judge his age with that beard; he was perhaps in his thirties, but he might have been younger. He watched her study him, his eyes amused now.

"Mademoiselle," he said in French. "I hope I meet with your approval."

She felt her cheeks go scarlet. None of the men Milford had brought here had looked like this.

"You speak French, right?" Milford asked her.

"Yes," she said.

"Talk to him," Milford said. "Find out his name, where he's from."

She raised her eyebrows. "You don't know who he is?"

"Two boys found him asleep in the old cottage. How would I know who he is?" Milford frowned at her, then gave a low grunt. "I didn't bring him here to see if he'd marry you, Eileen, if that's what you thought. And tell him to sit down."

Eileen nodded and sat on the bench next to the stranger, smoothing her skirts, trying to think of French verbs and not the man before her.

"Talk to him," Milford said, crossing his arms over his chest.

She did, haltingly at first, pausing because the stranger watched her with an intensity that was difficult to ignore. She found the situation unnerving.

"Welcome to Ronley Hall, sir," she said. "You obviously speak French."

"Oui, mademoiselle."

"And some English?"

"Un petit peu."

"What is he saying?" Milford demanded.

"I welcomed him. He says he speaks French and a little English."

"We knew that! Ask who he is."

"Your name, sir?" she asked the stranger in French.

"Belmond, mademoiselle."

"Is that his name? Belmond?" Milford asked. "What's the rest of it? Where's he from?"

She asked Belmond.

"Jean-Paul, miss. Jean-Paul Belmond."

"You are French, sir?"

"Oui."

"From?"

Belmond smiled slowly, showing a dimple in his left cheek. She caught her breath, saw him note that, and felt a wave of annoyance. This man was very assured of himself.

"London, mademoiselle."

Milford moved impatiently. "London! He's from London? What is he, one of those Huguenots?"

"Oui, monsieur," Belmond said to Milford. "Huguenot."

"From London. Where in London?"

"Spitalfields," Belmond answered, then glanced at Eileen. "I do speak some English, mademoiselle."

She nodded. Spitalfields was full of Huguenots, religious

refugees who had fled Louis XIV's France after he'd re-
voked the Edict of Nantes and removed their freedom of
worship. They'd been welcomed as fellow Protestants, as
supporters of King William.

"You don't look like a weaver," Milford said, then turned
to Eileen. "Tell him."

Belmond smiled again when she translated. "Not all
Huguenots are weavers, nor tailors, nor clockmakers, mademoiselle. I am a soldier."

"A soldier," Milford said when she told him. "Where is
he going to be a soldier?"

"Scotland. To offer my services to King William's army."

"What did he say about King William?" Milford asked.
"Tell him I fought with William at Maastricht, that I stayed
with him all the way through the Battle of the Boyne."

Eileen didn't need to tell him. Something, quickly suppressed, flashed in Belmond's eyes before she had said the
words in French. Anger? Why would Milford's words make
a Huguenot angry?

"A fellow soldier," Belmond said to Milford in heavily
accented English.

Milford nodded with a smile. "You'll find that William is
a fair commander. Where will you join his army?"

"Wherever I can find it," Belmond answered through
Eileen.

"You'll be there a good long while. Those damned Scots
won't accept that they've lost the throne for good."

"I suspect that while James Stuart lives, the fear that he'll
try again to regain his crown will live as well."

Eileen translated, then watched the two men look at each
other with approval. "Two mercenaries," she said with distaste. "You sell your ability to kill."

Belmond shrugged. "A man must eat."

"You do not look like a man without resources."

"I am a younger son, mademoiselle, so I became a soldier."

"A younger son of a nobleman?"

"Of a merchant."

"A merchant. From Brittany."

Belmond nodded.

Milford leaned forward. "Where's he from in Brittany?"

"A small town that no one would know," Belmond said.

"What is the name of the town, sir?" Eileen asked.

"St.-Sebastian."

"Where is it?"

"West of St.-Malo, which probably means nothing to you, mademoiselle."

"On the contrary, sir, it means a great deal. Is your home between Dinard and St.-Malo or between Dinard and St.-Brieuc?"

His surprise was quickly hidden. "West of Dinard," he said cautiously.

Milford's tone was annoyed. "What did he say?" When she told him, he grunted. "West of Dinard, east of Dinard, who cares? It's still France."

She smiled tentatively at the Frenchman and was rewarded with a flash of a smile in return.

Milford growled. "Don't make friends with him, girl, just ask him questions. If you want him when we're finished with him, you can have him. Or he you, I should say. Maybe he'll even marry you." He smirked and glanced at his men.

Eileen took a deep breath, reminding herself that it would do her no good to speak sharply to the man who let her keep a roof over her head. "You will keep a civil tongue, Milford, or I will not do this for you," she said as mildly as she could.

Milford laughed, but his men exchanged glances and looked uncomfortable. She looked into Belmond's eyes again. And realized, with a shock, that he had understood everything they'd said.

"He treats you with little courtesy," Belmond said in French. "One should not talk to a serving girl like that, miss, and I suspect you are not a serving girl. None of them speak French?"

Eileen shook her head.

"How is it you do?"

"I was well educated."

"Do you have French blood as well?"

She smiled, thinking of her lineage. "A long way back. You understand quite a lot of English, sir."

"One cannot help but pick up some of the language when one lives here."

"Then why do you not speak to them?"

"I tried. They did not understand me. I do not have all the words I need."

"How long have you been in England?"

"Almost a year."

"In London?"

"For the most part."

"Do you miss your home?"

For the briefest of moments, he had a wistful expression. "Very much."

"Where is home, sir?"

His expression was guarded again. "London now. Originally Brittany."

She shook her head. "You are not from Brittany, Monsieur Belmond. You might not even be French, although your French is excellent. And I suspect you are not a merchant's son."

"You doubt me, mademoiselle?"

"Yes."

"I have told you the truth."

"I would wager that you have not."

"Would you?" He watched her for a moment. "Is Milford Sir Adam's son?"

"No. Milford bought the property after Sir Adam's death."

Milford sat up straight. "Sir Adam? Did he ask about Sir Adam?"

Eileen nodded.

"Ask him why."

Belmond answered her translation in French. "I was told that Sir Adam owned Ronley Hall."

"Ask him who told him that, to ask for Sir Adam?"

Belmond repeated his answer. Eileen told Milford, then bit her lip.

"Why is it wrong to ask about Sir Adam?" Belmond asked her.

"The last man to ask for him by name was a follower of William's enemy."

"You cannot even say his name?"

"The deposed king? It's not wise."

"I don't understand. It was a simple question, with no special significance."

"The former owner of this property drowned in the Thames the day after he denounced King William. That was two years ago. Since his death the only travelers who have asked for him have been sympathizers of the deposed king."

"What are you saying?" Milford asked.

Belmond put both hands on the table and leaned forward to Milford. "I go to King William's army," he said in English.

Milford nodded, but his expression was skeptical.

"Who are you, miss?" Belmond asked her. "Are you his kin?"

"No."

"Are you his . . . ?" He let his words fade, but she understood his meaning.

"I am nothing to him. He was generous enough not to turn me out when he easily could have. I do small things, nothing of any worth. I am simply one more burden. He is trying to find someone to marry me, but it is unlikely; I have no dowry and no one wants a penniless wife."

He smiled again. "I should think many men would want to marry you, mademoiselle. Your lack of dowry is not the impediment you think it."

"It is when your father denounced the king and then was murdered for his rashness."

"Sir Adam was your father?"

"Yes."

"And your mother? Is she here with you?"

"She died with him. She was from the country to the north, sir, not a healthy thing to be in England in these times."

"Your mother was from Scotland?"

"Yes. From the Highlands. A MacKenzie."

"MacKenzie. Your mother was a MacKenzie. What was her name?"

"Catriona MacKenzie."

Belmond stared at her. And she knew.

Milford rose to his feet. "I don't like this. What are you talking about?"

"What he'll find in Scotland," Eileen said, trying to sound calm.

"Savages is what he'll find. What else are you talking about?"

"I told him my mother was Scottish."

"At least your mother was wise enough to leave Scotland and spend her life here," Milford said. "Too bad she wasn't wise enough to marry someone other than a mouthy bastard."

Eileen closed her eyes for a moment, fighting her anger. She had no retort. Milford was right; her father had been a bastard, born on the wrong side of the blanket. And his unguarded words had killed him, killed them both.

Belmond looked down at his gloves and then back at her as he stood. "Please tell Milford that I am grateful for the meal, and for the few hours of sleep I had in the cottage, but that I will now be going while it's daylight. Please tell him, mademoiselle. And thank you for your assistance."

When she'd translated, Milford shook his head. "No, he won't be leaving. I know you think I'm stupid, Eileen, but I'm not." He turned to his men. "Take him to the cellars. Search him."

Belmond took a step away from the table, drawing his sword. "Monsieur," he said to Milford in English. "I go to King William's army."

"Not yet you don't." Milford gestured to his men.

Belmond took a step backward. Eileen moved to her right, thinking to get out of his way. He moved in the same direction and smashed into her, catching her before she could fall. That simple gesture, of his hand on her arm, gave

Milford's men the opening they needed. Eileen watched in horror as they fell upon him.

It was over very quickly. He fought well, defending himself rather than assaulting, backing several of them against the wall. But there were ten of them and they attacked him from all sides. When one knocked him to the floor, the rest swarmed over him, beating him until he no longer moved. And then they dragged him across the floor to the cellar stairs.

Chapter Two

James MacCurrie stepped to the edge of the battlements of Castle Currie and looked over Loch Torridon. He did not see the frozen Highland landscape, still covered in snow from the storm that had battered them the day before, nor the ships that huddled together in the icy waters of the harbor below.

Neil was in danger.

In the last two months his twin brother had sent many messages, of frustration, anger, resignation, impatience. But not fear, not pain. Until this morning. James did not turn when his wife Ellen slipped up next to him, but he put his arm around her and pulled her against him.

"Is it Neil?" she asked, her tone quiet.

He nodded grimly, then leaned to kiss the top of her head. He didn't have to explain to her; Ellen knew he and his twin had a means of communication that needed neither words nor proximity. They'd always been like that, even as wee lads, had been able to send strong emotions to each other, had known when the other was in danger. The ability had saved the MacCurrie brothers more than once.

When James had met Ellen and fallen in love, the bond between the twins had been tested; not weakened, but altered. Even two years of war together, most of it spent away from home, had not restored what they'd had as boys. Which, he supposed, was natural. They were grown men, not lads anymore. It was time that the old days were gone, but he was still growing accustomed to the changes that the last two years had brought.

Two years ago their father Alistair had been alive; James Stuart had been on the throne of England, Ireland, and Scotland. Neil had been his twin, not his laird. And neither Ellen nor his son had been in his life. James glanced over his shoulder, to the bench where his grandmother Mairi held three-month-old John Alistair MacCurrie, and pulled his wife closer. His first allegiance now was to Ellen, this woman he loved beyond reason, and next to their son. Then to his older brother. It was a new way of thinking.

His son waved a chubby fist and James smiled at him. They'd named the babe after Ellen's cousin, John Graham, and after James's father. He'd not used Alistair as his son's first name; he'd left that for Neil, the Earl of Torridon, chief of clan MacCurrie. It was only right that his brother's son should carry the name forward. If Neil ever had a son. If Neil came home.

"What is it?" Ellen asked.

"I'm no' sure," he said. "Some sort of danger, something he dinna expect. He's displeased with himself."

"That means he's alive."

James nodded. She was right; silence from his brother was the real worry, for it would mean that Neil was seriously injured. Or dead.

"This one was stronger than the others," he said. "Anger. Then a jolt, as though he recognized he was in danger."

"And since then?"

"Nothing."

"Can you tell where he is?"

"No." He frowned. "He should ha' been home a month ago."

"These trips to France have been very uneven, my love. Some have been very quick, some overlong."

"They're all overlong," he said. "I should ha' gone."

Ellen looked from James to their son.

James kissed her forehead, drawing her attention back to him. "But how could I leave ye again after so much time apart, with ye about to have my child? I would no' have gone. And Neil kent that."

"Neil has been very generous in letting you stay here for all these months."

"No' as generous as ye might think. With me here he kent he could go roaming and still have someone to watch over Torridon." He laughed. "There are advantages to being a twin. I think he's been enjoying the traveling."

"Even with the danger."

"Especially with the danger, lass." His expression sobered. "At least until now. Something's happened, Ellen. I dinna ken what, but it's no' good. And I canna even go to him. We've no' kent for certain where he was since Duncan dropped him on the French coast. He could be anywhere between here and there."

"So what will we do?"

He pulled her closer. "Wait. We'll wait. I'm sure to hear from him soon."

"And if not?"

"If not . . ." James stared out over the water. "I dinna ken. I guess Duncan and I will go to France."

Neil opened his eyes slowly. They'd done their work well, the bastards; he hurt all over. He lay on his back in the dark, on a cold floor. His wrists and ankles were bound, his boots and stockings gone. He could feel the stone against his shoulder blade, the dried blood on his lips and in his mouth. His teeth were all there. It was a start.

He groaned as he turned on his side, and cursed himself. This was his own fault. He'd been a damned fool. He'd given himself away, had stopped thinking when he'd looked into her eyes. She was beautiful, yes, but he'd met women more striking than Eileen Ronley. A few.

She was tall, slender with full breasts and a trim waist, and an intriguing way of carrying herself, proud but not haughty. Direct. Her hair was golden, lit with copper and ginger and russet, thick and shining, framing an oval face with even features. Her mouth was lovely, pink lips that smiled easily, showing even teeth. Her straight nose and smooth cheeks were sprinkled with freckles even in the dark of winter. In the summer, he was sure, her hair would lighten and her freckles increase; she would be even more appealing.

All very pleasing, but it was her eyes that had entranced him. Gray eyes, lighter in the middle, a dark circle around the edge, traces of blue and gold, and framed by long lashes. Intelligent eyes, which had not hidden her interest, nor her disbelief, nor her pleasure and embarrassment when he'd told her a lack of dowry would be no impediment for her. Eyes that had widened when he'd asked her mother's name, when she'd recognized that he understood what Milford said.

He was a damned fool, losing track of what he was doing. He'd all but told Milford, who was untutored but not simple, that he was lying, that he was not the Huguenot he pretended to be. The ruse, invented in London when he'd not found a ship to take him to Scotland and realized he'd have to make his way through England, had seemed perfect. What better disguise than to speak the French he knew, and to act the part of a warrior? If he'd tried to pass as a weaver, no one would have believed him. He looked like what he was—a man who had lived with an army, who had fought his share of battles and lived.

As Milford had. Milford had been at the same battles as he and Jamie and Duncan, but on the opposing side. They'd stood on the same soil, seen the same horrors. Milford probably still heard the sounds of battle in his dreams, as Neil did. Not a man fooled by fancy dress and a French accent. He might not know who his visitor was, but given enough time, he'd figure it out.

Neil cursed his luck, then reconsidered. It had not been luck, nor coincidence, that had led him here. The same man who supplied him with the French sword he carried and the clothes that only a Londoner would wear, had given him Sir Adam's name, assuring Neil that Ronley Hall was a safe house, and that he'd be welcomed there.

Two years. Sir Adam had been dead for two years, long enough by tenfold for the news to have reached London and his source. Neil felt his anger rise; he'd take care of the man, find out why he'd lied, and decide what to do about it. Eventually. First he had to get out of this dank cellar, had to escape Ronley Hall.

Had to leave Catriona MacKenzie's daughter behind.

Everyone in the Western Highlands knew the story of beautiful Catriona, who had gone to London with her parents, fallen in love, and married a handsome stranger. Her father, Phelan MacKenzie of Glen Mothin, had disowned her, forbidden her name to be mentioned, ignored his wife's and sons' pleas to forgive the girl they loved. In true Phelan fashion, he was enraged, not that she'd married an Englishman, but that she had defied him. He had refused to speak of her, had forbidden those around him to mention her name. When word came that Catriona had had two daughters and wanted to visit, he gave his men orders to turn them away should she be foolish enough to travel to Glen Mothin.

For several years she'd written letters that he'd burned unopened while his wife wept. Then the letters had stopped. Phelan never spoke of her, had not written Catriona, even when her mother died, but her older brothers had never forgotten her. They had talked about her among themselves, speculating as to how she was now, where she was. They told their children about the aunt they'd never met, about the cousins who lived somewhere in England. Two girls; no one had ever known their names.

Duncan's father was the youngest of Catriona's brothers. He'd been a quiet man, his gentle demeanor hiding the steel beneath. He'd often defied Phelan, had even gone to see Catriona once, taking his wife and Duncan with him; and had paid the price. Phelan, infuriated yet again, had never forgiven his son, nor his grandson. Duncan's father had only laughed.

Duncan's mother Isabel had been Neil's and Jamie's aunt, their mother's younger sister. Isabel and Anne MacKenzie had been close as girls, their husbands fond of each other. When Isabel had died in childbirth, Anne and Alistair had gone to Glen Mothin to comfort him. And when, just a few years later, Duncan's father had died as well, and Phelan had rejected the boy, Anne and Alistair brought Duncan home to Torridon, to live with Neil and Jamie, raising him as their own. It was Duncan who had told the twins Catriona's story.

Eileen Ronley was Duncan's cousin.

Neil could see the resemblance. Her hair was a lighter color, golden rather than his russet, but the thickness, the fall of it, was like Duncan's. His eyes were the same shape, not nearly as lovely, but the same shape. He'd met Duncan's cousin, Catriona's daughter. Neil's cousin's cousin. Wait until Duncan heard.

They'd not talked of Catriona for years, but Neil knew Duncan had never forgotten her. How strange life was, how strange to find Catriona's daughter in this English backwater, and for her to be as kind as she had been to a stranger. And yet not a stranger. There was a connection between them, as though they'd met before. She seemed to have felt it too, even though it defied all sense.

The door opened, banging against the wall, bringing Neil back to the present with a jolt. Four men were silhouetted in the opening, two with torches that they stuck into sconces on the wall. Milford stood near the door watching while his men hauled Neil upright, holding him between them; Neil steeled himself.

"You have one chance to tell me what your name really is," Milford said.

Neil shook his head. *"Je ne comprend pas."*

Milford took a step into the room, then gestured to someone behind him. Eileen Ronley came around the corner, her eyes wide and fearful.

Eileen paused at the door, not sure what to expect. In her father's time this room had been stocked with Ronley Hall's own produce, and foodstuffs from the continent. Eileen had once, when she was ten, had an apple-eating contest with a friend here. She'd won, but at a cost; she'd been sick for days. Her mother had smoothed back her hair from her forehead and teased her.

She pushed the memories away. Her mother was gone, along with the life they'd led in London. She was at Ronley Hall now, in this cold cellar, with a man who pretended to be French. The room was almost empty, the barrels and casks of food gone, in their place the furniture that had been her parents', piled high and covered, stored to make room for Milford's heavier pieces.

In the space between the stacked furniture and the wall, Belmond watched Milford without expression. His coat was gone, his shirt torn from his shoulder, hanging in tatters from his left side, and gaping open in the front, revealing dark hair on a well-muscled chest and stomach. His legs were bare below the knee, his breeches torn along one long thigh. His face was battered, one eye almost shut, his lips swollen and crusted with dried blood, bruises beginning to appear on his neck and shoulder. But he was alive and standing. And angry.

"Mademoiselle," Belmond said in French, his tone belligerent. "Ask Milford what has happened to the hospitality I was led to believe the English showed to travelers? Why is it that a man cannot cross his lands without being captured like a criminal? Tell him I have done nothing that warrants this treatment."

Eileen translated, watching Milford's expression harden as he walked to stand before Belmond, gesturing for her to join him.

"Tell him," Milford said, staring into Belmond's eyes,

"that when he acted like a criminal, I treated him as one. No one draws a sword in my hall."

"You prevented me from leaving," Belmond said directly to Milford.

"Tell him I don't believe his story. Ask him what his name is, his real name."

"Belmond."

"Tell him the truth, sir," Ellen said in French. "Please. He can be violent."

"So can I. A Huguenot soldier has many friends. If I am harmed, my friends will discover who did it. They will come for him."

Milford grunted. "Ask him what his name is."

"Belmond, Jean-Paul Belmond."

Eileen took a deep breath, knowing what was next. Milford held his hand before him and opened it, showing Belmond the ring he had been holding, the ring he had shown Eileen upstairs, saying he would beat the truth out of the stranger. It was a signet ring, bearing a family seal, a ring only a nobleman would own.

"Who are you?" Milford growled.

"Jean-Paul Belmond. Huguenot," Belmond said. "Of Spitalfields."

"Why do you have this ring?"

"I won it in a card game in London," Belmond said when Eileen translated.

Milford held the ring up before Belmond. "It's a clan ring. From Scotland."

"I won it in London."

"Why did you have it hidden in your boot?"

"To keep it from thieves. I was going to sell it in Scotland. There are not many Scots in London these days."

Milford sneered when Eileen translated. "No, they ran away. Like their king."

"Like the English at Killiecrankie," Belmond said in English.

Milford hit him, hard, across the mouth, smearing blood across Belmond's cheek. Eileen gasped. Belmond raised his chin and glared at Milford.

"Who are you?" Milford shouted. "Why do you have this ring? Why are you going to Scotland? Why did you stop at Ronley Hall?"

"I go to William's army."

Milford hit him again.

Belmond closed his eyes for a moment, then opened them, his fury now visible. "Tell him," he said to Eileen, "that it takes a special kind of courage to hit an unarmed man who is tied hand and foot. Tell him that I invite him to untie me and then try to hit me again."

Milford swore when she told him, but before he could move, Eileen stepped between him and Belmond.

"Why are you doing this?" she demanded. "What difference does it make that he has the ring? Let the man go on his way! It doesn't matter!"

Milford pushed her aside and stared into Belmond's eyes. "I don't know who he is."

"Why does it matter?"

"Has it not occurred to you, Eileen, that he might be a spy? That he might be a Jacobite, carrying messages to Scotland from France, from King James's court? That he might, even now, be planning to kill King William, to bring James Stuart and his kind back?" Milford turned to glare at her. "You were talking to him about Scotland, about your mother. What else did you two say?"

"If he's a spy," she said, "would he have asked for my father?"

"Perhaps he'd been told that your father opened his door to all Jacobites."

"My father has been dead for two years. Surely they know that much."

"Perhaps his information was faulty."

"My father's death was well known."

"Your father was a well-known bastard. That was his only fame."

"As opposed to you, Milford. You're an unknown bastard."

Milford raised a hand as though to strike her, then lowered his hand and strode away. "You have an hour to discover the truth from him, Eileen." He gestured for his men to follow him. "Lock her in here with him."

"Milford!"

"What? He won't talk to me. You smile and flirt with him, Eileen, like you did in the hall. Tell him why your father is dead, tell him about your mother, about how many times you told me you wanted to go to Scotland."

"That was a long time ago. I was a child."

"Then tell him who your grandfather is. That should interest him. Tell him anything you want to, but find out who he is."

"And if he won't tell me?"

"Then I'll do it my way."

Milford strode out of the room. His men threw Belmond to the floor and followed, closing the door behind them with a thud, locking it from the outside. She stared at the door while Belmond struggled to a sitting position, leaning his head back against the wall and closing his eyes. With a sigh,

Eileen pulled a chair out from under its covering and sank into it, still trying to believe Milford had locked her in here. The torches wouldn't last an hour.

Cold air moved past her ankles and she looked around the room for its source. Belmond's boots and stockings leaned against his clothing near the door. If it got much colder, she'd give him his coat and pull some of the covers off the furniture to wrap around herself. They'd be dusty, but some protection from the chill. She glanced at Belmond, his face gaunt in the dim light, his cheeks pale under the bruises and scrapes. He must already be cold, she thought; he'd been on the stone floor for hours.

He opened his eyes. *"Merci, mademoiselle."*

She gave him a scornful look. "I hardly think the pretense is necessary any longer, Mr. Belmond. We can speak in English."

"I will speak in French, mademoiselle."

She sighed in exasperation. "Why are you thanking me?"

"For your kindnesses."

"I have done nothing." She paused. "Why did you come here?"

"I was searching for somewhere to sleep in the storm. I found the cottage."

"And knew to ask for Sir Adam Ronley."

"I'd asked in Warwick who lived along the way."

"Someone in Warwick told you that Sir Adam lived here?"

"Oui, I . . ."

She held up her hand. "Please do not lie to me. If you will not tell me the truth, tell me nothing."

He was silent then. After a few minutes she left her chair and untied his feet, then dug in her pocket for a handkerchief. She met his gaze briefly before she dabbed at the blood still dripping from his mouth. She frowned at him.

"If you think that I am questioning you to relay all you say to Milford, you are vastly mistaken. I did not tell him that you understand English, nor that I am quite sure that you are not French. And I will not tell him anything else you say. I am satisfying my own curiosity, not his. But you won't believe me, of course."

"Merci," he said.

"Why do you tell this ridiculous story? No one in Warwick would tell you that Sir Adam lived here."

"Perhaps I misunderstood."

"I doubt that."

Neil tried to move his legs, staring at his feet, anywhere but into her eyes. It was difficult to look at her and lie. She leaned over him, trying to unfasten the rope that held his wrists together. "Should you do that?" he asked in French.

She looked at him in surprise. "You don't want me to untie you?"

"I do not want you to pay a price for it, mademoiselle. You are correct; he is a violent man."

"Milford will not touch me."

"He almost did."

"And he remembered himself. He knows better than to mistreat me. His mother was our head gardener's daughter. He may now own Ronley Hall, but I grew up here and everyone here remembers that, including him."

"You are very familiar with each other."

"I've known him all my life."

"How did the grandson of a gardener become the owner of Ronley Hall?"

"When my father died we discovered that he had many debts. I had to sell all his properties to pay them."

"How did Milford have enough money to buy it?"

"From being in William's army."

"He fought with King William on the continent?"

"William wasn't king of England then, of course; he was merely William of Orange. Milford fought with him on the continent against France—William hates France—and with his army in Scotland."

"He was an officer? Did your family buy his commission?"

"No. I don't think he was any high rank. Why?"

"It's very unusual for a common soldier to earn enough money to buy a manor house. He must have done someone an extraordinary service."

"I have thought the same thing, but all I have been told is that he earned his money serving in William's army. I don't spend much time thinking about Milford."

"Why is it you are still here?"

"I had nowhere else to go. Milford let me stay on."

"I imagine it would have been difficult to leave your home."

"I had not lived here in years, but I spent my childhood here."

"With Milford."

"With Milford. And hundreds of others." She began to work the knots again.

"Interesting that he would leave you in here with me."

"Interesting? That is not how I would describe it."

"Where did you and your family live when you were not at Ronley Hall?"

"In London."

That explained her manner, Neil thought. This was no country lass. She'd been raised in wealth, then left to fend for herself. "Did you not have any family who could take you in? Sisters or brothers?"

She gave him a tight smile. "There is no one. My sister is dead. After my father's denouncement of William my cousins were loath to have me with them."

"You have no one else to turn to? What about your mother's people?"

"I know nothing of them. Probably they know nothing of me."

She bent to her task again. Neil watched the torchlight flicker across her golden hair. MacKenzie hair. Catriona's daughter was alone in the world.

"Are you not afraid of me, Miss Ronley?"

"No."

"Why not?"

"You will not harm me."

"How do you know that?"

She looked into his eyes. "I haven't the slightest idea how I know it, but I know you will not harm me, Monsieur Belmond, or whoever you actually are. I know I am quite safe with you." She blushed and continued in a brisk tone. "Besides, I could pound on the door and get out. They're waiting for me to ask."

"I could kill you before you could get to the door."

Eileen frowned at him again. "If you are trying to frighten me, you're failing. I think the only harm that might befall me is if you did tell me the truth; I might fall over dead from the shock of it, sir." She pulled the last strand of rope free. "There, Monsieur Belmond, you may move your hands." She rose to her feet and stepped away from him.

His hands hurt when he flexed his fingers. After a few attempts he could make them move freely; no permanent harm there. But he still couldn't feel his left foot, could not make the leg move. He pulled his knee to his chest.

"I suppose you will tell me nothing," she said in a weary tone. "Do you not trust anyone? I don't expect you to answer. I'm simply wondering what a man like you thinks."

"A man like me. What does that mean?"

"A man who kills to put bread on the table. I cannot imagine what it must be like to be you."

He blinked twice, released his left leg, and pulled his right up. *A man like me, who kills to put bread on the table.* Her disgust was visible and he felt a wrench at her low opinion of him, then laughed at himself. "Have you been to St.-Sebastian?"

"Yes. Unlike you, I do not invent stories."

"Did your parents take you there?"

"I went with my cousins."

"When were you there?"

"It does not matter."

"You will not tell me more, is that it?"

"I will not tell you more."

He grinned at her, suddenly amused. "You're withholding information?"

"As you are, sir."

"Am I?"

"Oh, yes. You may pretend you're French, but I'll warrant that you are no more a Huguenot than I am, despite your lovely clothes. I think you're Scottish."

He felt a jolt of alarm, but she continued as though it were the weather she were discussing.

"You were taught French by someone who spoke

Parisian French, not Breton French. And my mother's name means something to you."

"Are you really Catriona MacKenzie's daughter?"

"Yes. Are you a MacKenzie?"

He paused, too long, he realized as she lifted her chin. "No," he said.

"But you've heard the name."

"MacKenzie is a common name in Scotland."

"Which is not something I would expect a Frenchman to know. And please don't waste your breath telling me that the Scot you won the ring from was a MacKenzie. That is not a MacKenzie seal on it."

Neil rubbed his ankle. He stared down at his toes, willing them to move, then looked up as the light flickered in a sudden movement. She glanced at the torches.

"Who was your grandfather?" he asked.

"What does it matter? He's dead now."

"Sometimes the dead relatives are the most important. Why was your father murdered?"

She sighed. "I was told it was an accident. And perhaps it was. My father drank heavily."

"He died after denouncing King William."

"Yes, the next day."

"A coincidence, perhaps."

"Who can say? William and my father never got along."

"They knew each other?"

"Everyone knows the king."

"But the king does not know everyone. Why would King William have your parents murdered?"

"I don't know that he did. If William killed everyone who denounced him, he'd be busy for years. I do know, though, that my father's denouncement offended William greatly."

"Why?"

"My father did it publicly."

"So have many others."

"But my father was . . ." She stopped, then pressed her lips together.

"Who was your father?"

"It doesn't matter."

"I suspect it matters very much, Miss Ronley."

"Not to you, Monsieur Belmond."

He felt the first twinges of feeling in his foot. It hurt, but then, so did most of his body. Pain meant the limb was alive. He wiggled his toes, and almost smiled.

"You know he'll beat you again," she said.

"Yes."

"Why don't you tell me who you are? Your silence makes you seem guilty."

He gingerly explored his mouth, wiping dried blood from his lips. She was very calm for a lass who'd been looking at his bloody face for a while now. Not squeamish, this one. She leaned forward, her expression intent.

"He'll beat you again. I will not be able to stop it."

"Why would you try?" he asked.

"Why would I try?" she asked softly, then continued in a sterner tone. "Indeed, why would I? What a fool I am to think of it at all. It should mean nothing to me to see you beaten for your silence, even if you are innocent of Milford's suspicions. I won't know which it is, though, will I? All you have done is lie to me."

Neil took a deep breath, feeling the sharp pain of a broken rib. He hated to be called a liar, but she was correct; that was what he was. He licked his lips, feeling the bruises there. Speak French, he told himself.

"If I tell him a different story now, mademoiselle, he'll not believe that one either. He's convinced himself I'm a Jacobite spy."

"Are you?"

"No."

"You would say that, of course. You do know that spying is punishable by death."

"Not until after at least a hearing, perhaps a trial in your astonishing English courts. Is Milford the sheriff?"

"No, but he might send you to him."

"I'll face that if it comes."

"If you're still alive."

He was silent again, feeling his weariness start to carry him away. I am not here, he thought hazily. Because if I am, I dinna ken what to do about it.

Eileen stood up and whirled away from him. "How do you expect me to help you if you will not tell me the truth?"

He looked at her in surprise. "I do not expect you to help me."

She stalked across the room and scooped up his clothing, thrusting it at him. "Here, put these on. You may not have another chance." She watched as he pulled on his stockings and boots. "Why won't you trust me? Why won't you tell me the truth?"

He stood, slipping his arms into his coat. "You have said that you will not tell Milford what I say."

"I won't."

"And that he will not harm you."

"He won't."

"But you don't know that for sure. He hit me in anger; he almost did the same with you. What if he thought you knew something but wouldn't tell him?"

"He will not harm me."

"Who would stop him? There is a prize on Jacobite spies, mademoiselle; we all know that. I am not a spy, but Milford thinks I am. Even if you decide to say nothing, what might he do to get you to say that I did confess to being one?"

"So you will stay silent."

"Yes."

She stared into his eyes, and at last nodded. "All right. Do not tell me who you are. But please, if you know my mother's family, at least tell me that much."

He looked at the torches. A moment later she strode to the door.

Eileen pounded on the door, pleased when it was Jack's voice that answered her. Jack had worked for the Ronleys all his life, had given her father his complete loyalty. He was an old man now, but a reminder of the carefree days when she was a child here. "Jack, I'm freezing in here. Let me out, please."

"Just a moment, please, if you would, Miss Eileen. Milford's coming."

She heard Jack fumbling with the lock, then looked behind her as Belmond reached for his topcoat and pulled it on.

"*Merci*, Miss Ronley."

"*Merci,*" she muttered to the door with scorn, then jumped as Belmond suddenly moved toward her. He leaned low, his mouth next to her ear; she could feel his breath on her neck. His right hand was pressed against the door, long fingers, tapered and powerful. There was a band of skin lighter than the rest at the base of his third finger, as though a ring was normally worn.

She faced him, her heart pounding. He was taller than

she'd remembered, bigger. He leaned closer and lowered his head. For a long moment they stared into each other's eyes, then he smiled, the dimple flashing in his cheek.

"*Merci*, Eileen," he said, pushing back from her. "I am most grateful."

She could hear Milford in the hallway, then the lock clicked. Belmond took another step backward.

"Tell him I'm untied, Eileen."

"Milford," she said, still looking at Belmond. "The Frenchman is untied."

The door began to swing inward; she heard the sounds of weapons being drawn. Milford pulled her into the corridor.

"What were you thinking?" Milford growled at her.

Belmond held up both hands.

"Tie him up again," Milford told his men. He held Eileen's arm in a tight grip while his men bound Belmond's wrists before him. When they were finished, Milford pushed her before him toward the stairs.

"Put him in the priest hole," he said over his shoulder.

Chapter Three

Milford gestured to the desk. "That's everything he had with him."

Eileen picked up the shirt that had been flung over the edge of the desk, folding it absently as she looked at Belmond's belongings. The two pistols, his dagger and sword were laid next to a leather bag that had held the shirt, a coin purse, and a bandoleer strung with gunpowder charges. She emptied the purse onto the wood, counting the French and English coins it had held. He'd had very little money, and fewer possessions for a man starting a new life, especially one whose clothing was so expensive.

"What did he tell you?" Milford asked.

"Not much. He asked about you and about my family."

"What did you tell him about me?"

"That you fought with William on the continent and in Scotland. You'd already told him that yourself."

"What did you tell him about your family?"

"Very little."

"Did you tell him who your grandfather was?"

"No, of course not." She crossed her arms over her chest. "How could you have locked me in there with him?"

"He was bound hand and foot. Who knew you'd be stupid enough to untie him? Why did you?"

"I thought he might talk if I showed him some kindness."

"And did he?"

"No. May I see the ring again?"

Milford held out his hand. Eileen took the ring, holding it up to the light. It was made of fine gold; the seal, intricately carved, was of an oak tree silhouetted against the sea. The band showed some minor scratches.

She thought of the pale skin on Belmond's finger. "You think it's Scottish?"

"I've seen others like it in Scotland. It would belong to someone in the clan chief's family, perhaps the chief himself."

"Perhaps he did win it in a card game."

"He might have."

"What if he's telling the truth?"

Milford grunted.

"If he is telling the truth and he's well connected, you'll pay the price."

"I've already thought of that. He also could be a French spy going to Scotland with messages for the clans."

"Do you really think he is a spy?"

"I don't believe him, that's what's important."

"What will you do?"

"When the weather clears, I'll bring him to Warwick. They can question him."

"Getting him to Warwick won't be easy. You'll need several men."

Milford nodded, then gathered Belmond's things and stuffed them into the leather bag. He held out his hand for the ring. When she gave it back, he bounced it on his palm. "Perhaps I'll leave him here and just take this. They might know in Warwick what clan it's from and whether it's significant."

"What if he's telling the truth?"

"Then I'll apologize and let him go. It's not your concern. I don't need you anymore. Jack will keep him alive and that's all I need." He tossed the ring again and caught it, walking away without another word.

It snowed all night and well into the next day. Eileen sat before the window of her bedroom, staring at the white that blanketed everything, wondering if she'd lost her mind. Why had she not told Milford her suspicions about their visitor?

"I do not expect you to help me," Belmond had said. And why would she? Of the two, surely it was Milford who should command her loyalty, not a man who'd lied to her with every breath. Were blue eyes that seemed to hold the sea and sky in their depths the reason? A tall, lean body with long legs and wide shoulders? Was she that foolish, to have her head turned by a handsome face, by a man who knew what effect he had upon her? It seemed so. And if so, then she was a lonely, pathetic fool and it was time to face that.

Life at Ronley Hall stretched out before her, empty and unbearably alone. Next month Milford would marry the daughter of a wealthy Coventry merchant, would bring the spoiled girl here to be Ronley Hall's mistress. Eileen did not begrudge the girl the title, nor what would be a comfortable life—and certainly not Milford as a husband—but the girl had made it plain that she considered Eileen an unwelcome tenant. Life here would be even bleaker than before.

Eileen had almost resigned herself to her fate, had almost convinced herself that a loveless but companionable marriage might be tolerable, was preferable to growing old living on Milford's charity. And might be all she might be able to expect. She'd thought of accepting the next halfhearted offer for her hand. Until Belmond. Her response to him had made her reevaluate everything.

What should she do? Where could she go? Her former friends were either in exile with King James, or shunning her because of her father's rashness. There were no men her age who sought her company, only the few aging single men in the surrounding area who ogled her while conversing in a desultory manner, then closeted themselves with Milford, negotiating, no doubt, to ignore her father's illegitimacy for future favors from Milford.

She should not assume she could always live here. Milford had been kind, in his own fashion, but he might grow less charitable with a wife who disliked Eileen; he might grow weary of housing her. She should be considering her future, not mooning about Belmond. His was a handsome face, that was all. But how long had it been since a man had looked at her like that, as though he could devour her?

He was at least a liar, most likely the spy he'd denied being; but when he'd leaned over her at the door, she'd forgotten all that. For a moment she'd thought he was going to kiss her, and she'd raised her mouth to meet his like some ninny, offering herself to a stranger. She knew better, should know better, than to look no further than a man's appearance—but no one had ever made her heart beat so fast. Why was she so drawn to him? It was as though they had met before . . .

He was in the priest hole, had been since yesterday. She imagined him in the small stone room, pacing the floor. There was a bed there, long unused, but little else. And Milford would do nothing to make him comfortable. She crossed to the window, tracing a finger along the tiny drifts of snow that had gathered on the lead between the panes.

When the storm cleared, Milford would go to Warwick. She had no doubt what he'd be told, that the ring was Scottish; most likely so was the man in whose possession it had been found. Milford would be instructed to bring Belmond in for questioning. And then? She shook her head, telling herself it had nothing to do with her. If Belmond were a spy, if he were plotting against King William, or even simply carrying messages to and from Scotland, then he would pay the price. Imprisonment, interrogation, perhaps death.

It was not her concern; he'd told her that, more than once. Why then could she not stop worrying about him? Because she found him attractive? Or because he'd stirred something she'd consciously tamped down for two long years—her own loyalties? After her parents' deaths, Eileen had been evicted from their apartments in the palace, had been warned at midnight by her cousin Anne to leave London silently. She'd followed the advice, running to Ronley Hall and an uncertain future. William seemed to have forgotten about her, her cousins as well. Until recently.

Eileen looked at the letter she held, the second she'd received in a month. Her cousin Anne had written again, inviting Eileen to join Anne and her family for the Christmas season. To accept meant much more than simply where she would spend the winter holidays. To do so would mean Eileen would place herself firmly in William's camp, to forever turn her back on her father's views.

Did that matter to her? Did she have a choice?

What of the MacKenzies? She'd told Belmond that she knew nothing of them, but that was not true. Her mother had told Eileen and her sister hundreds of stories of growing up in the Highlands as the daughter of a powerful man, of the impulsive decision she'd made to marry Adam Ronley, knowing what her own father would say. Catriona had talked often of the pain of the separation from her mother and brothers. Of her unwavering support for King James.

In the last few years of her life, after Eileen's sister had sickened and died, her mother had withdrawn within herself, for the most part ignoring her flamboyant husband, or watching him with an indulgent smile. She'd never complained, though she'd had cause enough.

Eileen could go to Scotland and try to find her mother's people, but she had no assurance that she would be welcomed, and to do so would estrange her from her cousins Anne and Mary forever. It was time for her to rethink her future.

It was time to re-enter the world.

Duncan MacKenzie stroked his hand along the new mast. His ship had done well on the sea trial, was now ready for trips farther than the one up and down Scotland's western coast that he'd just taken. He moved to the rail and watched the *Isabel* glide into the harbor at Torridon, looking up at Castle Currie as he always did. Home, he thought, then frowned as he saw his cousin Jamie waiting on the shore. He knew that stance, saw the tension in Jamie's shoulders as the ship came closer. Duncan swore under his breath. Neil. He'd been expecting this.

Jamie must have gotten some message from Neil in that strange fashion the twins had. Duncan swore again. It had been two months since he'd rowed Neil ashore, two months that he'd been worrying about his cousin. He'd tried to talk Neil out of the trip, had argued with him that last morning, hoping he'd persuade Neil to stay on board. But Neil had laughed, saying that this trip would be just like all the others, and Duncan had let himself be convinced. But he'd known it; deep in his bones, he'd known something was different.

When they were lads, the three cousins had laughed at the twins' grandmother Mairi when she'd look off into the distance, then back at them with some dramatic announcement. The years had taught them to listen, though, for more often than not Mairi MacCurrie was right. And Duncan was learning to listen to that same voice that spoke to him, warning him that something was wrong. He'd ignored the voice this time, and it came back now to remind him of that.

Duncan had spent hours discussing his misgivings with Jamie. The two cousins had assured each other that his fears were unfounded, but when Duncan had gone to Oban, expecting to pick Neil up from the ship that was to bring him there from France, the ship had arrived without Neil, nor with any word of him. After a fortnight, Duncan had gone home to wait with Jamie, rarely leaving Castle Currie except to patrol the coastline, and this trip, to test *Isabel*'s seaworthiness.

He straightened his shoulders, willing his stomach to unknot. Whatever it was, they'd fix it. If he and Jamie had to go searching for Neil, they would. It wouldn't be the first time—nor most likely the last—that two of them got the third out of trouble.

But first he had to tell Jamie the news he brought, that Alexander MacGannon, chief of his clan, the older but still powerful Earl of Kilgannon, had decided to sign the oath of loyalty to King William. As had the MacDonalds, and Glengarrys. If the MacLeods did the same, and the MacCurries resisted, they'd be alone in this part of the world.

William would remain king whether they liked it or not,

Duncan thought, remembering the battles of Killiecrankie and the Boyne in which he'd fought with his cousins. After Dundee's death at Killiecrankie, the Jacobites had been poorly led. If John Graham, the Viscount of Dundee, had lived, James Stuart might have regained his throne, but with neither good leadership nor financial resources, the Jacobites' hopes seemed futile. The promised French assistance had never arrived and the Jacobites still left in Scotland and Ireland faced an uncertain future.

Neil had gone to France to discover James Stuart's intentions and his instructions to the clans who had fought so bravely for him. Other clans had sent representatives of their own, some of whom had returned with stories of a disheartened King James and a court in disarray at St. Germain-en-Laye. In London, King William grew stronger and ignored the harsh reprisals his army took on those who had backed James Stuart. And now they faced the deadline of declaring their loyalty. By January first all the Jacobites had to sign an oath of allegiance to King William or be declared enemies of the state.

Torridon had been protected from William's army by its remoteness—the mountains to the north, south, and east and the sea to the west were barriers that William's army would be unlikely to cross. William could confiscate the Torridon title that Neil held, but he'd never get the lands that went with it. The MacCurries had held this castle through attacks from others, and Duncan was confident they would repel William's forces if he were foolish enough to attack. It was unlikely, but they kept alert, and part of their vigilance included patrolling the seas around Loch Torridon—Duncan's current responsibility now that Jamie was a married man and spending his time with Ellen and their son here or at Netherby with her family.

He watched Jamie shift his weight and waved to his cousin. Duncan was the first off the ship, crossing the strand to meet Jamie. The cousins embraced, then stepped back.

"What did ye hear?" Duncan asked, noting the strain in Jamie's eyes. "And was it a real letter, or one of yer 'feelings'?"

Jamie grinned, but his smile faded as quickly as it had come. "A 'feeling,' of course. It's Neil."

"Aye?"

"I dinna ken. Danger is all."

"D'ye ken where he is?"

Jamie shook his head.

"Makes it a bit difficult to go after him," Duncan said mildly.

"Aye, but we need to be ready."

Duncan clapped him on the shoulder. "We will be, lad. Any other news here?"

"The north is backing William. They've mostly signed the oath a'ready. We've had three messengers reminding me that we havena signed."

"Which is what we expected. Is the deadline still the same?"

"Aye, January first. But I'm no' signing anything. Neil can sign or no, as he chooses. Depends on what he found out. Now come tell me yer news."

"Aye," Duncan said, not saying what they both wondered. What would they do if Neil did not return before the deadline?

*　　*　　*

Milford put a big hand on Eileen's shoulder, leaning low over her shoulder. She waved the liquor fumes that surrounded him away from her face.

"Come with me," he said and walked across the room without looking back to see if she followed.

Eileen rose from the chair, reaching for her shawl. She knew where they were going. Milford had been drinking since midmorning, the smell of it coming from his pores now. She followed him to the office, where he pushed the coins around on the desktop, then picked up Belmond's sword and led the way down the stairs to the priest hole, swinging the heavy oak door at the bottom open.

Jack nodded as they entered. Belmond was on his back on the bed, his wrists and ankles tied to its corners. His eye was no longer swollen, but his jaw and neck were covered with bruises. He stared at the ceiling and ignored Milford.

"Ask him why he has French coins," Milford said to her.

Eileen translated. Belmond did not respond and Milford told her to ask again. This time Belmond shifted his gaze from the ceiling to Eileen's face, but still he did not speak.

"Why do you have him bound like this?" she asked.

Milford leaned low over Belmond. "Answer me!"

Belmond looked from Eileen to Milford.

"Tell him," Milford said, slurring his words, "that I will give him one more chance to answer my questions. Ask him again."

Eileen repeated the question. "Please answer him," she added.

Belmond did not respond.

Milford belched and gave Eileen a slanted look. "There

is another way," he said, lowering the sword over Belmond's stomach.

Eileen gasped with horror. "No! What are you thinking?"

"I need answers!"

"Not this way!"

Milford gave her a crooked smile, then reached down to grab Belmond's shirt, lifting and slashing it from collarbone to waist. Belmond did not move as Milford threw the sides of the shirt open and lifted the sword high with both hands.

"Sir!" Jack cried. "Don't do it!"

Eileen threw herself to her knees, sliding her hands along Belmond's stomach until they were under the wavering sword. She glared up at Milford. "You will not do this!"

Milford kept his gaze locked with Belmond's. "Then ask him again. If he doesn't answer, you'd better move your hands, or prepare to lose a finger or two!"

Eileen turned to look at Belmond, ignoring his racing pulse under her hands. His stomach was taut, the skin smooth atop muscles that contracted as she spread her fingers. His expression was carefully blanked, but his body betrayed his alarm.

"Please, please, answer him," she said in French, hearing the tears in her voice. "He's drunk; he might do this. Please! I cannot bear it!"

She felt the intake of Belmond's breath, watched his chest rise, but he did not speak. "Please," she whispered.

He looked into her eyes, then nodded. "I will for you, mademoiselle, for you and no other," Belmond said. "Tell him that we use the French coins among ourselves. Many of the Huguenots still dream of returning to France. That is why they give King William such support in his war. We use the coins because they are still of value among those who hope to return to a France under King William's control. Tell Milford that once again he has proven himself master of an unarmed and bound man. Tell him I look forward to the day we meet as equals."

Eileen translated his answer in a trembling voice, afraid to watch Milford when she told him the last of Belmond's comments.

Milford grunted, slowly lowering the sword, his expression remorseless.

She straightened, pulling her hands back. "Milford, how could you be so vile? He's unarmed and you're drunk! Go upstairs and sleep it off."

Milford threw the sword to the floor. "It worked, didn't it?" He lurched across the room and up the stairs, leaving her alone with Jack and Belmond. For a moment she could hear nothing but the pounding of her heart.

Jack swore quietly and sank to the floor, leaning against the wall. "I thought he were going to do it."

"So did I," she said, staring at her trembling hands. Would she have left them on Belmond's skin, or would she have pulled them back as Milford lowered the sword? He wouldn't have done it, she told herself, wouldn't have plunged the sword into Belmond's stomach while she watched in horror.

"It was the drink, miss," Jack said.

She nodded.

"To think I would live to see Milford as master here." Jack rose to his feet slowly, groaning. "I'm too old for all this. He's getting worse. Maybe his new wife will mellow him."

I will not stay to find out, Eileen thought, glancing at Belmond. He met her gaze, his eyes very dark.

"*Merci* again, mademoiselle."

She pulled the tatters of his shirt over his chest, then laid his coat atop him.

"You were very brave, mademoiselle. I am grateful to you," he said in French.

"Anyone with a shred of decency would have done the same. He is taking your ring to Warwick, to see if anyone recognizes it. You are in grave danger if they do."

Belmond laughed softly. "I do understand that, mademoiselle. But I have nothing to hide. I am not plotting against your king."

"Are you bringing messages from King James's court to Scotland?"

"Why do you think that?"

She stared at him, her anger rising. "Why would I not? It is plausible. Well?"

"I am going to join William's army."

"Are you a spy?"

"No."

"Are you Scottish?"

He did not answer.

She sighed again. "I am a fool to even ask. The more important question is why I would think, even for a moment, that you would tell me the truth. I'm beginning to believe you are incapable of it." She rose to her feet and stared down at him. "*Bon chance*, Monsieur Belmond. Let's go, Jack."

Jack nodded and followed her up the stairs.

Eileen wrapped her cloak around her shoulders and stared into the last of the fire, pacing the length of her room again. It must be almost midnight, but she'd been unable to settle since Milford had gone. After he left Belmond, he'd closeted himself with the kitchen maid he currently favored, and soon fell asleep, his snores so loud they could be heard in the hall.

Three hours later he surfaced and staggered downstairs, announcing that the snow had stopped and he'd leave for Warwick at once. It had taken his men an hour to be ready; Milford spent it sitting sourly in the hall, barking orders. He'd taken most of them with him, leaving only a handful to guard Belmond and Ronley Hall. He would be back, he'd said, by the next afternoon.

She'd been wrestling with her decision for hours. It must be tonight.

The house was quiet when Eileen opened her door as noiselessly as she could, pausing on the threshold to listen. There were no sounds that were not typical of the wee hours at Ronley Hall, and she stepped into the corridor.

It only took a few minutes to get to Milford's office. Her heart was pounding as she closed the door behind her and fumbled on the mantel for the candle. She would do this, she told herself as the feeble light illuminated the room, in her mother's memory. Belmond's things were spread out on the desk and she gathered them quickly before her courage deserted her. She bundled the pistols and dagger into the open bag, and took a deep breath. It wouldn't get easier.

There was only one way into the priest hole from the house, through the door from Milford's office, the entrance hidden by the tapestry that had hung there for decades. Only one way to the priest hole from the house, but two ways out, one that Milford did not know. She'd only gone through the tunnel once, when she was a child, following her father down the stairs from his office and into the tiny room where the Ronleys had hidden priests in more turbulent days.

Her father had been drunk, she knew now, but at the time she had listened with a pounding heart to her father's wild stories of men hiding in the priest hole while overhead soldiers thrust pikes into mattresses and tore doors off locked rooms. Adam Ronley had leaned low to look into his daughters' faces, and told them that if they ever needed to run from Ronley Hall, there was a secret way.

He'd gone halfway back up the stairs to the office and pressed a stone high in the wall, then pushed against the side of the passageway. Eileen had giggled, thinking her father was joking, then gasped when the wall gave way and he disappeared into the dark hole that had opened in the wall. He led the frightened girls through a long tunnel, full of spiders and things that scurried out of their way, and at last up a flight of stairs to a trapdoor in an old potting shed.

The shed was still there, full, last time she'd looked, of unused gardening tools, the trap door covered with broken shovels and cracked stone pots. But it was still there.

Neil raised his head when she entered, looking at her, then behind her. He'd heard someone on the stairs and had braced himself for what was next. He'd not expected to see Eileen Ronley, her hair loose on her shoulders and her expression determined. She carried his bag before her, the handles of his pistols and dirk sticking up from it. She paused when she saw him watching her, then put the candle down next to the bed and dropped his things beside it.

"I'm alone," she said breathlessly in English. "And we haven't much time. I don't know if anyone saw me. Milford's gone to Warwick with your ring. He'll be back tomorrow, perhaps early, perhaps with the sheriff's men." She fumbled at the rope that held his right wrist. "It's started snowing again, but only lightly. It will be more difficult to get through, but you'll leave no tracks. I can't untie this!"

"What are you doing, mademois . . ."

"I would think it is obvious. I am setting you free, despite the fact that even now, when there is no one here but us, you're speaking French. I know you speak English. Would it kill you to do so?"

He laughed. "It might," he said in French. "Use the knife, Eileen."

She stared at him for a moment, her eyes dark, then reached behind her and pulled his dagger out of the bag. He felt no fear, though his mind told him he should. It made no sense, but it was as she'd told him; he knew she would not harm him, that he was safe with her. She began to saw at the knots.

"Why are you doing this?" he asked.

She concentrated on the knot.

"You won't tell me?"

She shook her head. "You'll have to wonder."

He laughed again, watching her intent expression as she sawed at the rope, the way she pressed her lips together, ignoring the lock of hair that fell forward to hug the curve of her cheek. When she'd severed the knot, freeing his hand, he took the dirk from her, cutting through the bond on his left wrist easily. He fought the lightheadedness that washed over him as he sat up, then attacked the ropes that held his ankles. They broke open easily and he tucked the knife in his belt, swung his legs over the side of the bed, praying that they'd work.

"Hurry," she said, giving him his bag.

He stood with a sigh of relief that his legs held him, then strapped on his sword when she handed it to him, taking the pistols from her and tucking them in his belt. She picked up the candle and gestured for him to follow. Halfway up the stairs that led to Milford's office, she stopped, holding the candle high and staring at the wall.

"Hold this," she said, handing him the candle and putting both hands on the wall, running her fingers along the top of the stones. With a murmured prayer she pushed something down, then stepped back. "Push."

"The wall?" he asked.

"Yes," she said, both hands pressing against the rock.

He leaned against it, expecting a heavy weight, but the rock moved easily aside, and he lurched into the dark. He regained his footing, then looked into what seemed to be a stone tunnel that angled upward.

"You go first," she whispered.

"Where does this go?"

"To an old shed, outside the walls. No one ever goes there. Hurry!"

"I'll guard your back in case they come."

"You go first. Please!"

He narrowed his eyes, wondering if this was a trap after all. Was he to be killed trying to escape? Would she do that to him, send him knowingly to his death? He looked into her eyes, saw the fear there, and something in him relaxed. This was the same lass who a few hours ago had tried to protect him with her bare hands. God help him, he trusted her.

"Why don't you lead the way, mademoiselle?"

She shook her head emphatically. "There might be spiders."

"Spiders? You're afraid of spiders?"

She raised her chin and handed him the candle. "You go first."

The tunnel was narrow, and she was right, there were many spiders. And rats; he saw the glint of eyes that disappeared with a scurrying sound. He held the candle before him, feeling the cold air rushing toward him from up above. She stayed close, not quite touching him, but just behind. At the foot of a short flight of stone steps, he stopped and turned to her.

"The shed is at the top of the stairs," she told him. "Just push the trapdoor open."

He took her hand. "Come with me. I'll take you to your mother's family."

"I . . . I cannot."

"Why not?" He held the candle high between them, trying to read her expression. Her eyes were dark in the dim light, her cheeks pale against the black of the tunnel behind her. "Come with me."

She shook her head. "I cannot. I don't know them, nor they me."

"I won't leave you here to face him alone. Let's go back."

"No!"

"What will he do when he discovers I'm gone? He'll know you helped me."

"I'll think of something. Milford wouldn't dare hurt me."

"Until he gets drunk again."

"Go, please, Belmond," she said, gesturing at the stairs behind him. "When you get to the top, push hard. There may be tools and things on top of the trapdoor, but you should be able to get through. The road to Coventry will be to your right, about a quarter mile, on the other side of the stone wall."

"I'm not leaving you here to face him."

"He won't be able to prove anything."

"Miss Eileen?"

The voice came from the end of the tunnel. They both turned to look.

Belmond pulled her behind him, drawing his sword. Eileen put a hand on his arm. "It's Jack," she whispered.

"Miss Eileen?"

She could see the light coming closer, then hear the scuffle of Jack's feet on the uneven stone. "I'm here, Jack," she called.

Belmond turned to stare at her.

"Go!" she whispered, pointing up the stairs. "Go!"

"I'll not leave you here to face this," he said.

"You must! Go!"

He shook his head.

"Can you get the trapdoor open?" Jack called.

"I don't know yet. I haven't tried," she said.

"Belmond is still here?" Jack came into view, a torch held high. He nodded when he saw them, his relief evident. "Oh, good. I knew you'd do something, Miss Eileen, but I've thought of an idea. Have Belmond come back and tie me up in Milford's office. Otherwise Milford will blame you. Better that he think Belmond broke loose on his own."

She gave Jack a tentative smile, then glanced at Belmond, who glared at the older man. Jack met his gaze without flinching.

"I think you understand me, Monsieur Belmond," Jack said. "Surely you cannot mean to let Miss Eileen pay the price for your freedom."

"No," Belmond said.

"Then come with me, please, sir. It'll be better this way."

"Why do you do this?" Belmond asked in English.

Jack chuckled. "Not for you, sir, that's for sure. This will infuriate Milford and please Miss Eileen, which pleases me. I think that's all the explanation you need. You should hit me in the face too, so I can say I were knocked unconscious."

Belmond stared at him. "I don't want to hit you."

"You should. If you don't, Milford will think I helped."

When Belmond looked at her, Eileen nodded, and at last he struck the older man on the cheekbone, hard enough to leave a red mark, but not hard enough to harm him.

Jack nodded, apparently pleased. "Now come on, you two," he said and led the way back up to Milford's office.

Belmond was silent as they trussed Jack thoroughly just inside the office door. Eileen told Jack that she hoped they were not hurting him and he assured her he was quite comfortable. Belmond looked at Jack, then thanked him quietly.

"Get away, sir, whoever you may be," Jack said with a nod of his head. "Godspeed."

"Thank you," Belmond said again, then led Eileen back down the stairs.

At the stone doorway, Eileen stopped, handing Belmond the candle. "Good-bye, Monsieur Belmond. Leave this in the shed, please."

"Come with me, mademoiselle. I will take you to the MacKenzies."

"I cannot."

"Why not? There is nothing for you here."

"I know what I face here. If I were to go with you . . ." She shrugged.

"I would keep you safe."

"You'll have enough to do to keep yourself safe, sir."

"Come with me. You know you can trust me."

She shook her head. "I don't know that. I don't know

who, or what, you really are. I wish you well, but I cannot go with you. Now, please, go."

"What can I say to convince you?"

She smiled sadly. "Nothing. Go, sir, before we are discovered. Please."

"I am in your debt, mademoiselle."

"*Adieu*, Belmond, or whatever your name is."

He looked at her as though he were memorizing her face, then leaned forward and slid his hand along her neck, pulling her mouth to meet his. It was a short kiss, but sweet nonetheless, his lips softer than she could have imagined, his touch gentle and somehow wistful. He lingered for a moment before pulling away from her, his finger tracing where his lips had just been. She stared at him, then put a hand to her mouth.

"Not *adieu*, Eileen Ronley; that means farewell. I will see you again."

He slid the stone door closed.

Chapter Four

"I left him tied hand and foot!" Milford shouted. The staff turned to watch, then scurried away when he glared at them. He whirled to face her. "You did this!"

Eileen folded her hands in her lap and tried to keep her tone calm. "Don't be absurd," she said. "What do you think I did—stole out of my room in the middle of the night, knocked Jack unconscious, then let Belmond out with no one seeing either of us? You had guards at every door to this house, and at every gate. How do you suggest I managed to evade all of them?"

Milford careened across the room, rubbing his stomach.

"What did the sheriff tell you?" she asked.

"To bring Belmond to him at once."

"Did he recognize the ring?"

"He agrees that it is a clan ring—a Highlander's ring, but he didn't know which clan it was. He took an imprint of it."

"Why? Why does the ring—or the man—matter?"

"King William's men are telling everyone that he will rid Britain of Jacobites once and for all. The sheriff will be furious that I lost Belmond. How did he get out?"

Eileen shook her head. Milford stormed around the room for several more minutes, then ordered her away. She escaped gladly, returning to her room to stare out at the frozen landscape. It had snowed all morning, enough to cover Belmond's tracks. At midday the snow had stopped, leaving the weather clear and still. She took a deep breath, letting relief flood through her. She'd been afraid Milford would bring her down to the priest hole again, that he'd press her to explain how Belmond could have escaped. She'd gone reluctantly last time, watching while he tossed the bed across the small space, demanding that she tell him where Belmond was. She'd told him that she did not know. That much, at least, was the truth.

What had she been thinking last night? In the cold light of day it seemed incredible that she'd crept along the corridors and down the stairs to help a stranger. And worse, that she'd do it again, even if it meant lying to Milford, even if it meant she was truly lacking judgment. That she'd not been alone, that Jack had joined her in her foolishness, was no consolation.

Why had she helped Belmond? What she'd felt—that something between them—was it nothing more than the reaction of a lonely woman to a handsome man who needed assistance? Or was it the ties she'd always felt to her mother's people, to the Scots? If he was a Jacobite, which she firmly believed, then he'd fought for the same cause her father had believed in. Was that it? She hoped so, for anything else left her wondering just how foolish she was capable of being.

She turned from the window and called for writing things, spreading the paper out on the table before her, then picked up her pen.

"My dear cousin Anne," she wrote. "Thank you for your invitation."

Neil's journey home was long and miserable, but uneventful. He met some of Glengarry's men outside York and traveled north with them, then caught a ride on a MacKenzie ship going up the coast. At Torridon, Jamie and Duncan were on the shingle waiting for him, as he'd known they would be, standing in the middle of a crowd of clansmen who welcomed their clan chief home, letting Neil know of their worry for him, their pleasure in his return, and assuring him that all had been well while Jamie had held his place.

It was some time before Neil was able to turn to his brother and cousin. They embraced him and clapped him on the back, making jokes about his long absence, jovial while the others watched, but they didn't fool him. He saw the worry in their eyes, knew the questions they would want answered as soon as the three were alone. And when they climbed the hill to the castle, the clansmen a respectful distance away, both Jamie and Duncan began their questioning.

"Dinna ask me what went wrong," Neil said with a wry smile. "What dinna go wrong is a much shorter story."

Duncan swore softly. "I kent I shouldna ha' let ye go alone!"

"Ye tried to warn me," Neil said mildly with a glance at his cousin. "I should ha' listened. Next time I will."

"I'll hold ye to that," Duncan said.

"I'll listen next time. How is it here?"

Jamie and Duncan exchanged a glance. "For the most part," Jamie said, "all is well. But we've someone stealing from among the men."

Neil's eyes narrowed. "Stealing. What is he stealing?"

"Coin. And anything easily sold," Duncan said. "We think it's one of the men on the ships—they're the only ones who leave. A sailor could sell things without causing suspicion. If it's one of mine, I'll string him up."

Neil nodded. This was new, and unpleasant. Stealing created an air of suspicion and distrust, the opposite of what he tried to achieve with his men.

"We're assuming ye did find the king," Jamie said.

Neil nodded. "I found him. He asked if we were at Killiecrankie and the Boyne. When I said we were, he thanked us for our contributions."

Jamie raised an eyebrow. "Our 'contributions'? Did we donate something I'm no' remembering?"

"We donated enough," Duncan said. "And I remember all of it, every wretched minute."

"We damn near donated ye," Neil said to Jamie, remembering almost losing his brother at Killiecrankie. "King James is . . . dispirited. He says to sign the oath. He thanked us for our help."

Jamie and Duncan stopped walking and stared at him.

"That was it?" Duncan's voice held the anger they all felt.

Neil nodded. "We're on our own, as far as I can see. For the time being, at least. There are many with the king who think he'll recover and start again. But for now . . ." He let his words trail off, remembering the pale and spent man he'd visited with. James Stuart was not ready to start another war, not against a strong and wealthy King William. For now they'd have to wait. Perhaps forever.

"So ye'll sign the oath?" Jamie asked.

"Aye," Neil said. "That's what the king wants us to do."

"So how was that dangerous?" Jamie demanded. "Ye sent messages that had me packing my bags. If I'd kent where ye were, we would ha' been on the road that night."

Neil laughed ruefully. "I could ha' used yer help. I was in Warwickshire."

"Warwickshire? What were ye doing there? Ye were supposed to sail home."

"Which I would ha' done, had I no' been a month behind schedule. I got as far as London by water, then had to come north through England. I was . . . detained . . . in Warwickshire."

"Ye sent a message that had Jamie climbing the walls," Duncan said.

"Aye, well," Neil said with a shrug. "I was somewhat concerned m'self." He studied Duncan for a moment. "I met yer cousin."

"Ye did? Which one? Who was in France?"

"I met her in Warwickshire."

"Her? Who? I dinna have any cousins in Warwickshire, Neil."

"Aye, but ye do. I met Catriona's daughter. Her name is Eileen Ronley."

Duncan's mouth fell open.

Neil spent half the night telling his story to his family, glancing often at Duncan, seeing the resemblance between him and Eileen. Her eyes were rounder, her hair lighter; she was soft and feminine and lovely and Duncan, well, Duncan was a man and she was a beautiful woman. But there was a blood link that could not be denied. He should have tried harder to convince her to come with him. She should be here now with him, safe and protected.

He'd told himself on the journey home that he was merely grateful to her for risking her own safety to let him escape and for concealing what she suspected about him. But he knew there was more than that, something that he could not explain, did not understand. It was as if he'd known her before, as though they were not strangers. It must be the MacKenzie blood they shared. That must be it. That MacKenzie blood had been much on his mind on the trip home.

Neil's and Jamie's mother was a MacKenzie, a distant relative of the powerful Earl of Seaforth, leader of the MacKenzie clan, and the ties between the clans were strong. Seaforth was imprisoned now, one of the handful of titled Scots who had paid a high price for backing King James. For years Neil and Seaforth had discussed Neil marrying one of Seaforth's cousins, Fiona MacKenzie. Most of the Highlands thought the match had been decided, and Fiona herself behaved as though it were, as had he and Seaforth. But the agreement had never been finalized. Now Neil questioned its wisdom. Or necessity.

He needed, now more than ever, to marry carefully. Two years ago both MacCurrie brothers had been available to make alliances through marriage that would ensure the future of the clan. But Jamie had married Ellen, cousin to Dundee, who had led King James's army in Scotland against King William's forces. In the aftermath of Dundee's death and the collapse of the Jacobite movement, Jamie's marriage was a detriment, not an advantage. Neil could not begrudge his brother the happiness he'd found with Ellen, but it meant that Neil would have to think carefully about his marriage plans. And perhaps Duncan's.

They talked about his trip for hours, he and Jamie and Ellen, Duncan, and his mother and grandmother, about King James and the future of the Jacobite cause, about how dangerous London was now for a Scot, and how many former backers of King James were flocking to King William's court and swearing their loyalty.

About Eileen Ronley. And Catriona MacKenzie's marriage to Adam Ronley. It was the twins' grandmother Mairi who recalled the most.

"Catriona married an English bastard, which set her father off, is all I ever kent," Mairi said. "Of course, it never did take much to set Phelan off, then or now. Your grandfather never forgave her, Duncan, but apparently Ronley had some powerful connections. They lived in London the last I heard."

Duncan nodded. "I remember my mother telling me some of it."

"Ye should write to this Eileen," Mairi said to Duncan. "Tell the lass who ye are. Invite her here."

Neil shook his head. "He canna write to her, Grandmother, or Milford will ken who I am and guess that she helped me escape."

Mairi nodded. "Aye, that's true. But poor lass, all alone in the world. Was she surprised to hear that she had a cousin who was also yer cousin?"

"I dinna tell her who I was. And I dinna mention Duncan at all, just offered to bring her to the MacKenzies."

"Who did ye tell her ye were?" Duncan asked.

"A Huguenot, heading for William's army."

"Well, no wonder the lass dinna come north wi' ye. Why would she want to travel with a stranger? A French stranger?"

"Why would she want to meet the grandfather who disowned her mother?" Anne, the twins' mother, asked. "No doubt she was raised on the stories of his cruelty." She looked at Duncan. "Yer father told us dreadful stories about yer grandfather. I don't remember the details; I only have a feeling of distaste."

"I only met Phelan MacKenzie the once," Mairi said. "Miserable man."

"He was the last time I saw him," Duncan agreed. "I'm sure he still is."

"Phelan's no doubt planning something now that Seaforth's away," Mairi said.

"To save his own skin," Neil said. "He dinna join Dundee, and I'm sure he now thinks that was a bonnie choice."

Anne looked at her oldest son. "What is she like, Neil, this Eileen Ronley?"

"She reminds me of Duncan. She's verra tall for a woman, but she's much prettier than he is. And she's clever."

Jamie laughed. "Are ye sure they're cousins then?"

"Eileen," Anne said, her expression thoughtful. "The same name as Ellen." Duncan and Jamie exchanged a grin. Neil groaned.

"It was a chance meeting is all, Mother," he said lightly. "It's no' the legend."

Mairi snorted. "Chance meeting? No such thing, laddie."

"She's from the east," Anne said. "Ye ken . . ."

"Aye, Mother, we all ken that the Brahan Seer predicted that Jamie and I would marry lasses from the east with the same name. I am no' going to marry the lass; I'll probably ne'er see her again. I'm promised to Fiona MacKenzie, if ye remember. She's from the east as well."

"Ye have no' signed the papers yet," Mairi said. "Perhaps ye should not now that things have changed. Did ye see Fiona when ye were in France?" Mairi asked.

"Aye. She's fine."

"That's it? 'She's fine'?"

Neil gave his grandmother a grin. "She's fine."

"I ha' a feeling about this, Neil," Anne said. "Ye met Eileen for a reason."

"If I did, it was only to bring word to Duncan that he has another cousin."

"I wouldna be so sure," Mairi said. "It was ye who met her, not Duncan."

Neil nodded, looking down at his finger where his ring should be, feeling his amusement drain away. "Aye, I ken that. And I've wondered why she would risk so much to help me. She saved my life and I am in her debt for it."

"Perhaps it was yer ring," Mairi said. "Perhaps she recognized it."

"She dinna ken I was a MacCurrie, Grandmother, but I think ye're right, that she recognized it as a clan ring."

"I remember when yer father had the rings made," Anne said wistfully. "Ye were only three, the both of ye. I never thought the ring would help to save yer life." She sighed. "It's a shame it's gone, but if ye had no' had it with ye, Eileen wouldna have suspected ye were a Scot."

"She would ha' saved his life even without it, I'm thinking," Mairi said. "Look at him. What lass wouldna be affected by that face?" She ignored the twins' and Duncan's laughter. "I do think ye met the lass for a reason, Neil. This dinna just happen. Ye owe her a debt, laddie."

Neil met his grandmother's gaze. He agreed with her, that he'd met Eileen Ronley for a reason. He just didn't know what it was.

"I ha' two debts to pay in England," he said. "One to Miss Ronley, and one to Milford. I intend to pay them both in full."

*   *   *

The morning brought sun and a clear sky, both welcome after the recent brutal storms. Neil was busy discovering what had happened in his absence, meeting with the clansmen, and roaming Torridon territory. The MacLeods of Gairloch, whose lands were north of theirs, were quiet, a blessing, for he had no stomach for more combat between the clans.

For decades there had been unrest between the MacCurries and a small group of MacLeods who lived near Torridon's border. The laird was a MacKenzie, and the MacCurries were closely allied with him, but some of the MacLeods had never recognized Torridon's ownership of certain lands.

There had been many violent incidents between the Mac-Curries and those MacLeods, the most notable an ambush of the twins' father. Alistair had killed a man as he defended himself, and the death had never been forgotten—nor forgiven—by the MacLeods. Two years ago they'd tried to ambush Jamie and Ellen at the same spot and failed again.

Neil had made peace with the MacLeods' leader, but had kept his grandson Calum as a hostage to guarantee that the peace would be kept. Calum had stayed willingly, even long after Neil had offered to send him home. He'd gone to war with the MacCurries, fighting with distinction at Killiecrankie and the Boyne, and had become a trusted part of Neil's retinue.

But all was not well in Torridon; the thief Jamie and Duncan had spoken of had struck again. Someone was looking for money. A man who stole from his companions had little sense of loyalty—not to his friends, and perhaps not to his clan. He might even, for a little more coin, be willing to sell information to the highest bidder, a dangerous thing in these unsettled times. He'd have to discover who the thief was, and quickly; a distasteful task, but if Jamie and Duncan were right, not a difficult one. The thief was someone neither stealthy nor very clever—he'd left an obvious trail. It would be only a matter of time before Neil found him.

And there was the decision whether to sign the oath of allegiance to William to be made. Over the midday meal, Neil, Jamie, and Duncan decided that Calum would accompany Duncan on the *Isabel* for a series of short trips to the Outer Islands, to Inverness, and south to talk with the MacDonalds and MacGannons. The Highlands, still healing from the losses sustained in backing King James, seethed with talk, and the MacCurries needed to know what was being said.

The three cousins and Calum headed down to the harbor so Neil could see the latest repairs to the *Isabel* and to review his own ships. On their way down the hill, Ellen joined them, falling into step next to Neil, chatting about the baby. As they passed through the gatehouse, she put her hand on his arm, and outside the wall, she stopped, turning to him. Neil met his sister-in-law's gaze, then looked at the oak tree, the symbol of the legend of the MacCurries, a physical reminder that the stories were more than just talk. Ellen looked up at him with a faint smile.

"I know you dislike to talk about the legend," she said, "but so much of it has come true."

Neil looked at his brother, but Jamie refused to rescue Neil, grinning over his shoulder as he and Duncan continued down the hill. Neil nodded slowly, giving Ellen his attention. He'd grown fond of her in the last two years; he respected her views and her love for Jamie, but he hated talking about the legend.

"It's difficult to accept," he said, "that a man kent what my life would be like before I was born."

"Look at the tree and tell me you don't believe any of it."

Neil sighed. He didn't need to look at the ancient tree. He'd seen it all of his life, and even when he was away, he wore the ring that bore its image. Had worn the ring, he corrected himself, feeling the spot where it should be now.

The tree had already been old when it had been split by lightning the night that he and Jamie had been conceived, just as the Brahan Seer had predicted. And both halves had lived, and their father had died on his birthday, as their grandfather and great-grandfather had, three generations of MacCurrie lairds, just as the Seer had foretold. The twins had played their own part in the legend, leading the clan to war, and then home to peace. Many of the MacCurries assumed the rest of the legend would come true as well, that the twins would each rule Torridon, but never together, that their children's children would end the peace because of an alliance formed by marriage generations earlier.

He knew all that; he just didn't know what he was to do about it.

Ellen gestured to the tree again. "It happened just as the Seer said. All of it. You have only to look at this tree to know something extraordinary happened here. And something is happening again. I know you feel it. We all do."

"Aye, Ellen, both halves of the tree lived, and we led the clan to war. And now, supposedly, we've begun the fifty years of peace."

"And you'll both marry women from the east," she said.

"Which is no' difficult, considering we're on the west coast."

"Scoff all you want. I believe that James and I were

meant to meet and spend our lives together. Just think how easily we could have missed each other! If he'd been five minutes later on his way to Dunfallandy, I'd be dead. If I'd tarried, he would have arrived without me. I didn't understand it when it was happening, but now I know it was my fate to meet your brother and fall in love with him."

Neil grinned. "How could ye resist? He's verra handsome."

She laughed. "Yes, isn't he? But you need to listen to what I'm saying."

"Are ye saying we dinna have free will, Ellen?"

"No, I'm saying that some things are meant to be."

"Preordained. We dinna have a choice."

"Put it any way you like. I believe that we have many choices in life, but not in all things. I believe, with all my heart, that I was meant to spend my life with your brother. Think of how strange it is that we met at all—how many things that had to fall in place just so for us to be in the same place at the same time. We never should have met. He is from here, I'm from Dundee, on the other side of the country. He's a Highlander; I'm a Lowlander. If not for my cousin John and the plot against him, we never would have been brought together. But, as unlikely as it was, we did meet on that road to Dunfallandy. Those few minutes changed both of our lives forever. And now I have a feeling about Eileen Ronley."

"A 'feeling'?"

"Like you and James get when you communicate without words."

"I hear ye, Ellen." He glanced up at the tree. "God kens there's enough that's happened in my life that canna be explained. But I dinna think things are preordained."

"Neither did I," Ellen said, looking into his eyes. "Neither did I."

Later that day Neil leaned on the stone battlements and took a deep breath as he looked across the water. Except for sleep, he'd not been alone since he'd gotten home, and it felt good to have a quiet moment to just think. It was cold inside the castle, despite the roaring fires and covered windows, and the warm sun up here was welcome. And rare this winter. Below him Loch Shieldaig swirled into Loch Torridon, the dark blue water surging westward with the tide.

He was home.

The mountains opposite were shrouded in white, as were those behind him, to the north and east, their gray and rosy sandstone peaks covered now with deep snow. They prevented all but the most hardy from reaching Torridon, which was exactly what had been intended when the site had been chosen all those years ago. The MacCurries lived on the water as much as the land, using the sea lochs as highways, as they had for centuries.

And would continue to do so, if Neil had anything to say about it. He'd die before he let William's men take this land from his clan. And he'd have plenty of company. He didn't fear losing his title, for that was only something recognized outside Torridon; and he didn't need London's approval to continue as chief of the MacCurries. But like it or not, he had to live in the world. And soon he'd have to leave again, to sign the oath to King William. It was difficult, standing here in the warm sunlight, to remind himself of what could happen to his home if he refused to do it. He raised his face to the sun.

Was it sunny at Ronley Hall? What was Eileen Ronley

doing this late December afternoon? He'd thought of her every day since he'd left her, wondering if she'd paid a price for setting him free. And where, he wondered as he looked down at his hand, was his ring now? Had it already been melted down, the gold refigured?

After Christmas, after they'd come back from signing the oath, he'd talk with Duncan about going to England to meet his cousin. The two should meet, he told himself. It had nothing to do with him wanting to see her again. He smiled wryly, thinking of Duncan's laughter if he was to tell him that. But they should meet; for they had Phelan in common, a grandfather who had disowned his children and never bothered to know his grandchildren. Neil stroked his hand over the ancient stones, remembering his own grandfather and how much a part of Neil's life he'd been.

Someday—soon, if his mother and grandmother had their way—he'd have children to run along these battlements with Jamie's, sons and daughters who would be raised with love and firmness, as he and Jamie had been, who would bring joy to their father. Someday. And their mother? He shook his head to clear the vision that had come unbidden, of Eileen Ronley standing here with him, her golden hair gleaming in the sun, her beautiful eyes merry as their children played.

It would more likely be Fiona. Fiona of the long sighs and bored, slow lift to her lashes; who had never, in all the years he'd kent her, looked at him the way Eileen had. Fiona, who tolerated his company, talking endlessly of clothing and hairstyles, gossiping about other women, never asking anything of his life, interrupting when he tried to tell her. Fiona of the lackluster hair and even more boring character.

Would she like Castle Currie? Would she love it here, as he did, see the beauty in this rugged land? Stand here with him and watch the light transform the water, the mountains change with the seasons? Sail into the harbor and feel the same surge of fierce pride at the sight of Castle Currie silhouetted against the sky? Or would she sigh as she had in France, bemoaning the loss of King James's power, of her social status, of her apartments in London?

Could he marry her? Did he have to?

They left just after Christmas, Neil, Jamie, Duncan, and Calum MacLeod, battling the deep snow together. Neil signed the oath of allegiance to King William with three days to spare, and without comment, Jamie on one side of him, Duncan on the other, handing the pen back to King William's man and ignoring the snickers of the soldiers who had watched them. He kept his back straight as they walked away, but part of him had died with every pen stroke.

Neil had fought for what he'd thought was right, for James Stuart who, like the man or not, was the rightful king. He should be grateful that he'd been allowed to keep his land and his title, that he wasn't imprisoned like Seaforth. Small consolation, he thought, listening to the talk about the forts that King William was building in the Highlands, one at Inverness, the other near the northern end of Loch Linnhe, tangible reminders that the Jacobites had lost.

They spent that night at an inn, drinking far into the wee hours with other Highland chiefs and their clansmen. At last they withdrew to their room, where Jamie and Calum fell asleep immediately, but Duncan stayed awake with Neil, sitting silently now while Neil stood before the fire and thought about the alliance with France that had been discussed downstairs, one that would support a new attempt at reclaiming the throne of Scotland, but not England, for James Stuart.

Some of the chiefs were heading to France to see if there was anything to it. They'd invited Neil to join them. Duncan tossed the cork into the air and caught it, then again, watching his cousin absently touch the spot on his finger where his ring should be.

"Do ye think I should go?" Neil asked him, still looking into the fire.

"Not the now," Duncan said. "Go when winter's over; let them do the traveling for a change. Ye can trust Kilgannon, at least, to report honestly."

"He's no' going. Neither is Glengarry."

Duncan swore softly. They needed someone to bring home an unbiased and complete report of the latest happenings at King James's court.

"I dinna think we've anything to gain by it," Neil said, turning to him. "From what I saw, King James is no' likely to order up an army, and even if he did, I dinna ken who would lead it. But we should ken what's going on."

"I'll come with ye."

"I've no' yet decided if I'm going."

Duncan laughed. "Aye, ye have. I'll come with ye."

"On the way home, I thought we'd stop in Warwickshire."

"At Ronley Hall."

"Aye."

"For?"

"I left my ring there."

"Which may now be in Warwick. Or London. Or melted."

"Milford kens where it is. He can tell me."

"Oh, aye. If he's been told who ye are, ye'd be warmly

welcomed. It's a brilliant plan. Why no' write to him and tell when ye're coming?"

"I wasna planning an announced visit."

"Dinna be a fool, Neil," Duncan said without heat. "Have another made."

"My da gave that one to me."

"And yer da wouldna want ye risking yer life for it. That's no' why ye're going back."

"I'm thinking that ye might want to meet yer cousin."

Duncan grinned. "Ah, the real reason. She must be an interesting lass."

"She is. I owe her my life and I mean to pay my debt to her."

"And Milford, ye said."

"Aye, and Milford. Perhaps she'd like to come to Scotland and meet her mother's people."

"Ha' ye told Jamie? Or do ye ha' to?"

"I dinna have to."

"What did he say?"

"He agrees we should go to France." Neil grinned. "And he laughed when I said that we might stop in Warwickshire."

"When do we leave? I'll need a fortnight."

"Ye'll have a week."

Duncan shook his head. "I'm going for sainthood."

Chapter Five

Kilgannon sat heavily on the stone bench overlooking King James's gardens at the palace of St.-Germain, then turned to Neil. "I'm ready to go home, Torridon. What about ye?"

Neil nodded, watching Duncan circle them, keeping any would-be listeners at bay. They'd left the palace, hoping to find privacy, but even the chilly gardens were crowded with those who would be only too happy to repeat an overheard conversation between the two Highland chiefs.

"This trip has been a waste of time," said the older man. "I should ha' stayed home instead of letting Glengarry convince me to come at the last minute. If I'd kent ye were going to be here, I would have skipped."

"Aye," Neil said. "I'd ha' done the same if I'd kent ye decided to come after all. Waste of time is right. There was nothing for us here."

"Hasna been for a while. I'm done wi' the Stuarts, laddie, done wi' coming to France. I signed the oath to King William, and I'll live up to it. And ye?"

"We'll do the same. "

"I'll no' be back."

"Nor I."

"Not even to see yer betrothed?" Kilgannon paused, then laughed. "Do I sense a hesitation?"

Neil studied him. Kilgannon was a forthright man and had been a reliable ally in the last few years. Neil had been glad to find him here, as part of the Highland delegation to King James's court. And Kilgannon was right—the trip had been a waste of time. King James had listened disinterestedly, then waved away all discussion, saying he'd be king of all Britain or none of it. Neil had left the audience wishing he'd stayed home.

It had been the same when he saw Fiona. She greeted him with her usual ennui, seeming neither surprised nor pleased to see him again. He'd told himself to be charming, to give her a chance to change his mind about her. But nothing seemed to affect Fiona. It made no difference to her mood if he was garrulous or silent; she accepted his compliments with a smug expression, but never offered any in return. She'd not, he suddenly realized, even asked him why he was there.

Yes, Kilgannon did sense a hesitation. But as much as he liked the MacGannon chieftain, Neil had no intention of discussing this with him. Or anyone.

"What do ye ken about a Sir Adam Ronley?" he asked.

Kilgannon chuckled. "A'right, laddie, dinna answer me. I'm no matchmaker; marry where ye wish. But I'm wondering if ye need another alliance with Seaforth. If I had anyone marriageable, I'd be talking to ye myself. Ye ken that if ye dinna marry Fiona, it might be wise to marry one of Gairloch's lasses."

"Aye."

Kilgannon laughed again. "I see ye're taking my advice to heart. Sir Adam Ronley, eh? William stripped him of his title and lands, so he must ha' died as Sir Adam. He was the Duke of Whitby when I kent him."

Neil stared at the older man, his mind racing. "Whitby! I thought Whitby was one of King Charles's by-blows."

"Aye. Same man. Adam Ronley was the first of his bastards that Charles deuce recognized. For a while Ronley was noisily claiming that his mother and Charles had been married."

"Aye, I remember. King Charles denied the marriage."

"Aye, and after a while, Ronley was silent on the subject."

"Silent or no', someone killed him," Neil said.

"Aye, some said that. But that was years later, and just after he'd denounced King William."

"Do ye think William had Ronley murdered?"

"Hard to say. Having another bastard of King Charles's who claimed to be legitimate, this one the oldest, would most likely not please William. But Ronley had been quiet about that in the years before he died, even when King James took the throne. Was he murdered? Could ha' been. Verra strange way he died, drowning in the Thames on a clear night, taking his wife with him. There are those who might do such a thing, hoping to find favor with William. William wouldna complain—he has a way of ignoring unpleasant things that benefit him—but I dinna think he would worry enough about Ronley to have him killed. Whatever happened, it's been forgotten now, after two years. Why are ye asking about Adam Ronley?"

"I met his daughter."

"I dinna ken he had one."

"He had two. One died."

"And?"

"And her mother was Catriona MacKenzie, Phelan's daughter, Duncan's cousin, which is why I'm asking about her father."

"Phelan's granddaughter. And King Charles II's granddaughter as well," Kilgannon said thoughtfully. "Which means that if Whitby hadna lost his title before he died, she'd be the Duchess of Whitby now." He turned to look into Neil's eyes. "And if Adam was legitimate . . . I doubt her cousins will be too pleased."

Her cousins. Neil swore softly. Of course. The king and queen, William and Mary, were Eileen's cousins, as was Mary's sister Anne, all grandchildren of Charles II. If the letter that proved Charles had married Sir Adam's mother did exist, then it meant that Eileen was Charles's legitimate heir and should have the throne instead of her cousins.

Eileen should be the queen of England. Neil met Duncan's gaze.

James MacCurrie stared into the fire. Neil had sent word that they were well, but there was more that James could not understand, an excitement, a tension that was both pleasurable and unsettling. A woman. Not Fiona, surely, he thought. He'd never felt this sort of emotion from Neil—a wonderment almost. And a message about the legend, about a plan. Destiny. England. And a crown.

He frowned to himself, then glanced at his wife. Ellen held their son in her arms and rocked him as she sang softly, bits of her lullaby wafting to him as he came back to the present, to this warm room he shared with Ellen at Castle Currie.

What was Neil trying to tell him? A crown? Was King James planning another campaign to regain his throne? But no, he'd not gotten any sense of James Stuart from Neil, no hint that he needed to prepare the Torridon men for another war. Destiny. The legend. A woman. Eileen Ronley?

What he was certain of was that Neil and Duncan would

not be home any time soon. The legend. He looked at his wife again.

Eileen climbed the stone steps carefully. January had been bitterly cold in London, the wind finding paths into the snuggest of rooms, snow arriving every day or so, thawing, then refreezing at night to form yet another layer of ice that slowed all passage. Even here within walls the stairs were slick with frost.

She glanced behind her, where Celia Lockwood followed, still talking. Playing nursemaid to her cousin's fourteen-year-old lady-in-waiting was not what she'd thought would await her in Anne's household. Still, Celia was a sweet girl and Eileen could not help but like her. She should have known that Anne's invitation would have a hidden purpose. Not a malicious one, for Anne had meant, no doubt, to be kind to both Eileen and Celia by pairing them. But some days it was tedious nonetheless. She'd barely seen Anne. Her cousin was busy with her husband, her ailing child, and her current feud with her sister and brother-in-law.

"And he has the most amazing eyes," Celia said. "Brown, but not actually brown, more of an amber . . ."

Eileen stopped listening. She didn't need to respond, just occasionally nod or murmur something. Had she ever been that young? The girl had not stopped talking since they'd left the chapel, chattering endlessly about the young man she'd seen there. He was, apparently, the most perfect male that had ever lived.

He was only the latest in a score or so who had earned that title since Eileen had arrived. No wonder Anne had felt Celia needed watching. There had been the Dutch youth, the son of one of the ambassadors from Spain, the messenger from Norwich, the footman who had helped Celia from a carriage, the youngest—and perpetually drunk—son of one of Anne's retainers. She'd lost track of them all. Celia made her feel ancient.

Eileen had known she would be considered insignificant at best when she came back to court, that some would shun her simply because she was her father's daughter, and others would fear her lineage. She'd been more warmly welcomed than she had expected to be, but now, six weeks later, had grown as invisible as many of the women who served in the household. She did Anne's bidding willingly, both out of gratitude for her cousin's generosity to her and out of affection, but being here was nothing like what she'd expected.

Mary and Anne had been so close when Eileen had been with them before, especially at the last, when the sisters had been united in opposing their father's continued reign, sure that William would be a better king than James Stuart, that he would bring order to Britain.

Eileen had disagreed with them then—and been privately horrified that they could turn on their own father, even a man as unlovable as King James. Neither Mary nor Anne had seemed then to mind that Eileen had not shared their views, nor did they now seem to remember her opposition—or her father's denouncement of Mary and William's ascension.

Everything was so different than when she'd been here last. Mary was now queen, and acted like one, informing the world of her every opinion. Her husband, Prince William of Orange, had refused to be anything but king, and although Mary's claim was stronger than his own, everyone had agreed to make them co-monarchs, even Anne, who had waived her own rights to the crown in favor of William. But all that was forgotten now.

Anne, though still a royal princess, had been relegated to the level of a poor relation. Her allowance had been drastically curtailed and her household had suffered as a result. Her guards had been reduced and Anne had even been the victim of robbery shortly before Eileen had arrived. The princess was growing bitter. And vocal in her disparagement of her sister.

Anne's closest friend and staunch ally, Sarah Churchill, the Duchess of Marlborough, had been tireless in her criticism of William and Mary and had recently gone to Parliament to complain about Anne's allowance, which had unleashed a new storm of resentment between the sisters. Much of Eileen's time was absorbed in listening to Anne and Sarah bemoan the state of Anne's finances, or in carrying terse messages and even terser replies between Anne and Mary. More than once she'd wondered if in leaving Ronley Hall she'd merely exchanged one kind of prison for another.

Eileen waited for Celia at the top of the stairs, taking a moment to wipe the frost off the window next to her. The windows of the room she shared with Celia were shuttered and covered with tapestries to keep out the bitter cold, and while she was glad the drafts had been blocked, living in closed-in spaces constantly was dreary. The afternoon was gray and already growing dark, but she could at least see the gardens, barren as they were now. She suppressed the wave of longing, which came so often now, for the old days, when her parents were alive, when London was a playground for her. When she did not know all she knew now.

"And then," Celia said as she joined Eileen, "the duke

proposed that we all ride off to Cornwall and slay the dragon."

"Mmmm," Eileen said.

"You weren't listening, were you?" Celia pretended to pout, but her eyes were dancing. "You're as bad as my stepmother. She says I rattle on so that she has to think of other things or go mad."

Eileen laughed with her, but she heard the bitter note in Celia's voice. The girl might make light of her stepmother's caustic remarks, but the woman was the reason that Celia had come alone to court. Her father's new wife had made sure that her pretty—and maturing—stepdaughter was removed as soon as possible.

Unwanted women, Eileen thought as she led Celia through the heavy door to their wing. That's what we both are. Women with no place in the world, reduced to living on the charity of others. She smoothed a hand along her skirts, feeling the worn texture of the silk. There would be no new clothing anytime soon.

She'd pretended since she'd returned to London and to court that she did not notice what the other women were wearing, that it did not bother her to have to wear her few gowns over and over. She had her mother's pearls and drop earrings, still fashionable, and she and Celia could update their hair, but neither of them could compete with the well-heeled women of William and Mary's court unless they married well, which was unlikely in her case. Celia, with her youth and beauty and cheerfulness, would catch someone's eye, and Eileen would be left alone with only dour Bess for company. She should have gone with him.

She'd thought of Belmond every day since he'd left Ronley Hall, wondering where she would be now if she'd accepted his offer to take her to the MacKenzies. Would she have been welcomed by her grandfather, her mother's unfortunate marriage forgotten? Would she have found a home at Glen Mothin, surrounded by her mother's brothers and their families? Had she let her fear of the unknown deprive her of all that? Would the air still be alive with whatever flowed between Belmond and her? Or would that have been short-lived; had it been intensified by the knowledge that they'd probably never see each other again?

"Not adieu," he'd said. "I will see you again." She put her finger to her lips, remembering his touch, then forcing herself to stop thinking about him, to stop wondering if his words had only been just that—words. She turned the last corner and opened the door to their rooms.

As the welcomed warmth surrounded them, Eileen lifted her heavy cloak from her shoulders, shaking her hair free, watching Bess hurry over. Another unwanted woman. Bess was the widow of one of Anne's Dutch contacts, a round young woman who pretended to assist everyone while her eyes showed her sour view of the world.

"You have a visitor," she said to Eileen.

Eileen's heart leapt. Belmond. Don't be ridiculous, she told herself. He wouldn't be here in London. If he was who she thought he was—a Highlander—London would be a dangerous and foolish place for him to be. And no matter what he'd said, there would be no reason for him to come and find her. "Who is it?"

"Howard Templeton."

Howard Templeton, Eileen thought. She'd not heard that name in a very long time. Howard had been her father's constant companion here in London, accompanying him on his days-long bouts of drinking. He'd always been kind to

Eileen and her mother, and had been one of the few who'd dared to attend her parents' funeral. What had brought him here? She turned from Bess's curious stare and went to find out.

He waited in the tiny dark sitting room of Anne's apartments, his handsome face creased with worry. His welcome was perfunctory.

"It's all over London that you're here, and that you're the go-between for your cousins," he'd said, then paused and glanced around them, as though there might be listeners even here. "Eileen, you should not be here. Do you not realize how dangerous London is for you?"

"Dangerous? Howard, surely you're not serious."

"I am very serious. You are your father's daughter; that's enough for some."

"What do you mean?"

"Your parents were murdered here."

"You told me it was an accident."

He paused and blinked. "Yes. We'd always thought it was. But what if it were not? You should go back to Ronley Hall and stay there."

"I cannot," she'd said.

"Has Milford . . . ?"

"No, nothing like that. But he's married now and I am not wanted there. I have nowhere else to go."

"You'd be safe there."

"No harm will come to me in Anne's house."

"Anne herself was attacked."

"That was months ago. He was simply a thief, nothing more."

"She was attacked, Eileen."

"Because William and Mary have cut her allowance so

strongly that Anne could not keep all of her guardsmen. Nothing has happened since."

"London is full of thieves. Why do you think you're safe?"

"I have little money and rarely go anywhere but to court."

"Why don't you come and stay with me?"

Eileen put a hand to her throat. Was he offering . . . ? But no, he quickly understood her hesitation.

"I'm a changed man. I have a wife and child now. My carousing days are over. I am offering a safe place to stay, nothing more."

She tried to smile. "I thank you for the offer, Howard, but I cannot. I have promised to stay with my cousin Anne. You know that her son is often ill."

"Yes, and that she lost another child at birth last year. What does that have to do with you?"

"I cannot abandon her, Howard. She needs me."

He sighed heavily, then handed her a piece of paper. "My address. These days I am usually home. If anything frightens you . . . if you hear something unsettling, Eileen, come to us."

The cold grew even more bitter, keeping everyone indoors, which suited Eileen. She spent her days with Bess and Celia or with Anne, listening to her cousin's long list of physical complaints. Anne, who had grown very heavy, was having stomach problems again. She often wanted Eileen to read to her, or sit with them while she and Sarah Churchill discussed how badly William and Mary were treating her. Anne's husband floated in and out, but rarely contributed.

During the day Eileen could pretend that Howard's warnings did not worry her, but at night, closeted with the others, she would stare into the fire and wonder what would become of her. Had she been foolish to leave the relative security of Ronley Hall? Was she in danger here in London?

Did anyone even remember her father, let alone his protests of legitimacy and his screeching denouncement of William? It had been years since her father had told the world that King Charles had married his mother, years in which many others had made the same announcement, all denied by Charles. When King James had taken the throne, Adam Ronley had not pursued his claim, and since his death, she'd assumed the memory of him had faded as well.

What if she'd been mistaken? What if Howard was right, that there were those who thought she'd returned to London to raise the issue again? If her father had been legitimate, she'd have a stronger claim to the throne than William and Mary and Anne. But if that was the case, why would Charles have not recognized his own son? Her father had only talked about it when he was well into his cups, and she had always dismissed it as the ravings of a drunk.

What if others had listened and given credence to him? But no, Howard was completely wrong. She'd drawn no attention on her return, fading into the woodwork with a speed that had amazed her. He had been her father's friend, and was only trying to protect her, but Howard's warnings were absurd. Why then did they so unnerve her? She needed to be made of sterner stuff.

She dug through her clothing chest, and brought out the velvet drawstring sack, opening it slowly and holding its contents up to the light, watching the two rings glisten in the glow from the flames. Her mother's wedding band, a too tangible reminder of the mother she'd loved and lost, of the father for whom she'd had such mixed feelings.

If there had ever been any doubt as to who Adam Ronley's father was, the London wags said, one had only to look at his sexual habits. Charles II had slept with almost any woman who was willing; his oldest son had done the same. Eileen had watched her mother fade under the constant barrage of his infidelity. This ring was symbol of their union—and a reminder that marriages do not always remain what they begin.

The second ring was Belmond's. She'd stolen it from Milford's office before she'd left, telling no one. Absurd, she told herself, this feeling that she was keeping it safe until Belmond could come for it. She held the signet ring up to the light again, the carved oak tree elegant in its simplicity. Inside the band, which she had not noticed at home, two initials were engraved: N. M.

It was time to ask some questions.

The next morning she sent a note to Howard, asking him to visit again. When he did, she told him briefly of Belmond's visit to Ronley Hall, with her own emotions carefully edited, then showed him the ring. He held it up to the light and confirmed that it was indeed a Highland clan ring, but he wasn't sure which clan. He would, he'd said, make inquiries.

Five days later Howard returned, refusing to talk in Anne's apartments, taking Eileen by coach to his home. She hid her surprise when they stopped at an elegant—and costly— townhouse in a fashionable part of the city. When he'd been her father's friend, Howard had had very little money; her father had paid for most of their adventures. Obviously the last two years had been very good to him; or perhaps this expensive home, his well-cut clothes, and general air of wealth were nothing more than the result of an advantageous match.

Eileen settled herself on the sofa and watched Howard dismiss his lovely and very young wife, saying he needed to talk with Eileen alone. His expression was very serious while he waited for his wife to close the door behind her.

"Torridon," he said when they were alone. "The ring you showed me bears the Earl of Torridon's emblem."

Her heart leapt. She'd been correct; Belmond—Torridon—was no more the son of a Breton merchant than she was. "Torridon is in Scotland, I assume?"

"On the western shore, in the Highlands. Torridon is a Jacobite," Howard said. "His name is Neil MacCurrie; he is the chieftain of a very powerful clan. His forces stayed with King James's army until the end. If Torridon was in England, there are many people who would like to know why."

"We don't know if the man was Torridon, Howard. He said he was French, a Huguenot, from London. He might have won the ring as he said he did."

"Torridon is said to be tall, lean, very dark, with a fierce look about him. What did this Belmond look like?"

"That description would fit him, but a thousand other men as well."

Howard rose to pace the room. "It might not have been Torridon himself, for he has a brother who looks much like him—no doubt half the clan looks like him; those Scots breed like rabbits. I beg your pardon. I always forget your mother was one. Who else have you showed the ring to?"

"No one in London. Milford saw it and made some inquiries in Warwick, but discovered nothing."

"Tell no one else about it, Eileen. Torridon is a dangerous

man. He signed the oath to King William, but who can trust Highlanders? Torridon's mother is a MacKenzie as well, a Seaforth MacKenzie, and Seaforth is currently in prison for his treason. Tell me again why Torridon said he was at Ronley Hall."

"He said he'd been told it was a safe place to rest."

"Did he talk to you about King James? Or your father?"

"He asked for my father, which is why Milford was suspicious of him."

"What else did he say?"

"I've told you everything, Howard. He said he was a mercenary, going to join William's army in Scotland."

"I'm told he is a spy for King James, that he travels between Scotland and France, trying to raise interest and money for King James's next attempt on the throne. Why would Torridon be in England?"

"We don't know that he was."

"Either your visitor was Torridon himself, or Torridon was in London losing at cards, which doesn't fit what I've heard of the man. I'm told Neil MacCurrie neither drinks heavily nor gambles, which makes the story about losing his ring at cards unlikely. He's said to be fearless and ruthless. And not above seducing women for information, despite his wife and children at home. He's married to a relative of Seaforth's, but that doesn't stop him from using his looks to get into beds of women who might help his king. You were fortunate, Eileen. You could have been one more victim in a long chain."

She willed her cheeks not to redden, her mind not to remember Belmond's kiss—Neil MacCurrie's kiss—his whisper of "I will see you again."

"Has he contacted you here?"

"No," she said. "Why would he?"

"He knows who you are."

"He knows I am Sir Adam's daughter, nothing more. And even if he knew all about me, why would he seek me out?"

Howard gave a harsh laugh. "The granddaughter of King Charles II? Possibly the legitimate heir of King Charles? What Jacobite would not want to seek you out? Has anyone contacted you about that?"

Eileen forced a smile and kept her tone light. "About me claiming the throne? Surely you don't believe my father's fantastic claims? I am no threat to William and Mary. If I were, would they have invited me here?"

"Princess Anne invited you. And she is feuding with Queen Mary."

"What are you suggesting?"

"Anne must be feeling injured after giving her support for William to be king. She even let his claim supplant her own, and her children's. And in return what she has received is a reduction in her allowance and a cold shoulder from the queen."

"You seem to have a wealth of knowledge."

"Everyone in London is saying the same."

"Everyone in London is speculating."

Howard almost smiled. "Am I correct?"

"Anne has never led me to believe she has regretted William becoming king."

"Has she been approached by the Jacobites?"

"Not to my knowledge. Why would she be? King James is said to be very bitter about his daughters deserting him."

"Perhaps he thinks to divide the sisters and have Anne join forces with him."

"How would that help? William and Mary are on the throne."

"Perhaps it is his revenge."

"No, Anne won't join her father, Howard. She's next in line to the throne now, and not likely to relinquish her chance at ruling."

"She will rule only if William and Mary do not have children. And there is no sign of a child yet."

"Mary is only twenty-six. She may still bear ten children. Howard, this makes no sense to me."

He took a deep breath and smiled tightly. "No, I suppose not. But if Torridon—or any of the Jacobites—contacts you or Princess Anne, let me know immediately. Don't trust him, Eileen. I would hope you would be wise enough not to fall prey to such a man after all your mother went through. You know that I loved your father, but I saw what his behavior cost her. She suffered, child, and I'd hate to see you as foolish. If Torridon contacts you, send me word at once."

He turned the subject to other topics then, and very shortly thereafter, returned her to Anne's. She thanked him for his information, let him hand her out of his coach, and waved as he left. But it was with a heavy heart that she turned to go inside. Howard had frightened her more than she'd let on.

She had thought Anne's invitation to be an escape from an untenable position at Ronley Hall. It had not occurred to her then that some could misinterpret her return to London, that they would whisper and wonder about her intentions, that even now murderers could be watching her for any signs of ambition, watching Anne for signs of unrest and plotting against William and Mary.

She closed her eyes for a moment, wishing her parents

were alive. Her father, even drunk, would have laid the rumors to rest with a few amusing quips. How was she to do the same?

And Belmond—Neil MacCurrie, she corrected herself. She felt the familiar longing for him, mixed now with anger. She'd kept his secrets and protected him; all she'd gotten in return was lies. And a kiss she would never forget.

The Earl of Torridon, the son of a MacKenzie. Why had he not told her? No wonder he'd been dumbstruck when she'd said her father was Adam Ronley and her mother a MacKenzie. Of course the MacKenzie name had meant something to him. How could it have endangered him to tell her something of her own mother's people? Could he have not thrown her a crumb of information, not even when they'd been alone, when it was clear that she was setting him free?

Fearless, Howard had said of him. And ruthless. And not above seducing women for information, despite his wife and children at home. What a fool she'd been. Had she learned nothing from watching her father soothe her mother's tears after a night away from home? She thought of kneeling beside the bed in the priest hole, stretching her hands wide to protect Neil MacCurrie from Milford's drunken mood, his skin smooth beneath her fingers.

She would not be so foolish again. The past was past. She was alone in London, alone in the world, and she'd do well to remember that. She would trust no one except those who had proven themselves, and even then, she'd watch them, knowing she could not read their hearts.

*　　*　　*

Neil pushed the door of the cabin open, leading Duncan inside. "Another waste of time," he said, peeling the sodden topcoat from his shoulders.

They'd arrived in London late the night before, weary and battered from the rough crossing from France. The storms had been relentless, the seas huge and pounding, but Duncan's *Isabel* had kept them safe, and Neil was glad to be back aboard her now after this useless day. They'd spent most of it in the city, trying to find the man who had told him Ronley Hall was safe. They'd found the shop, boarded up, and neighbors who would not answer their questions, but nothing else.

Duncan wiped his wet hair back from his eyes, then poured them each a whisky and handed Neil a glass. "So when are we going to Warwickshire?"

Neil took a sip. Duncan's russet hair was brown with moisture, his freckles dark on his pale skin; there were lines of weariness around his eyes. Neil owed his cousin much; Duncan's humor and calm had been steadfast, a welcome change from the melancholy and furtive intrigue that surrounded King James. He shouldn't ask any more of his cousin; Neil could stay in England on his own.

"Ye can go home as soon as ye're ready," Neil said softly.

"Without visiting Eileen Ronley?"

"Aye."

"And ye would come with me?"

Neil shook his head. "I'm going to Warwickshire. But there's no reason ye need to come as well."

"Ye want me to leave ye here?" Duncan's words were measured.

"I'm saying ye can go home, lad, that ye have done enough."

"What happened the last time I let ye travel alone?"

"I ken what I'm walking into this time."

Duncan's face grew red. "Either I go wi' ye, Neil, or ye dinna go at all."

"Oh, aye?" Neil sipped his whisky, amused. Duncan, irate, was always interesting, but Duncan was rarely irate for a selfish reason, which made it difficult to summon any anger to fight him. "Duncan, ye and the men are tired. I'm saying ye can go home."

"No. If ye stay, I stay."

Neil laughed.

"What if I told ye I want to go to Warwickshire?" Duncan asked.

"Why would ye?"

"I ha' a cousin there. I should at least meet the lass and introduce myself."

"She might no' want to meet ye."

"She might no' want to see ye again, Monsieur Belmond."

Neil thought of Eileen Ronley's eyes assessing him, of her hand touching her mouth after he'd kissed it. "Aye, it might be another waste of time, but I'm going."

"Then it will match the rest of the trip." Duncan leaned forward. "Look, Neil, ye told me she asked about her mother's family. That's me. I want to meet her. I'm damned curious about this lassie. So we're going, right, both of us?"

"Ye dinna need to come," Neil said mildly.

Duncan grinned at him. "Someone has to watch yer back; God kens ye do a poor job of it. I'm coming. Just tell me when."

Neil laughed. "We'll go tomorrow. And I'm grateful to ye."

Duncan waved his words away. Neil took another sip of whisky. Soon he would see Eileen again, thank her, tell her who he was, who Duncan was, offer to escort her to the MacKenzies.

See if she was worth all the time he'd spent thinking of her.

"Tell me again how we thought this was a good idea," Duncan whispered.

Neil laughed softly and closed the door to the stairs up from the priest hole, letting the tapestry that covered it fall into place. They'd crept through the night to the potting shed, lifting the trapdoor and making their way through the tunnel without mishap. They were in Milford's office now, in the dark.

In the priest hole Neil had held the candle high, looking at the bed, remembering lying there wondering if this was where he'd die. It was dusty and barren now, no trace of him here. Duncan had met his gaze, for once no trace of humor in his eyes, and Neil knew his cousin was here as much for revenge as to meet Eileen.

Now to find her. He waited as his eyes adjusted to the dim light. He could make out the large desk in the middle of the room and the door to the corridor. If his memory was correct, that corridor branched two ways, one to the stairs to the hall, the other to another wing, most likely where the bedrooms were. Eileen had been the daughter of the house; unless Milford had turned her out of her rooms, her bedroom was in the wing with the others. Of course, most likely, so was Milford's. And where, he wondered, did Milford's guards sleep?

He started at the sound of leather on stone in the corridor outside, darting to join Duncan behind the door. Who was coming to Milford's office at this hour? The door opened slowly, light from a single candle spilling across the stone floor and lighting the Persian rug. There was a yawn and the scuffle of feet not picked up.

Neil let his breath out as he saw Jack move slowly toward the fireplace, and glanced through the edge of the doorjamb; the corridor was dark. He closed the door silently as Jack fumbled with the coals. When the tiniest of flames licked at the logs, Neil moved into the center of the room.

"Jack," he whispered.

The older man froze, then turned his head stiffly. He smothered a cry when he saw Neil.

"We wish ye no harm," Neil said.

"I won't tell no one you're here. I'll help you again."

"Go and get Miss Eileen, then would ye, please? Or show us where she is."

"She's gone."

"Gone?"

Jack nodded, his eyes growing even wider as he saw Duncan. "Aye, sir. She left before Christmas. It were good she went. Milford's new wife didn't like her."

Neil tried to set aside his sense of loss. He'd spent a good part of the time they'd waited imagining what Eileen would say when she saw him again.

"Where did she go?"

"Someone's coming," Duncan whispered.

"It'll be Milford," Jack said. "He's always up with the

dawn. He'll be alone. Get your sword out, sir, and threaten me."

Neil fought his laughter as he drew his sword, pushing the older man next to Duncan. The door swung inward.

Milford paused on the threshold, then moved forward. "Jack?" He spun around when Duncan swung the door closed, his expression hardening as he looked from Duncan to Neil. "You! How did you get in here?"

"Dinna make a sound, Milford," Neil said. "We can kill ye before yer men could get here."

"What do you want?"

"My ring."

"It's not here. I think Eileen has it."

"Where is she?"

"I don't keep tabs on the woman."

"Why would she take it?"

"Probably to sell it."

"Where is she?"

"I don't know, Torridon."

Neil raised an eyebrow. "Verra good. Ye found someone to identify the ring."

"Yes. And you, Monsieur Belmond. Or should I say Mac-Currie?"

"Ye've made inquiries, I see. Bonnie effort, Milford. Where is she?"

"In London, with her cousins. I'm sure she'll welcome you."

Neil sneered at him. "Oh, aye, I'm likely to go to King William's London just the now. Ye ken as well as I do that Highlanders are no' more welcome there than I was here. We're hunted for sport."

"Perhaps it'll teach your kind to stay at home. I thought

we'd taught you that at the Boyne. Were you one of those who ran in Ireland, Highlander?"

"Were ye one of those who ran at Killiecrankie, Englishman?"

"No. I was one of those who danced on Dundee's grave."

Neil raised his sword, fighting to control his anger. It would feel wonderful to run the bastard through, but he would not do it. It was a lie. Dundee's grave had been well protected. Still battling for control, he stepped forward.

Milford stepped back. "I'm unarmed, Torridon."

"As I was when I was here. At least ye're not bound hand and foot." Neil sheathed his sword and held his hands high. "Go ahead, Milford, do yer best. Ye were a soldier before ye got old and fat. Have at me."

Milford glared at him.

"If ye're no' interested, then get my ring and I'll be off."

"I don't have it."

"I dinna believe ye."

"Are you calling me a liar?"

"I believe I am. And a coward."

Milford barreled forward, arms flailing. Neil ducked away, then lunged, throwing all of his weight into the blow he delivered with his right fist. He caught Milford on the cheek and nose, but Milford kicked him in the stomach and jumped back out of Neil's reach.

"Come on, Highlander. Let's see what you can do."

"Ye might want to wipe the blood off yer face, Englishman."

Milford swiped at the stream of blood pouring from his nose. "Lucky blow."

Neil leapt forward and struck Milford again, hitting his

chin and cheek this time; Milford reeled backward. "More than luck."

As Neil moved toward him again, Milford raised an arm to protect his face. Neil dropped his arms, his stomach for the fight suddenly gone. He swung a leg behind the backs of Milford's knees, knocking his feet out from under him. Milford went down heavily, landing on his back with a grunt.

Neil bent over him. "Ye tried, I'll give ye that at least."

"How did you get in here?"

"Ye should ha' yer guards stay awake."

"I doubled the guards."

"Perhaps I can make myself invisible."

Milford glared at him.

"Where is Eileen?"

"I thought it was your ring you came for."

Milford grabbed at Neil's ankle, but Neil jumped out of his grasp, drawing his sword as he moved. Neil bent over Milford, seized his shirt and sliced it from neck to waist. "Do ye remember doing this to me?"

"I was drunk."

"Which doesna change that ye did it."

"You were a stranger in my house, Highlander, pretending to be French, but carrying a Scottish ring. Who wouldn't be suspicious?"

"Suspicious is one thing, holding a sword to me when I'm bound is another. Ye're a brave man when ye ha' no opponent."

"I didn't kill you."

"Nor will I ye."

Neil gestured to Duncan to help him. They tied Milford's hands and stuffed pieces of his shirt into his mouth, then pulled him down the stairs to the priest hole, where they tied him to the bed while Jack watched. When they were finished, Neil stepped back and looked into Milford's eyes.

"I'll release Jack when we're outside yer walls," he said. "And if I discover ye've lied to me, I'll come back and kill ye. Understood?" He walked away, not looking back as he closed the heavy wooden door behind him.

Chapter Six

Bess entered the room with her usual gloom. "The queen has sent for you," she told Eileen. "Her men are waiting. She wants you to attend her at once."

Eileen nodded, trying to conceal her dismay. There had been a time when the same request from her cousin Mary would have pleased her. Had pleased her, when, just days after she'd arrived in London, Mary had demanded that Eileen attend her. Eileen had ignored the haughtiness of the request, assuming that Mary's minions had not transmitted the warmth Mary must have sent.

How wrong she'd been. She'd stood before her cousin and listened not to the speech of welcome she'd expected, but to a tirade of complaints against Anne, against Sarah Churchill, against Parliament for granting Anne's allowance requests. Not once had Mary even hinted at being pleased to see her cousin again; there was no recognition of a shared history. Eileen might have been a stranger.

Nothing had changed since that day. Every ten days or so, Mary demanded that Eileen visit her, but never once had she showed any affection. King William, when he was there, nodded vaguely, his manner distant, as though he'd not known Eileen for most of her life, with no acknowledgment that they, too, were cousins.

This would be another session of standing while Mary ranted about Anne's behavior. And on her return, Anne would question her, asking for every nuance of Mary's voice, every gesture, every hidden meaning. But Eileen could not refuse the summons. She pushed the surge of resentment aside and nodded at Bess.

"Tell them I'll be right down."

"Do you want me to come with you?" Celia asked. "She'll ask about Sarah."

"The duchess," Bess said, her disapproval patent. "She's the Duchess of Marlborough. You should call her by her title."

Celia shrugged. "I think of her as Sarah. I'll come, Eileen, and wait in the audience hall while you're with her. It's always amusing to see who's there."

Eileen smiled gratefully. "Thank you."

Celia talked all the way to the palace, chattering as they climbed the stairs and were admitted to the audience hall, still talking when Eileen left her to go into the anteroom, where only those with appointments with the king were allowed to enter. Her wait was blessedly short; she stood quietly alone, aware of the glances and comments passed behind the hands of the courtiers lounging on the long sofas and gossiping in small groups by the massive fireplace.

It was worse than all the other visits. Mary did not even greet Eileen, just waved all of her attendants away, waited until the room was cleared, then launched into an enraged harangue. She had been told that Anne had said William was an unfit king; she ranted, then questioned Eileen at great length.

Eileen shook her head. "I have never heard Anne say anything like that, Mary. Never. Her only complaint about you is her allowance."

"Does she not resent that we have the throne and not her?"

"She has never said anything like that to me. Mary, people are telling you things that have no basis in fact. They're trying to destroy your relationship with your sister. Anne relinquished her claim in favor of William's; is that the action of someone who doesn't think he'd be a good king?"

Mary sighed, and looked off into the distance for several minutes, then turned to look at Eileen again, her eyes suddenly moist. "This unhappiness between Anne and me is God's punishment."

"For?"

"For us being unnatural daughters. We deserted our own father and now we are paying the price. You would not desert your father."

Eileen was silent, thinking of her father's merriness, of his drinking, of his casual betrayals of her mother, of his words that had led to their deaths.

"Would you, Eileen?" Mary's tone was sharp now. Her mood, so easily altered, had shifted again.

"My father opposed you both," Eileen said. "But I am here."

"Because you have nowhere else to go. Which reminds us—we have decided we cannot restore your title and the Whitby lands. I'm sure you understand."

Eileen stared at her cousin, horrified. She'd asked so many times, and each time Mary had led her to believe that it was only a matter of time before her father's title and lands would be hers again. All she wanted was a home of her own. Whitby's lands, while lovely, would provide her with little more than a roof over her head, but they would be hers. Restoration of them to her would mean that Eileen could leave London, would be dependent on no one, would never again have to stand before the queen like a beggar.

She found her voice at last. "Why? But, Mary, why?"

"If we restore the lands, everyone will think that denouncing us is acceptable. It's bad enough that you have been welcomed back into my sister's household. We cannot make you a duchess as though your father had done nothing."

"Mary, please! I will retire to Yorkshire and everyone will forget me. No one will think anything of it except that you are generous."

"They will think we bought your loyalty."

"You have my loyalty now."

"Do I? I hardly know anymore. We have been king and queen for three years and still we have Jacobites climbing out of the woodwork! Every day I hear of another plot against us—some said to be initiated by my sister." Her tone deepened. "Some that feature you."

"I have no ambitions, Mary."

"So you say. But every day I hear stories. I am weary of it. No, your lands will not be restored. You have a home with Anne; do not ask more. Now leave us."

Eileen had forced her tears back as she walked stiffly through the anteroom, ignoring the curious glances thrown at her. They'd hear soon; by nightfall everyone in London would know that Eileen Ronley's request had been turned down, that the queen was not sure whether she was trustworthy. She even managed to smile at acquaintances as she made her way to the passage behind the audience hall, closing the door to the narrow unadorned hallway behind her with a sigh. No one would bother her here; few but the servants even knew of its existence.

She stopped before a window, leaning her head against the heavy velvet draperies and willing herself not to cry. It took several moments to regain her calm, to control her anger. What difference could it possibly make to William and Mary to restore her title and lands? Or just the lands, so she might have some way of supporting herself? They were still held by the crown, and if her information was correct, were being neglected. How could refusing her benefit anyone? She was no Jacobite, no plotter against the throne.

If she were queen, she would never have refused her cousin this request. If she were queen, London would be a very different place.

An interesting thought.

Eileen raised her head and took several deep breaths, ready to face the audience hall. She must seem unaffected as she passed through the huge room, must stop and chat with those she knew, smile and toss her head and pretend she had not a care in the world. If they smelled her distress, sensed her weakness, she would be eaten alive by the gossips within a week. She'd learned long ago, at her mother's knee, how to behave. Never let them know what was in her heart, in her mind. She fluffed her skirts, straightened her back, then wiped the moisture from her cheeks, pinching them to bring some color. She was ready to find Celia.

Eileen saw Celia on the far side of the audience hall, talking with three men whose backs were to the room. She started through the crowds, stopping now and then to chat with someone she knew, but more often just winding through the tightly packed throngs. It was often this way lately, masses of people waiting for an audience with William or Mary, hoping to bribe or talk their way in.

One could barely even see the beautiful room, its high

ceilings ornate with paintings of biblical scenes, its walls lined with large portraits and windows heavy with draperies, pulled now to keep out the cold. A chandelier, heavy with dripping crystals, lit the center of the room with a soft glow; crystal sconces lined the walls, and all the people heated the space. It was, Eileen thought as she saw Celia coming toward her, the only good thing about being here—one was warm.

"I've just met an astonishing man!" Celia cried.

Eileen laughed, her mood lightening. "Let me guess— he's the most handsome man in the world."

Celia beamed. "But of course! He's perfect. Come and see for yourself."

The three men Celia led her to were tall and very well dressed, the quality of their long coats and wigs visible even from here. One of them turned, scanning the room, his young face curious. He smiled with pleasure as he saw Celia.

"There he is," Celia said, waving gaily. "His friend says he knows you."

That was unlikely, Eileen thought. The two other men, their backs still to her, wore ornate brown wigs, the curls lush and heavy on their shoulders. Their long legs were encased in tight silk stockings, their shoes fashionably adorned with silver buckles. Men with money to spend on luxuries. She knew no one who fit that description.

"They're French." Celia stopped next to the young man. "Miss Ronley, may I present Francois Reynard?"

The young Monsieur Reynard bowed and smiled. "Mademoiselle Ronley, it is a pleasure to meet you."

Eileen smiled in return, then turned to the second man, who studied her with unabashed curiosity, his green eyes frank with interest, his smile wide, wisps of dark red hair straying out from under his wig. He smiled and she gave him a polite smile, thinking he was a bit too curious about her—he must have heard something about her father. She turned to the third man and her heart lurched.

Belmond. Here, in William and Mary's audience hall.

"Mademoiselle Ronley," Belmond said with a smile, "we meet again."

His eyes, amused now, were as blue as she'd recalled, his black hair hidden under the elaborate brown wig. He was clean shaven and for the first time she saw the well-defined line of his jaw, the outline of his mouth. She watched him smile, remembering those lips on hers. And Howard's words.

This was Neil MacCurrie, the Earl of Torridon. Or was it?

"Where did you meet Monsieur Belmond?" Celia demanded of Eileen. "I don't remember you mentioning him."

"It was not here in London, mademoiselle," Belmond said to Celia, his smile wide. "It was at Ronley Hall. An unforgettable experience."

Eileen clasped her hands together and willed her heart to stop pounding.

"Miss Ronley," Belmond said, "may I present my cousin, Armand Delacroix?"

She turned to look at Neil MacCurrie's cousin. "Monsieur Delacroix," she said. "Also from Brittany, no doubt, where the Celtic influence is so strong. Which would explain the red hair and the freckles."

Armand grinned at her, his eyes merry. "Mademoiselle Ronley."

She turned to Belmond. "I thought you were joining William's army in Scotland."

He shrugged. "They had no need for my services."

"Is Scotland calm again?" Celia asked.

"I'm not sure Scotland will ever be calm," he said.

"Lord Wilmot says there are Jacobite spies everywhere," Celia said. "He says the Scots are just waiting for a chance to attack London and take back the throne."

"Does he?" Belmond asked, looking from Celia to Eileen with a grin. "Imagine that."

"Yes," Eileen said archly. "Imagine a Jacobite so bold as to come here, to the palace, to stand in this very hall as though he were welcome?"

"Wouldn't one think they'd see the futility of their cause?" Celia asked.

"I have heard that they are very persistent," Eileen said.

"Is that wrong, mademoiselle," he asked, "to be persistent?"

Eileen raised an eyebrow. "When the goal is hopeless, the persistence begins to look . . . foolish."

"Perhaps the goal is not hopeless. Perhaps it simply requires more effort."

"Surely you don't mean to suggest that the Jacobites should try harder? Or that it would be wise for them to send someone to London?"

"I would think that most unwise. Only a fool would do that."

"On that, then, we agree. But the world seems to be populated by fools."

Belmond looked around the room. "Is it suddenly cold in here? I feel a chill."

"Perhaps you are accustomed to a warmer climate, sir. Is Brittany warmer than London?"

"Just now anywhere is warmer than London. I am quite surprised; I had expected the opposite."

"Had you? And why would you expect that?"

"Past experience," he said.

"One is sometimes surprised to discover that things are not what one thought."

"Sometimes it is not always possible to correct a misimpression."

"Sometimes the misimpression is intentional. Sometimes it is not only possible to correct it, but wise."

Armand laughed behind his hand, then turned away, pretending to cough. Eileen could see his shoulders shaking, see the glance he shot at Belmond before he walked two paces away.

"Your cousin is amused, sir," Eileen said.

"So it would seem."

"Are you selling your services in London now?"

"No, Mademoiselle Ronley. I am simply observing."

"Observing," she said, tapping her lips. "What else could that be called?"

Francois took Celia's elbow. "Miss Lockwood, that's a most interesting portrait. Let's look at it more closely."

Celia looked from Belmond to Eileen with a wide-eyed stare before letting Francois lead her away. Eileen looked around her to be sure no one could hear, then turned back to Belmond, flicking her fan open and waving it before her with tiny, jumpy movements.

"What are you doing here?" she hissed. "Are you mad?"

Neil watched the color rise, then fade in Eileen Ronley's cheeks. She might pretend to be unaffected, but her body betrayed her. As did his. When he'd realized that her brittle tone masked anger, he'd felt a wave of the same, followed by a wry amusement. Milford must have told her who he was.

He leaned over her, close enough to smell her scent. In the middle of an icy winter, surrounded by unwashed bodies and overworn clothing, she managed to smell like roses. And she was beautiful, her blue bodice and looped overskirt atop a creamy white petticoat simple in contrast with the other women's heavily ribboned and laced gowns. She'd dressed her hair in a strange way, piled atop her head with a tall comb. It was probably the latest fashion—many of the women wore their hair the same—but he preferred her as he'd last seen her, her golden hair tumbling across her shoulders, her manner warm.

"I came to see ye," he said, not bothering to disguise his accent.

Startled, she looked into his eyes, then abruptly away.

"Why so cold, Miss Ronley?"

"Why did you come here? This is a dangerous place for you, Lord Torridon."

He leaned back from her, studying her face. She was angry, yes, but there was something more in her manner. "Ah, Milford told ye who I am."

"No, he did not. Does he know?"

"Aye, he does. I just had a lovely visit with him."

"You went to Ronley Hall?"

"I did. I went to find ye. Why are ye here in London instead?"

"There was nothing for me there; I was living on Milford's charity."

"And now ye live on yer cousin Anne's charity."

"How did you find me here?"

"It's no' difficult to discover where Princess Anne lives. Once I kent who yer cousins were, the rest was easy."

"And how did you find that out? Who talked to you about me?"

"All of London is talking about ye, wondering why Adam Ronley's daughter has come back."

"Why did you not tell me who you are? Why say you were a Huguenot?"

"A Scotsman is no' welcome in yer England just the now. And ye never believed my story. We both ken that."

"You could have trusted me."

"I did, lassie. I let ye ken more than I should ha'."

"Are you Neil MacCurrie?"

"Aye."

"The Earl of Torridon?"

"Aye."

"Not a mercenary."

"No."

"But you let me believe that of you."

"Aye."

"Interesting vocation you chose for yourself, sir."

"I look more like a soldier than a weaver," he said calmly.

"Are you a Jacobite?"

"I was."

"Suddenly loyal to William and Mary? And 'observing' their court? You told me you were not a spy."

"I am not."

"Then why are you in London? Who are you 'observing'?"

"Ye, Miss Ronley. Ye and no other. I couldna forget ye."

"Did you try?"

"No."

Her eyes flashed. She was very angry, and somehow his words were making it worse. Why?

"What is to stop me from turning to the room and telling everyone that a Jacobite, fresh from King James's court, is here at William and Mary's court? Let us see what conclusions they would draw."

Neil stared at her, his dismay overwhelming. He'd spent hours thinking of meeting Eileen Ronley again, had braved the icy wind dressed like a French fop, then waited for days in this stuffy crowded hall for just a moment with her.

He'd not expected her to throw herself in his arms, and had known he'd have to explain his presence in London, but he'd not imagined that she'd be like this. What had happened to the warm lass he'd met at Ronley Hall? What had she been told that had so changed her manner toward him? Perhaps, he thought wryly, he was not the only one with a twin. He looked into her eyes.

"Suit yourself, lass. Ye can tell them all who I am and watch as they drag me away. But before ye do that, perhaps ye'd like to meet yer cousin?"

Eileen's heart gave another thud as she followed his gaze to the man he'd called Armand. "You said he was your cousin."

Neil MacCurrie nodded. "He is, but on the other side. His mother was my mother's sister. His father was your mother's brother. Eileen, meet Duncan MacKenzie."

Eileen looked up into Duncan's green eyes. She could see the resemblance to her mother, the hint of shared blood in the spare cheekbones and wide mouth. Duncan was a handsome man, as her mother had been beautiful.

"Miss Ronley," Duncan MacKenzie said. "We came here

so that I could meet ye. We ken it's dangerous, but ye are so closely kept at Princess Anne's that we couldna get near to ye. How are ye, cousin?"

"You should not be here," she whispered.

"We have company," Neil said under his breath as Madam Landers and Lady Newcombe, two of London's most voluble gossips, approached them with wide smiles and open curiosity.

"Miss Ronley, dear," Madam Landers said, waving her fan coquettishly at the men. "Do introduce us."

Eileen raised her eyebrows at MacCurrie and waited to see what he would do. With a smile, he bent low over Madam Landers's hand.

"Jean-Paul Belmond," he said in heavily accented English. "At your service."

"A lovely thought," Madam Landers said.

"Madam Landers, Lady Newcombe," Eileen said crisply, "may I present Monsieurs Belmond and Delacroix, originally of Brittany, now of London."

Duncan bowed to both women, smiling widely. Eileen could see his amusement and hoped the women mistook it for pleasure in meeting them.

"Ah," said Lady Newcombe, "the French have such a way about them, don't they? What a pity we're going to war with them. We have our Huguenots here, of course, but I do miss the old days when the court was full of Frenchmen."

"That would be in your grandfather's day," Madam Landers said to Eileen. "King James had such a dour court. I do not miss the man in the least. You seem to have survived your father's . . . indiscretions, my dear."

Eileen smiled tightly.

"Miss Ronley seems to find her feet every time," Lady

Newcombe said, "although we've just heard that you won't be regaining your Yorkshire lands. You must be so distraught."

Neil MacCurrie looked from Lady Newcombe to Eileen.

"I am quite content here, madam," Eileen said.

"Of course you are."

Madam Landers was busy assessing Duncan, beginning with his toes and ending at his face. Duncan's smile widened. It was obvious, Eileen thought, that this was not the first time he'd been scrutinized by a woman. Madam Landers then did the same to Neil MacCurrie, who watched her with visible amusement.

"You must call on me so we can become better acquainted," Madam Landers said. "Both of you. I insist. Tomorrow."

"Are we free, Monsieur Belmond?" Duncan asked, his accent heavy.

"But of course," Neil said. "I shall be honored to escort Miss Ronley."

"Yes, all right, but no one else," said Madam Landers. "Miss Ronley, do not bring that Dutch cow or the Lockwood chit. Just these two most welcome men."

"Princess Anne cannot spare me," Eileen said.

"What a shame," Madam Landers said. "Gentlemen, we shall be delighted to receive you. Say, midafternoon?"

Lady Newcombe threaded her arm through Neil's. "We've had the most dreadful winter," she said. "One wonders if it will ever get warm."

Neil looked over his shoulder at Eileen. "One does wonder."

Madam Landers and Lady Newcombe shouldered her aside easily, introducing the men to several groups and excluding Eileen. She'd often wondered if the two gossips, fixtures in the audience hall, had been planted to mingle with visitors and report who was there. Now she was sure of it. But to whom would they report? William and Mary? Anne? Or to other forces in London?

Eileen watched their progress with a sinking heart. If Neil or Duncan slipped in his accent or demeanor, these two would notice. And talk. But neither man seemed to be at all worried; they smiled and laughed as Madam Landers paraded them about the room.

She should be raising the alarm, letting William and Mary know who was in their hall. But she could not do that to him. Whatever he might be, she would not be the one to reveal him. Neil MacCurrie bent over a blond woman's hand while smiling into her eyes and leaning her head closer to his. She could not stay and watch this.

She found Celia deep in conversation with Francois, or whatever his real name was. "Stay if you like," Eileen said, hearing how brittle her voice sounded. "I must leave."

"Oh, not yet," Celia said. "A while longer."

"I have to go."

Celia's forehead wrinkled with worry. "Of course. Monsieur Reynard, you are welcome to call upon us during your visit."

"I would be delighted, mademoiselle," Francois said with a smile. He lifted her hand to his mouth. "Until then."

Celia sighed, but followed when Eileen walked toward the door, leaning to ask her what all that had been about with Monsieur Belmond and why Eileen had not told her about him, and why they had to leave so abruptly when Francois was being so charming. Had something happened?

"Miss Ronley! Eileen!"

Eileen heard his voice easily over the din, turned to see MacCurrie striding toward her, ignoring the now hushed throngs who watched with avid interest.

"We will accompany you," he said as he reached her.

"I thank you, sir, but that is not necessary."

"*Oui, mademoiselle,* it is. Delacroix, Reynard, we leave at once. Come."

He took her arm and escorted her through the door and down the wide staircase, not acknowledging the curious who followed them to watch. He waited in the foyer, ignoring the watchers, while Eileen's cloak was brought, taking it from the footman and laying it on her shoulders, his hand tarrying just the slightest moment. He took her arm and led her to the door.

Outside, the icy wind hit them at once, creeping up Eileen's skirts and chilling her ankles, but she hardly noticed. MacCurrie, his arm around her back, led a fast pace down the line of waiting coaches; Celia, huddled under her coat, hurried to keep up, Reynard and Duncan at her heels. MacCurrie stopped abruptly at a coach and threw open the door, gesturing for Eileen to climb inside.

She shook her head. "We can walk, sir."

"Of course you can. But you'll take the ride I'm offering."

"Thank you, Monsieur Belmond, but we will walk. It's not far."

"It's almost dark, mademoiselle," he said as though speaking to a child. "You have no guards with you. Why do you take chances with your safety? Get in the coach. Please."

"We will walk."

"Eileen . . ."

"Sir," she said in French, "we do not know each other well enough for you to presume to use my given name, especially before the entire assembly. Surely you know what they will think!"

"They'll think I know your name," he answered in French.

"They'll think much more than that and you know it."

"Why do you care? They're nothing but nattering gossips. They would have talked about us anyway. Any new face at court is discussed for hours if not days, and from what I heard they discuss you daily. Why do you care what they say?"

"I have nothing else, sir. This court—this life—is everything I have, everything I ever will have. I must make my way in their company."

He was quiet for several moments, his expression thoughtful. "I'd not thought of that," he said at last.

"No."

"I owe you an apology."

She looked away, dangerously close to tears. It was suddenly all too much, the audience with Mary, discovering that her father's lands would not be hers, finding him here in London, seemingly oblivious to the danger he was in. She took a deep breath, aware that her emotions were much too close to the surface.

"Miss Ronley," he said, still in French, his voice low and earnest. "Let us drive you home. I mean no harm to you. I came to thank you and to introduce Duncan to you, not to destroy your life here."

She looked into his eyes, saw only concern, and felt suddenly too weary to argue. What further harm could it do to let him take them home? He was right—it was dangerous for her and Celia to walk these streets without protection, even for such a short distance. And she would have another few minutes with him.

"I . . . I thank you, sir. We will accept your kind offer," she said.

He nodded, visibly relieved, and handed her into the coach, then Celia. The men followed. Duncan knocked on the roof and the coach lurched forward. She sat silently, trying to control her tumbling emotions, to control the urge to throw herself into Neil MacCurrie's arms, to let him comfort her. To trust him. She could feel him beside her, his shoulder just inches from her own, his thigh next to her skirts. He seemed outsized in the small carriage.

As did Duncan MacKenzie. Was it possible that she was related to him? How different he was from the cousins on her father's side. William was sturdy, despite his asthma, but not tall, and certainly not imposing. Mary was bosomy and pretty, Anne larger and not as pretty. And Eileen looked like none of them.

She looked, she realized with a start, like Duncan. It was more than the height and freckles that they had in common—the wisps of hair visible under the wig and his eyebrows, arched now under her scrutiny, were auburn, the same russet as her mother's hair had been. Her own was much lighter, but the texture was the same. Duncan looked like her mother. He could well be her cousin.

And he might be Neil MacCurrie's cousin as well. The two men had the same long elegant bones and lean cheeks, the same shape to their shoulders, and assurance in their bearing. Both men, even dressed in silk and brocade, made her think of open spaces, of mountains and the sea. And of more.

"Where are you taking us?" Celia asked, her voice tremulous.

"Home, mademoiselle," Neil said.

"To France?"

He smiled slightly. "We are not abducting you, mademoiselle. We are taking you back to your lodgings."

"Oh." Celia sounded almost disappointed.

"Despite what Miss Ronley has told you, I am not a marauder."

"Miss Ronley has told me nothing of you, sir," Celia said.

"Ah. I must be very forgettable."

"I do not know how anyone could forget you," Celia said. "Any of you."

"I will take that as a compliment, mademoiselle," Neil said.

"How long are you visiting London?"

"We live here."

"Here? In London? Are you Huguenots?"

"Yes."

"Was it terrible, having to leave your home and come to England?"

He glanced at Eileen. "Yes," he said, the tiniest trace of humor in his tone.

"Do you think you will ever return to your home?"

"I intend to, mademoiselle."

Celia looked at Francois. "It will be England's loss."

Duncan grinned. The corners of Neil's mouth moved.

"Merci, mademoiselle," Francois said calmly.

"You don't look like craftsmen. Aren't all Huguenots watchmakers? Or weavers?"

"We are not," Francois said. "We are soldiers."

Celia's eyes widened. "Soldiers? Will you go to France to fight in King William's army?"

"No," Neil said. "We'll go to Scotland."

"Scotland! Oh!"

They were silent for the remainder of the ride. When the coach stopped, Duncan flung the door wide and looked out cautiously, one hand hovering over the hilt of his pistol. Eileen, watching him, realized anew how little she knew of these men. Had they stood in her cousins' audience hall with loaded pistols? Would they have used them? Milford's words came to her: "He might, even now, be planning to kill King William, to bring James Stuart and his kind back."

She stared at the leather window coverings, feeling incredibly foolish. Howard had warned her, Milford had warned her. But just being in Neil's presence, looking into his very blue eyes, had rendered her witless. As he had at Ronley Hall.

Francois handed Celia down and followed her up the stairs to the door. She knocked, then talked quietly with him while she waited.

Neil leapt from the coach and offered his hand to Eileen. "We must talk, Miss Ronley," he said in English.

Eileen stepped onto the frozen snow and withdrew her hand at once. "What can we have to say to each other? I thank you for the ride, sir."

He glanced around them. "Eil . . . Miss Ronley, we need to talk."

"You have put me in a difficult position," she said quietly. "Do you really expect that I will lie to my cousins to protect you while you spy on their court? You are very bold, sir."

He frowned. "I have to explain all of this. I'll come for

ye tomorrow, about the same time, and we'll go somewhere that we can talk without interruptions, a'right? Please."

She looked up into his eyes. How she wanted to believe him. But Howard's words tumbled in her head. Fearless. And ruthless. And not above seducing women for information. She shook her head. "There is nothing more to say."

Duncan leaned to her then. "Lass, we mean ye no harm. Will ye no' at least talk wi' me? Let me tell ye about yer mother's family."

"Mr. Delacroix, or MacKenzie, I have no way of knowing if yours is another fiction. No, gentlemen, I will not see you again. Thank you for the ride home."

"Ye ha' to listen to us, Eileen!" Neil said, his voice tight with anger.

"Do I? I think not. Please do not come tomorrow. And do not go to court again. You should not rely upon my continued silence. I too have my loyalties."

"If ye willna see us here, then we will go back to court," Neil said. "We'll be there every day until ye talk wi' us."

"I am warning you not to put me in that position. The world is populated by fools, but I am not one of them."

Neil's eyes flashed. He looked away, then back, his lips drawn thin, his expression cold. "Then may I have my ring, Miss Ronley?"

His ring. She'd forgotten his ring. Of course. Milford would have realized that she'd taken it, and obviously had told Neil MacCurrie. She felt a wave of humiliation. It had been his ring that he was after all along, not her company.

"But of course," she said, her tone as icy as she could manage. "You came for your property."

"I came to find ye, Eileen, no' for the ring. I told ye the truth."

"Which time? Which of your stories is the truth? The Huguenot who was driven out of his home by an intolerant king and now offers his sword to feed himself? Or the Scottish earl who roams England looking for Jacobite sympathizers and then appears at court? Is this man your cousin, or mine? Which is the truth? Did you really think I would see no more than your handsome face, that I am one of those women so witless that they succumb to a few smiles? I have to admit that for a moment, Lord Torridon—or is it Monsieur Belmond?—I almost believed that you came to have me meet Duncan. What about Francois? Surely I must be related to him as well."

"No."

"What is his real name?"

"Calum MacLeod."

Before Eileen could reply, the door swung wide, revealing Bess, her face anxious. "Oh, thank God you're back! Come at once—Anne's son is ill again and we need you!"

Celia, with a glance at Francois, scurried inside. Eileen picked up her skirts to follow. Neil put a hand on her arm, his voice just above a whisper.

"Let us not leave it at this. I will come for ye tomorrow and we'll talk."

"No. I will have your ring waiting for you with Anne's man. You may ask for the package for Monsieur Belmond."

"Eileen . . ."

"Do not make it worse. Please . . . I am glad you are alive. And I do not wish you harm. But I have all I can bear just now. Do not ask me to keep your secret here. Please."

"We must talk, lassie. Let me come to ye."

She shook her head. "I would we had met some other

time, or that we were other than who we are. As it is . . ." Her lips trembled. "You ask too much. Good-bye."

They were silent for most of the ride to the ship, Neil staring at the door of the coach as though it transfixed him. Duncan had never seen his cousin so affected by a lass. They'd spent time with many women over the years, he and Neil and Jamie. He was familiar with Neil's bantering flirtations, with his easy manner around women, and their willing acceptance of his company. He'd been with Jamie when Jamie had met Ellen Graham, had seen the same intensity between them that he saw between Neil and Eileen now. There was something almost uncanny about them, as though they'd known each other before, as though this was a reprise of an ancient pattern. He swore softly. Damn Celtic blood.

"An interesting welcome, Neil," he said, keeping his tone light. "It must ha' been yer handsome face. And, Calum, it'll be England's loss when ye leave, laddie. I think ye may expect to visit again. The two of us will ha' to wait for an invitation."

Neil stared at the window for several minutes, then turned to look at Duncan. "We have an invitation already. Tomorrow we'll call on Madam Landers and see what she has to say."

Chapter Seven

Eileen closed her eyes and willed her body to relax. Their prayers had been answered, at least for now. Anne's two-year-old son was out of danger. His fever had broken at last in the wee hours and he rested easily now. Perhaps he, unlike the rest of Anne's children, would survive.

When the doctor told them that the worst of the danger was over, Anne and her husband had collapsed in each other's arms. Eileen, Celia, and Bess had crept away then. She'd found her bed, but not sleep, and had been lying in the dark for hours, thinking about all that had happened in the last day, about Mary's suspicions, and the refusal to give her her father's lands.

About Belmond, or Neil MacCurrie, or whoever he was. Whatever he was.

Was he the rogue Howard had described? Had he really come to London to see her—or simply to reclaim his ring? Why had he not come here to Anne's rather than wait for her in the audience hall? Had he even known she was in London? Or had he, upon finding her at the palace, smoothly covered his surprise and presence with his tale of going to Ronley Hall? Was he here spying on William and Mary? Had he hoped that Eileen would be a source of information?

She would not be, of course, but he'd quickly find someone else. More than one woman, if she'd correctly read the looks thrown him, would be willing to report to him. He would have women falling all over him, and soon, if Madam Landers and Lady Newcombe were any indication. His informant might not be cousin to the king and queen, but he would find all the information he needed in exchange for a few smiles. Or more.

Eileen turned on her side, willing back the image she'd conjured, of him in another woman's bed. She was being ridiculous. Of course he'd bedded women. One could see it in the way his gaze caressed her without a touch, the way he'd sat too close to her in the coach. Neil MacCurrie was no innocent. And, if she spent much more time around him, neither would she be. She did not need to lie with a man to know how complicated it could make her life.

Her life—how absurd, as if this were a status worth defending. What was her life now? Would her future mean endless shuttling between feuding sisters? Would she grow old here, an unwanted, untouched woman tucked away in Anne's household, never knowing carnal joys, never knowing what parents shared when they looked at their child?

No one had been willing to marry her at Ronley Hall. Would it be the same here? Would she and Bess and Celia age together? But no, Celia would not last long. Some wealthy man would whisk her away to decorate his home and brighten his old age. Celia, sweet, innocent Celia, who deserved a man to love her, would probably never have that. Nor, most likely, would she herself.

Why was it that the only man to stir her senses in years had to be not only married, but a man who could lie with impunity, who made her believe anything he said without effort? She could not be the only woman he had that effect on. Neil MacCurrie would quickly find someone to tell him what he wanted to know.

She turned again, trying to quell the flash of jealousy she felt at the thought of him with another woman. And to destroy the vision of Neil naked, his long limbs stretched out beside her, his lips hovering above hers. His body would be beautiful, she had no doubt of that, and he would know how to make her respond, would teach her what lovers knew.

Perhaps she'd been the greatest fool of all, keeping her body intact. For whom? For what? To age slowly in this dark room, to lie awake at night, yearning for the touch of a man who would never care for her, who only wanted to use her? He was a liar, a spy, a seducer of women; she must concentrate on that, not on imagining what his skin would feel like under her fingers.

Howard had said that Neil MacCurrie had a wife waiting at home, children as well. What was wrong with her that she could even consider ignoring all that she believed him to be? Just to see his smiles, to feel his touch? Had she inherited some flaw from her father, from her grandfather, that made her so carnal?

But what if even some of what Neil said was true? Duncan might even be her cousin; that much could be true. Still, it changed nothing. He shared Neil's politics and might share his principles. Duncan seemed forthright, but he could be cut from the same cloth, could be as deceitful as she feared Neil to be.

And what if Milford was right? What if Neil MacCurrie was in London to kill William? A widowed Mary, queen though she was, would be no match for a determined King James, and Neil might well know that. Was he ruthless enough to kill William? He'd admitted to being a Jacobite, a soldier—that he'd fought against William's men. Or was it less sinister? Was he in London not to murder anyone, but simply to hear the latest and then report it to King James in France, or his fellow Jacobites in Scotland? Didn't that still make him a spy and a traitor?

She'd been right to send him away. She should have done more, should have done exactly what she'd threatened in the hall, to turn to the crowd behind her and denounce him for what he was.

And yet . . .

If he was a liar, he was a very good one. What if some of what he said was true? He was, as she'd guessed at Ronley Hall, a Scot, and he obviously knew the MacKenzies—his reaction to her mother's name had not been feigned. What if Neil MacCurrie was just what he'd claimed? Had he traveled all the way from Scotland just to see her again? But if he was not a spy, why was he here in London? To see her, to thank her, as he'd said? If that was true, then how unkind she'd been.

And Duncan? It was difficult to believe that Duncan, with his clear green eyes, could plot and deceive. What if the two men were no more than they claimed, and she was tossing aside a chance to know her cousin, to learn about her mother's family? To see Neil MacCurrie again? And she might never know. She sat up, staring through the thin muslin bedhangings, feeling the cold air rush to meet her.

He would come for his ring. And she would talk to him then.

Neil looked through the windows of the public room of the Pegasus Inn with narrowed eyes. At his side the landlord spoke in a quiet voice.

"He's been there since yesterday, sir. Him or someone just like him." The landlord nodded at the man who stood in the shadow of the doorway opposite. "And last night three men pretending to be Jacobites tried to get me to talk about King James. I told them we were faithful servants of William and Mary. And then I led them in a toast to their royal majesties' health. How could they refuse?"

"Did they ask about yer guests?"

"Aye. I said I had some Frenchies here who were wearing me out with their demands." He gave Neil a glance. "It might be coincidence."

"Or it might be me," Neil said. "D'ye want us to leave?"

"No' the now. I'll let ye ken if I'm overworried. Let 'em watch all they wish."

"Thank ye."

"Ye're welcome to stay as long as ye'd wish, Torridon, but I'd prefer ye to take the back door in the future, aye?"

Neil nodded, looking through the window at the waiting man. "Aye. And I think I need to ask a few questions of my own. Who would ken who the friends of Adam Ronley would ha' been?"

"Adam Ronley? One of King Charles's get? Dinna he drown in the Thames?"

"Aye, two years ago."

The landlord rubbed his chin, then nodded. "I ken who could tell ye."

Duncan looked over his shoulder as he followed Neil down the dark close, half expecting to see someone following. But no one crept along the dank passageway after them. He didn't blame them; water dripped from the stones overhead and the footing was icy. Not a place many would want to be. Calum led the way, the lad coming out into the dim daylight and looking above him with a grim expression. A moment later Duncan stepped into the courtyard and looked up at the items of clothing pinned to lines strung overhead. They'd been there for some time, the tattered shirts and breeches stiff with age and cold. Most of the windows that faced the courtyard were barred, or broken, open to the wind that screamed through the narrow passage. There was no sign of anyone living here.

"Are ye sure we need to do this?" he whispered.

"We'll make it a short visit," Neil said, looking at the paper in his hand. "It's that one." He led the way to a door at the far side of the courtyard.

Duncan put his hand over the hilt of his sword and followed. He did not like this place, not even with three armed men. Neil's knock was unanswered, but a moment later an old woman thrust her head through the window above them. Her gray hair was thinning, her headdress threadbare. Her gnarled hands gripped the windowsill as she leaned out to look at them.

"Who's there? What do you want at this time of the morning?"

"I ha' some questions, mistress," Neil said. "And some coin for answers."

"What kind of questions, Scotsman?"

"The kind best asked quietly."

She cackled. "There's no one here but me and the rats, and they won't be listening."

Neil pointed to the clothing hanging above them. "Who wears those?"

"No one. My man left me years ago. I leave them there so people will think I'm not alone. What d'you want to know?"

"May we come inside?"

"Three men with swords at their hips and pistols in their belts? Not likely, sir. Ask your questions from here, or go away."

Neil frowned and exchanged a glance with Duncan. Duncan shrugged. If it was up to him, they'd leave, but he knew that set to Neil's jaw. He motioned to Calum to stand by the entrance to the close, so the lad could warn them if anyone approached.

"D'ye ken who Adam Ronley was?" Neil asked.

"I do. Who's asking?"

"I'll no' be telling ye my name, nor asking yers."

"Fair enough. Yes, I know who Ronley was."

"D'ye ken which of his friends might still be in London?"

"I do. Show me the coin and I'll decide what I'll tell you."

Neil held up a coin, then put it on the doorstep.

"Toss it up, handsome."

She caught it easily, and bit it before she nodded. "Give me another just like it and I'll give you your answer." She caught the second one and bit it as well. "A third will get you a juicy story."

Neil sighed but tossed the third to her, watching her repeat her testing of it.

"His closest friend was Howard Templeton."

"And the juicy story?"

"Templeton used to bring Ronley to my place—no, I didn't live here then; I had my own establishment, a lovely one. Ronley drank a great deal and was always swearing that he should have been king but that Charles wouldn't tell the world the truth. After King James left, Templeton started being not so nice to Ronley, making fun of him a lot."

"And?"

"And another coin will help my memory."

"It's the last one ye'll get," Neil said as he tossed it to her.

"You'll get your money's worth. Then William and Mary took the throne. The day after Ronley denounced William, Templeton brought him to my place and paid for all his drinks. That was unusual; Ronley usually paid for everything. And when Ronley started his moaning about being king, Templeton told him to be quiet. And that afternoon Ronley drowned in the Thames."

"Do you think Templeton did it?"

"Not alone. Ronley was a big man and hard to manage when he was drunk."

"Ye think it was murder, then?"

"I think Templeton knows what happened. I never saw him again, but I heard he has a wife and a big house now."

"Do you know where he lives?"

"No." She ducked back inside and closed the window.

Neil turned to Duncan. "Howard Templeton. Remember the name."

Neil and Duncan spent the rest of the morning visiting men who had been Jacobites, who had once welcomed Neil. Some still did, but others refused to even talk to him, let alone entertain him. London was even more dangerous than he'd thought. They risked much to stay, even for a few days.

In the afternoon they went to Madam Landers's, where their reception was much warmer. Duncan was immediately whisked away by their hostess, leaving Neil to talk with Lady Newcombe. She was a willing informant, and might have become more had Neil not pretended to misunderstand her blatant invitation to become a bedmate. There were men, he knew, who would not quibble with her offer, accepting her embraces for what they were and realizing an exchange had been made—his attentions for her information. He was not one of them. Nor was Duncan, who met his gaze over Madam Landers's head, his amusement manifest.

Keeping Lady Newcombe on the subject was difficult at times, and Neil had to keep steering the conversation back to the court of King Charles II.

"King Charles had many children, is that not so?" he asked.

"Oh, yes, many. None legitimate, of course, though Monmouth and Adam Ronley both liked to say that they were legitimate, but it was all nonsense. Adam always swore he had a letter and a marriage license that proved his claim, but he never produced them. And the king always denied it. You may imagine who was believed, not that it mattered. Charles was very generous; he gave his children titles and property. Adam got the Whitby lands and the title."

"He married a Scottish woman, I'm told," Neil said.

"Oh, yes. Catriona someone. He was nineteen—her father refused to allow the marriage, but King Charles ordered it done, so that was that. Her father went home to Scotland even before the wedding. We rarely saw her—she almost never came to court. Adam was never happy with her."

She flicked her fan rapidly, smiling coquettishly at him. "Adam was a man who needed merry company, and there were many who were happy to provide it. Oh, he was fun to be with! It was a sad day."

"He and his wife died together, did they not?"

"Yes, drowned in the Thames. They said an accident, but no one believed it! Murdered, he was, both of them. I'm sure of it, everyone was." She sighed. "Not that long ago—just two years—but it seems an age. William and Mary's court is nothing like Charles's, but at least it's better than King James's. That was dismal!"

"Did Sir Adam ever bring Miss Ronley to court?"

"Occasionally. He shouldn't have. She was only a child, and her grandfather's court was a wild place—I'm not sure I was old enough to be there—but I learned astonishing things and still remember most of them. She spent more time with her grandfather than with her father. Now tell me, Monsieur Belmond, just how well you know Miss Ronley. Or should I say 'Eileen'?"

Neil forced a smile. Such a little thing, to call a woman by her given name, he thought, and yet, to most of society, so important. It signified that they were well acquainted, likely that they were lovers. Some married couples never called each other by their given names, not even after a life spent together. He'd not considered what it would mean to the listeners to have him shout her name across the room as though he had a right to do so. He had little regard for the trappings of the court; fewer for those who hungered for gossip. But Eileen Ronley lived in that world and he must acknowledge that.

"Not well enough to use her name, I assure, madam. But 'Ronley' is not a fluid name, you know. It does not slip easily off the tongue. Miss Ronley let me know exactly how displeased she was." He smiled again, ruefully this time. "I am still learning your English ways."

She looked at his mouth and tilted her head and Neil steeled himself. He knew what was next. "If you need any . . . instruction, Monsieur Belmond, you have only to ask."

"I will keep that in mind, madam."

*   *   *

The wind howled for most of the day, the frozen rain lashing the icy drops against the windows; they seeped inside, bringing the frigid air with them. Eileen spent the hours with Bess and Celia, closeted away in their room, answering Celia's endless questions about Belmond with as much truth as she dared.

She longed to trust the girl, to tell her everything, but she did not dare. Celia's mind—and heart—was too easy to read. That would change if she stayed here at court. In time, the openness that was so charming would be replaced by the same jaded weariness Eileen felt.

Anne had not called for any of them today. Nor had anyone else. Eileen had talked to the footmen, had left instructions with all the staff to fetch her if a Monsieur Belmond came for a package. The day was drawing to a close and still he had not come.

She sighed now, reaching to feel, as she had so many times, that his ring was still tucked within her handkerchief in her pocket. She could feel its shape beneath the material, could visualize the gold gleaming in the light. An oak tree. The sea. What did they represent? She knew precious little of her mother's people and nothing of the other clans.

"I shine, not burn" was all she remembered—the MacKenzie motto. And some vague stories of the Brahan Seer, who had predicted so many things that had come true. Her mother had told her some of them over the years. If she concentrated, perhaps she'd remember more. But why bother? What difference could it make now? He wasn't coming.

She lifted her head as Celia rose to answer the door.

"He's here," Celia said.

*   *   *

Neil circled the dark room again. Princess Anne's lodgings were far from luxurious: ancient tapestries, worn and thin, hung against walnut-paneled walls pocked with dents, punctuated by heavily covered windows that might as well have been open for all the air they leaked. The furniture was old, stiff and unyielding, which was why he paced the room. That, and his worry that Eileen would not see him again.

He had to talk to Eileen, to discover why she'd been angry with him, even before he'd used her given name. She'd obviously found out who he was—from whom? Milford? She'd known he was a Scot before he left Ronley Hall, so why the sudden coldness? It should make no difference to him what she thought of him, but it did. Which had led him here, despite his own anger at her coldness and rejection of him. He had to at least try.

He turned when the door opened, hoping it would be Eileen, but was disappointed when the girl said that Princess Anne would receive him now.

"I have come to see Miss Ronley," he said, careful to keep his accent French.

"You are to follow me, sir," the girl said.

His wariness increased as she led him down the dark corridors. The girl opened a door and gestured him inside. The woman who awaited him was about his own age. She glared at him and waved him forward.

"Come closer, I cannot see you," she said. He stood before her while she squinted at him, then leaned back against the chair with a sigh. "Who are you, Monsieur Belmond?"

"Pardon, madam?"

"You heard me. Who are you, sir, that you call upon my cousin here? That you call my cousin by her given name in the middle of my sister's audience hall? You do know that all of London is talking about you now."

So this was Princess Anne, he thought. He bowed politely.

"My name is Jean-Paul Belmond, madam."

"Of?"

"London."

"London. I've never heard of you."

"It is unlikely that you would, madam. I am seldom at court."

"No more seldom than I, sir. And to my knowledge, you have never been here to this house, but you know Eileen."

"We have met."

"Where?"

"At Ronley Hall. I was traveling and spent the night there."

"How well do you know her, Monsieur Belmond?"

"Not well enough to use her name. That was both unintentional and unforgivable."

Anne's expression relaxed; she almost smiled. "My cousin is under my protection. Her reputation has been unsoiled until now. You caused quite a stir yesterday."

"Not by design."

"I am glad to hear it. I am not without power, Monsieur Belmond, and I would be most unhappy if anyone were to harm Eileen."

"I do not wish to harm her in any way."

"I am glad to hear that as well, and wondering why I have not heard of you before this." She looked behind him. "Why have you not mentioned him, Eileen?"

Neil spun around to see Eileen standing behind him, her face impassive. His heart, which had lurched, settled into a dull pounding as Eileen moved forward, to stand next to him. She did not look at him.

"I did not think to see Monsieur Belmond again, Anne," Eileen said.

"He lives here in London."

"I thought he was traveling elsewhere."

"He has come to apologize," Anne said. "It that not so, Belmond?"

"It is."

"Then do so."

Neil turned to Eileen again, startled to see not anger, but amusement, in her eyes. "I am sorry to have discomforted you, Miss Ronley."

"Thank you, Monsieur Belmond. I accept your apology."

"Thank you, Miss Ronley."

She smiled at him then, a real smile, before turning to her cousin. "Anne, if you are quite finished interrogating Monsieur Belmond . . . ?"

Anne nodded. "But leave the door open, Eileen. There has been enough talk already. We don't need any of our servants adding to it."

She led him to a long, narrow room, where the walls were lined with walnut paneling and cushioned benches, the windows covered tightly here also. Closets lined the end of the room, the top half of each caned. Eileen closed the door firmly behind them, lit several candles that waited on a sideboard, and turned to him.

"I am sorry that Anne questioned you so vigorously. I did not know she would do that. I had not complained to her; I'd not even told her we'd met."

He spread his hands wide before him. "I dinna mean to

make ye the subject of gossip by calling yer name at court, Miss Ronley. I just dinna want ye to leave without me talking to ye; I dinna think that anyone would be listening. I dinna care what other people think of me and sometimes I forget that other mightna feel the same way. Truthfully, lass, in Scotland no one would ha' blinked."

She waved his words away. "In a few hours they will be discussing someone else. It doesn't matter."

"I suspect it does; yer cousin thinks it does. Someone told her about it."

"It was not me."

"Thank ye for keeping yer silence, at Ronley Hall, and yesterday at court, and today wi' yer cousin. I am once again in yer debt."

She shook her head. "There is no debt, sir."

"Aye, there is. Ye saved my life and I came to acknowledge it."

"Who told you where to find me?"

"Milford. Who told ye who I was?"

"Does it matter?"

"Aye. Ye are welcome in London. I am not. And if any of yer cousins were to ken who I am . . . well, it might not be too healthy for me."

She settled herself on one of the benches and folded her hands in her lap. "I haven't told my cousins about meeting you."

"Thank ye for that."

"I only asked one man about your ring, one of my father's friends. He told me that it was the Torridon crest and that you were probably the Earl of Torridon."

"I am."

"He says you are a spy for King James. Are you?"

She asked it so mildly that he looked into her eyes, wondering if her pleasant manner concealed something else. Was someone listening? Was she amused because she thought he was about to incriminate himself? Was this her revenge for embarrassing her yesterday? He glanced behind her, at the closets. Men could hide in the three closets, could even now be watching him through the cane.

"There is no one in the closets, sir," she said, her tone much cooler. She crossed the room and flung the cabinets open one by one, facing him with heightened color. "See? You are very nervous for an innocent man."

"Ye said yerself it is dangerous for me in London."

"So I did. Why are you in London, Lord Torridon?"

"To see ye, not to spy on yer cousins. What d'ye want me to tell ye, that I'm planning to murder William and Mary in the middle of their own palace, wi' hundreds of people watching? D'ye take me for a fool?"

Eileen laughed, surprising him. He sat down on the bench and watched her, his expression apparently making her laugh again. She sat near him and smiled.

"I'm sorry," she said, "but you made it sound so witless."

"Aye, well, it would be, wouldn't it? Look, lassie, I fought for James Stuart, I'll no' deny it. But we lost. And I'll make no pretense—I dinna like that William is king, but I ha' accepted that he is."

"A wise choice."

"A necessary one." He leaned forward. "I ha' told ye the truth. I came to thank ye for saving my life. If ye had gone to Bristol, we would ha' gone there. Ye went to London; I followed ye. I went to Princess Anne's, but they wouldna let me see ye, so I went to court to find ye. It's that simple. I came to thank ye, and to see if ye'd paid any price for setting me free. Did ye?"

She shook her head. "No. Milford was suspicious that I'd helped you leave, but he could not prove anything."

"Good. I also came to ha' ye meet Duncan. He's wanted to meet ye ever since I went home and told him about ye."

"Oh."

"Aye."

"Why didn't you tell me about him at Ronley Hall? Why didn't you tell me who you were? Did you think I would tell Milford?"

"Ye had no reason not to. Ye've kent him yer whole life. Why would ye no' tell him if he asked?"

"I would not have told him."

"I dinna ken that, though, did I? Ye could ha' easily told him all ye kent, or suspected. Why did ye not?"

"I . . ." Her cheeks colored. "I'm not sure myself."

He suppressed his smile. It was all right. Eileen Ronley was not as unaffected by him as she pretended. Nor he to her. "And I came to see ye today to find out why ye were so angry yesterday at court. Even before I used yer name, ye were angry, lass. Why?"

"I was told that you were . . . I thought you should have told me who you were at Ronley Hall, or told me something of my mother's people."

"I'm sorry I dinna. Had I kent I could trust ye, I would ha'. We were strangers then."

"We still are."

"Are we, lassie?"

She straightened her back. "London is very dangerous for you. If I was able to discover who you are, so will others."

"I will leave soon."

"And go . . . ?"

"Home. To Torridon."

"And then what?"

He gave her a puzzled look. "And then I'll live there."

"With your family."

"Aye."

"Tell me about Duncan," she said briskly. "He is your cousin as well as mine? Does that mean that you and I are related?"

"No. Duncan's father was yer mother's brother. His mother was my mother's sister."

"Was. Are they all dead, then? His parents and yours?"

"My mother is alive. Duncan's parents are not. When he was fourteen he came to live at Torridon and was raised with my brother and me. He's a good man, Eileen, Miss Ronley. He'd like to talk wi' ye before we leave. Will ye meet wi' him, just for an hour?"

She looked across the room. While he waited, he watched her profile, the glint of candlelight on her golden hair. She'd closed the door despite Princess Anne's warning, but she was still wary of him. Why then did he feel as though he knew her, as though he'd always known her, that somehow Eileen Ronley had always been a part of his life? He should leave her now, should leave London. And if she refused to meet Duncan, he would. They'd leave at first light. And eventually he'd forget her. She turned to look into his eyes.

"Yes," she said. "I'd like to talk to Duncan."

"Tomorrow?"

"Where?"

"We'll come for ye. In the morning. Will ye do that?"

"Yes."

He stood. "Until tomorrow then, Miss Ronley."

"Wait." She reached into her pocket and held out her hand. "Your ring, sir."

"I'd forgotten ye had it. Thank ye." He took the ring and slipped it on his finger, feeling its welcome weight. "May I ask ye, lass . . . why did ye bring it here with ye?"

"I . . . I didn't want to leave it with Milford. It's very beautiful."

"Aye, it is."

She met his gaze. "And I wanted to know who you were. I knew someone would recognize the crest. The design is very distinctive."

"It's the MacCurrie crest."

"An oak tree and water?"

"Aye, land and sea. Who was it who recognized it?"

"I'm not sure. It was my father's friend, Howard Templeton, who told me."

Neil felt his blood chill. "Templeton told ye who I was?"

"He made some inquiries after I showed him the ring."

"Ha' ye told him ye've seen me again?"

She colored again. "No. Nor shall I."

"I thank ye for that."

"Do you know him, Neil, um, Lord Torridon?"

He grinned at her. "I'm shocked at ye, Miss Ronley. Such improprieties! Neil will do just fine, lass."

She smiled softly. "You need to leave London."

"I will." He looked at his hand, at his ring, with its reminders of his past, then at her. "Do ye believe in destiny, Miss Ronley?"

"Destiny?"

"Aye. Fate. That things were meant to happen."

"Why do you ask me that?"

"I think we were fated to meet, ye and I."

"Why would we be?"

"That I dinna ken. But it's passing strange that I should end up at yer home."

"You said you'd been sent there."

"I was given the names of two safe places. I chose Ronley Hall."

"Perhaps both of them were dangerous."

"Quite possibly. But I think that we were destined to meet."

She smiled distantly. "Do you know how many times I've heard that?"

He raised an eyebrow.

"I came to court when I was twelve, Lord Torridon. I've heard this, and every other possible seduction scheme, before, many times. 'We are brought together by fate. You must be mine.' No, I do not believe in destiny."

"Then why did we meet?"

"Chance."

"Ye dinna believe that and we both ken it. Ye may scoff—God kens I would were I ye—but whether it makes sense or no', there is a thread between us, a connection. I dinna understand it, but I feel it. And I think ye do too." He touched the corner of her mouth and traced his finger along her lips. "Go ahead, tell me there's nothing between us, that when ye look at me, when I touch ye, ye feel nothing."

She leaned away from his touch.

"Ye're verra beautiful, lassie; most men would admire ye for that alone—and I do—but it's no' that that pulls me to ye. There is something between us. And ye canna tell me different, can ye?"

She stared at him with wide eyes. He bowed to her.

"Until tomorrow, Miss Ronley. Sleep well, lassie."

*   *   *

Neil smiled to himself as he made his way through the dark corridors and finally out into the street, where snow swirled into drifts, and the footing was treacherous. He'd see her again. It would have to be enough to last the rest of his life. He'd go home to Torridon, marry Fiona, and behave responsibly. But not yet.

Chapter Eight

Eileen tugged the brush through her hair, trying to control her anger. "Why does she want to see me again so soon? Tell her no."

"Tell the queen no?" Bess shook her head. "What are you thinking?"

She'd been thinking she was about to meet Neil and Duncan. She'd spent the early morning preparing for the meeting, trying on every piece of clothing she owned, pairing bodices and overskirts, dressing her hair different ways. She told herself that her efforts were for herself. Not to please Neil. He was married and she wasn't a fool. Or much of one. She had just decided—again—that her hair would not do when the summons came that the queen wanted to see her at once. Eileen frowned at her image.

She knew why she had been summoned. She'd be asked to explain why it was that a stranger named Belmond spoke to her so familiarly in the hall, why everyone at court was talking about her. Could she face them all again, walk through those halls with her chin high, pretending that her heart wasn't pounding?

What would she tell Mary? That she had planned to meet a Jacobite who had fought against William's army, who even now, despite his protests, might harbor hope that one day King James might regain his throne? That she was so willing to spend an hour in his company that she was willing to overlook everything her mind told her, ignore the warnings she'd been given, just to see him again? That even if he'd harbored ill will toward William and Mary, she would at least talk with him and the man he said was her cousin? She might as well sign her own death warrant.

Eileen hurried along the street, huddling inside her cloak, scolding herself for not insisting that she be escorted. She looked over her shoulder, hoping that she was simply being overly nervous. The man who had followed her was still there, the same distance behind her no matter whether she slowed her steps or sped them up. At first she'd paid him no mind, even when he'd moved forward from the building across the street from Anne's lodgings, falling in behind her as though he'd been waiting for her.

Mary was having her followed.

Perhaps he had waited for anyone who left Anne's, and Eileen just happened to be the first. Perhaps Mary had employed him to tell her of all the comings and goings at her sister's. That was certainly possible, given Mary's remarks at their last meeting. Someone was filling Mary with tales about Anne, someone who did not want the animosity between the sisters to end. Who? And why?

Eileen looked over her shoulder. He was still there, matching her pace. What if he was following her, just her? What if Mary believed those who were apparently spreading rumors that she had returned to London to further her father's claim to the throne?

Or did it have to do with Torridon, with Neil MacCurrie's visit? She'd been in London for two months without being followed; he'd been here for just a few days and now she had a man dodging her footsteps. Should she turn and confront him, ask him what he was doing?

Perhaps she was being targeted for a simple robbery. Many people in London knew where Princess Anne lived. Few would suspect her household to be as impoverished as it was. Perhaps he thought to abduct Eileen, to hold her for ransom, thinking that she would have a family who would pay for her safe return. If that was the case, he would be unpleasantly surprised. No one, beside those in Anne's household, would even miss her if she were to disappear. And there was no money to pay a ransom, even if Anne wished to. She allowed herself a wry laugh at the thought that being attacked for her money or her pearls was preferable than any other scenario she could devise.

She started to run. If he meant her harm, he'd have to do it soon; she was almost at the palace. She looked over her shoulder. He'd begun to trot. She began to pray aloud, continuing until she saw the guards at the palace gates, until they waved her in.

She slowly climbed the steps, trying to catch her breath and still her heart, then turned to look back. The man was standing outside the fence, watching her, his expression impassive. For just a moment their gazes locked and held, then she turned away. She would know him again, would remember his round face and those dark eyes that watched her without wavering. She pulled her cloak tighter.

The audience hall was just as crowded as the day before, with many of the same people there. The whispers started as soon as she entered the room. She kept her chin high and her manner breezy as she stopped to chat with several acquaintances, hoping for an opening to use the remarks about Monsieur Belmond that she'd practiced. Everyone stared at her, but no one spoke to her beyond the most cursory greeting until Lord Wilmot, standing with Lady Newcombe, stopped her. For once she was pleased to see the gossips—and ready for them.

"On your way to see the queen?" he asked.

"Yes," she said, preparing to launch into her explanation.

"See what you can discover about Scotland," Lady Newcombe said.

"Scotland?" Eileen asked, her voice much too high.

"Glencoe," Lord Wilmot said.

"Messengers have come in every hour or so," Lady Newcombe said. "See what the queen will tell you."

"Mary never discusses politics with me."

"Politics?" Lady Newcombe cried. "Hundreds were murdered in their beds and you call it politics?"

"Hundreds murdered? Whatever do you mean, madam?"

"You've not heard?" Lord Wilmot asked.

Eileen shook her head.

Lady Newcombe sighed. "Princess Anne never seems to know anything happening in court. How would anyone in her household know?"

"The Earl of Stair ordered his men to Glencoe," Lord Wilmot told Eileen.

"Billeted them in people's homes," Lady Newcombe said. "For weeks!"

"And then, in the dark of the night, they rose up and murdered everyone they could set their hands on, all of MacDonald's people," Lord Wilmot said. "I am no friend of Scotland, even less of Highlanders, but this is not right."

"How horrible," Eileen cried. "Why would Stair do such a thing?"

Lady Newcombe leaned closer. "He's saying King William ordered it, to punish one of the chieftains who did not sign the Articles of Allegiance to him."

"Mark my words," Lord Wilmot said. "The Scots will not stand idle. They will avenge this. The Highlands could rise again."

"We could be murdered in our beds!" Lady Newcombe looked around her as though expecting an attack any moment.

"I'm sure we're safe here," Wilmot said dryly.

"Hurry back to tell us what the queen says, Miss Ronley," Lady Newcombe said. "We'll be waiting."

Eileen murmured something vague as she left them, to see the queen, her heart pounding. Glencoe. Scotland. Neil. She had to warn him.

Duncan looked around the room with interest. So these were Princess Anne's lodgings, where his cousin Eileen lived. He hoped that her rooms were more comfortable than this dank little one. Celia Lockwood talked in the corner with Calum, their heads bent close together, oblivious to the cold air that seeped in through the heavy window coverings. Good that they'd be getting the lad away from here soon. He had no need of a lovesick companion on the trip home. He shot a glance at Neil. Nor of two.

Neil was quiet, not surprising with what they'd discovered earlier this morning. The man who had sent Neil to Ronley Hall was dead, murdered, rumor said, by a Jacobite who had not been pleased with the information he'd received. The city was seething with stories of King James's imminent return, of Highlanders ready to sack and pillage all of England. It was not a good time to be a Scot in London. They'd been told, more than once, that they should leave immediately. Which they would, after they talked to Eileen.

He'd kent, the minute he'd seen her, that he and Eileen Ronley were related. She had Catriona's eyes and lithe grace. He remembered his young aunt from his visit to England with his parents. He'd been seven, and Eileen, several years his junior, must have been a bairn. He'd not seen her, or did not remember her if he had. It had been Catriona, with her easy laughter and warm manner, who had entranced him. And now he'd found her daughter. He wished his da were here to know this. Or Neil's and Jamie's father.

He watched Neil absently trace a hand along the top of a battered chair. They'd waited for Eileen to return from the palace for over an hour. It was time to do something.

Mary waited with a sour expression, her silk gown crumbled where she had gathered the material in bunches. The room was uncomfortable, too warm, too crowded with furniture and food. A long table had been set before the row of lead-paned windows, silver and gold trays heavily laden with fruit and meats shimmering in pale broth. Eileen thought of the many times Anne had carefully cut away spoiled sections of fruit, handing what little was left to her small son. It had been a very long time since Eileen had seen so much food, let alone such a lavish display. Pheasant and quail and venison shared the table with fruits from every part of the world. All for Mary. No one else would dine from this selection, and little of this would be touched.

The queen's questions were sharp, her interest in Belmond dimmed only when Eileen had told her the same story she'd told everyone, that she'd met Belmond when he had spent the night at Ronley Hall. The man was overly bold, she told Mary, but there was nothing between them. What else could one expect of the French?

Mary refused to answer any questions about Glencoe, though Eileen tried several times to discover what had happened. Something dreadful had happened, that much was certain, something momentous enough to require all these messengers, coming in to see Mary with long faces and travel-stained clothing, but Mary would tell her nothing. And where was William?

The queen frowned as she nibbled on the sweetmeats piled on the silver tray at her elbow. She took a bite of several, then threw them on the floor with a disgusted look. Her dogs scrambled for the treats, snarling and smearing bits of food across the Persian rug.

"I cannot get anything decent from this kitchen," Mary snarled, knocking the tray to the floor with a petulant flip of her hand. The dogs fell upon the tidbits.

Mary took a deep breath. "We have reached a decision and know you will be as pleased with it as we. Monsieur Belmond's attentions to you made us realize that you need a husband. We have arranged for you to marry Henrick von Hapeman. Your wedding will be in three days. We will provide everything for it. And then you will go to live with him in Holland. Tell my sister that I expect her to attend your wedding."

Eileen gaped at her. Henrick von Hapeman! He was the second son of one of William's Dutch retainers, a close advisor of the king. Henrick was several years younger than she, a lazy drunkard who had only his extensive holdings in the Low Countries to recommend him. He was handsome in a dissolute sort of way, but his wife would spend a life of waiting for him to return from his carousings.

She would be her mother all over again. She would live in Holland, cut off from everything she knew, everyone she loved. In exile. Mary must believe the stories of Eileen's ambitions.

"No!" Eileen whispered.

"Yes," Mary said, her tone sterner. "Belmond's actions made you the talk of London, and I will not have that. We'll get you safely married. What you make of your marriage will be your business. I trust that you will not continue your liaison with Belmond, but if you do, I expect you to be more discreet. I was surprised—and disappointed—to hear your name linked with this sort of behavior. We do not wish for our court to be compared to your grandfather's. I am saving you from scandal, Eileen. I expected gratitude. You will be the wife of a wealthy man."

"Mary, I beg you not to do this!"

"It is done. The contracts have been signed."

"I have signed nothing."

"Your signature was not needed. William signed as your closest male relative. You have only to make yourself beautiful. I'll send my seamstresses over to help. And a hairdresser. Leave us."

Eileen stumbled out into the anteroom, then paused, gathering her wits enough to slow her steps and pretend that she was not thoroughly shaken. She'd used every argument she could think of, but Mary had been firm. The wedding had been arranged and would take place as scheduled. William had decided.

She felt a wave of rage. It did not matter what William had decided! She would not marry Henrick, not in three days, not in three hundred years. This might be William and Mary's choice for her, but it was not hers. She would not be exiled, would not be whisked away to oblivion.

Lord Wilmot and Lady Newcombe hovered near the door to the audience hall, but they'd not seen her yet. She darted to the side of the room, leaning against the wall and taking several deep breaths, willing herself to be calm. Think, she told herself. There must be a way out of this.

"Miss Ronley." Duncan MacKenzie's quiet voice came from behind her.

Eileen spun around. He stood alone, smiling at her. She clutched his arm, torn between relief that he was alive—and so calm—and a wave of frenzied fear.

"Why are you here?" she whispered.

"To see ye, of course. Neil's here too. We waited at Princess Anne's for a while, then discovered that the queen had called for ye, so we came to the palace. Ye might notice we're no' easily dissuaded."

"Do you have any idea of how dangerous it is?" She grabbed his arm and pulled him after her, staying close to the wall, then ducking through the almost invisible doorway to the service hallway, blessedly empty. She closed the door behind them and faced him. "We have to get you and Neil out of here. Have you not heard what happened at Glencoe?"

Duncan shook his head, frowning. "Glencoe? No. What?"

"Where is it? How close is it to MacKenzie lands? Who lives there?"

"Old MacIain . . ." As the door behind her opened, Duncan paused, his hand hovering over the hilt of his sword.

A pistol came through first, and Duncan pushed Eileen

behind him as he yanked his own gun out of his belt, then relaxed as Neil slipped through the opening, closing it behind him. When Neil said something in Gaelic, Duncan's expression grew grim.

Eileen stepped forward. "You can talk later. Have you heard . . . ?"

"About Glencoe?" Neil asked. "Aye."

"I've got to get you out of here," she said. "Follow me."

"We can go out the way we came in," he said.

"No, it's not safe. Please trust me, Neil."

"Do I not always, Eileen?"

"Come," she said, starting down the hall. "Be very quiet. If I introduce you to anyone, simply smile and bow. Do not speak."

The men exchanged a glance and nodded. She led the way, following the hallway for several turns, then hurrying down the service staircase and along the passage that at last led them to the guardroom. The guards leapt to their feet as they entered. Eileen smiled at them and gestured to Neil and Duncan.

"These are the Huguenot merchants that the queen received privately. Would you show them out, please? I must return to Her Majesty."

The guards, who had relaxed as she spoke, nodded. Eileen turned to Neil and Duncan, thanking them for their time. She gathered her skirts to leave, but paused as Neil put a hand on her arm.

"Mademoiselle," he said in French. "Once again I am in your debt."

"I wish you safe journey home," she whispered and hurried up the stairs. She could feel their gazes on her back, but did not turn. If they were wise, Neil and Duncan would leave London today. And she? At the top of the stairs, she had to stand for several minutes while the tears overwhelmed her.

She got away from court with surprisingly little difficulty. Lord Wilmot and Lady Newcombe were on the far side of the audience hall when she entered it, deep in conversation, and she quickly passed through the room before they could see her. Madam Landers was blessedly nowhere to be seen.

Once on the street, she wrapped her cloak around her and hurried away from the palace. The sky, still gray, hung above her, its looming presence perfect accompaniment to her mood. She would not marry Henrick. She'd apply to Anne for her help, even though it was a weak gesture at best. Two years ago she could have counted on Mary granting any request Anne asked of her. But now . . . perhaps asking Anne was the worst thing she could do.

A carriage clattered behind her and she stepped to the side of the narrow street, taking refuge in a doorway. Instead of passing, the carriage slowed, then stopped, directly in front of her, sealing her into the small space. She backed against the door, suddenly remembering the man who had followed her from Anne's to the palace. The carriage door swung open.

Neil MacCurrie leaned forward, Duncan visible behind him. "We'll take ye home, lass," Neil said. "Come on."

Without another thought, she got in.

Neil watched her settle herself on the opposite seat. Something had frightened her badly. Her face was pale; her eyes red, as though she'd been crying. She twisted her hands together, then clutched at her skirts, relaxing her grip when she saw him watching. "Are ye a'right?" he asked.

She nodded.

"Thank ye for spiriting us out, Miss Ronley."

"Had you not heard what happened at Glencoe?" she asked.

"Only just in the hall."

"Is it true, then, that this MacIain did not sign the oath?"

"He did sign. But he was late."

"Did you sign it?"

Neil thought of the smug smile of William's man in Inverness. "Aye."

"Where is Glencoe?"

"At the edge of the Highlands. East of Loch Linnhe."

"Nowhere near MacKenzie lands," Duncan said. "It was no' our people."

Our people, she thought. "Are you not worried about Torridon?"

"My brother's there," Neil said. "He says all is well."

She raised her eyebrows. "He says all is well? Is he here in London?"

"No, he's at Torridon."

Duncan laughed softly. "Neil and Jamie have a way of communicating, Miss Ronley. They dinna need words. If Jamie says all is well at home, then all is well."

Eileen looked from Duncan to Neil with a puzzled expression. "I don't understand."

"Aye, well, ye're no' alone," Duncan said. "But I've seen it, so I believe it."

"Duncan's correct," Neil said. "I canna explain it, but my brother and I can send messages to each other."

"Without words," Duncan said.

"You can read each other's thoughts?"

"It's more like waves of emotion. I ken if something's wrong wi' him, and he wi' me, or if something's verra good, but we dinna ken exactly what it is. Jamie's telling me that everything is fine at Torridon, so I do need to get home, but no' just the now. Torridon is remote, and we'd ha' a lot of warning from the inland clans if troops were heading there."

"What about ships? Could they not simply sail there?"

"Aye, they could, but Duncan's men are guarding the coast, so they'd not land. Torridon's safe for now, lass."

"But London is not. What if it's true, what people are saying, that William allowed this massacre? What else will happen in Scotland? What would happen to you if anyone discovered who you are? You must leave immediately!"

"Aye, we're going," Neil said. "And we want ye to come with us."

"Come with you? To Scotland?"

"Aye. My mother's a MacKenzie. She'd welcome ye."

"I can show ye where yer mother came from," Duncan said. "Ye can meet our grandfather, for what that's worth."

"Our grandfather? He's still alive?"

"Did ye no' ken that?"

"No! I thought he'd died years ago."

Duncan laughed. "Just his heart. I dinna ken what kind of reception we'd get. My father defied him as well as yer mother, and I've no' seen him in years. But if ye wish to go to Glen Mothin, we'll take ye. Come on home wi' us, lass."

Neil nodded. "And if ye dinna wish to go to Glen Mothin, ye're welcome at Torridon. Let us show ye Scottish hospitality. It's no' like Milford's. Let me repay yer kindnesses somehow."

"There is no debt, sir. I did exactly what I chose to do."

"Then I thank ye for choosing to help us. Let us repay yer generosity by taking ye to yer mother's people. Come with us."

"I cannot."

"Why?"

"I . . . I have my own responsibilities, sir. I cannot leave Anne."

"We'll bring ye back to London when ye're ready."

The carriage jerked to a stop before her lodgings and Neil leapt out to help her down. "Eileen, think on it at least, will ye no'?"

"I cannot. Thank you, but I cannot."

"D'ye ken the Pegasus Inn, near St. Paul's? For the next two days we'll be there. If ye send word, I'll come to ye at once. Day or night."

"Two days? Why are you not leaving at once? Why wait two days?"

"Because I owe ye a debt, lass. I owe ye my life. Ye're unhappy here, Eileen. Let us take ye away from all this."

"Why would you do this for me?"

"When I was in the priest hole, did ye flinch at helping me?"

"I thought long and hard before I did."

"Aye, well, I gave this some thought as well, and I thought ye might like to meet yer mother's people."

"I could travel to Scotland on my own later."

"Lass, it's no' safe. If ye think London dangerous, ye should see Scotland. After word spreads of Glencoe, no Englishwoman will be welcome in the Highlands. And while yer mother might ha' been Scottish, ye look and sound like an Englishwoman. No, either ye come wi' Duncan and me, or ye dinna go at all."

Her eyes flashed. "I will decide that."

He laughed as he stepped back from her, suppressing the urge to bundle her into the coach and ride like hell for the border. "No doubt ye will. I only meant that ye need to be careful."

"Thank you, then, both of you, for the offer and for the ride home."

Duncan nodded. "Pegasus Inn, cousin."

She lifted her skirts and climbed the stairs. The door opened as she reached the top, and after a glance at them, she went inside. Neil turned to Duncan.

"Something else happened. We'll ha' Calum come and visit Miss Lockwood this evening."

Duncan nodded. "My thoughts exactly."

Eileen closed her eyes and leaned her head against the chair. She'd been listening to the stories Bess and Celia had brought back from their trip into the city. London was horrified by the attack on Glencoe, and most blamed the king, saying Stair would not have acted without William's approval. The talk, Celia said, was that William had sent word to squelch rebellion in the Highlands by any means. There were those who applauded such tactics, but many more who whispered behind hands that perhaps they'd been too hasty in welcoming William and Mary to the throne, and wondering if there was another choice. For the first time in months people were wondering if King James should return.

Was it possible that William had ordered the massacre? Or turned a blind eye to it? What kind of man took revenge for a petty offense by ordering soldiers to murder people in their beds? What kind of king approved such a thing?

She'd tried to be calm, but she'd cried as she told Bess

and Celia about Glencoe and the forced marriage William and Mary planned for her. Eileen dreaded telling Anne, who would be very angry with Mary. This would be another log on the bonfire that raged between them, but she could not marry Henrick.

What should she do? She could not approach the queen again; any request to delay the marriage would only be met with curt refusal. Should she take Neil and Duncan's offer and go to Scotland, to her mother's people? But no, it was unthinkable, for so many reasons. Only a fool would go to a country that might erupt into violence again.

And she couldn't even, for a moment, consider leaving Anne, who had only been kind, who had offered her a home when no one else would. How could she leave Anne now, with Mary suspecting her own sister of plotting behind her back? How could she leave Celia, a mere child, in the midst of all this intrigue? And how could she travel unescorted with her cousin and Neil? *Her cousin and Neil.* When had she slipped into thinking of them that way?

If she did nothing, she'd be married in a few days and whisked off to Holland to rot while Henrick neglected her. She had to decide her future, and now. Should she go to Ronley Hall, ask Milford to take her in, then wait for an enraged William and Mary to find her and drag her back to London? That was unlikely to please her proposed husband.

Henrick might be as unhappy with the match as she, for his father had most likely arranged it with William. No doubt there had been an exchange—Henrick would marry Eileen and receive something in return. Money? Property? Henrick's father was known to be a shrewd businessman; he would not have made this arrangement without compensation. She had no money to top William's offer. How else could she stop the marriage? What if she approached Henrick herself?

Henrick lived not with his father, but in an impoverished part of the city, in tiny rooms atop a rickety house. Eileen had told no one of her visit and had used the servant's entrance as she left, to be sure she was not followed. She wondered now, as she climbed the grimy stairs, if she had not been foolish. She could easily disappear in this quarter, and no one would ever know what had become of her.

She knocked on the door to his rooms, bracing herself for the discussion. But Henrick did not answer the door; a thin young girl peered out with a fearful expression.

"Yes?" the girl asked.

"I am Eileen Ronley," she said. "I'm looking for Henrick von Hapeman."

"You're the one his father wants him to marry?"

"Yes."

"Oh." The girl swung the door open and waved Eileen inside.

The small room was crowded with furniture, a couch and table, piled high with dirty dishes, under the filthy curtainless window. A chair, its coverings torn, leaned against the tiny fireplace. The rest of the room was filled by the bed, on which Henrick lay on his back, asleep, his naked chest rising with each snore, his long, matted hair only slightly darker than the pillow beneath it.

"He's been drinking since his father told him," the girl said, her tone a mix of defiance and fear. Her heart-shaped face was gaunt, her eyes angry. "He told me he'll still see me . . . He said he'll take me to Holland with him." She paused. "He loves me. He doesn't want to marry you, miss."

Eileen looked at Henrick again. "If he opposes this marriage, then he must talk to his father at once. I will not object if we do not wed. You are welcome to him."

The girl's defiance melted at once. "Oh, thank you, Miss Ronley! You are so kind! Thank you, thank you!"

The girl's voice followed her as Eileen went down the stairs and into the street. Marry that animal? Never. She had a sudden memory of Neil leaning to kiss her at Ronley Hall, and shook her head to clear the vision. She would not think of him now. She had to use all her energy to find a way to prevent this marriage, or delay it until she could decide what to do.

Henrick would probably be of little help. She had no faith in his ability to dissuade his father, even less in his father's ability to dissuade William. She fished the piece of paper from her pocket. Howard's address. It would be a long walk, but she had much to think about on the way. She would throw herself on his mercy. If he let her stay for a few days, she might be able to come up with a better plan.

Howard gave her a warm welcome, leaning back on brocade silk in his lavish parlor, his expression growing remote as she told him about the marriage. When she'd finished pouring out her story, he spread his hands wide.

"I do not see that you have a choice," he said. "Surely you do not expect to successfully defy the king and queen? Nor to ask me to? I have worked hard to find a place in this court, Eileen."

"You earlier offered me a safe place to stay."

"Yes, of course, but this changes everything. I cannot help you hide from the king. I have a family to consider. Surely you understand."

"I only need a few days, Howard."

"I'm so sorry, my dear. Perhaps the marriage will not be as distasteful as you imagine. You will be a wealthy woman."

"My husband will be a wealthy man, Howard. That is not the same thing."

He shrugged. "You will live in Holland, which is said to be lovely in the spring. You may find you enjoy it."

There was a long pause, during which she waited, hoping that he would reconsider and offer her his help. But he said nothing, simply watched her with a solemn expression, and at last Eileen rose to her feet, thanking him for his time.

Neil's eyes narrowed as he watched Eileen leave Templeton's house. She looked neither right nor left, just rushed away. She did not see him, nor the man who stepped away from the building next door and fell into place behind her. At the corner she stopped and stood still staring into the distance. Her follower staring into the distance moved into the shadows, watching.

Neil swore softly. It had been Howard Templeton he'd been watching, not Eileen, and he'd not been pleased to see her rush up to Templeton's door. Miss Ronley was welcomed and brought inside; obviously this was not the first time she'd come to this house. Why was she there? Discussing the Earl of Torridon? She'd told him she would not tell Templeton that she'd seen him in London.

He was a fool. He'd let himself believe her when she'd looked into his eyes and said she would not tell anyone he'd visited her, ignoring what he knew—that a woman can lie as well as a man. And simply because a woman was beautiful did not mean he should relax his guard. Something in his gut twisted at the thought of her betrayal. What kind of woman was she, who could lie so convincingly? What kind of a man was he, to be so easily duped?

And yet . . .

There might be a number of reasons, none of them having anything to do with him, that would cause her to visit her father's old friend. Did she suspect that Templeton might have had something to do with her parents' deaths? Did she trust him? Was this just a social visit to Templeton and his wife, a duty call? Or was she involved in something completely different, something to do with William and Mary and Anne? Was she delivering a message from Anne to Templeton? What possible connection could the two of them have?

He frowned again. He did not know this woman; the absurd feeling that he did was not based in reality. He should have brought Duncan or Calum with him instead of having Duncan lead their own watcher on a wild goose chase through the streets of London and Calum go to visit Celia Lockwood. It was time to leave this city before he went completely mad. Fiona and he might bore each other, but he knew who she was.

Eileen was still standing at the corner, fishing now in her pocket while her shoulders shook. She turned to glance behind her now, a handkerchief to her eyes, then started forward again. She was crying. He took a step forward, then ducked back into a doorway as the man who had been following her came out of the shadows. She turned the corner; the man turned it ten seconds later.

He should turn around, Neil told himself as he walked forward. Eileen Ronley's life had nothing to do with him. He'd come to London to see if she'd paid a price for setting him free and he'd done that. There was no reason to stay any longer. But she was crying. He started after her.

He heard her frightened voice before he reached the corner.

Chapter Nine

Eileen stood in the middle of the street, facing her pursuer. The few people on the street had stopped to watch, forming a circle around her and the man.

"Who are you, sir? Why do you follow me?" she cried.

The man stood motionless, his back to Neil; he spread his hands wide and said something too low for Neil to hear.

"Yes, you are, and you followed me yesterday. I want to know why!"

Neil moved forward, pushing through the people. French accent, he reminded himself. "Mademoiselle," he said, "do you have need of assistance?"

Eileen's eyes widened as Neil came to stand just behind the man following her. The other man was smaller, but Neil knew that meant little. Round eyes shifted from Eileen to him, the man's hand moving backward to his hip, where a pistol was holstered.

"Dinna even consider it," Neil said quietly to him. He held the man's gaze while he spoke loudly to Eileen. "Are you having difficulty, mademoiselle?"

"He's been following me for two days," she said.

"She is mistaken," the man said. "I'm not following her."

"You were following her, sir; I saw you," Neil said. "Why?"

The onlookers gasped as the man darted backward, yanking his pistol out and pointing it at Neil; Eileen gasped. Neil gauged the distance between them. There was no fear in the other man's eyes, only a steely determination; he could pull the trigger without hesitation.

Neil put his hand on the hilt of his sword. "Lower the gun, sir."

"I am being accosted!" the man shouted. "Someone come to my aid!"

"No!" Eileen cried. "Do not help him!"

When the man tightened his finger on the trigger, Neil threw himself forward, reaching for the pistol that now waved wildly at the end of an outstretched arm. They struggled, twisting from side to side. Neil pulled back, then threw himself forward, knocking the other man off balance. The man staggered, flapping his arms to keep his feet. And the pistol discharged.

A woman screamed. Eileen gave a hoarse cry; there was a sudden rush of people toward her, but Neil saw only his opponent. The man drew his sword and Neil did the same, leaping forward with a roar. The man was a skilled swordsman, fending off blows and delivering his own with practiced ease. The onlookers scurried out of the way as the two men battled across the street.

When the ruffian lunged, aiming for Neil's stomach, Neil stepped to the side, feeling the blade cut into his coat but not his skin. The man lunged again, too far this time, and Neil took the opportunity, knocking the man's sword from his hand. It clattered on the stone and for a second Neil thought the battle was won, but then the man yanked a shorter blade from his belt.

Neil lifted his sword to meet the man's charge, but long before the short blade could reach him, Neil thrust his sword in the man's chest, and watched as he fell to his knees. It was a long moment before the man fell forward onto the stones, blood seeping from his wound.

One of the onlookers darted forward to lean over the man. "He's dead!"

"Call the watch!" someone cried.

Several women screamed and men began to murmur, but Neil ignored them as he searched for Eileen in the crowd. Her face was ashen, one arm held tightly over her chest. A large red stain seeped into the cloth of her bodice. Neil stared with horror.

"Eileen!" he said hoarsely. "Dear God, lassie, how badly are ye hurt?"

She looked down at her arm and bodice, then stretched out her arm. Her sleeve was ripped open. Neil, hearing a roaring in his head, took her hand in his and gently moved the material away from the wound.

Blood covered the skin of her forearm; he tore the lace from his throat and gently mopped it away from the wound, a channel cut into her skin where the pistol's charge had plowed through her flesh. It must be painful, and there would be a jagged scar, but her arm was intact.

He looked into her eyes, then at her bodice, expecting to see what he dreaded; but there was no hole in her clothing, no gaping wound in her chest, and he began to breathe again.

"Lassie, Eileen," he said, "are ye hurt anywhere else?"

Her eyes were dark in her pale face. "No. Just my arm."

"Just yer arm," he whispered. "Dear God, I never thought ye'd be hurt."

She reached up to touch his cheek with her uninjured hand, almost smiling. "You saved my life, Neil." She began to tremble and he pulled her to his chest while he watched the crowd over her head, his sword still ready.

The man who had bent over the dead man straightened and spoke quietly. "Get away with you, Scotsman. Go, both of you, before the watch comes."

Neil met the man's gaze, then nodded. "Thank ye, sir," he said, tightening his arm around Eileen and pushing through the people. No one stopped them.

They ran for several minutes, in the direction of the river, away from the crowd, slowing when they realized that people were staring at them. Neil stopped, releasing her to wipe the blade of his sword on his handkerchief and resheath it, then reaching for her arm.

"Let me look at it again," he said, gently pushing the material back from her wound. "It hurts, aye?"

She nodded.

"It needs to be cleaned. We'll pour some whisky on it. It'll sting, but it'll help. Come, I'll take ye home and attend to it."

"Neil," she whispered, her eyes filling with tears. "You saved my life. I thought he would kill you!"

He gave her a crooked smile. "No' likely, lassie. It would take more than the likes of him to kill me. Do ye ha' any idea who he was?"

"No. I saw him yesterday, when I went to the palace."

"The same man?"

"Yes."

"Eileen, ye must leave London. Come with us to Scotland." He pulled her to his chest, leaning his cheek against her hair. "It was a warning. Come with us to Scotland. Come, lassie, let me take ye home."

He tipped her chin up and brushed his lips atop hers. She

leaned into him, and for the briefest of moments pressed her lips against his; then she pulled back.

"Neil?" she said softly. "Were you following me?"

He took a deep breath. "Why were ye at Templeton's, Eileen?"

"Were you following me?" Her tone was icy.

"No. I was finding out who this Templeton was who told ye about me. I dinna expect ye to be visiting him. Why were ye?"

She straightened her back and raised her chin. He could see her drawing away from him. She didn't trust him. He felt his triumph and fear and anger draining away, replaced by a sense of loss.

"He told ye who I was, Eileen. I wanted to ken who he was."

"Yes, of course," she said. "And what did you find out?"

"That ye were with him. Is he . . . are ye his . . . ?"

"Lover? Is that what you're asking me, Neil, whether Howard Templeton is my lover? He's married. I don't consort with married men," she said in the prim tone he despised.

He sighed. They were strangers. How many times did he need reminding of that? "Where were ye going next?"

"Home."

"I'll take ye."

"Thank you."

Neil put an arm around her stiff shoulders. He'd see that she got safely home, and then he'd go back to the Pegasus and tell Duncan and Calum to start packing.

Eileen leaned against the bedroom door and let her tears flow. Her arm ached and she would probably have a horrible scar, but she was alive, and so was Neil. If he'd not been there, what would have happened to her today? But . . . he had only been there because he was following her. She didn't believe he'd been watching Howard. No, he'd been following her, and he'd lied. Again. Howard had warned her, Milford had warned her. Still . . .

Neil had saved her life, had let his fear for her show in his eyes. His touch had been gentle, his concern obvious; but she needed to remember that it was not love he was offering, nor had he ever pretended that it was. He'd offered an escort north, nothing more. Destiny, he'd said. How had her life become so complicated?

Enough, she told herself. Crying and cowering in her bedroom wouldn't help. The problem that had led her to seek out Henrick and then Howard was still there. If she did nothing, she'd be a married woman in two days. Henrick would be powerless to stop this match, and Howard would not help.

Neil. Glen Mothin. She pushed the images the words brought aside. To travel north with Neil and Duncan, to see the mountains and castle her mother had talked about so often, to hear bagpipes skirl across a glen, or above a silver river. To see Neil MacCurrie, his dark hair gleaming in the sun, turn and smile at her, and pull her into his arms.

Unthinkable.

"Come closer, Eileen," Anne said crossly. "You know I cannot see you back there." Her expression darkened as Eileen came to stand before her. "What is the matter, child? Why do you hold your arm so strangely? What has happened to you? You look quite dreadful!"

Eileen forced a smile. She was sure Anne was right; Bess

and Celia had told her the same thing when she arrived home. She'd told them only that she'd been followed from Howard's house, not why she'd gone there, and that her arm had been injured in the melee. They'd been all sympathy, at least Celia had. Bess had watched her with an expression that let Eileen know Bess thought her a witless fool. And perhaps she was.

"Eileen?" Anne's gentle tone brought her back to the present. "What is it?"

"I have hurt my arm. And William and Mary want me to marry Henrick von Hapeman. In two days."

"What happened to your arm? And they want you to marry von Hapeman's scrat? You cannot be serious!"

Eileen nodded, unable to speak as tears spilled down her face.

Anne patted the cushion next to her. "Sit down, child. Start at the beginning."

Neil came back to the Pegasus to find both Calum and Duncan gone. He poured a whisky, then stirred the fire, telling himself he felt chilled because of the weather, because he'd killed a man today, because Eileen had been hurt, not because she shut him out of her thoughts and rejected his offers. It was time to go home and forget her. He'd paid any debt he owed her today.

He drained the glass and poured another. Fiona would be a good wife, a dutiful one if not entertaining. He'd make it work, as had all those other men who had married to protect their clans rather than their hearts. And in time . . .

Who was he fooling? He wouldn't forget Eileen Ronley. He'd just learn to live without her. In a few years he'd hear that King Charles's oldest granddaughter had married some duke somewhere and had nine children. All with her eyes and hair.

He swore aloud and then again, going to the window and throwing it open, leaning out into the chilled air. There was a movement in the doorway opposite, as though someone shrank back into the shadows. It was time to get out of London. How many warnings did he need?

Hours later, Calum burst into the room, dripping from the icy rain outside. He slammed the door behind him and tossed his topcoat aside. Neil and Duncan, sitting before the fire, exchanged a glance. Calum's mood was always easy to read. If he was angry, he stomped; if happy, his feet did not touch the floor. His latest visit with Celia Lockwood must have not been pleasant.

"Well?" Neil asked. "Anyone out there watching?"

"He's still there. I came in the back way."

"And Miss Lockwood?"

"Celia's fine. She's grand, in fact. I'm going to see her again tomorrow." Calum crossed to the fire, holding his hands to its warmth. "I have news, but ye willna like it. Eileen Ronley has been followed several times, and ye ken all about her getting injured today. And she's getting married in two days."

"Married!" Duncan cried.

Neil sat up straight. "What the hell? She said nothing of this!"

"She dinna ken until yesterday. The queen ordered it. Apparently when she saw ye at court she'd just been told."

Neil thought of Eileen's brittle mood the day before; fragile, he realized now. When he'd flung the carriage door open, her eyes had been wild. But to not mention this marriage then, or today, when . . . why would she not have told him, especially after this afternoon?

But then, why would she? She'd made it clear that she didn't trust him. He was a fool. The notion that he was not to part from her was unreasonable; there was no fate at play here, just more basic urges. He liked to watch her move, he thought she was beautiful. He was grateful that she'd saved his life at Ronley Hall.

He wanted to bed her. Was that all it was? Was it nothing more than a very strong attraction that would fade if it were sated, disappearing as thoroughly and as quickly as it had overwhelmed him?

"Who is he?" His question was brusquer than he'd intended; he ignored the look Duncan and Calum exchanged.

"Henrick von Hapeman. Younger son of one of William's retainers, a Dutchman, close advisor to the king."

"And?"

"Henrick is a gambler, a drunkard, a womanizer. Celia says he's more experienced at twenty-one than many men twice his age. His father has much wealth and vast holdings, but no title. She'll bring him her lineage, he'll bring the coin. And they'll live in Holland."

"Holland!"

"They'll leave right after the wedding."

Duncan frowned. "Is she willing?"

"No. Celia says Eileen asked Princess Anne to intercede. They went to see the queen this evening, but it was a disaster. Anne and Mary argued and King William got involved. He's furious that Eileen is unwilling—he says he'll throw her in the Tower if she refuses."

"The king is furious?" Neil asked, his eyes narrowing. "A

strong reaction." He stood, then paced before the hearth. "How many bastards did King Charles have?"

Duncan turned sharply to meet Neil's gaze, and Neil knew he was wondering the same thing. Why were William and Mary forcing this marriage, why so suddenly? London was in an uproar, the criticism of the king over the Glencoe massacre growing by the hour. They had to know what was being said about William in the streets. King James was no real threat to their throne now. But Eileen might be.

Were William and Mary trying to diffuse any following that King Charles's granddaughter might have by marrying her to this von Hapeman? She would have no base of power, no military might that would be hers through a husband with English or Scottish blood, no ties to Kings James or Charles. And she'd live in Holland, where William was from, cut off from all who might think to embroil her in a plot against him and Mary. She would be surrounded by her husband's family and countrymen. Her every movement could be controlled.

He'd never see her again.

If King Charles had married Eileen's grandmother, then this was a master stroke. And if not, what loss to them? Eileen would be away from court, away from any ambitious nobles who were dissatisfied with William on the throne.

No wonder she'd been distracted yesterday; he'd be willing to wager that she'd thrown herself on Templeton's mercy, asking him to help her stop this match. And the bastard had refused.

"When is the wedding?" Neil demanded.

"Day after tomorrow," Calum said.

"When? Where?"

"I dinna ken."

Neil rose to cross the room, reaching for his topcoat.

"Where are ye going?" Duncan asked, standing.

"To see Eileen."

"I'll come wi' ye."

Bess touched Eileen's shoulder. "Wake up."

Eileen turned over, coming out of sleep slowly. She'd taken refuge in her bed shortly after sundown, too weary to face her future. "What is it?"

"Monsieur Belmond is here."

"Belmond? Here?"

"Downstairs. With Monsieur Delacroix."

Eileen sat up, throwing the bedcovers aside and slipping from the bed quietly. Celia slept on, her hand pressed under her cheek like a child. She was a child, Eileen reminded herself. A pawn. Like herself.

"What did he say?" she asked Bess as she wrapped her cloak around her.

"Eileen, who are these men?"

"Huguenots. How do I look?"

"You cannot receive them at this hour!"

"What time is it?"

"Half nine."

"Not an ungodly hour, Bess. Many people are just sitting down to dinner." She reached for her hairbrush, wincing as the wound on her arm burned.

"You should not receive them alone."

"I will be fine."

"Princess Anne should be told."

"Then tell her," Eileen said. "You know where I will be."

She paused outside the parlor, trying to compose herself. She could hear the soft murmur of male voices, the tap of heels on the wooden floor, muted suddenly, then sharp again. Someone was moving across the room. Neil said something in Gaelic; Duncan replied.

She pushed the door open. Both men turned as she closed the door behind her. "Good evening, gentlemen."

Neil scowled at her. "Eileen, are ye marrying this von Hapeman man?"

"How do you know that?"

"It's all over London. Are ye?"

"That is what the king has arranged."

"Have ye agreed?" Duncan asked.

"Why did ye no' tell me?" Neil asked. "Yesterday when we brought ye home, today . . . why did ye no' tell me?"

"I . . . I needed time to think."

"I am yer cousin," Duncan said. "I could ha' thought wi' ye."

"Do ye no' wonder," Neil said, "why the king and queen are marrying you off like this? Are ye no' wondering why?"

"Yes, of course I am. I'm sure William has his reasons."

"Aye, like the reasons he had for Glencoe."

"I doubt he's planning to have me murdered."

"Ye'll be surrounded by men who owe him allegiance. Every part of yer life will be controlled."

She nodded. "Yes, but . . ."

Neil came to tower over her. "Are ye considering the marriage? It's a sham!"

"It would not be the first marriage to be so."

"Nor the last. But why would ye do it? Do ye want to marry him? Stay here with Anne."

"In direct defiance of the king? How long do you think it would be before he cut Anne's allowance even further or punished her some other way? Or sent soldiers for me? You saw what happened yesterday. What would he have done if you'd not been there? No, I cannot stay here—Anne has offered me a home, not a sanctuary. I cannot abuse her generosity and ask her to risk even more enmity with her sister. How can I ask more of her? What can I do? Shall I retire to one of my properties? Go live with my many relatives?"

"Then ye must delay the wedding."

"How? I went to see Henrick. He was drunk; his mistress told me he didn't want this marriage any more than I, but he's weak. He'll never convince his father otherwise. I even considered running to Ronley Hall. Tell me what I can do."

"Come to Scotland with us."

"I cannot leave Anne. I cannot, Neil."

"Ye mean ye will not. London is no longer safe for ye, ye've seen that. It's only a matter of time before the noose tightens. Come wi' us."

"I . . ." She wiped her sudden tears away.

"What, ye dinna trust me? Even now? Convince her, Duncan!"

Duncan spread his hands wide. "We'll protect ye, Eileen. Come wi' us, let us take ye home and keep ye safe. We're cousins, lass!"

"Oh, Duncan, I would love to believe that!"

"Why d'ye not?"

"I don't know who to believe anymore," she said softly.

Duncan crossed his arms over his chest. "Our grandfather's name is Phelan MacKenzie. My father was the youngest of his three sons, yer mother the only daughter. When yer mother was sixteen, she came to London with our grandfather, and she met yer da. Grandfather opposed the marriage, but the king approved it. D'ye ken the MacKenzie motto?"

She nodded.

"Many people do, ye're thinking, aye? But no' many people say it wrong, do they? It's 'I shine, not burn.' When yer mother was little, she couldna remember that. She always said it 'I burn, not shine.' My da teased her about it often."

Eileen stared at him, hearing her mother's laughter as Catriona told the story of how unmerciful her brother's teasing had been. And how she'd loved him.

Duncan's eyes flickered. "Ye're remembering, aren't ye? My da called yer mother 'Cat.' No one else ever did. Our grandfather hated that name. Yer mother had a scar under her chin, a long thin scar. D'ye ken how she got it?"

Eileen nodded again.

"So do I," Duncan said. "It was an accident, but the man responsible for harming her was killed. Did she tell ye that?"

"Yes."

"Did she tell ye how?"

"Yes."

"He was cut into ten pieces. Slowly. Our grandfather is a vindictive man."

Eileen swallowed. Her mother had only told her that the man had been killed in a dreadful way, and that Phelan had made her watch.

"The only time I saw yer mother I was seven, when I went to England with my da. Ye and yer sister were wee bairns, I guess; I dinna even remember ye." Duncan's expression softened. "She taught me how to play chess. She never took the first move, but she always won. And she hummed while she decided what she'd do next. I remember falling asleep next to my da while he talked with her. I thought she was wonderful; I dinna ken we'd never see her again. She glowed, Eileen, like she was lit by the sun."

Eileen put her hand to her mouth and stepped away from

him. Duncan was right—he had known her mother, whose glow had faded with the years and her father's betrayals. She turned, finding herself in front of Neil, and looked into his eyes, then lower, her emotions tumbling as she watched the lace at his throat rise and fall with his breathing. She took a deep breath.

"Eileen," Duncan said softly. "I am truly yer cousin. And I wish ye no harm. Neither does Neil. Come home to Scotland wi' me, wi' us."

"Come wi' us, lass," Neil said softly. "We'll keep ye safe."

The door opened with a creak of complaint from the unoiled hinges. Princess Anne stood in the doorway, Bess behind her. "This is late for a social call, gentlemen! Miss Ronley is no longer receiving guests tonight."

"Madam, we only need a few more minutes," Neil said.

"You must leave now, Monsieur Belmond, or shall I call the guard?"

"We will return tomorrow, madam."

Anne nodded regally, watching them gather their things, then standing aside to let them pass. Duncan bowed to Eileen, then to Anne.

"Pegasus," Neil whispered as he bowed over Eileen's hand.

"Good night, gentlemen," Anne said, waiting until the outer door was closed.

Bess drifted away then, as did the footmen, but Anne lingered. When everyone else was gone, she stepped into the parlor and closed the door, leaning against it, giving Eileen a long, appraising look.

"I heard everything," Anne said.

Eileen took a deep breath and waited.

"After your Monsieur Belmond was here the first time, I did some investigating and discovered that he is the Earl of Torridon. If I was able to find that out so easily, so can others. Two days is too long for Torridon to be in London. The Glencoe massacre has distracted William and Mary, but soon they will find out who he is, and they will act."

She crossed to the fireplace. "William would be delighted to have the court talking about something besides Glencoe, to be able to tell the world that Torridon was here as part of a murder plot against him, that what happened in Scotland was necessary to protect the throne from another Jacobite rebellion.

"And that you are part of it. Everyone is talking about you and Belmond, and that he came here, to talk to me. Torridon must leave, if not for his own sake, then for mine. He taints me—and you—with his presence. And soon, if they all have not already, the gossips will remember that your father opposed William and Mary's ascension.

"You are in more danger than from a bad marriage, Eileen, and you being here in my household puts me at risk. I have a son and a husband to consider, even if I do not think of myself.

"Going to Scotland with them may be your best choice."

It was still dark when Eileen slipped out of the bedroom she shared with Celia and Bess. She'd hardly slept last night, and at last had made her decision. Quietly closing the door behind her, she crossed the sitting-room floor and knelt before the chest that held her things. She emptied it quickly, putting everything into her satchels, then prying up the false bottom from the base of the chest.

Careful not to split the aging wood, she pulled the oiled

leather pouch out from its hiding place, holding her breath as she unfolded the letter it contained. She did not need to read it; she knew every word by heart. It was dated December 3, 1646, and signed by her grandmother, Jane Ronley.

"My dear husband, I have this day been delivered of a son and have named him, as we agreed, Adam Charles Ronley Stuart. I consign him into your care, dear love, for I am not well. Please come to me."

Eileen had never intended to produce the letter, had never planned to pursue the throne. But now, after all that had happened in the last week, she would reconsider. If it was true, if Adam had been legitimate . . . it changed everything.

She wrote letters to Anne, Bess and Celia, saying little more than that she needed time to decide her future—which was true—and that she'd write to them when she could. And then she slung her bags onto her shoulders and left the silent house. She would miss Anne, and Celia, but little else in London, certainly not William and Mary, nor Bess, nor the court.

Outside in the street she paused. The doorway opposite was empty and she looked around, half expecting to be pounced upon. But no man with a round face accosted her, and after a few hesitant steps, she readjusted the bags on her shoulders and began her journey.

Neil threw the window open, stretching his arms over his head, heedless of the cold air on his naked skin. London at dawn. The city was quiet now, the streets almost empty. In an hour they would teem with life, vendors hawking their wares, merchants opening their shops for the day, footmen and messengers scurrying through the throngs. And in an hour, he and Duncan would be gone, back to the *Isabel,* to sail with the tide.

Below him, a woman picked her way carefully through the refuse. She carried a large leather bag in front of her, another on her shoulder. She paused now at the corner, pushing her hood back, looking at the signs that lined the front of the buildings. He leaned forward to see her better and she looked up at him.

Eileen Ronley.

They stared at each other for a moment, then he grinned. Her gaze flickered lower, to his chest and stomach, and back to his face. She smiled.

"Stay right there, lass," he called to her, then closed the shutters and crossed the room to shake his cousin's shoulder. "Duncan, she's here!"

He grabbed some clothing, throwing it on as quickly as he could, not bothering to tuck in his shirt, nor to put on shoes. Duncan, who had jumped from his bed, was doing the same. There wasn't time to shave. He threw water on his face and dried it hastily, then pounded down the stairs, Duncan at his heels. He opened the door, half expecting her to be gone, but she waited on the step, her face pale.

"Welcome!" he said. "I'm verra glad ye came, lass."

"Are ye going wi' us?" Duncan cried.

She nodded.

Duncan gave a loud whoop and swung Eileen in a circle, then set her down. "I'm glad ye trusted us, Eileen."

Neil touched her cheek and smiled. "Ye willna regret it."

Chapter Ten

They headed immediately for the docks from the Pegasus, which pleased her. Now that she'd made her decision to leave, she could not wait to be on her way. She would miss Celia and Anne, but no one else; her relief in finally leaving was mixed with regret that she had so little to leave.

What would William and Mary say when they discovered she'd left? She imagined William's face growing bright red, as it always did when he was enraged, and she prayed that Anne would not suffer for this. In her letters, Eileen had done what she could to make it plain that no one knew that she was leaving, and certainly not Anne. She said a prayer now for her cousin, who had nowhere else to go, no handsome cousin swooping in from Scotland to whisk her away to safety.

Was it safety she fled to? She rubbed her injured arm, careful not to touch the wound. At least it was not a marriage with Henrick, not a place where she was followed and spied upon to see if she had ambitions for the throne. What lay ahead would be a whole new world.

Even at this early hour the docks swarmed with men, for the tide was about to turn and many ships would leave with its flow, letting the Thames do much of the work of bringing them to the open sea. She was hustled aboard the *Isabel* and left to stand alone at the railing while the final preparations were made. Duncan had introduced her to the crewmen as his cousin. They'd told her their names, and seemed pleased to meet her; many of them were MacKenzies.

Duncan stood at the foot of the gangplank, Neil at the entrance of the dock with Calum, waiting, Duncan told her, for the last few crewmen to be rounded up from the nearby stews and brothels. The men stopped to talk with Neil as they returned, then ran toward the ship, their manner agitated.

A few moments later Neil said something to Calum, who nodded and raced to Duncan. Duncan nodded as well, then gave orders with a calm assurance. Crewmen leapt to action, swarming up into the stays as though born there. The huge sails were lowered, hanging limp for a few moments, then rising high into the air with a snap as they caught the wind.

With a glance behind him, Neil broke into a run. As he reached the gangplank, a troop of red-coated soldiers rounded the corner. Duncan and Neil sprang up to the ship and leaned with two other men to pull the gangplank aboard. The soldiers paused, then moved forward quickly. Eileen gripped the railing, looking from the soldiers to Neil and Duncan, who watched the troop approach, their manner giving her no hint of their thoughts.

The *Isabel* gave a shudder, then glided away from the dock. The soldiers watched, but did not move as the ship moved into the middle of the crowded Thames with a surprising grace. Duncan came to stand by Eileen, then grinned at her.

"Were they trying to stop us from leaving?" she asked.

"If so, they dinna try verra hard, did they? No, lass, I think they were just letting us ken that they kent we were leaving. Which means they ken who we are—and that ye're with us. Ye'll notice they dinna have their weapons drawn."

Eileen gave him a shaky smile. "So we're safe now."

He shook his head. "The Thames takes its own sweet time getting to the sea. When we pass Greenwich we will start to breathe easier. But until we hit the open water, we'll not ken what they ha' planned for us."

"Are you worried?"

Duncan laughed. "The *Isabel* was built for speed, lassie. We ha' twenty guns and a well-trained crew. If they try to take us, they'll have a battle they dinna count on. We'll be fine. Dinna fash yerself."

He left her then, to talk to the men. At first Eileen watched every ship in the river, but no one approached them. No one seemed to pay the *Isabel* any special attention at all and as the minutes passed without incident, Eileen began to relax and watch London pass before her, and the water traffic around them. Ships, huge and small, sailed in both directions, lighters and shore boats and ferries racing between the larger craft. Why there was not a collision every other moment amazed her.

Under her hands the wood of the railing was smooth, well tended, as was everything on this tidy ship, and from this perspective the city looked as orderly. She knew better; under its serene surface, London seethed with plots and schemes, deceptions and betrayals. And still she loved this city, where so much of her own history had been set, where generations of her family had lived their own dramas.

It was Calum who led her belowdecks, to the small cabin that would be hers for the voyage. It was sparsely furnished in a practical but pleasing manner, with a long berth against the hull, drawers underneath the mattress. At the side of the bed was a low cabinet and next to the door hooks on the wall above a long bench. Calum had deposited her bags on the bench and waved at the room.

"It's Duncan's cabin," he said. "But it's yers for the voyage."

"Where will he sleep?"

"With Neil, in the big cabin. They're used to it, miss. Usually they spend most of their time there anyway, looking over the charts and talking."

"I'm sorry to put him out of his own cabin."

"I'm sure he doesna mind, Miss Ronley, he's that pleased ye're coming with us. And we're all glad to be leaving London. Did ye ken we were watched the whole time we were here? We changed the ship's name, and changed her flag to England's, but still we had the men watching us. Now, come back up on deck wi' me if ye would, miss. Neil said ye might want to see us leaving."

She followed him topside, where he left her again at the railing to watch the shoreline and all the activity on the ship. It was a masculine world, and Eileen the only woman aboard, but she felt safe, and with every mile that brought her closer to the Atlantic, lighter. She was no longer Eileen Ronley of Ronley Hall, no longer the poor relation of a besieged princess. She was Catriona's daughter, going to see her mother's home. And leaving all this behind, perhaps forever.

Neil was right—she did want to see the last of London, a bittersweet sight. The sun, weak in the cloudy sky, lit the eastern windows and cast the western side of buildings into deep shadow. Here at the end of the city, houses and warehouses were built high above the tidal reaches, docks stretching into the water like fingers, hampering the traffic that never seemed to dwindle.

This city had been such a large part of her life; she would miss it. She hoped she would not regret the impulse that had led her to abandon everything she knew and throw herself into the hands of these strangers. But they were not strangers, certainly not Duncan, who seemed so genuine, who reminded her of her mother. And not Neil, not after all they'd been through.

As though she conjured him, Neil joined her now with a smile, standing next to her, seemingly oblivious to the cold wind ruffling his hair, silent, as he'd been since they'd left the Pegasus. Occasionally he threw her a glance, or looked down at his hand, twisting the signet ring while his expression grew thoughtful, but for the most part he watched London as they moved eastward to the open sea.

After several minutes, she turned to Neil. "Do you think we're safely away?"

"Aye. If they'd meant to stop us, they'd ha' done it before now. We'll ken for sure when we hit the sea, but I think we're fine."

"Are all these men from Torridon?"

"Aye."

"I don't understand why they are following Duncan's orders and not yours."

"On board ship there can only be one master. This is Duncan's ship; he commands her and all aboard. On the *Isabel* I am a passenger."

"Does that not bother you?"

"No. Why would it?"

She thought of the men she'd known at court. "Not everyone would relinquish power so easily."

He smiled slightly. "It is no' a relinquishment of power. At Torridon I make the final decisions; on the *Isabel*, Duncan does. We're both content wi' the arrangement. How's yer arm, lassie?"

"It hurts, but at least it has stopped bleeding."

"We were fortunate that the charge only scraped ye. If it had hit the bone . . ." He let his words trail off. "Ha' ye ever seen London from the water?"

"Yes, but it's been a long time. The city has grown since I sailed past it. I don't remember the city extending this far."

"When were ye on the river last?"

"It's been years. We were on our way to France, to Brittany."

"Oh, aye, Brittany. I would meet the only lass in Warwickshire with an intimate knowledge of the coast of Brittany. Ye said ye went with yer cousins."

"I went with Anne several times; Mary came with us once, but then she married William and didn't travel with us. I was too young for the parties, but at least I got to see some of the coast."

"Is that where ye learned yer French?"

"No, I studied with Anne and Mary. And was I right, that you were taught by a Parisian?"

He nodded. "Ye were. Da had a tutor brought to us; Duncan and Jamie and I all learned French at the same time, like we did everathing."

"You are very close to your brother and cousin."

"Aye. Jamie might as well be me, and Duncan a near second. Has been, almost since the day he came to live with us."

"Why did Duncan live with you at Torridon rather than with his mother's people after his father died? Or with his grandfather?"

"They were all gone except for my mother. And Phelan wouldna have him."

"Really?"

"Really. Yer grandfather is a difficult man, lass. Ye should ken that he may no' welcome ye. He might even be angry that ye came to see him."

So much for her dream of a warm welcome, of a safe haven, she thought. "Does Duncan see him often?"

"No. It's been years. Guard yer back wi' him; he'll use ye if he can." He paused. "Did ye ever meet yer other grandfather, King Charles?"

She tried to keep her tone light. "Yes. Many times."

"What was he like?"

"He was kind to me."

"Did he acknowledge you as his granddaughter?"

"Yes. I was a favorite because I liked his dogs."

"His dogs?"

"Spaniels. Surely you've heard he bred them? His rooms were full of them; they even slept on his bed. He was very pleased that I liked them; not everyone did. His rooms often stank; my father complained of it, but I loved those dogs."

"And the man?"

A sudden memory came to her, of sitting on her grandfather's bed, the dogs piled on top of the two of them, while they played their favorite game. Charles called it "If I were Queen". He would throw a problem at her; she had to pretend to be the queen and solve it. She'd not thought of it in years, but the memory came back now, full-blown. She could smell the tobacco, the dogs, the stale wine; remembered her grandfather throwing the windows wide open, saying to her, "London is burning. What would you do if you were queen?"

He'd told her then about 1666, the year of the plague and then the Great Fire, about what had been done, the successes, his mistakes. She'd thought it only a fascinating story, had not recognized it for what it was, a lesson in leadership, a history of their own family. And there had been so many other times.

He'd known. Her grandfather had known, that this day might come, that she might discover the truth. Eileen put her hand to her waist, felt the leather pouch that held her grandmother's letter there. What was she to do about it? One letter would prove nothing.

Neil shifted his weight and she realized he was waiting for her answer.

"My grandfather was kind to me," she said, her voice sounding hollow.

He did not pursue the topic farther, but pointed at the shore. "We're almost at the last of the city; after those warehouses there's little more."

"You seem to know London well."

"I ha' been here many times."

"In the last two years?"

"No, lass, no' in the last two years. I've only been here twice since yer cousins took the throne, and it wasna to spy on them. The first time it was simply to reach land. I had planned to go home by ship, but that dinna work, which is why I ended up at Ronley Hall."

"Where were you coming from?"

"France. I went to see what King James had to say about us signing the oath to William."

"What did he say?"

"To sign it. So I went home. But I had to go overland, went to Ronley Hall, so that ye could save my life, more than once. That time, in the priest hole, when he was drunk, he might well have killed me with my own sword if ye'd no' stopped him. I'll never forget lying there with yer hands on me and his drunken face above us. I ha' been in yer debt since the moment I met ye, but never more than right then."

Eileen pressed her lips together, hoping she did not look as embarrassed as she felt. She'd not thought that he might remember the incident as vividly as she did. "There is no debt. And even if there had been, you've more than paid it now, by saving my life on the street."

"Ye'll ha' a scar to remember the day by."

"I'm here to remember it, Neil, that's what matters. And now you've let me come with you."

"I'm glad ye did. I only wish it had been me that convinced ye to come, and no' Duncan."

"What do you mean?"

"He convinced ye that the two of ye are cousins and that made ye trust him."

"That was part of it."

"And the rest?"

She looked into his eyes. "Was you, Neil. It was you I trusted."

"And I ye, lass. Doesna make any sense—we're strangers—but there it is."

There it is, she thought, nodding. Part of her knew Neil as she knew herself, as though she'd always known him. And part of her was amazed that she'd trusted him so completely. But not completely, she reminded herself. She'd not told him, nor Duncan, about her grandmother's letter, about her suspicion that it was true, that Charles had married her grandmother, which would mean that her father had been legitimate, Charles's only legitimate child.

Had her grandmother been mad? Had she imagined a wedding that had never happened? Or was she sane and Charles, knowing the truth, had denied the marriage for his own reasons? Had Charles feared that his firstborn, the son of a commoner, was inadequate for the task of being king? If so, he must be spinning in his grave after the recent performances of his brother and niece and nephew. And if that was not his reason for not acknowledging Adam, what was?

Charles had seen, as a very young man, his own father beheaded. Was he, in some strange way, trying to protect his son? Or was he, as he'd been for most of his life, considering only himself? She tried to remember everything she could about her grandfather—the dogs, the constant stream of women, the smell of alcohol and tobacco, and the late hours. A rumpled bed, so innocuous to a little girl, became, in retrospect, a symbol of what her grandfather was—a self-absorbed man who never reined in his appetites. It was impossible to imagine him considering Adam's well-being over his own.

Had the letter she carried been the only one, or were there others that had survived all these years? Was there a marriage license somewhere? Had something surfaced that had brought William and Mary's fear of Eileen to a fever pitch, or had they already known—or feared—that her father was legitimate? Was that why she'd been followed, why she'd been suddenly betrothed to a man who would isolate her in Holland for the rest of her life? Had she herself precipitated all this by returning to London? And if, after Glen Mothin, she returned to London, what would she face? Would they hesitate to remove her?

What should she do now? Did she want to tell the world? Or did she want to slip the letter, still folded in its pouch, into the depths of the sea one night on this voyage? She didn't know what she felt, what she wanted for her future, and whether anything she did could change it. Even if the letter was destroyed, William and Mary might continue to suspect her ambitions, which would mean she would never be safe while they were on the throne.

She would think about all this, but not now, not until she went to Glen Mothin. There would be time enough then to decide what was next. In the meantime, she would do her best to forget it, difficult as that was with her grandmother's letter wrapped at her waist, heavy against her skin.

Eileen was startled out of her thought when a small boat came much too close to the *Isabel*. One of the crew leaned over to curse at the boatman, who answered in kind. Eileen gasped, but Neil only laughed.

"Will ye miss all this?" he asked.

"Not the river traffic."

"Reminds me of yer cousin's audience hall, everaone makin' his own way through the chaos."

"Do you know," she said, turning to look at him, "that my heart almost stopped when I saw you there? I could not believe you would be so foolish."

He shrugged. "It wasna foolish. Arrogant, perhaps."

"You were outnumbered by hundreds to one. How can that not be foolish?"

"They're courtiers, not soldiers. Duncan and I ken our way across a battlefield; we werena worried about a few men in wigs. Most of them lift a fork more often than a sword."

"Some of those men have been in war, and most of them were armed. It was a very dangerous thing to do."

He smiled slowly. "It was the simplest way to find ye. I came to London to find ye, Miss Ronley, and I did."

She ignored his smile, and the way he leaned close to her. Surely he was not planning to kiss her here, on this crowded deck? "You could have waited at Anne's," she said, disappointed when he leaned away from her, shaking his head.

"Anne's men wouldna even take a message to ye. On her orders, I suspect. So we went to court and found ye. I wouldn't trust her, lass."

"Anne told me to go to Scotland with you."

"Because it suited her."

"That's rather harsh."

He gave her a long measuring look. "Eileen, ye are the direct descendent of King Charles, not yer cousins. I suspect they are all verra aware of how tenuous William's claim to the throne is."

"I am not a threat to them."

"Perhaps they think ye are. Are ye no' suspicious as to why they wanted ye married off in such a rush, and to a man who will make sure ye spend yer time holed up in some country estate with not a penny to yer name? As long as ye stayed at Ronley Hall, ye were no' a threat. But when ye came to London and were openly recognized as Charles's granddaughter, and remembered as one of his favorites, ye became a possible one."

Her heart began to pound. She'd not realized he had pieced this all together. *If I were queen.* She tried to keep her tone light. "How?"

"Ye are now someone for those dissatisfied with William, and there are many, especially after Glencoe to rally around. Trust me, there are many who would take delight in replacing William. D'ye no' think William and Mary's haste to have ye marry Henrick was unseemly? But practical, ye must admit. It would solve a problem for all of yer cousins."

"Just William and Mary."

"Anne is third in line to the throne."

"Only if William and Mary do not have children."

"Which they havena, even after all these years. Anne's next, and her son after her. A new dynasty."

"If he lives. He's a frail little boy."

"And if it turned out that yer claim to the throne was stronger than hers . . . lass, it doesna take a wizard to realize she might want ye gone."

"I cannot believe my cousin Anne would do anything to harm me. She has never been anything but kind to me."

He shrugged. "Aye, well, maybe I'm wrong. But were I ye, I wouldna trust any of them."

They were silent while his words echoed in her mind, then he put a hand atop hers on the railing, as he looked into her eyes.

"I willna let them harm ye, Eileen. I swear it," he said softly.

"Thank you," she whispered, unnerved again. "Tell me about Torridon," she said, to still the emotions that flooded her, to stop her mind from wondering.

"Torridon? The land?"

"Start with that. What is it like? Is it near the coast?"

"Loch Torridon comes in from the sea and turns to the right, where it joins Loch Shieldaig. The castle, Castle Currie, overlooks the water there, atop a high bluff. There is some level land near the shore, but behind that, wrapping around the whole of Torridon, like arms around a lover, are the mountains. In the summer the low ones are purple with heather, in the winter all are white with the snow. And in spring, when the snow is melting, thousands of waterfalls rush down their sides and pour into the loch. They guard Torridon from the rest of the world. And after the last few years, I'm glad of it."

"What do you mean?"

He spoke slowly. "I've seen war, lass. I've buried men I played with when I was a lad, had to go home to their families and explain why I asked them to go with me. They never said it, but I could see them wondering why the man they loved dinna come home and I did. I nearly lost my brother at Killiecrankie. I'll never forget wondering if I'd have to go on without him; I canna imagine life without Jamie. Nothing has looked the same to me since then."

He continued, his tone edged with sadness. "I've seen the best leader I've ever kent struck down, and a king who dinna deserve the sacrifices he was given. And seen greed and selfishness in the aftermath, evil things done for personal gain, good men ignored in favor of unwise ones. And two kings, James and William, living in luxury while those who backed them pay the price for loyalty. The Stuarts ha' no' been good for my country. I ha' no regrets that the Jacobite cause is over." He took a deep breath, then cleared his throat. "Which is no' what ye asked, is it? Torridon . . . aye, well, it's home, ye ken? I'm ready to go back."

"You must love it very much."

"I do. I've been gone much in the last few years, far too much. Now it's time to go home and make a life." He met her gaze. "I'd like to show it to ye."

"I'd like to see it," she said quietly. "How long will it take us to get there?"

"We'll go to Glen Mothin first. We'll sail to Loch Carron and take horses from there; it's the fastest way. Torridon has too many mountains to cross and after the winter we've had, they'll be full of snow. Glen Mothin is surrounded by mountains as well, but ye can ride in from the west without having to climb them. Ye'll have an easier trip that way."

"Aren't you coming to Glen Mothin with us?"

"I'll see ye there, but I'm no' sure I'll be welcomed to stay. Phelan and I dinna get along."

"Why?"

"I ha' given my loyalty to the Earl of Seaforth. Phelan would like to replace him, especially now, when Seaforth is in prison."

"For?"

"For backing King James. That's another thing ye need to ken, that yer grandfather backed King William."

"Could the same thing happen to you?"

"That I would back King William? No' likely."

"I meant, sir, as you well know, whether you could be imprisoned for backing King James."

"Aye, I could, if William and Mary thought I was important enough."

"If Milford had taken you to Warwick, I'm sure you would have been thrown into jail. Which makes you going to court even more audacious."

"Perhaps, but effective; I found ye, didna I?"

"You enjoyed the danger."

He grinned. "I wanted to find ye, lass, and I did."

"Do you really think the Jacobite cause is over?" she asked.

"For the MacCurries it is."

"What about Glencoe?"

"There will be a lot of talk—William and Mary are no' widely loved, ye ken—but I doubt that the Highlands will rise again. We ha' no leader, and without a strong man at the helm, we'd only fail again. If King James were otherwise . . . but he's not, so nothing will change from what it is now. Ah, here's Duncan."

"And Greenwich," Duncan said as he joined them. "I think we're safely away. Look, ye can see the Royal Observatory that yer grandfather built, Eileen. I've heard that he was very proud of it."

"Yes, he was," she said.

"As well he should have been."

"What would ye build if ye were queen?" Neil asked her, his tone mild.

She gave him a sharp glance. "If I were queen?"

"If I were king, I'd build a decent set of docks for visitors," Duncan said, "so I wouldna ha' to pay moorage."

"If you were king," Eileen said with a laugh, "you wouldn't have to pay for moorage."

"Aye, well, there is that." Duncan grinned at her. "And Neil would no doubt build another wing for Torridon. He has grand ideas for Castle Currie. He wants to move the outer wall north and add a new wing."

"Some of the old part is falling around our ears," Neil said.

"Ye'll have plenty of time to do yer building," Duncan said. "If the Seer's right, it'll be fifty years before we go to war again."

Eileen threw him a puzzled look. "What do you mean?"

"Has Neil no' told ye about the MacCurrie legend?"

"No. What legend?"

Neil groaned. "Duncan, give it a rest . . ."

"She needs to ken it, lad," Duncan said, laughing. He leaned back against the railing. "Years before Neil and

Jamie were born—on the same night—did he tell ye they were twins?"

"No."

"Well, they are, though it's easy enough to tell them apart." He told her the story while Neil stared across the water, ignoring them. "Neil and Jamie took the clan to war, so now it's time for the fifty years of peace," Duncan finished.

"Do people believe this legend?" she asked.

"Aye, many do. Including me," Duncan said.

"Really? How extraordinary."

Duncan laughed. "Ye'll ha' to let go of yer London thinking, Eileen. In Scotland there are many extraordinary things that are quite real."

Like the men, she thought.

"Duncan's right, lassie," Neil said, his tone light. "It's time we broadened yer thinking." He looked up as the first drops of rain hit them. "But first we'd best get ye below; this storm has been chasing us and now it's here."

Chapter Eleven

Neil led Eileen and Duncan below, into the *Isabel*'s large cabin, the staccato beating of the rain on the deck fainter now. He settled himself in one of Duncan's comfortable chairs while Duncan explained the cabin to Eileen, showing her the many features he'd had specially built. She listened attentively, seemed quite interested, until the rolling began that meant they'd hit the open sea. She grabbed onto the table then, her eyes wide.

"Do you think the storm will get worse?" she asked.

"This?" Duncan said. "It's nothing. Wait until we get around to the west."

To distract her, Neil spread nautical charts across the table that served as a desk, and lit the lamp above it. "Here's where we are now," he said, leaning over the charts. "And here's Torridon."

She came to stand at his side. "We'll sail up the western shore of England?"

"There's no sense in going around the north," Duncan said. He looked up at the sound of a thump from above and headed for the door. "I'd best see what they're doing," he said and disappeared through the doorway.

Neil pointed to the chart again. "Here's Loch Carron, where we'll land, and here is Glen Mothin. That will give ye a sense of where we're going," he said, straightening.

She still leaned over the chart, tracing the route with her

finger. He brushed her hair over her shoulder, and she looked up at him.

"Is it true, that there is a legend about your family?" she asked softly.

"Aye, there is one."

"Do you believe it?"

"Some of it has already happened."

"Like the tree?"

"Aye. And my father and grandfather and great-grandfather all dying on their birthdays. And the war."

"So now all that is left is the fifty years of peace," she said.

"There are a few other things that havena happened yet."

"Such as?"

"Such as Jamie and I are supposed to marry women with the same name. Jamie's married Ellen. According to the legend I need to find a woman with the same name."

She straightened and stared at him. "Are you not already married?"

"No. Why would ye think that?"

He saw the jolt that shook her, but her voice was very quiet. "I was told . . . You talked about your family, about building a new wing . . . that you would live at Torridon with your family . . . I thought . . . that you were married. I've thought all along that you were married."

"And still telling ye how beautiful ye are, and letting ye ken that I admire ye? If I were married, lass, I wouldna ha' done that. Who told ye I was?"

"I . . . I don't remember."

"Ah. Which means it was Templeton, right?"

"Yes. He must have gotten it wrong."

"Oh, aye," he said, letting his scorn show. "A mistake.

Aye, I believe that. No, I'm no' married, Eileen, never ha' been. And I ha' no children. What else were ye told about me?"

She smiled. "That you were fierce and fearless."

He raised an eyebrow, surprised at her teasing tone. "Really? Shows what he kens. I'm none of them—not fierce, nor fearless, nor married. But I do ha' to find a lass whose name is Ellen, or something similar."

She looked down at the chart without saying it: Eileen was the same name in a different form. He looked at the curve of her neck, at her lashes, dark on her cheeks. He should tell her about Fiona.

"We have a long way to go," she said, tracing a finger along the shore of Loch Carron and up to Glen Mothin, then looking up at him.

Soon, he told himself. He'd tell her soon, but not now, when her mood was so warm. She'd retreat from him again. He'd tell her soon. Or perhaps he should talk to Fiona first?

"I suspect it will go quickly," he said. "And now ye ken where we're headed." He reached to touch her cheek, but withdrew his hand as Duncan thundered down the stairs and into the cabin.

"Wet, but no' bad," Duncan said, closing the door. He stopped, looking from Neil to Eileen, then crossed to stand with them. Neil ignored Duncan's speculative look, and pointed to the chart again. "This is Gairloch, where Calum is from."

"He's not from Torridon?" she asked.

"Not originally," Duncan said. "Neil brought him there as a hostage."

Her eyes widened. "A hostage?"

"Aye, in exchange for good behavior from the MacLeods."

"Is he still a hostage?"

Neil laughed. "No' for years. He's been with us since. Went to war and all."

"I doubt we could get rid of him if we tried," Duncan said. "Come and sit down; we'll be more comfortable. I think ye'll be surprised at Scotland, cousin. It's verra different from one part of it to another. If ye were to go to the east, where Jamie's Ellen is from, it's rolling hills and verra green. As ye head west and north, the mountains are everywhere, and when ye get to the coast, to a place like Torridon, ye have the mountains and the sea together. Ye'll ne'er see the like."

"It sounds wonderful."

"Just wait."

Her accommodations were not spacious, but comfortable and clean, and despite the heavy seas, she slept well that first night. She pulled the covers tighter against the damp and studied the wood grain of the ceiling boards of her cabin in the light that spilled from under the door, hearing occasional footsteps and calm voices as the crew changed position. In an amazingly short time the creaking of the ship around her became familiar and she started to relax.

The last thing she heard was Neil and Duncan talking easily together in Gaelic in the large cabin next door. How wonderful it must be to have someone to trust completely, she thought. She refused to think of how alone she felt, and let the *Isabel* rock her to sleep.

The next morning the sky was clear, the air crisp, snapping the sails overhead when she came on deck. The crewmembers she'd met on her way up had greeted her with friendly smiles, as though she were an honored guest. She smiled in return, shivering when the wind pulled at her hair and found her ankles. Summer was still a long way away, but the sun was bright and she stepped out of the shadow of the hatch.

Neil and Duncan stood together near the forward mast, their heads bent over some navigational instrument, Duncan's russet bright against Neil's darker hair. Both men were in Scottish clothing, the first time she'd seen them wear it—saffron shirts topped by waistcoats, Duncan's green, Neil's a deep blue. They wore long, close-fitting tartan pants that displayed long legs and strong muscles. This was their own clothing, she thought as she moved closer. They'd both been handsome in their city clothes, but they looked even more wonderful now.

Duncan pointed to the horizon, Neil to the sky, and they laughed together. She paused before joining them, enjoying the sight of them together, the colors of their clothing bright against the varnished wood of the boat and the cobalt of the water behind them.

"Good morning, gentlemen. We must be out of English waters," she said.

They looked up with puzzled expressions.

"Your clothing. You don't look French at all."

Neil grinned and waved a hand at the crew. "Good morning, Eileen. They can stand us pretending we're civilized for only so long, and then they want us to become who we are again."

"And who are you?"

"Scotsmen, lass, Highlanders, who are damned proud of the fact."

"Ye'll need to get used to us like this," Duncan said. "No more wigs until we ha' to go to court again."

Eileen laughed. "Good! But I suppose I'll hear bagpipes next."

"And drums."

"London seems a long way away."

"That it is, lassie," Neil said. "That it is."

The days passed without event, quickly forming a pattern. Her arm was healing at last, but the scar would stay with her, a reminder, she told herself, of why she'd left England. The weather had been blessedly calm and she was welcome on deck anytime she chose, which was preferable to spending long hours in her tiny cabin. She loved being on the water, had learned to trust the *Isabel*. The sturdy little ship rose high on each swell, but Duncan glided her down with ease. Eileen soon felt growing affection for her temporary home. And its captain.

And Neil? In the evenings she would sit with him and Duncan, listening to stories of them growing up together, of their families, of going to war, of how James and Ellen met. But Neil never talked of the future except in the broadest of terms. "Now ye ken where we're headed," he'd said. But she didn't, not at all.

She told herself to guard her heart. At times she listened to her own warnings; but there were other moments when she forgot to be wary, when she talked with Neil without measuring every word, simply enjoying his company. She tried to memorize the way his sudden smile would change his face from serious and intimidating to lighthearted, the dimple she loved softening his features; that burst of laughter he'd give when she or Duncan amused him; the humor in his eyes when Calum said something that showed how very young he was.

Neil watched her as well; she often caught him at it. Sometimes he'd stare at her, then away, and she'd wonder what he was thinking. At other times he let her see the desire in his eyes, then laugh and tease her about something, hiding his emotions again. Each night he'd show her where they were on Duncan's charts, and each night she'd watch his long fingers move across the page and wonder what they would feel like on her skin.

Despite her vow not to think about it, she found herself constantly wondering what was ahead. A visit with a grandfather who by all accounts was, at best, bad-tempered? And when her visit to Glen Mothin was over, would she go to Torridon? And then? Eventually she would have to face her future, decide whether to reveal her secret, to face all that would entail.

If she decided to make her grandmother's letter public, if she made a claim to the throne, there would be war; William and Mary would not step aside. She knew the devastation that hostilities could bring to her country. She would not be responsible for bringing that to England. After Torridon she would have to find a safe corner somewhere in William's kingdom and live a quiet life. By herself.

Or was there, perhaps, another choice? Might there be a future with Neil, or was she mistaking his kindness for something more? She'd not imagined him kissing her at Ronley Hall, nor the way he touched her occasionally, letting his fingers linger on her skin. Was she reading much too much into what might be nothing more than simple desire, and a slight fondness for her? Was he now realizing that they were strangers brought together by chance, not destiny—two people with little in common and only shared blood with Duncan to bind them? Had she misunderstood everything?

She'd thought their first landfall would be at Loch Carron, but Duncan explained that he and Neil had decided to make a stop at Linmargen, a small fishing village in MacLean territory, to see whether the massacre at Glencoe had started something in the Highlands while they'd traveled. They turned toward the shore, slipping easily into a sea loch, and she saw Neil's eyes narrow.

Ahead lay a wide path of water, long and deep from the color of it, flat land around it that suddenly rose into a thick band of trees and then into heights that were still covered with snow. But it wasn't the calm scene, the men singing on the shingle as they repaired a fishing net, that had caught Neil's attention. It was the two frigates in the bay, and the red-coated soldiers who milled under the trees and along the shore. The cousins stood quietly at the rail as the *Isabel* glided forward.

Duncan's voice was a whisper. "They're English."

"Aye," Neil said. "I count twenty-four guns on the near one."

"And nearly the same on the second," Duncan said.

The English frigates filled the landing area, but the Scots on shore did not seem to be troubled by it. The docks were busy with what seemed to be normal activity despite the cluster of soldiers near the larger frigate. Surely if all seemed so calm, Eileen told herself, there could be no danger; but the two men next to her stood stiffly, Duncan's whisper a reminder of their tension.

"What d'ye think?"

"MacLean's ships are here," Neil said. "It canna be too

terrible. Go on in. There's no law yet that says we canna visit a friend."

"Aye," Duncan said.

Neil gave her a glance. "Eileen, lass, will ye go below and out of sight until we can sort this out? Calum, stay with her." He added something in Gaelic and Calum nodded, gesturing to his sword.

"Be careful," she said, looking from Neil to Duncan. They nodded and she followed Calum down to the large cabin.

Duncan gave the order to his men to proceed into the harbor, and a moment later men climbed into a shore boat and shoved off the shingle. "They're coming out to welcome us," he said to Neil. "Shall I introduce ye as Monsieur Belmond? Can ye remember to speak French?"

Neil gestured to his trews. "I'm no' dressed for the part, and I dinna ha' time to change before they reach us. We'll just be ourselves."

"I dinna want my ship blown apart because some Englishman's nervous."

"Then charm them, Captain MacKenzie."

"I'd rather blow them off the earth."

"Ye'd rather keep both yer ship and yer skin. Remember that."

"Ye may need to remind me again," Duncan growled and gave the order to lower the anchors.

The cousins waited silently as the shore boat approached, then drew alongside. Four men climbed aboard the *Isabel*, dressed in long red coats with blue facings. Neil had not paid attention to English uniforms since his days with Dundee, and he did not recognize the uniform. He doubted

it would help their cause to mention to these English soldiers that he fought against them at Killiecrankie or at the
Boyne. Three of the men gazed around with open curiosity.
The fourth, the officer, looked down his nose with a haughty
demeanor.

"Welcome aboard the *Isabel*," Duncan said.

"Sir," the officer said, "I am Captain Asher. Who are you
and why have you come to Linmargen?"

"To visit MacLean," Duncan said evenly.

"Your name, sir?"

"Why?"

"I am under orders to ask, sir, the king's orders. Your
name?"

"Duncan MacKenzie."

"From?"

"Pardon?" Duncan asked, stalling while he looked at
Neil.

"You are from what port, sir?"

"Torridon," Neil said.

Asher gave Neil a cold look. "I asked the captain, sir.
Kindly be good enough to let us speak."

Neil raised an eyebrow, but was silent.

"From Torridon," Duncan said.

"And bound for?"

"Linmargen."

"Does MacLean expect you?"

"No' unless he has second sight."

"Your business with him, sir?"

"Is it suddenly against the law to visit a friend?" Neil
asked.

Asher ignored him. "For what purpose, sir?"

"To visit a friend," Duncan said. "Why are ye asking all these questions?"

"We need your answers for our records."

"Ye're keeping records on us now?"

"How long will your visit be?"

"Depends on when I wear out my welcome."

"Would you answer please, Captain MacKenzie?"

"I dinna ken how long I'll be here. Depends on if I'm ever allowed to land."

"How many men do you have aboard?"

"Four hundred and twelve," Duncan said. "Give or take a score."

"Not amusing, Captain MacKenzie."

Neil crossed his arms over his chest. "Why do ye need to ken all this, Asher?"

Asher turned to look at him. "Who are you, sir?"

"Neil MacCurrie. Why are ye asking these questions?"

"MacCurrie." He shuffled through his papers. "You are the Earl of Torridon?"

"I am. Why are ye asking Captain MacKenzie these questions?"

"Have you signed the Articles of Allegiance, my lord Torridon?"

"I have, but I dinna remember signing away my right to travel."

"We are noting all movements of former hostiles."

"Former hostiles," Neil repeated, letting his amusement be heard.

Asher turned back to Duncan. "How many men do you have aboard?"

"I dinna remember the exact number," Duncan said.

"Captain MacKenzie, are you refusing to answer my question?"

"I'll line them up, if ye like, and we can count them together."

Asher pressed his lips together. "You cannot be serious. Your uncooperative manner will be reported to my superior."

"Of that I ha' no doubt," Duncan said.

"You may land," Asher said grandly, then signaled to his men to follow him back into the shoreboat. Neil and Duncan watched silently while they pushed off.

"Glad ye charmed them," Neil said.

"Glad ye helped."

"Aye, well, short of prostrating ourselves, we couldna ha' pleased him."

"Lovely welcome back to the Highlands," Duncan said, watching the soldiers land and disappear into the trees. "Will we still go to see MacLean?"

"I will; ye need to stay wi' yer ship."

"Ye canna go alone. I'll come wi' ye."

Neil shook his head. "Ye'll no' go ashore, Duncan. If I ha' to make it an order, I will. Dinna look daggers at me, laddie. One of us has to stay here. It's yer ship; ye'll stay wi' her."

"I dinna like this."

"I ken that. Nor will ye like it when I tell ye that if I dinna come back, ye're to head for home."

"Without ye?"

"Aye."

Before Duncan could protest, Eileen's angry voice came from behind them. They turned to see her striding across the deck.

"What an odious man! He was unbelievably offensive!"

Neil shrugged. "We've seen worse."

"He spoke to you as though you were simpletons."

"He dinna consider that he was speaking to equals."

"You are an earl! Duncan is the captain of this ship!"

"And ye've seen with what regard that's considered."

"Surely you don't need to talk with MacLean badly enough to tolerate this."

"And let them drive us off? No' likely. It'll take more than the likes of Asher. What if MacLean needs us? I'll talk wi' the man, then we'll go."

"I'm sure William doesn't know his officers are being so rude."

"Aye, and he dinna ken about Glencoe. Yer cousin is amazingly uninformed."

She paused, then lowered her voice. "Neil, please don't go."

"I'll be back, lassie," he said softly, then turned to face Duncan and the men, raising his voice. "Calum will come wi' me. Give me three hours. Then sail."

It had been well over three hours since Neil and Calum walked into the trees and disappeared. A score of English soldiers, all heavily armed, clustered together on the shore, watching the road and the ship. Eileen stood at the railing with Duncan, gnawing on her nail and considering all the horrible things that could have happened.

Neil could be dead.

There, that was the worst. Or he could be bound now, waiting for eventual transport to some filthy prison and then to trial for treason. She shook her head to clear her frightening thoughts. He also could be sitting safely before a fire with this MacLean and trading stories.

"Why did he go?" she asked Duncan. "Why not send some of the men?"

"Neil always goes himself."

"He should be more cautious. How does he know it's not a trap?"

"How could it be a trap when no one kent we were coming?"

Eileen almost smiled. "Well, there is that. But he shouldn't go himself; he's too important."

"He'd tell ye that Jamie could take his place in a heartbeat."

"Could he?"

Duncan shrugged. "Probably, but I'd rather no' find out if it's true. Besides, MacLean is more likely to talk candidly to Neil than to someone else. If MacLean says all is well despite the soldiers being here, then we'll go to Glen Mothin."

"And if he says all is not well?"

"Then we'll go to Torridon. We'll ken soon."

"Can Calum fight? Can he defend Neil?"

Duncan laughed softly. "Oh, aye, the lad can fight. Dinna worry, they willna be battling their way out." He gestured to the fishermen, still mending nets on the shingle. "They let us ken things were a'right."

"How?"

"A song, sung in Gaelic, telling us that the English were here making noise but little else. It helps that none of the redcoats speaks the Gaelic."

"Yes," she said softly, somewhat comforted. "Do you think there are English ships like this at Torridon?"

"No. If the English sent a man like Asher to Torridon,

Jamie would ha' told Neil. And he would ha' sank all their ships in our harbor, King William or no."

"It's over three hours now. You're not going to leave, are you?"

"No."

"Even though Neil said . . ."

He gave her a slow smile. "I dinna hear anything about leaving. Did ye?"

She smiled with him, much relieved at his attitude. "No, nothing," she said, then stood on her toes to kiss his cheek. "Good."

He grinned at her.

They were silent then, the minutes slowly ticking by. She watched the shadows grow long on the eastern side of the small houses, watched the fishermen bundle up their nets and move toward the road as the soldiers under the trees stood straighter.

A moment later, Neil walked out of the shadows, his pace measured. He looked calm, but at his side Calum walked with stiff movements, his tension obvious even from this distance. Eileen let out the breath she'd not even realized she was holding, sighing a prayer of thanks. Duncan raised an arm in greeting and Neil returned the wave.

"Make ready," Duncan called over his shoulder. The men leapt to action, lowering sails and standing by the anchor lines.

Neil looked unconcerned as he was rowed to the *Isabel* and swung himself aboard, then leaned over the rail and thanked the Linmargen men in Gaelic. They answered in kind and pushed away. Neil turned to Duncan and Eileen.

"Let's get out of here," he said.

Duncan gave the order to raise the anchors. "Well?"

Neil sighed. "MacLean's no' happy about the soldiers being here, but he says it's just for show; they've no' made it farther than five miles inland. And Asher is the man in charge, so his claiming to report us to his superior is meaningless."

"And?"

Neil looked at Duncan, Eileen, and the waiting clansmen. He would tell them what he'd heard from MacLean—but not every detail. Some of it he would never repeat. He felt immeasurably weary. He'd wanted the reports to be exaggerated, to be wildly overstated. What he'd discovered was the opposite. The *Isabel* swung to face the entrance of the loch, waiting, motionless, for the wind to find her.

"What we heard about Glencoe was true. It was a massacre, and it was planned. Stair sent soldiers to be billeted with the MacDonalds; they stayed in the houses for days, living wi' the people, eating their food, sitting before their fires. One night the soldiers rose up and killed everaone they could get their hands on. Men, women, children, murdered in their beds, in their sleep. Parents watched their bairns killed before them, children watched their mothers and fathers die. Old MacIain's dead; his wife as well. The village is destroyed and many of those that werena slaughtered froze in the snow in the next few days. Those who lived— and at least one of his sons did—got to the next clan and raised the alarm."

He paused for a moment. The *Isabel* gave a shudder as her sails filled, then leapt forward as though anxious to reach the open sea. "It's said that King William signed the order himself." He looked back at Asher's soldiers gathered on the shore, standing in a clot of crimson uniforms. "What kind of men can do such a thing? What was gained? I dinna understand."

He turned from all of them then, standing silently at the rail while the *Isabel* raced through the arms of land at the loch's entrance and into the deep water beyond. The sky overhead was clear, the sea indigo, lashed to foamy peaks by the wind. If he lived to be a thousand, he'd never understand men who kill unarmed people in their beds, men who could order them done.

Her cousin had done this.

If Dundee had lived, if King James had been a different man, if he and the other Jacobites had not failed . . . but there was no sense in thinking about what might have been.

Neil stood alone, trying to make his mind stop visualizing what he'd heard, concentrating on the horizon, slowly aware that Eileen had come to stand at his side. He turned to look at her, hoping she wouldn't tell him that all would be well, that it wasn't William's fault.

She was crying silently, tears streaming down her cheeks. She put a hand on top of his. He felt his own eyes fill, and wrapped his arm around her, pulling her close. She slid her arm around his waist and settled her head in the hollow at his shoulder with a sigh. He looked out over the water again, then kissed the top of her head.

Chapter Twelve

It was two hours before Duncan returned to his cabin. He'd left Eileen still on deck, where she'd stayed after Neil had gone below. He'd watched them at the railing with a feeling of inevitability. It was hardly a surprise that whatever was between them had intensified on this voyage. He should be pleased that his cousins had found each other. And he was. But damn, this would be thorny.

Neil was awake, lying on his berth, staring at the ceiling. Duncan didn't look at him as he crossed the room and rolled up the charts that he wouldn't be needing. He put them in the vertical bin before he met his cousin's gaze.

"Do ye ken what ye're doing—with Eileen? D'ye ken how complicated this can become?"

Neil sat up, swinging his feet over the edge of the berth. "Aye."

"Ye ken they'll all think ye just want to be king, that when ye found out her father might be legitimate, ye decided to woo her."

"I dinna care what they think."

"Doesna matter. That's what they'll think in London. And so will Seaforth and Phelan. And Kilgannon and Sleat. And King James."

"Aye, Duncan, and Lochiel and whoever else ye can think of. I dinna care what they'll think."

"Ye should. They'll think ye abandoned King James."

"I'll no' fight again for the man."

Duncan crossed his arms over his chest. "Nor I."

"The only one of those that matters is Seaforth," Neil said. "And ye're right, Seaforth willna understand. I ken that, Duncan. In his place I'd think the same thing—he's rotting in prison and suddenly I want to end the agreement to marry Fiona, even though I've said for years I would. He'll assume that I'm forsaking her for Eileen because I'm shifting my loyalty from him and King James to William. He'll consider it a personal betrayal. And I canna blame him." He sighed. "And Fiona will think I've deserted her because King James lost—how can I tell her it's worse than that, that I dinna want to marry her because another woman is more precious to me? What am I going to say to her?"

"Ha' ye told Eileen about her?"

"No."

"Ye might want to do that," Duncan said mildly, then frowned. "Neil, d'ye ken what ye're doing?"

Neil gave a wry laugh. "Bowing to the inevitable? I want her, Duncan." He spread his hands wide. "Perhaps this is how the legend comes true after all."

Duncan tilted his head. "I assume ye're no' just amusing yerself, that there's more here than . . . I've grown fond of the lass, and I willna take it well if ye . . ."

Neil's eyes narrowed. "Have I ever?"

"No. But I've never seen ye like this."

"What d'ye mean?"

"I see how the two of ye look at each other. We can all see it; there's no one been in the same room wi' the two of ye without kenning that something's going on between ye. I dinna ken where ye go from here, but if ye havena told her about Fiona she'll no' likely be pleased to hear of it now."

"No."

Duncan moved the remaining charts around on his desk, then looked up at Neil again. "Are we still going to Glen Mothin?"

"Aye. Why would we no'?"

"Dinna bristle at me, Neil. Ye dinna say whether ye'd heard if it was safe to travel. That's why ye went to see MacLean, remember?"

"Aye. We're going. We'll see it through." Neil stood. "What would ye say if I wanted to marry her?"

"If the world was different, it would be a fine match. But as it is—just tell me why ye and Jamie ha' to make life so damned difficult for yerselves in the women ye pick?"

"Jamie's happy."

"Oh, aye, he is now, but ye werena there for most of it. Trust me, it wasna enjoyable when he was in the middle of it. When I pick a woman, it'll be different, ye can count on that."

Neil grinned. "Will it? Fine words; I'll be waiting to see if they come true."

Duncan and Calum went back on deck immediately after their evening meal, jumping up from the table together, as though they'd planned to leave her alone with Neil. Eileen felt suddenly shy, thinking about this afternoon. Neil had kept his arm around her for some time, then kissed her forehead, saying he was going below. That was all, just that he was going below. She had watched him go, not knowing if that had been an invitation to join him, or a warning to leave him alone. She'd decided the latter, but had wondered if she'd been right.

All through dinner the three men had watched her. She folded her hands in her lap now and waited, not sure of his mood. Neil played with his silverware, then looked up at her, his eyes very dark. His tone was quiet.

"D'ye have any idea of how good ye looked, standing at the rail, waiting for me to come back on the ship this afternoon, Eileen? Ye just may be the bonniest lassie who ever lived, and ye were standing there, yer hair catching the sun, waiting for me to come back."

"I was so worried about you."

"Were ye? No need, lassie. There was no danger for me."

"If you had been hurt . . ." She shook her head, remembering her fears. "You were gone so long that I wasn't sure if you were coming back. I thought perhaps the soldiers were holding you."

"I gave orders that if I dinna return, Duncan was to sail."

"We wouldn't have left; you know that. We would have gone to find you."

"Would ye have? Glad to ken everaone obeys my orders so well."

"I would not have left you there, Neil."

He smiled. "What did ye think ye could do if they were holding me, lassie?"

He leaned back. "When I was talking wi' MacLean, even as compelling as his story was, all I could think of was gettin' back to see ye."

"And all I could think of was having you back with me, safe and sound."

He stretched his hand across the table, palm up. She put hers atop his, watching as he closed his fingers around hers.

"I dinna understand it, lass, but there's something verra powerful between us . . . has been from the first."

"Yes."

"I'm glad ye dinna pretend it's no' there."

"How could I? I've never felt anything like this."

"Nor I."

He was the first to stand, but she joined him without thinking, lifting her face to him as he pulled her into his arms. His kiss was hungry and searching; his lips were soft, and he tasted like the whisky he'd had with his meal. When he slipped his tongue into her mouth, she stiffened, then relaxed. This was what she'd wanted for some time and she wasn't going to play the offended virgin. She wrapped her arms around his shoulders. At last he leaned back, smiling into her eyes.

"I ha' wanted to kiss ye like that for a verra long time, Eileen."

"And I you."

"When ye gave me that appraisal at Ronley Hall, I damn near threw ye over my shoulder and hauled ye away right then. Expect it the next time ye look at me like that."

"I thought you were splendid. I didn't realize I was so transparent."

He laughed softly. "I was verra complimented, lassie. And I thought ye were splendid as well. D'ye have any idea how beautiful ye are? I'll tell ye, when ye came to the Pegasus that morning, ye damn near stopped my heart."

"You? What did you do to me, the handsomest man who has ever lived, leaning out, half-naked, to look at me?"

He laughed deep in his throat. "All naked."

"Were you? It's just as well I didn't know that then. Kiss me again."

He kissed her, both of them braver now in their exploration of each other. She lost track of everything but the sensation of his mouth on hers, his shoulders beneath her hands, his body hard against her stomach. She ran her hands along his back, to his waist, arching against him.

"Eileen . . . God help me, I want ye."

"And I you."

He drew back from her, taking deep breaths. "But we canna. We ha' things we must talk about first."

"Yes, we'll talk," she said, pulling his mouth down to hers, "but kiss me first."

He kissed her again, his tongue probing her mouth as one hand cradled her breast, and the other held her tight against his loins. She bent her neck to allow him access, leaning back against his arm as he traced a line of kisses from her chin to the tops of her breasts, shivering with pleasure when his fingers dipped below the lace of her neckline. She moaned softly and ran her hands through his hair, pulling its thickness from its bindings and let the dark locks fall around them like a veil. His hand was inside her bodice now, then on her breast, creating sensations she'd never known could exist.

"So soft," he murmured.

She put a hand to his throat, letting her fingers trail down the base of his neck, to run along his collarbone, then inside his shirt. She pushed the linen back, putting both hands on his chest, feeling the springy hairs there, and his heart beating under her fingers. She unfastened his waistcoat, then the laces on his shirt, spreading it to the side, leaning into him, to press her lips against his skin and slide her hands along his sides.

He let her explore him for another minute, his breath shallow, his heart pounding under her hands. He slipped her bodice off her shoulders, pushing it and her chemise down, first to the tips of her breasts, then below.

"Ye are so beautiful," he whispered. "So bonnie, Eileen."

She smiled, and he put a hand on her breast, bending to kiss her mouth.

From the deck above came shouts, then the sound of

pounding footsteps. Neil raised his head, staring at the ceiling. Eileen could hear Duncan now, shouting orders, then suddenly all was quiet. She met Neil's gaze.

"What is it?" she whispered. He shook his head, then looked down at his hand on her breast. "You have to go see," she said, drawing back from him.

He nodded, but hesitated, and she smiled. She did not want this moment to end either, but there were raised voices on deck now. She pulled his mouth to hers, in a brief but searing kiss, then he stepped back from her, yanking his shirt closed. He turned at the door.

"I want ye, Eileen, more than I've ever wanted any woman."

And then he was gone. She pulled her chemise over her breasts and tugged her bodice back in place. She could hear Neil's calm voice now, and Duncan's, angry but controlled, mixed with the sailors' outraged tones. What could it be?

No one saw her when she came on deck, pausing as the wind caught at her clothing. The men were gathered by the forward mast, the scene lit by the last of the daylight and torches that had been attached to the mast.

The wind-torn light flickered across the angry faces of several men who talked to Duncan and Neil in heated tones, in Gaelic, pointing fingers at a man who stood sullenly off to the side, a leather bag at his feet, its contents strewn across the deck. They were accusing him of something, but the man was arguing, pulling out his pockets until they hung from the sides of his trews.

Duncan held both hands high and made a pronouncement. The men looked from him to Neil, who nodded, then talked for several minutes, his hair, still loose, flying around his head. Whatever he said placated them and the men began to turn away, but not before making several more remarks to the accused man.

As the deck cleared, Eileen moved forward into the light. Calum, who she'd not even seen, moved from the shadows near the railing to stand next to the accused man. In his hands were two pistols, and his expression was grim. Duncan and Neil, who had exchanged a glance as she approached, faced her now.

"Go on below, Eileen," Neil said quietly.

"What happened here?" she asked.

Duncan looked at the accused man. "Someone's been stealing and some of the men think it's Desmond here."

"Ye found nothing on me!" Desmond shouted.

"No," Duncan said. "But ye'll no' go back with the others."

"They only accuse me because I'm a MacLeod." He glared at Neil, then spat at his feet.

Neil watched impassively, but Calum took a step forward, saying something low and fierce to Desmond, who sullenly looked away. Calum made a remark to Neil, who nodded and patted the younger man on the shoulder.

"What will you do?" Eileen asked Duncan.

Duncan looked at Eileen for the first time, his eyes narrowing for a moment before he threw a glance at Neil. He gestured to Desmond. "He'll spend the night in a sail locker. We'll be at Loch Carron in a day and a half. Get yerself into yer cabin, Eileen. The men are in a foul mood and I want ye safe."

She looked at Neil, who nodded, then went below. Alone in her cabin, she began to undress, discovering as she did that her bodice was wildly askew. She looked into the small mirror above the chest, seeing her hair, half torn from its pins. No wonder Duncan had given her such a sharp look.

*   *   *

She woke just after dawn to the clatter of boots on the stairs. Men, many of them, were moving quickly across the deck. Eileen sat up when she heard Neil's voice, just outside her cabin.

"Eileen?"

She flew across the small space to fling the door wide. His shirt hung loose over his trews, and he was fastening on his baldric, arranging his sword at his hip while he spoke.

"Ye need to get dressed. There's an English frigate been following us all night. I dinna ken if we'll engage, but ye should be ready."

"I thought something else had happened with Desmond."

"Desmond? Och, lass, he's no' worth all the noise. Get yerself dressed and dinna worry about Desmond MacLeod."

She nodded. "Be careful, Neil. Please be careful."

He smiled, then bent to slip his hand behind her neck, kissing her for the briefest of moments. "Dinna fear. Duncan's verra good at this. Stay here."

She watched him stride along the corridor and disappear up the stairs, then dressed quickly, throwing the blue muslin of her worn bodice over her head. A shout from above was muffled by the cloth; she wasn't sure what had been said, but when it was followed by laughter, she stayed calm and finished pulling on her clothing, making sure this time that she'd done it correctly.

On deck she stood near the hatch, out of the way of the men who hurried past her and into the rigging above. The seas were high, and she had to steady herself as she moved to join Neil and Duncan at the railing.

"Ye should've stayed below," Neil said, putting an arm around her.

She shook her head, looking at the English ship that followed them. "I want to know what's happening, not hide and wonder."

"What's happening is that we're letting her gain on us so we can figure out what her game is," Duncan said.

"What do you think it is?" she asked.

Duncan shrugged. "We'll ken in short order. If we tell ye to get below, ye'll do so, aye?"

"Yes," she said, looking from his stern expression to the frigate.

"Show them our guns," Neil said. "Let them see we're ready!"

Duncan called the order.

"They should be able to easily see the gun doors opening and the cannons rolling into place," Neil told her.

Duncan shouted an order in Gaelic and the *Isabel* slowed. The English ship drew closer, off their stern quarter now. Eileen could see her flag, the men in her rigging. Her aft deck was crowded with soldiers in red uniforms.

"It's one of the frigates from Linmargen," Neil said and swore. "Why is she heading north wi' soldiers all over her decks?"

Duncan called something to his men. The ships were close enough now for Eileen to make out individual faces on the English ship. Her men were watching the *Isabel*, many of them pointing to her guns and shouting over their shoulders.

"Must be a fresh recruit at the helm," Neil said. "She shouldn't be this close; she's no' ready and we are. She's within range now."

A hush fell over both ships as the distance closed. Duncan raised his arm, ready to give the order to fire. Neil put his hands on Eileen's shoulders and pushed her down to the deck, sheltering her with his body. She looked through the railing and waited. The frigate slid forward, much too close. Her gun doors were just beginning to open and Eileen could look through them to the men scurrying to get the cannons into place.

Duncan called to his men in Gaelic and began to count. The frigate shuddered and veered to the left, jibing sharply away from the *Isabel* and out to sea. Eileen watched to see if she'd swing back to face them, but she continued away, the soldiers' pale faces staring at them from her stern.

Neil said something to Duncan before helping Eileen to her feet, but kept his arm around her. They waited, still watching to see if the frigate would turn and make a run at them, but she continued west, growing smaller by the minute. After another few moments, Duncan called something to his men in Gaelic, who burst into laughter.

Neil joined them and turned to her, still laughing as he caught her hand in his. "And that, lassie, I willna translate."

She smiled at him. "I don't think you have to."

He tightened his grip on her hand. "Lass, ye're verra braw. Most women would ha' cowered down below."

"My lord Torridon, you'll discover that I am not most women."

"Miss Ronley, I kent that the first time I saw ye." His expression grew serious as he looked around the deck, crowded with men who watched them. "Come below, lass. We need to talk."

She looked into his eyes. "Of course."

In Duncan's cabin she was less tranquil. He closed the door and leaned against it, looking at her. She could not read his expression, but he'd not touched her, which said volumes.

"Eileen, I . . . I ha' only the most respect for ye. I want ye to ken that."

She nodded. "And I for you."

"We'll be at Loch Carron soon."

"Yes."

"Will ye come to my home after ye visit at Glen Mothin?"

She nodded, barely daring to breathe. He let out a huff of air.

"Good. I'll leave ye there while I go away for a while."

"Where will you go?"

"I ha' to talk to some people, but I'll come back. So ye'll come to Torridon?"

"I don't understand."

"I have to talk to some people; I'll explain it all later. Will ye come to Torridon, lass?"

"Yes." She waited, but he added nothing else. "Thank you for the invitation."

He nodded awkwardly and left. She stared at the door for a moment, then burst into tears. She had expected a declaration of love, recognition that this powerful bond between them should be solidified. Not an invitation to see his castle. What had happened to the man who had kissed her so fervently just a day ago? Had she been too willing, too obvious in her affection?

Who did he have to talk to? Did he need permission to declare himself to her? He'd said he wasn't married—and he was an earl, the chief of his clan. Who could he possibly need to talk to but her? She put a hand over her mouth to stifle her sobs. She didn't understand any of this.

Loch Carron, Neil thought as the *Isabel* slipped into the calmer waters of the sea loch. Almost there. The voyage was over; he'd not wanted it to end. On shore they would face the world as it was, not as he'd like it to be, and all the cares that had been suspended during this trip would settle on them again.

He'd had a lot of time to think last night; he and Duncan and Calum had taken turns checking on Desmond, not worried that he could go anywhere, but that some of the men might come after him. They'd found none of the things the men said were missing on Desmond's person, nor among his possessions, but there was a furtiveness, a sullen glowering about Desmond that made Neil distrust him. He was a MacLeod, which several of the MacCurries had mentioned with derision, but that wasn't it; Calum was a MacLeod and Neil had rarely trusted a man more.

It was not Desmond he'd thought about in the long dark hours. It was Eileen. He wanted her; intended to make her his own, and as soon as he was free to ask her, he would do so. He thought it would be wise to let her know he'd like to bring her to Torridon after Glen Mothin, but obviously he'd gone about it completely wrong. She'd been cheerful since he'd invited her, but there was a reserve now in her manner that hadn't been there before. This Eileen was always polite, but it was as though something had been extinguished.

He didn't know what else he could have done. He'd wanted to tell her how much he cared for her, how much a part of his every thought she'd become, but until he was free of the entanglements of Fiona and Seaforth, he didn't think he should speak of his feelings. As it was, he'd lost control that day in Duncan's cabin. If they'd not been interrupted, he would happily have made love to her right then.

He'd never felt anything like this, the mixture of lust and simple pleasure in Eileen's company, amusement at her remarks, pride in her fearlessness. He should have told her earlier about Fiona, and he would as soon as he had it settled. He'd get Eileen safely to Torridon, then he'd have to tell Seaforth and Fiona.

Telling Seaforth would be difficult, for the imprisoned earl was likely to consider it a personal betrayal. He would assume—as would many in the Highlands—that Neil had deserted him and was now giving his support to William. And Phelan. Telling Fiona would be just as miserable. He felt like a scoundrel for letting the match be supposed for years and then ending it with little warning.

Perhaps Fiona would be as glad of the release as he, but he doubted it. He'd seen her wrathful before. She was at King James's court, where she could, and most likely would, do all she could do to damage him.

And that was the least of it.

Eileen's kisses might be sweet, but her lack of trust was bitter indeed. She'd never told him herself that her father might have been legitimate, had still never told him why she'd been at Howard Templeton's house, or what she thought of her cousins having her followed. She must know, at least suspect, that she could be the true heir to the throne.

Did she want the power? Was the Stuart blood strong enough in her to make her want to be queen? Had he been wrong in assuming she was leaving London for good—or was this trip merely a convenient means to establish a base in Scotland from which she could try for the throne? He wanted none of it. He was weary of the struggling for power, of the schemes and intrigues he'd seen.

What he wanted, he'd realized in the last few months, and never more than in the last few days, was to go home, to live with a woman he loved, to start a family. He wanted what his brother had; Jamie was more than content, he was elated. Neil wanted to find out what that felt like.

If Eileen were willing, he'd marry her and take her home to Torridon where he could keep her safe, no matter if all the world were banging on his door for her. He pictured her on the walls of Castle Currie, her hair pulling sunbeams out of the sky. And at night he'd feel her beneath him, her soft breasts in his hands and his mouth. And under him as he filled her, her long legs wrapped around him.

If she were willing. She might not be. She'd not trusted Duncan either, surprising that, since she and her cousin had grown fond of each other. Or at least he thought she was fond of Duncan. Maybe he didn't know the lass at all. He hated doubting her, but what was he to think when she'd shut him out so effectively? He'd get her to Glen Mothin and then see what happened.

Glen Mothin. How would Phelan react to Catriona's daughter appearing out of thin air? Would he reject Eileen as he had her mother? Or would he, as Neil suspected, give her a lukewarm welcome that heated up as Phelan realized how strategically important she might be?

If Phelan considered nothing else, he would recognize that Eileen was Charles II's oldest grandchild, and had been one of his favorites. William and Mary had no heir, and Anne, next in line, had only one sickly son. It was possible, likely even, that if Anne died without an heir, people would remember that Eileen carried Charles's bloodline forward. Even if Eileen wanted none of it, Phelan might attempt to use her as a pawn in his own games, to gain more power, if not in England, then at least in Scotland. Who Eileen married, who she bore, could change the future.

And if Adam had been legitimate? Would Phelan push her

to try to retake the throne? Even Phelan would know that meant war.

Would the Highlanders, as weary of conflict as he was, be willing to arm again for the half-English granddaughter of Phelan MacKenzie? It was unlikely that anyone would even listen to Phelan—he'd burned a lot of bridges over the years. There would be those who would take his news as the ravings of an old man. Would the English be willing to have their land in turmoil and an unknown, untested, half-Scottish queen put in place?

What if she was willing to marry Neil, but still wanted to be queen? He would marry her, even knowing that the world would be saying, for the rest of his life, that Torridon wanted to be king, and that he could only get there through a woman. Like William.

And what if she rejected him? She'd know how unlikely it was that England would accept a Scot as her consort. Was she now thinking of the men she'd known at court, deciding which of them would bring her the most power, the most money? Was that why she'd run from the marriage to von Hapeman, not because of the man, but because he wasn't strong enough to further her goal? Was that why she was so distant now?

It might even be simpler than all this. It was, loath as he was to face it, possible that she did not return his ardor, that hers had been a very brief infatuation that cooled with more contact. He might have failed to win her heart, as he'd done with Fiona. Perhaps no woman would ever love him.

If she would not have him, he'd go home, build the new wing, and find a woman to share it with him. Not Fiona; that much he'd already decided. In time, his fascination with Eileen would fade; she'd become a memory.

He lifted his face to the cold wind and took a deep breath of the pine-scented air. He'd know soon enough.

Loch Carron, Eileen thought as she came on deck. The last leg of their journey. Glen Mothin was a long day's ride through the foothills and along the river. There were only a handful of hours left before she'd have to face her grandfather and what the future would bring.

She moved to stand at the railing next to Neil. He gave her a faint smile, then looked out over the water again, distant, as he'd been all day. She sighed and looked across the loch. The hills around them were deep blue, those farther away even darker, the sky a rosy lavender in the early morning light. The water was quiet as it flowed around the many tiny islets and sinuously passed headlands loaded with trees.

The *Isabel* was not alone on the loch, even at this hour; fishing boats were heading out to sea. Duncan leaned low from the bow to talk to the men on them. When he straightened, his expression was grim.

"We may ha' to change our plans," Duncan said as he joined them. "The English frigate we saw at sea has been visiting here often while the soldiers go inland. The fishermen dinna ken where they go."

"We'll land at the next village," Neil said. "And ask the crofters."

"Aye," Duncan said, "but I'll no' leave my ship where she can be taken."

Neil nodded. "We'll find a safe place, or we willna leave her."

The news at the village was mixed. The crofters said the frigate had visited many times in the last few weeks; some said that one of the English officers had a sweetheart in an inland village. There had been no incidents along the water, but no one thought it a good idea to leave the *Isabel* there for very long.

And there was another problem; there were only two horses left in the whole district. Their owner would sell both, but there wasn't another one for miles; the English had bought them all. The crofters recommended that Duncan buy fresh horses farther up the loch and ride down to the entrance of the glen. They were sure the villagers in the north would have at least one horse available.

Neil and Duncan had looked askance at the only horses that the tacksman could provide, exchanging glances that left no doubt of their dissatisfaction. Eileen had expected Highland ponies, those short but sturdy beasts that roamed the mountains. These two were horses, old mares, weary even before they'd taken a step. And small. Neil's or Duncan's legs would dangle below the stomach of the larger mare, would hit the ground if either rode the smaller one.

After some discussion, they decided that she and Neil should take the mares and begin the journey. Duncan and Calum would find more horses somewhere and catch up with them. It would be easy enough, Neil said; their progress would be sluggish at best. He said little else, and neither did she, but her heart beat faster.

They'd be alone together, and perhaps now they could talk without interruption. Before she got to Glen Mothin she would know what Neil MacCurrie felt for her.

Chapter Thirteen

The wind whispered through the trees, mournful notes followed by long sighs that made Eileen wonder if they were alone in the forest. The trees—rowans, beech, fir, and pine, mixed with others she didn't recognize—were thick here, their crowns forming a canopy over the luxuriant undergrowth. Ferns grew huge in the shade below, moss layered beneath them. Left alone, the forest would, she suspected, claim the pathway in very short time.

Neil had called it a road, but anywhere else in the world it would be called a track or a path. No carriage could pass this way, only horses, and not more than two abreast. It kept the English out, he'd told her with a smile, the first smile he'd given her that day. He'd been polite, as she had, but nothing more. There had been no recognition of anything special between them, no renewal of the awareness of her that had marked his earlier behavior. She'd felt a sense of loss that had overwhelmed her. Apparently she had misunderstood everything.

They'd ridden for most of the morning without seeing anyone, but if the hair standing up on the back of her neck was any indication, that would soon change. Neil rode ahead of her, his back straight, his head turning to scan the trees as they passed. She moved her horse alongside his now, leaning to whisper to him.

"I think we're being watched," she said.

"Aye," he answered calmly. "I'm sure ye're right."

"What should we do?"

"Pour some wine on the ground at our midday meal."

"What?"

He laughed. "Dinna look so askance, lass. We told ye on the ship, that ye'd have to let go of yer London thinking."

"What does that mean?"

"That ye're right; we're no' alone, and we are being watched."

"By whom?"

"Ah, now there's the real question. People call them many things. I dinna ken what they are—spirits of the wood, or ghosts, or people so cautious that they dinna let us see them—but I sense it too, that they're there watching."

"Spirits? Ghosts? Surely you do not believe such things."

"In London I would not; there I am in the world of man. But here, where the very earth is different, I'm no' sure what to believe. This is an old land, Eileen, and we are no' the first to live in it. D'ye hear the wind through the trees?"

"Yes."

"I hear it too; no' everyone does, ye ken. But is there any wind blowing past ye? Are yer clothes moving? D'ye feel the breeze on yer face?"

"No."

"Then what is it, lass? Simply wind that's higher than we are?"

"Possibly."

"Aye, but look up—see any branches moving? Any leaves twisting?"

She did; the trees overhead were still, their branches quiet. "No."

"Then ye tell me what it is we hear."

"People? Hiding?"

"Unlikely. There are villages ahead, but no' for some miles. Ye'll notice the difference when we get close to people."

"Is it only here?"

"Och, no. It's here less than many other places. Some spots just have a . . . a spirit, I guess ye'd call it, a character of their own."

"Does Torridon have it?"

He paused, considering. "Torridon lets ye ken it's strong, that it willna be dominated. It's the mountains all around, I think."

"Or the men." She smiled at her words.

"Or the men. My grandda and my da were quite formidable."

"So are you."

He smiled back at her and she realized that she was no longer afraid. Above her, the trees sighed again, this time the sound comforting rather than unsettling. London seemed very far away.

They ate their midday meal seated on rocks next to a tumbling stream. The foliage was thick here as well, but not as tall, bushes and plants growing down into the water itself, colorful with the first of the spring flowers; tiny wild roses mixed with purple flowers that she did not recognize and ferns, masses of ferns. She spread their food out on a plaid he'd brought while he tended the horses. A moment later he settled himself next to her, handing her a fistful of flowers.

"For the fairest lassie in the land."

She smiled and took the flowers, hiding her surprise. He

leaned back against the rock and talked of simple things— the waterfall they could see farther up the river, the rabbit that peaked at them from beneath the closest fern, the clouds that were scudding across the sky. He took a swig of whisky, then uncorked the wine, pouring several drops of it onto the ground.

"For the local gods," he said, laughing, "in case what we were taught in church was wrong."

She laughed with him, thinking how unlikely this all would have been to her a month before. She sat in a pool of light in a forest, the boulder beneath her growing warm as the sun beat on them. Her clothes were her oldest, thread-bare, faded and splattered with mud; her leather shoes were scratched and filthy; her hair was windblown. If only Madam Landers could see her now.

Neil cut the bread and cheese that would be their meal, his dark head bent to the task, hair gleaming in the light, looking more blue than black. His lashes were lowered against his cheeks, his fingers long and lean as they moved. She looked away, images of what those hands could do to her making her flush. He smiled as he handed her a piece of bread, letting his hand linger on hers for longer than neces-sary. He might be, she thought, the most handsome man who had ever lived. Even the most innocent of touches made her think wild thoughts, of throwing herself atop him and dis-covering where that might lead.

Was the moment all the sweeter for how quickly it would pass? She would think no further than now, would enjoy this lunch, this day; this man and his untroubled mood. For how-ever long their time together was, she would savor all three. Soon they'd arrive at Glen Mothin and this golden meal would be only a reminiscence.

"Tell me about your family," she said, to distract her own thoughts.

"My family. Well, ye ken Duncan. And my brother Jamie is much like me. There's his wife, Ellen, who disliked me verra much at first. And I her."

"And now?"

"Now I've come to prize her. Jamie and Ellen ha' a son, John, a wee babe now, but growing. And there's my mother, Anne, and my grandmother, Mairi."

"And your father?"

"Died several years ago. Just as the troubles with William began. He was a good man, a bonnie leader."

"You miss him."

"I do. But he visits now and then."

"Really?"

He nodded. "I feel his spirit at Torridon, lass; I dinna ken how else to explain it. When I leave, I always ask my da to watch over the clan and the family."

"And does he?"

"So far. I dinna ken if he's really there, or if it's all his teachings, or just my own memories. But I try to do what he would ha' done."

"Did he believe in the legend?"

"No' at first. No', I think, until the night that the tree was split. I think he believed after that." He laughed. "I think everaone believed after that."

"And now you'll have fifty years of peace."

He shrugged. "Perhaps. I can only tell ye what has happened, no' what will."

"So you don't believe it?"

He looked into her eyes. "I'd like to think that I'll go home and live peacefully, that the MacCurries will have fifty years without war, and that I helped to start it. But did the Seer mean fifty years starting right after the first time I took the clan to war—or after a period of years of warfare? I dinna ken."

"Do you think you will go to war again?"

"Only for a damned good reason."

She was silent then, feeling the pouch with her grandmother's letter at her ribs.

"Yer turn," Neil said. "Tell me about yer mother. Was she like Duncan?"

"Somewhat. She was tall, and their hair is the same shade of red, or collection of shades, I should say. He has a smile very like hers, that wide grin that is so contagious. And he laughs often, which she did when we were young."

"That must ha' been difficult, to lose yer mother."

"It was. But she'd started to leave years earlier, when my sister died. That was the beginning of the end of everything."

"What happened to yer sister?"

"Smallpox. My mother always blamed London for it, but it was everywhere. My sister was twelve; I was fourteen. We were both ill with it, but I lived and she . . . didn't." She looked into the trees, remembering. "I loved her very much. I always thought I should have protected her, that somehow it was my fault."

"Ye were but a lass yerself. It wasna yer fault."

She smiled sadly. "I know that now. But I always wondered why I lived. It was as though I'd been saved for a reason, as though there was something I was to do . . ." She let her words drift off. "Are Duncan and I Phelan's only grandchildren?" she asked hurriedly.

Neil shook his head. "No. Duncan's the only grandson,

but Phelan has five, maybe six, granddaughters other than ye."

"So I have other cousins."

"Aye."

"What are their names?"

"I dinna remember them all, lassie." He handed her a hunk of cheese and took a bite of his own. "The only one I remember clearly is Adara."

She gave him a sharp look. "Why?"

He chewed slowly, then took a drink of whisky before he answered her. "Why do I remember Adara?"

"Yes."

"Most likely because she's the one closest to my age."

"And?"

He grinned. "She was a cheerful companion when we were younger."

"Cheerful. How like 'willing' is that?"

He looked into her eyes, his merry now. "Verra."

"I see."

"No doubt she's married with a handful of bairns by now."

"No doubt."

"And doesna remember me."

"Oh, yes, you're eminently forgettable."

"Am I?"

"No." She tilted her head. "Adara, eh?"

"Ye sound jealous," he said playfully.

"I think I am," she said.

He laughed and slid a hand behind her neck, pulling her toward him. His kiss was gentle; he tasted like whisky, and she leaned closer, willing him to forget Adara and think only of her. Behind them the trees rustled and pine needles fell around them. A benediction, she thought. She let the cheese slip from her hand and concentrated on his kiss.

"Eileen," he sighed, one hand roaming lower to her breast, the other drawing her to her knees to press against him. If she'd had any doubt of his interest—or his readiness—his arousal soon removed it. "Eileen, ye are so bonnie."

He moved his hand higher, pausing above the pleated lace of her neckline, looking into her eyes as his fingers slipped between the silk and her skin, pushing the thin chemise she wore aside to find her breast, cupping her. She bent her head to give him access to her neck. He kissed her neck, then her mouth, then the top of her breasts, stopping only to move her bodice aside.

She stroked his back, letting her hands roam lower, to his waist, then to his buttocks. She'd never touched a man in this way. She stretched her arm and ran her hand the length of his leg, bending to feel every muscle of his thigh under the fine wool of his trews, wondering what his skin would feel like.

His lips found her breast and drew her nipple into his mouth. She moaned softly, threading her hands through his hair, pulling it from its bindings, and kissed the side of his neck. "Oh, lass," he said. "Ye are so sweet."

"Neil," she said.

She was vaguely aware of him sweeping the food aside, of the stone bottle bouncing down the boulders unheeded, landing with a dull thud among the ferns, of the clouds moving overhead, cooling them one minute, then allowing the sun to heat their bodies. Or was it their own heat?

She was bolder now, letting him touch her leg, and running her hands along his side, to his hip and lower, down to his knee, pulling his shirt from his belt, slipping her hands beneath it and up his chest.

He pulled the pins from her hair, drawing each lock from its prison slowly, laying it on her shoulders, then kissing the spot where it landed before doing the same with the next until her hair tumbled around her shoulders, wild now in the breeze that had freshened. She reached to pull him down to her, with a sigh.

James MacCurrie looked up from his paperwork, rising from Neil's desk to walk to the window that overlooked the waters of Loch Torridon, hearing not the familiar sounds of the harbor below, but the rustle of wind moving through trees.

And a woman's sigh.

Neil. The break in the link between the brothers was almost tangible. Neil had shut him out, closed the portal through which they sent each other messages.

It had happened before, but then it was he who had kept Neil out of his thoughts. He put his hands on the warm stones of the windowsill.

Eileen Ronley.

He had no doubt that Neil went looking for her, and obviously had found her. There was no need for his brother to rush home. All was well in Torridon, despite Glencoe, despite the English frigates that roamed the coast.

He heard the sigh again, then the murmur of his brother's voice, speaking words of love in Gaelic. Did Eileen understand what he said to her? James wished his brother the same joy he'd found with Ellen. But God help him—Neil was in for an education.

Neil would have to be home by summer, to take the reins

of ruling Torridon and the clan, while he and Ellen would be off for Netherby, her mother's home, as he'd promised her they would be. Now, despite the unrest throughout the rest of the Highlands, Castle Currie was placid. He did not know what was to come. The fifty years of peace that had been promised? Or would that, like everything else in the legend, be fulfilled, but not as one would guess?

He sent his brother a message, of calm. And approval.

Duncan swore as he looked at the sky. Rain before nightfall. That's all he needed now, something to slow him down even more. He'd secured the *Isabel* at an inlet not too many miles from the first village, then began the search for a horse. It took hours, while people talked incessantly of who might be able to help. He'd gritted his teeth and tried to smile. They were trying to be helpful, he told himself, and he was grateful.

He had his horse by midafternoon, a tall strong Highland pony actually, built for the mountains. He'd asked Calum to stay with the *Isabel*, knowing the lad would care for her as his own. He bid Calum farewell, slung his pack over his shoulder, and took off for the road to the glen.

Somewhere out there ahead of him were Neil and Eileen. It had seemed at first a bonnie idea to let them go alone, but as the hours passed he had misgivings that grew into apprehension. They should have taken a score of men with them. Phelan was unpredictable, and somewhere that English officer had a sweetheart. Wouldn't it be braw to meet a party of soldiers on the road? He felt the temperature drop as he entered the trees.

He frowned as he looked up at the road ahead. At the end of it was his grandfather. He was not sure Phelan would welcome him, or Eileen. This trip may have been a dreadful mistake. Too late, he told himself. He was going to Glen Mothin, his grandfather be damned if he didn't like it.

Neil looked up and into the trees. The wind was increasing, the branches moving, rustling, but he thought he'd heard the snap of a twig.

Eileen laughed softly. "Ghosts. Spirits, Neil. Nothing more."

He leaned up on one elbow, his finger tracing the outline of her mouth, his lips following the same trail. He wanted her, wanted to make love here, now, in the wind that was growing stronger by the minute, in the sunshine, outside where the ghosts and spirits could watch if they chose.

But he couldn't. He pulled back from her, looking into her eyes and hating himself for what he was about to do, wondering why he'd not told her earlier. How he had let it come to this? What had he been thinking, to talk to anyone before Eileen?

"Lassie, I ha' to tell ye something."

Her smile faded, the wary look that he hated back in place. She took her arm from his neck and pulled her bodice over her breasts. "What?"

"I want ye, lass, but I canna make love to ye."

"Why?"

"I'm no' married. But I'm no' exactly free either."

She stared at him. "What do you mean?"

He swallowed, then sat up, looking over the stream. The clouds had pushed the sun away and the water was no longer cobalt, but gray, the color of steel.

"For several years now I ha' had an understanding with Seaforth, that I would marry his cousin Fiona. We've signed no contract, but there is this . . . agreement." He turned to look at her, hoping she'd laugh and say she understood.

She sat up. "An agreement," she said, her tone flat.

"Aye. I've no' signed anything, but . . ."

"For years. You've known about this for years."

"Aye."

"And didn't tell me, even when I asked you if you were married."

He shook his head, miserable.

"You kissed me, knowing you would marry this Fiona."

"No . . ."

"Yes." She put a hand to her waist, her eyes as cold as her tone. "How could you let me think you cared for me?"

"I do, Eileen."

"Oh, yes, I can tell." She rose to her feet and glared at him. "You take your promises much more lightly than I do."

"I break no promises."

"No? Are you not promised to Fiona?"

"I've signed no contract."

"But there is an understanding. Thank you for having the courtesy to tell me before we made love. This way I have only a few kisses to regret, not a child."

He scrambled up to face her. "I'm sorry I dinna tell ye. I tried to tell ye, Eileen, several times; there dinna seem to be a right moment."

"Before you kissed me the first time, Neil, that would have been the right moment! Before you used my name in the audience hall, before everyone in London thought we were lovers, before you offered to bring me to Scotland and I broke every rule of society by traveling with you without a chaperone! Before all that, you should have told me that you were not free to . . ." She took a deep breath and continued, her tone much quieter now. "I thought you cared for me, that we had something very special that we shared. All your talk of destiny, of a connection between us . . . is that what you say to everyone?"

"No. Only to ye, Eileen. Ye and no other."

"What a fool I am! I was warned about you; I should have listened. I suppose everyone else in the world knew that you were promised except me."

"I'm not promised."

"How could you spend each day with me, how could you talk and laugh and kiss me, let me love you, when all the while you had this secret that affected everything between us? How could you not tell me everything?"

"The same way ye have not told me everything."

"What have I not told you?"

"That ye think yer father might have been legitimate, with all that that means, and that ye suspect that William and Mary think the same. But ye wouldna talk to me about it, would ye? I'm good enough to kiss, good enough to even share yer body wi', but no' yer mind, no' yer heart?"

She took a step back from him.

"How could ye no' talk to me, Eileen? How could ye let me kiss ye when ye dinna think I was worthy enough to ken who ye might be? Did ye think I would use ye? Did ye think that I was worthy enough to share yer bed, but no' yer life? Will ye look for an Englishman with great wealth, who will back yer bid for the throne? Or maybe ye'll look for a prince, or a king? Was that it, lass, that I'm no' good enough for yer royal blood? And if ye're unhappy, then ye're no' alone. Perhaps this has been a mistake from the start."

"Perhaps it was," she said, her tone cold.

He pushed past her and leapt to the ground, turning at the

edge of the trees to watch as she sank to the rock and put her hands over her face.

The afternoon sun was cooler when she woke. And she was alone, lying on the stones that now seemed so hard. She'd cried until she had no more tears, then wrapped herself in his plaid and closed her eyes. He'd been back while she slept. The stone bottle was stoppered and placed neatly beside the wrapped bread and cheese. The horses were tethered nearby.

And Neil was standing in the deepening shadows under the trees, looking at her. He moved silently forward now, his expression grim, his finger on his lips.

"Quiet, lass," he whispered. "We're no' alone anymore. There are soldiers on the road."

"Neil," she said. "I never meant to hurt you."

"Nor I ye, Eileen. Never."

"Where do we go from here?"

"To Glen Mothin."

"You know what I mean."

He sat down next to her and sighed. "I dinna ken, lassie."

"Do you . . ." She stopped as a bird screeched overhead, as though frightened from its nest.

Neil reached for his sword, drawing it as he slid off the boulder and faced the trees. He stood for a moment, then handed her one of his pistols, and crept forward slowly in the forest until she was alone, listening to the sounds of the wind and the water. And her heart.

There were at least twenty men on the road ahead of them, Neil said when he returned. English soldiers, well armed. Heading toward Phelan's.

"Could they be going past Glen Mothin?" she asked, handing him his pistol.

"There are only mountains past it."

"My grandfather backed King William. Perhaps he's billeting them."

"Could be. In fact, that's likely."

"We shouldn't go then. We'll go back and find Duncan."

"I dinna think there's any danger for ye, lassie."

"But there might be for you."

He shook his head. "Phelan willna harm me, Eileen. He kens it would get through the Highlands in verra short order. Jamie would avenge me, and he'd have half the western seaboard as his allies."

"Seaforth is in prison. He couldn't help you."

"There are other clans. I'm no' worried about myself."

"We should wait then, so we don't catch up with them."

He looked over her shoulder at the horses and gave a snort of derision. "I dinna think that'll be a worry for us."

He was right. They made extremely slow progress. The day was drawing to an end and they had only gone a few miles. She didn't mind. Reaching Glen Mothin and meeting her grandfather were no longer very important. Being with Neil was. Trying to find a way through their anger, back to their earlier happiness, was important. All her former worries seemed absurd now. She'd been a fool not to tell him about the letter.

Or had she been? She'd seen many at court who swore eternal love to one another, but many of those loves did not last the month. Was that what this was, a quick-growing passion that had already, for Neil at least, begun to die? Was that why he told her she was beautiful, kissed her with fervor, but could not bring himself to declare love for her? Was he waiting to see if he had a future with her before ending the match with Fiona?

She had no good example of long-lasting love. Her grandfather must have loved his queen, for though she was childless he never set her aside, even while he'd taken his pleasure with whomever he chose. Her father had done much the same, swearing his love for her mother, then leaving her weeping while he and Howard spent their nights with other women.

Jack. The thought of him came from nowhere, but there he was. Jack, from Ronley Hall, who would never be a wealthy man, who had accepted his place in society with quiet grace. Jack loved his Emmy and she him. It was possible, then, to find a love that could last. Jack had found it.

Her father's mother certainly had not. Her life had been brief, and her last few months must have been sad for her, married to a prince, then left behind to bear his son and die in secrecy. But perhaps secrecy no more. The letter Eileen carried with her might be the key to a new future, if she chose. Was that good for England, for its people? Is that what she wanted? Or was Neil what she wanted?

Was that the basis of his anger, not that she had not confided in him, but resentment that she had not asked him to be her consort? He was capable enough, she was sure, to lead the army she'd need to take the throne. Did he love her? Or was she nothing more to him than the woman who might make him king?

If she could believe that William and Mary could discover the truth, why was it far-fetched that Neil had heard the same thing? Was his talk of destiny just nonsense? Had he appeared at Ronley Hall not by chance, nor by any divine intervention, but as part of a coldhearted attempt to win her affection before she knew who she was?

And who was she? She had no raging desire to rule, no need for courtiers to fawn over her, and kings and ministers to negotiate with her. What she wanted was much less grand—a home, and a man who would love her faithfully. She wanted Neil, had wanted him from the first moment she'd seen him at Ronley Hall. She wanted to trust him, to throw herself headlong into a love that would last forever, but how did one know? Did her very questioning of it mean that what she now felt for him would fade, had already begun to fade?

He rode ahead of her now, his back stiff. A warrior, a leader. A proud man. She could not believe any of her suspicions about his ambitions, could not believe he would smile into her eyes and lie. If she was wrong to love this man, then wrong she would be.

Sudden love, steady sorrow. Did the axiom always prove true?

The pounding of hooves behind them startled her out of her thoughts. She threw a look over her shoulder. This was no sighing of the trees, no spirits of the forest. Horses, several of them from the noise, were swiftly bearing down on them.

Neil heard them too, for he looked around as though searching for somewhere to hide. There was nowhere. To their left was a series of boulders, too steep for even a strong horse to climb, let alone these two. To their right was the stream, deep here and flowing swiftly; the horses would never make it through the torrent. Ahead the road rose gradually, the trees thinner there. If they could make it to the top of the rise, they might find somewhere to shelter them while whoever it was thundered past.

Neil drew his sword and gestured for her to go before him. As she passed him, he swatted her mare, sending the horse jumping forward at a quicker pace that only lasted a few feet before she settled back into her ponderous walk.

"Kick her, lass. See if ye can get her to move!"

Eileen did, but to no avail. He had no success with his horse either, swearing as the sound of pounding hooves got louder. He jumped from the saddle and pulled Eileen from her horse, shoving her to the side of the road. He pulled her bags from the horse and threw them, with his pack, into the bushes that grew next to the pathway.

"Go," he whispered, half lifting her up on a boulder.

She clambered up as he instructed; he was behind her, then in front of her, yanking her into the shadow of the trees as the first horse came into view. English soldiers, five of them riding together, thundered past, another five just behind. And still another group, too many to count, thundering out of sight. She heard men shouting, heard the sudden whinny of a surprised horse.

She could hear the soldiers talking now, their voices carrying to her, but not their words. English, it sounded like, but what was it they said? Neil leaned forward, then stood up, gesturing for her to stay where she was. She nodded and watched him climb up the boulders above her.

She was shaking. She wanted Neil safe; nothing else mattered. There were at least twenty men ahead, armed soldiers, and only one Neil. Why had she let him leave her? They could have hidden together in these shadows, could have waited until the soldiers had gone.

Their horses, no doubt, had been trudging along the road,

letting the men know that two people had been there, and were probably still nearby. But the soldiers had been moving quickly and perhaps would not have taken the time to investigate. Surely Neil would not try to take them on himself.

Eileen closed her eyes, straining to hear human sounds. The forest was hushed, as though it listened with her. And then, from behind her, up the hill, she heard the sound of dry leaves scraping together. She turned, her heart in her throat, but saw no one. The hair on the back of her neck rose. She was being watched. She began to pray.

Duncan leaned low over the horse's neck so the branches wouldn't knock him off the horse. There was no way to hurry on this stretch that eventually led him to the main road to Glen Mothin. The trees bent over the pathway, all but blocking it. He'd not been the first to take this route, slow as it was. Tiny twigs littered the road, fallen from the branches above, where horses had pushed through the overhang, the first smudged by those that had followed. Many who had followed. Why were so many people traveling these Highland tracks?

He'd thought he'd be alone on this path that led from the village on the north end of Loch Carron. Just a few miles ahead, he'd been told, the track would split. He was to go north, to meet the wider path that would lead to Glen Mothin. He told himself that surely those who had gone before him would take the southern route. He would only start worrying if they continued to head for Glen Mothin.

He wouldn't wonder whether the English frigate had landed and whether the soldiers rode inland to meet the officer's sweetheart, or if that sweetheart was in Glen Mothin. And he wouldn't wonder what would happen if Neil and

Eileen, mounted on those miserable beasts, were to be over-taken by those same soldiers.

Neil wouldn't have a chance. And it would have been his fault for thinking they should travel alone, that it would give them time to talk before they reached Phelan. Duncan bent even lower, hurrying his horse.

Neil leaned forward, brushing the leaves to the side. He was stretched on his stomach across a boulder that over-looked the road. Below him were the soldiers, gathered around the two horses he and Eileen had been riding. One of the soldiers raced back down the road, then returned, hold-ing one of Eileen's bags over his head like a prize. He turned the bag upside down, spilling its contents onto the road, slid-ing to the ground to rummage through them. Several men joined him.

Her shoes were kicked to the side, her silver hairbrush tucked into a soldier's belt, her chemise held up while the others hooted and made lewd suggestions, then tossed aside with the rest of her clothing, left strewn on the mud. But Neil paid little attention to the soldiers, annoying as they were. He strained forward to look across the group of men, to where the two officers sat astride watching, with a third man. A Scot, dressed in trews.

The Scot moved forward, out of the shadows, at first in profile, then full-faced. Neil swore to himself and gripped his pistol hilt tighter. What the hell was Desmond MacLeod doing here? The last time he'd seen Desmond was on board the *Isabel*, just before he and Duncan and Eileen had gone to search for horses.

Desmond had asked to be put ashore, to leave Duncan's service. Duncan had refused, saying Desmond would be safe enough on the ship and that when he returned they'd sort it all out. Surely Duncan had not released him? Or had Desmond found a way off the ship himself?

They'd not found evidence that Desmond was the thief, but Neil would put money on the fact that he was. Put money on it, he thought. Was Desmond working for the English soldiers? Would he do that? But why else would he be traveling with them?

Neil swore. They had a traitor among the Torridon men, a Judas, who would sell himself to the highest bidder. That explained Desmond's sullenness, the men's antipathy. And now Desmond was heading toward Glen Mothin, would arrive there before he and Eileen did, would tell Phelan of their imminent arrival. What else did he know? Neil started to rise, to find another vantage point. A hand on his shoulder pushed him back onto the boulder.

"Stay still," the man whispered in Gaelic.

Chapter Fourteen

Neil felt the cool metal of a gun touch his ear, and stiffened. If the man was alone, he might be able to take him, but Neil quickly realized that there were others moving behind him as well.

"Back slowly off this rock, sir," the man said.

Neil did as he was told, standing when he could, to face the man with the gun. The man was no longer young, but still lean and fit, his weathered face calm, but his eyes wary. Behind him four other men waited, all much younger; they looked like the first man. His sons, Neil thought.

"Who are ye?" Neil whispered.

"I was going to ask ye the same. We live here, in the village a mile up the road. I dinna need a hothead inciting the English soldiers just before they ride through my home. We saw the two of ye ride past us and then hurry up into the rock. Who are ye, sir?"

"Neil MacCurrie. Of Torridon."

"Torridon. Ye fought for King James."

Neil was silent, wondering what would happen if he agreed. The man laughed softly.

"It was no' a question, Torridon. It was a statement. So did we."

"Phelan's people didna fight for James."

"No, they didna. But we are no' Phelan's people. We share

the MacKenzie name, and the same damned glen, but we're no' Phelan's people."

"What do ye want from me?"

"The promise that ye will no' attack the soldiers unless they do more than strew yer woman's things about."

"Given."

"Then follow me away from the road and we will talk."

MacKenzie gestured for Neil to follow one of his sons, falling into place behind them. Two others stayed, crawling up on the rock where he'd been; the fourth took off at a run, heading north, on a path parallel to the road. They walked away from the road for several minutes before MacKenzie stopped and faced him.

"Why are ye going to Glen Mothin?" MacKenzie asked.

"To visit Phelan. Is this usual, for all these soldiers to be on the road? Is Phelan billeting them?"

"Only for a very short time. They're going to the wedding."

"What wedding?"

"Phelan's youngest granddaughter is getting married to an English soldier. They're attending." His eyes narrowed. "Obviously ye've changed allegiances since Killiecrankie."

"I have not."

"Torridon, ye're riding to Phelan's with yer woman. Ye wouldna ha' brought her here, traveling wi' only the two of ye, unless ye thought it was safe. I think ye're going to the wedding."

"We didna even ken about the wedding, just chose a bad time to come."

MacKenzie rubbed his chin. "Ye might say so. Now, tell me, sir, what is a clan chief from the west doing visiting Phelan MacKenzie?"

"My cousin is his grandson."

"Phelan has only one grandson and we've no' seen him in years."

"Aye. He's been living at Torridon."

"His name?"

"Duncan MacKenzie."

"He's no' wi' ye."

"He's behind us somewhere. We had problems getting horses."

"Long trip from Torridon."

"Aye, and we picked a poor time. Lower the gun, MacKenzie. I'm no threat to ye and yers. I'll just gather our things and we'll be on our way."

"Ye can spend the night wi' us. We'll take ye the rest of the way tomorrow."

"What about the soldiers riding through yer village?"

"They've been doing it for months now. If no one bothers them, they just keep riding, which is how we like it."

"They found our horses. They'll know someone was traveling."

"Like as no', they'll think ye're going to the wedding. My lads will tell us if they stop."

"How many people d'ye ha'?"

MacKenzie grinned. "More than ye, Torridon. Now, laddie, ye ha' little choice. Will ye be taking me up on my hospitality, or should I just shoot ye here?"

"If ye shoot me, the soldiers will hear it."

"They've gone by now. There's naught left here but us, and none of us would mourn ye. Ye'll come home and we'll wait and see who's coming behind ye. There are those in the village who ken Duncan MacKenzie. We'll see if he comes—and if he vouches for ye." He waved the pistol down the hill. "Ye first, sir, if ye would. We need to get yer woman."

Eileen crept forward another two feet, then paused, listening. She'd watched as the soldier had raced back along the road and found one of her bags, raising it above his head and turning to join his companions. It did not matter. They would learn little from ransacking it; it held only her clothing. She had the letter at her waist and what little jewelry she owned was tucked into her pocket. All they'd learn was that there was a woman somewhere about.

The shouting had quieted, the laughter as well. Either something was absorbing their interest, or they'd moved on. Had they found Neil? Were they, even now, hurting him? Or was he already dead? She moved another few feet, waiting to hear the now familiar sound of someone creeping stealthily behind her. She'd heard him several times now, but hadn't seen him yet. So far he was only watching as she made her way to where she thought Neil might be.

She reached the rocks at the top of the hill and ran along them, the trees screening her from the road. When the rocks ended, she jumped down into the underbrush, pushing her way through the knee-high ferns, keeping the road at her right. Another ten yards. She could see the road now.

It was empty, except for her clothing thrown into a pile, her bag on its side, gaping open. The slope was gentler here and she half slid, half ran down it, to the side of the road, hiding behind a tree, waiting while her heart slowed. She took a step onto the road. The dirt where the soldiers had paused was trampled. There was no sign of the horses she and Neil had ridden. And no sign of Neil.

She took another step onto the pathway, and looked in the

direction they'd come, freezing as she saw a young man, a boy really, walking toward her, swinging her second bag and Neil's pack. He was a Highlander, dressed in a kilt and bonnet and leather vest. He drew a pistol from his belt and pointed it at her.

The boy said something in Gaelic to her, then waited for her reply while she stared at him. From up the hill, where she'd just been, came a man's voice; a moment later he emerged from the trees, dressed in the same fashion, barely older than the boy. He moved to stand before her, gesturing for the boy to put the pistol away. He bowed slightly to her and smiled.

She swallowed; they did not seem to be threatening her. "Who are you, sir?"

The taller man spread his hands, obviously not understanding her.

"Neil? MacCurrie? Torridon? Did you see him?"

The young man gestured in the direction of Glen Mothin and indicated that she should walk with him. She reached for her bag, but the boy shook his head and pointed down the road. Obviously she was to go somewhere with these two. But how could she leave until she knew where Neil was, if he was all right?

She turned to the taller man, intending to make him understand that she would not leave until she knew where Neil was, but he and the boy were now picking up her clothing from the mud and putting it in her second bag.

They found her walking the road to Glen Mothin, flanked by the Scots, a man and a boy, each carrying one of her bags. Her back was straight, her head high. Her skirts were muddied and torn, her hair half down her back.

"Eileen," Neil called.

She turned, her expression lightening when she saw him. "Neil! Oh, thank God you're all right! I heard all the shouting; I thought . . ."

"Aye. The English found the horses and yer bag."

"I watched him carry it away."

He reached her and took her hand in his. "Are ye a'right, lassie?"

She nodded, then spoke in French. "I believe that we are prisoners."

He answered in the same language. "Of a sort. They say they know Duncan; we've been invited to spend the night. They'll wait for Duncan to vouch for us."

"Who are they?"

"MacKenzies. They say they're not your grandfather's people, that they fought for King James."

"Do you believe them?"

"We'll see. I don't see what choice we have just now. There's a wedding at Glen Mothin, one of Phelan's granddaughters, to an English soldier, which is why all the soldiers are going there."

"What about Duncan?"

"Duncan is clever; he'll take care." He looked up as the rain that had threatened began to fall. "A good night to spend inside, aye?"

Duncan pulled his plaid over his head as the rain intensified. He was on the main road to Glen Mothin now, making better time, except for the few minutes when he'd hidden in the trees and watched the soldiers pound by. They were making enough noise to warn anyone ahead of them of their approach. Which was good. Neil was sure to hear them before they were on top of him.

He'd hoped to find Neil and Eileen before nightfall, but the afternoon had darkened and with the rain it would soon be too dark to travel quickly. If this rain worsened they'd have to find a place for the night. But where? He lifted the edge of the plaid; he'd start looking for places where Neil might have found shelter.

From behind him he heard the noise of horses. More soldiers? What the hell were they all riding into? He guided his horse off the road.

The road ran through the MacKenzie village and lifted on the other side to start the climb to Glen Mothin. Sentries called to them as they reached the first houses, speaking in Gaelic to the MacKenzie who led them into the deep shade of the trees, where the rain had not yet reached.

Eileen pushed the hood of her cloak back, turning to look at Neil. He nodded to her, not willing to risk more conversation, even in French, until he had a better idea of who these people were. Nine men walked with them now, the others having fallen into step with them on the way to the village.

He'd heard that Phelan's control was slipping, that there were many MacKenzies who, though nominally loyal, were discontent, had been since Phelan had changed sides in the fight for the throne. It had been a gamble then, one that many in the Highlands were sure would fail, but Phelan had been proved right.

He'd already told them his allegiance. If these men were loyal to Phelan and pretending not to be, they'd not be well disposed to him. And if, as he suspected, they were not loyal to Phelan, he'd better not let them know that Eileen was Phelan's granddaughter. And how to warn Duncan? Each step that took them away from the road made it more difficult to warn Duncan, not only of these men, but of the soldiers ahead.

MacKenzie led the way now into the yard of a large croft-house. A tacksman's house, Neil realized from the size and obvious prosperity of the holding.

"Welcome to my home," MacKenzie said to Eileen in English, smiling and waving his hand to the open door where a woman stood waiting. "My wife. Come in, madam. Torridon, my lads will wait for yer cousin. Come in, sir."

An hour later Neil was beginning to relax. He and Eileen had been treated with courtesy, as though they were treasured guests, fed and handed wine and whisky, shown good seats before the fire while MacKenzie's children watched them. MacKenzie's wife spoke no English, the man said, then told her in Gaelic what had happened, including that Eileen's clothes had been rummaged and left in the mud.

The woman and her daughters had insisted on pulling Eileen's rumpled clothing from the bag and cleaning it. Eileen sat with them now, trying to talk despite the language barrier. Neil looked from Eileen to MacKenzie.

"How long were ye watching us?" he asked in Gaelic.

"Only a few minutes, sir. Since Glencoe we keep a close watch on everaone who comes up the road." MacKenzie looked into Neil's eyes. "I kent yer father. Met him at a gathering."

"Did ye?"

"Aye. I was wi' Phelan then, thought he might be a good leader. He wasna. But yer da, he was a good man."

"He was."

"Heard he died just before Dundee raised the flag for the king."

"Aye, about that time."

"We lost another good one when Dundee died. I was there, ye ken, at Killiecrankie. I dinna remember seeing ye, but I heard about yer brother getting shot. I was glad to hear that he lived. He married Dundee's cousin?"

"He did."

MacKenzie raised his glass high. "To Dundee. To yer da. To yer brother living. To King James."

Neil repeated the toast and threw down the whisky, gritting his teeth as the fiery liquor went down his throat.

"And now, sir, tell me the news of London."

Neil raised an eyebrow. MacKenzie gestured to Eileen. "Ye'll not be pretending that yer woman is a Highlander, will ye, sir? She may ha' the coloring and the height, but the lass doesna speak a word of Gaelic and she doesna ken our ways. Ye've got yerself an Englishwoman."

"She's half Scots."

"Who's her family?"

"Is that important?"

"Might be. And I think I've a right to ken who I'm extending hospitality to."

"Ye ken who I am."

"I ken who ye tell me ye are. But I'm thinking ye've no' told me all of it—and I ask myself why ye're traveling wi' an Englishwoman to see Phelan."

Neil grinned. "Do ye? And I'm asking myself why ye're blowing hot and cold. When my cousin comes, we'll see what happens."

MacKenzie laughed. "Fair enough."

* * *

Duncan slowed as he came into the village, pushing his plaid back from his head and arms and letting his hand drift to the hilt of his pistol. The men who watched him moved forward now, three of them on his right, two more on his left.

"Evening, sir," they said. "Where are ye traveling to?"

"Glen Mothin."

"Would ye wait a minute, sir?"

Duncan frowned as one of the men took off at a run into the trees. "Where is he going?" he asked the others.

"To get the tacksman, sir."

"Ye ha' three minutes," Duncan said. "Then I'm off."

"It won't take that long, sir."

Duncan sat stiffly, looking around him. The villager had been polite, friendly even, but he did not like this. He'd seen no more soldiers as the day drew to a close, but he was getting close to Glen Mothin. He knew his grandfather's politics; if Phelan was billeting soldiers, Duncan was riding into a nest of them. And Neil and Eileen already had. "Ha' ye seen other travelers today?" he asked.

"Some." The man turned as several men came out of the trees.

"Duncan MacKenzie!"

Duncan leaned forward, straining in the dim light to recognize the man who had called to him. "Sir?"

A middle-aged man with ruddy skin and a wide smile approached, his hand outstretched. "It's been years, but I would ha' kent ye anywhere, laddie. Come on in. I ha' a man here who says he's yer cousin."

"Beathan MacKenzie!" Duncan laughed, feeling his spirits revive. He'd known this man years ago, when Beathan had lived at Glen Mothin. He looked over Beathan's head as Neil came into the dim light and grinned.

"Him? Never saw him before in my life, Beathan."

They drank and talked well into the night, long after all the women retired. Beathan told them that he'd left Castle Mothin years before, when Phelan had backed King William and Beathan had stayed loyal to King James. Beathan had left the Jacobites after Dundee's death, coming home to Glen Mothin and trying since to outlive Phelan.

"It's been a hard few years," Beathan said. "Weather's been bad; we've no' had a good crop since Killiecrankie. All in all, though, we're doing a'right here, but we've had to learn to live wi' all the soldiers riding through. They've no' bothered us, much to my surprise, but ye'll understand that after Glencoe we're a bit wary."

He gave Duncan a speculative look. "I'd heard ye'd gone to Torridon after yer da died. And now ye've come home— and brought Torridon's English lassie wi' ye, just in time for the wedding."

Duncan exchanged a look with Neil and saw his agreement. "She's no' just any English lassie, Beathan. She's Catriona's daughter."

Beathan's mouth dropped open; he turned to stare at Neil. "I'll be damned."

"Probably," Duncan agreed.

Several hours and whiskies later, Neil asked him to walk outside for a minute before going to bed, and Duncan rose to his feet. He knew that tone; something needed to be said. He followed his cousin out into the rain, standing with him beneath a wide-spreading fir that somewhat sheltered them. Neil's face was in the shadows, but Duncan could see the set to his jaw.

"Well?" Duncan asked.

"Two things," Neil said. "I told Eileen about Fiona."

"And?"

"It dinna go well. She's verra angry."

"She seemed a'right."

"Aye, well, she's no'."

"And the other thing?"

"Desmond was riding wi' some of the soldiers. He was talking wi' the officers while the men went through Eileen's things; he dinna look like a prisoner."

"Last time I saw him . . . no, come to think of it, I dinna see him after ye left." Duncan met Neil's gaze. "He must ha' slipped off the *Isabel* when we were looking for the horses. D'ye suppose Desmond's services were . . . ?"

"Bought?" Neil finished. "We'll ha' to find out. And if he was, he'll pay."

Eileen rode behind Duncan and ahead of Neil as they traveled the last few miles to Glen Mothin. The road had risen sharply after the village, the air growing colder as they climbed. There were still patches of snow on the ground, and the trees thinned as the mountains grew taller.

A harsh land, she thought, trying to reconcile the landscape with the stories her mother had told her, of streams that raced downhill, cloaked with trees, of meadows filled with flowers, and slopes covered by heather. But there had been other stories as well, of the towers of Castle Mothin, grim and gray above the green countryside, a fortress tucked in a mountain glen, far from the rest of the world.

She'd slept in a box bed in Beathan MacKenzie's house, tucked into a corner of a back room that also served as a laundry. Beathan was a wealthy man by Highland standards, Neil had explained, during the few minutes they'd had together since their arrival. She'd not minded having the other people around. Being alone with Neil tonight would have been unbearable.

He'd marry Fiona. She'd be the woman to share his bed, bear his children, reach for him in the night. She'd take his name, and his seed. And Eileen would wonder, whenever she saw a dark-haired child, what Neil MacCurrie's children looked like, whether they'd have his blue eyes and his easy grace.

He'd taken her hand on the road, which had seemed right at the time, and he'd kept it in his while they walked into the village, releasing it only when they reached MacKenzie's home. It might be, she told herself, the last time he would touch her, the last time she'd welcome his touch. Or should be, unless her heart won over her mind.

The MacKenzies had been kind, and very hospitable, even more so when Duncan arrived. She'd been pleased to see him unscathed, but only had a moment to tell him that before he'd been swept away with Beathan and his sons. This morning she'd woken to a whirlwind of activity. Beathan, it had been decided the night before, would ride with them to Castle Mothin, bringing several men with him—just in case their reception was not warm.

She'd spent little time actually thinking about the moment when she would meet her grandfather, and now that it was upon her found herself growing nervous. Would he reject her as he had her mother? Would he be angry that she'd arrived in the middle of the wedding festivities, a reminder of the daughter who had so displeased him with her own wedding? Or would he throw his arms wide and welcome her to Glen Mothin?

She knew that her grandmother had died years before, and that Phelan had not remarried, that he'd had three sons and one daughter, and one grandson and several granddaughters—but little else about the man. She did not even know, she realized, as she watched Duncan's back, whether Phelan was tall, or fair, or anything about him except that he was an unpleasant man.

Perhaps this was where she was supposed to be, back in Scotland, with her mother's people, far from London and its turmoil, safe among the mountains and clansmen. She'd have cousins, almost sisters, to replace the ones she'd lost . . . or was she about to be more rebuffed than even she could imagine? What then?

Then she'd go back to London and face the future. If William and Mary tried to marry her off again, she'd use her grandmother's letter as a weapon, would threaten to make it public if they persisted. She'd ask for the Whitby lands to be returned to her, or to be reinstated in Anne's household.

Would she grow old, a spinster who spurned all suitors because they did not live up to her memories of a tall Highlander? Or would she eventually marry, reconciled to her fate, as so many others had done, making the most of a match that might be suitable, but never loving?

Or would she drown in the Thames, as her parents had done?

Her thoughts startled her, and she turned to look at Neil without meaning to. He looked off into the distance, his face pensive. She turned forward again, knowing her heart had betrayed her again.

Beathan's fine ponies were a far cry from the horses she and Neil had ridden the day before, and in less than an hour the first wide meadow appeared, suddenly laid out before them like a carpet of green. The air was cool and crisp, somehow lighter, and a few minutes later the mountains eased away to reveal a crescent-shaped valley that wrapped around a silver river. And above the river, on a knoll that lifted it even higher from the valley floor, was Castle Mothin.

It was rectangular, a graceless but formidable structure with gray stone curtain walls that rose forty feet into the air, penetrated by shot holes, a square tower at each corner. The walls were steep and buttressed at the corners, the stone upon which it stood the same color as the rock of the castle, making it seem all of a piece with the earth. Beyond the curtain walls a crow-stepped garret story was visible at each end of the building, banners flying from its peak.

In contrast to the forbidding castle, the village at its feet was crowded with people and rich with color, the tartan of the plaids that the Scots wore mixing with the red uniforms of the English soldiers. The mood here was celebratory. They were welcomed and invited to join the festivities as they slowly made their way through the village. They left Beathan's horses with his men and made the last part of the journey on foot.

At the base of the stairs that led up to the entrance of the castle they paused, Eileen between Neil and Duncan, waiting while the singing and drums they'd heard for some time grew louder, the revelers approaching them now. The drummers were first around the corner, leading the procession. The singers came next, all of them women, all dancing, hands clapping above their heads, skirts swaying with the movements of their hips.

The crowd stepped back as the women stopped for a moment, dancing intricate steps, then swinging through a pattern that changed their order. At the head of the dancers was a lovely woman a few years older than Eileen, with ginger hair and green eyes that lit as she spotted Duncan. And glowed when she saw Neil. She threw herself at Duncan, arms and smile wide.

"Duncan! Neil!" she cried, then spoke rapidly in Gaelic, obviously welcoming them to Castle Mothin.

Duncan laughed and embraced her in return, letting her pull him into the dancers with her. She twirled around him while the other women welcomed him, laughing as they enveloped him in their midst. The woman turned to Neil, her smile more private now as she reached to him, beckoning him with her fingers and words, then, when he did not respond, putting her hands on his waist and pulling him into the dancers, her hips swaying more, her lips curving in a very warm greeting. She put a hand on his cheek and stroked it along his jaw.

"And that," Beathan said at Eileen's side, "would be yer cousin Adara. She always did like a dark-haired man."

Neil reached back through the tangle of arms to pull Eileen with him into the crowd of dancers. "Come, lassie," he said.

"She knows you," Eileen said, raising her voice to be heard over the music.

"Aye," he said.

"And verra well," Adara said, laughing as she draped her arm around him, beckoning Beathan to join them.

Eileen let herself be borne up the stairs by the dancers and drummers, half the village behind them. The entrance to the castle was over a wooden bridge that echoed the sound of their footsteps to the stones above, then through an arched tunnel that landed them in a large courtyard.

The dancers continued toward the large square keep, the

building she'd seen from the road, leading the procession into the building, through the barrel-vaulted room on the ground floor, and up a staircase in the corner. English soldiers, officers among them, crowded into the stairway, smiling at Eileen when they bumped her, polite enough on the surface, but letting their gazes drift to her breasts and waist in a manner that left little doubt of what they were thinking.

Upstairs they tumbled into the center of a large hall with plastered walls, a timbered ceiling, and high windows that looked out to the clouds. At the end of the hall sat an older man in a huge carved wooden chair, like a king on his throne, watching with hooded eyes and a measured smile.

Phelan MacKenzie. Her grandfather.

He was no longer young. His hair was silver, thick, drawn back from a strong face that had once been very handsome. His arched eyebrows were raised over dark eyes as he watched Adara take Neil's hand, then Duncan's, and lead them toward him.

The music faded while all watched the two men Adara pulled forward. She dropped their hands and spoke, her voice rich and pleased, her words in Gaelic.

"What is she saying?" Eileen asked Beathan.

"She's calling for quiet. And telling her grandfather that she found two urchins on the road and brought them home with her for his approval."

Adara waved a hand at Duncan and said his name, then turned to Neil. "Neil MacCurrie," she said. "Torridon."

Phelan's expression did not change. He nodded, saying something quietly in Gaelic that sounded like a welcome, if a lukewarm one. Then he stood, stretching his arm and pointing at Eileen. Everyone in the room followed his gaze.

"And who are you?" he asked in English.

Chapter Fifteen

Eileen stepped forward to stand between Neil and Duncan before Phelan. Neil wondered if she was frightened, but her voice was calm.

"I am Eileen Ronley," she said. "Catriona's daughter. Your granddaughter."

Neil could hear the murmur of conversation behind him as her words were translated into Gaelic. Adara turned to stare at Eileen, but Phelan showed no surprise, watching her without expression while the seconds ticked by.

Eileen did not move, simply stood still under his scrutiny, and Neil felt a wave of pride in her, quickly overtaken by his annoyance that Phelan had obviously been warned of their arrival, thanks to Desmond. It would have been interesting to see Phelan's unguarded reaction. He took a step closer to Eileen.

"So," Phelan said, his words measured, "after years of neglect, my grandson graces me with his presence, bringing the Earl of Torridon. And you." He paused, looking around the room, then back at Eileen. "You have arrived at Castle Mothin in the middle of a celebration, when my home is filled with guests. You are welcome to join us for this wedding. Afterward, you and I will become acquainted." He looked at Duncan. "And you and I reacquainted. Welcome."

Eileen nodded. "Thank you."

Duncan echoed her words. Neil inclined his head, not

sure he could speak without showing his anger. Eileen might believe that she'd been genuinely welcomed, but he had seen Phelan's calculated assessment of who was listening. This display of charm was for the English soldiers, not Eileen.

Neil looked around the hall. It was as he'd thought; the English frigate that had followed them up the coast had brought these soldiers—and Captain Asher—to Glen Mothin. Asher met Neil's gaze with a frigid nod.

Phelan clapped his hands and called for music. Adara turned, smiling at Neil, pulling him toward her.

Eileen was introduced to her cousins, Phelan's other granddaughters, who welcomed her with different levels of warmth. The bride was too overwhelmed to even notice Eileen, but the others, including Adara, flocked around her, finding similarities in their coloring, height, and features.

She smiled and chatted the best she could; not all of them spoke English and there were awkward moments when the women simply stared at each other, waiting until someone could translate. Beathan, who knew everyone, had been very willing to do just that, standing with her while the dancing continued. Duncan came over to join them several times, then let himself be swept away by the women again, obviously a favorite of theirs. As was Neil.

She turned to look for him, finding him deep in conversation with a tall man dressed in Highland clothing. Neil turned from the man, to look at the English soldiers, then back at the man he spoke with, his expression guarded. Was there danger for him here? she wondered. Surely Phelan would respect the laws of Scottish hospitality, which protected both host and visitor. But then, she reminded herself, that was what the MacDonalds of Glencoe had thought as well.

During the meal she sat with the other women, but she watched Neil and Duncan, who sat with Phelan's clansmen. She watched them later as well, when Neil rose from the table and left the room, Duncan at his heels. They returned later with grim expressions.

It was Adara who had been the friendliest, Adara who insisted that Eileen sleep with the women, Adara who introduced her husband with a wide smile, saying they were all related now. And Adara who passed behind Neil, letting her fingers drape across his shoulders, then, her gaze darting across the room to see who might have seen, and finding Eileen watching, did the same to Duncan.

That night Eileen slept on a pallet on the floor of a large chamber, with eleven other women. Neil and Duncan had still been downstairs in the hall, talking with the other Highlanders, when she'd left; she didn't think they'd even noticed her leave. The English soldiers were mixing with Phelan's people, but both Neil and Duncan kept their distance.

The wedding was to be at mid-morning, and the women began their preparations just after dawn. Eileen was grateful that Beathan's wife had been kind enough to clean her soiled clothing, but even with the best she could do, her clothes were old and tattered. She sighed as she looked at her reflection, telling herself it did not matter; no one would be watching her. She'd just finished her preparations when one of the younger girls called to Eileen.

"Torridon," the girl said and giggled as she pointed at the door.

Eileen peeked around the open door and drew a deep breath. Neil stood in the corridor, his face in profile, his expression stern. He was resplendent in a clean white shirt under a fitted blue silk jacket, slashed to show the white silk lining underneath. The end of his plaid was thrown over his shoulder and held in place by a large sapphire brooch; the tartan was blue and green. She'd not seen him like this before, every inch an earl, a man of wealth and power.

He turned to look at her, his eyes very dark. "Good morning, Eileen. Would ye come and talk with me?"

"What do we have to say to each other, Neil?"

He scowled at her. "Damn it, lass, we need to talk. Will ye come? Please?"

She nodded and closed the door behind her, following him up the stairs and outside, onto the parapet that topped the curtain walls. He ignored the curious glances of the guards and frowned across the battlements while Eileen stood at his side, waiting.

Glen Mothin lay before her, the steep village streets slipping into the green valley floor. The mountains rose in sharp contrast to the wide meadows of fertile land, their rocky faces turned to each other in a circle; in the center of the ring, her grandfather's castle rose on its upthrust of rock to dominate all below. No wonder her mother had stayed in England, she thought. Only creatures of the cold would find this place welcoming.

Neil cleared his throat and turned to her. "Thank ye for coming wi' me."

"What did you want to tell me?"

"I want ye to be careful. Of what ye say, of who ye trust."

"Good advice, my lord Torridon," she said coolly. "I will do just that. Trusting unwisely is never prudent."

His cheeks flushed. "I ken ye're still angry wi' me, and that we've hurt each other. But we should be able to talk, lass. We've shared much. Surely that means something to ye."

She looked into his eyes, saw his concern, and something more, something that made her look at his mouth, remembering his kisses and his lips on her breasts. "Yes," she said softly. "It means something to me."

"I do care for ye, lass. Dinna think I do not."

"And I for you." She held up a hand. "But, please, let us not talk of it. We will only argue and neither of us wants that. Things are as they are, Neil."

"Things will change, Eileen."

"What does that mean?"

"It means I'll go and talk with Seaforth and Fiona. I'll end the agreement."

She pressed her lips together, willing her tears away, while he watched her with drawn brows.

"Have ye naught to say to that, lassie?"

"When that is done, then we'll talk. Until then, I cannot . . ." She wiped away her tears, annoyed that her body betrayed her so easily. "We'll talk about it then, Neil," she said, trying to sound calmer.

He nodded slowly. "Aye, all right." With a glance at the guards, whose attention had shifted to the courtyard below. "D'ye remember Desmond MacLeod, from the *Isabel*, the one accused of stealing?"

"Yes, of course."

"I saw him wi' the soldiers on the road yesterday."

"Why would he be with English soldiers?"

"We were watched in London, both at the ship and at the Pegasus, lass. I dinna ken which of yer cousins it was—

could be any of them. Ye saw the troops at the dock." He gestured to her arm. "And ye were followed, more than once. I think William put the word out that he'd pay for information on me, perhaps on both of us, and Desmond was greedy enough to accept."

"They must know who you are."

"Aye. And that ye're wi' me. It's good ye left London."

She stared off into the distance. It was time to put it into words. "My parents were murdered. I suppose I knew it all along."

"Aye, I think so. It may ha' been William, or his henchmen, like at Glencoe, but it may ha' been someone else. Who stood to gain by yer father's death?"

"William would have removed a thorn from his side."

"Aye, and we shouldna belittle that. William had many thorns in his side just then; he dinna need his own cousin saying he shouldna be king. But yer father hadna done anything more than to denounce him when he'd died. D'ye suppose yer da was about to try to claim the throne?"

"I would hope he was not that foolish. Even he must have known that he could not gather enough support to fend off William by himself."

"So who benefited by his death?"

"Milford got Ronley Hall. Templeton has a lovely house."

He nodded. "Aye, and there's more." He told her the story the woman in the close had told him and Duncan. She listened carefully. Some part of her had known Howard had to be part of her parents' deaths. She just did not want to believe it, not then. Not now. One of the guards was strolling along the parapet toward them now and she gestured to Neil.

He looked over his shoulder, then turned back to her, his words hurried.

"Lass, these men dinna toy. They kill. Ye need to be careful."

He pointed across the valley as the guard neared them. "And that," he said in a normal tone, "is the River Mothin. It starts just above us, in the mountains here, and travels all the way to Loch Carron."

"Lovely," she said, nodding at the guard as he passed; he nodded in return.

"Thank you for showing me the view, Lord Torridon."

"My pleasure, Miss Ronley."

When she was sure the guard was gone, she spoke again. "What will you do about Desmond?"

Neil's expression hardened. "I'll find him, lass."

"And?"

"And then I'll deal wi' him. Dinna worry, Desmond willna do us any more harm." He sighed. "Now I'd better get ye back downstairs."

She followed him into the stairwell, surprised when, about ten steps down, Neil stopped and turned to face her, his expression so serious that she put a hand to her throat, wondering what else he had to tell her.

"Eileen," he said solemnly, "I will talk to Seaforth and Fiona."

She nodded, quite unable to speak. He put his hand on her cheek and leaned forward, brushing his lips against hers.

"Lassie, trust me, just once again. Tell me ye believe me."

She looked into his eyes and nodded. "I believe you."

"Thank ye for that." He nodded to himself, as though

he'd made a decision, then gave her a wide smile. "I love ye, Eileen Ronley."

She could hardly breathe. "And I you, Neil."

He laughed softly. "Aye, I ken ye do. It's time for the silence to be over between us, lassie. I love ye, lass, and I'll let the world ken it soon. I canna yet; it's wrong not to tell Seaforth and Fiona first, but soon."

"Soon," she whispered.

When he reached for her, she let herself be pulled into his embrace, wrapping her arms around his neck and raising her mouth to his. His kiss was deep, searching, and long. She stroked his neck, then slipped her hand between the laces of his shirt, finding his warm skin. His heart pounded under her caress.

"Oh, Neil," she whispered.

"Aye, love," he murmured, then pressed his lips to her neck.

She no longer felt the cold stone behind her back, nor the ridges of the step pressing on her ankle, did not smell the mix of crisp mountain air from above and the damp coolness of the stairwell. She ran a hand along his thigh, then withdrew her hand as voices drifted up from below. He drew away with a rueful smile.

"Just once," he whispered, "I'd like to kiss ye without interruption."

"Tell me again," she said.

He did not pretend to misunderstand. "I love ye, Eileen Ronley."

She laughed. "I know. And I you."

He kissed her again, then led the way down the stairs.

*   *   *

Eileen sat with the other women at the wedding, but she paid scant attention to the lovely ceremony. She watched Neil, sitting with Duncan on the other side of the aisle. And she watched Phelan. Her grandfather missed little, his hooded gaze sliding from the bride and groom to the attendees, roaming along the pews like a predator. He stood and knelt at all the appropriate times, and smiled as the priest declared the pair wed, but there was no warmth in his expression.

The celebrations, held in the hall immediately after the wedding, were well attended, the villagers and clansmen crowded in with the soldiers for the meal and the music. The assembly was in high spirits, the music and dancing lively, and Eileen, sitting between Neil and Duncan, tapped her feet in time with the rhythm.

Phelan was enthroned on the dais, watching the revelry, not participating. But at the end of the meal, he left his chair, coming to claim her, saying that it was time she met his guests. As Eileen rose to her feet, she saw the cold look he exchanged with Neil, and the way he ignored Duncan. She looked at Duncan for direction, but he smiled, nodding for her to go.

Her grandfather led her to a group of Highlanders, introducing her as his "own Eileen" to the visiting Munroes, explaining to her that they had much in common with him. She smiled, but she knew what it was they shared with Phelan: they'd all backed William's bid for the throne. The oldest Munro, a small man with bright eyes and a quick smile, looked over her shoulder at Neil.

"I did not expect to find Torridon here," he said.

Phelan smiled. "He came with my grandson. One cannot

choose his grandchildren's companions, but one can hope to influence them."

Munro gave a snort of derision. "Ye'll have no luck changing Torridon."

"No," Phelan said thinly. "But Eileen will be staying with me now. I've not seen her in years."

Never would be more accurate, she thought, but said nothing, simply smiling as the Munro talked pleasantly with Eileen and Phelan. She knew that it was more than simple courtesy that had led Phelan to introduce her to this man. Probably Munro was looking for a wife to raise his six unruly children, or something similar. She'd seen the same false cheerfulness in Milford when he was trying to marry her off. Coming to Glen Mothin might have been a dreadful waste of time.

A few moments later, when there was a pause in the music, Neil strode across the hall to join them. His conversation with Phelan and the Munro was polite, and in Gaelic. Whatever it was they discussed was quickly exhausted, for almost immediately Neil bowed to Eileen and asked her to dance.

She accepted with a smile and let him lead her away from Phelan and the Munros to the center of the room. Neil called to the musicians in Gaelic. They nodded, laughing, but when Eileen asked him what he had said to them, Neil just smiled, showing her instead the first steps of the dance.

The music was sinuous, the rhythm deep. The beginning steps were simple, but other movements were added one by one, until the mix was quite complex. Neil's leg touched hers as he moved, his hands circled her waist, his fingers caressed her neck when he lifted his arm for her to turn under.

She abandoned herself to the rhythm, ignoring her grandfather watching them, everyone in the room watching them. She loved and was loved and this moment, this man, was all that mattered. Neil lifted his arm and twirled her in a circle, drawing her very close to him, then stepping back with slow grace, his leg rubbing slowly along the length of hers, his fingers draping down her arm.

As the music faded, he kissed her, his lips there and gone so quickly that she almost thought she'd imagined it. One look at Phelan, who was bearing down on them, let her know she hadn't. His face was flushed, his lips drawn back from his teeth, until he glanced around the room, noting all those who watched them; his expression lightened, but his tone was malignant.

"Torridon," he hissed, "what the devil do ye think ye're doing? Ye're promised to one of Seaforth's lasses!"

"I've signed no contract, Phelan."

"Ah. Seaforth's in prison. Perhaps the match is no longer wise, nor necessary, is that what ye're thinking?"

"Perhaps."

"If yer politics change, ye'll have many choices, but my granddaughter will never be one of them. Am I clear?"

"Aye."

"Ye'll do well to remember it."

Neil smiled coldly. "Phelan, ye are as charming as I remember ye."

"And ye, Torridon, as arrogant."

"Then we understand each other, sir."

Phelan glared. "Dinna touch her again."

"That's no' for ye to say," Neil said. "Ye've no' been any part of her life, Phelan. Dinna play the grandfather now. Ye fool none of us."

Eileen stepped between them. "It was only a dance," she said.

"A dance!" Phelan cried. "Ye dinna ken what that was, ye fool."

"Then explain it. What was it?" she asked.

"A declaration of possession."

Eileen looked at Neil, who met her gaze evenly.

"When he twirled ye like that," Phelan said, "and pulled ye against him, he lifted his hand and showed everaone his ring."

"So?"

"It's a gesture telling every other man to leave ye be. I'll no' have it."

"It's no' yer decision, Phelan," Neil said.

"Ah, but it is." Phelan took Eileen's arm and pulled her away with him.

She looked over her shoulder at Neil, then at the assembly, all watching them. This was neither the time nor place to confront Phelan, she told herself, and let him lead her to the side of the room. Neil strode to stand next to Duncan.

It was well after midnight when Eileen left the hall for a breath of fresh air and some quiet. Phelan had kept her close to him for hours and she was very weary of him. She would have escaped long before this had she had anywhere to go. Neil and Duncan had vanished ages ago without a word to her, and she had only the crowded room she shared with all the other women for refuge, so she had stayed.

Her thoughts had tumbled while Phelan had kept her near him, as he'd introduced her to more Munros, and Frasers, and even some of the soldiers. Captain Asher, without Neil and Duncan to irritate him, had proved to be very polite.

Cold and haughty, but polite. But it was not Phelan's guests who had occupied most of her mind.

What had Neil meant by that dance? Was it a declaration of intent, meant to warn off other suitors, or had he meant it simply for Phelan? Did he think she would know its significance? His motives baffled her, once again, but nothing could remove the glow she still felt from his kisses and his vow of love. Nothing.

She was tired now. It had been a long and difficult day, filled with emotion, and she needed to sleep, which would be difficult in that crowded chamber. She longed for her small cabin aboard the *Isabel*. She slowly climbed the stairs, too weary to hurry, even though the castle was filled with men who had had much to drink, and she would be wise to make haste.

At the top of the second flight of stairs she paused, suddenly aware that someone was behind her, his soft treads coming closer. Ahead the corridor was wreathed in shadow; behind her the stairs were well lighted but lonely. She stood still, then turned to face whoever it was.

Neil.

He lifted his head to meet her gaze and gave her a grin. "I thought ye'd never leave the hall."

"Were you waiting for me?"

"Aye."

"I didn't see you in there. You should have come to me."

"I wasn't in there," he said as he came to her side. He glanced down the stairs, then gave her another grin. "I was hoping to find ye alone, lassie."

"Why?"

"I have a room."

Her heart began a slow pounding.

"Duncan and I were given a room, just the two of us. And Duncan is . . . otherwise occupied. He willna be back until morning."

"Oh."

"It's no' how I'd planned it, but . . ."

"You planned . . . what, Neil?"

He laughed, deep in his throat, then took her hand. "Come wi' me, lassie, and find out." His expression sobered. "Eileen, will ye come? At least for a while? Will ye . . . ?" He let his words hang in the air and waited.

She shouldn't. She should go to the room with the other women, should spend the night on a pallet on the floor. She should tell him to talk to Fiona, who still had a claim to him, one that went back years.

He loved her, he'd said.

Suddenly all her fears, all her doubts of him, seemed so petty, so foolish. This was Neil, with whom she'd had, from the first moment, a connection that could not be explained, could not be analyzed. She could not believe she was wrong in trusting him. It no longer mattered what she should do. To go with him now made more sense than anything she'd ever done in her life. She smiled.

"Yes."

One word, she thought, hearing it bounce back to her from the stones. One word, and her life had changed forever.

Neil laughed and wrapped an arm around her shoulders, leading her down the corridor and up a flight of stairs to a wing she'd not been in. It was even quieter here in this narrow hallway, and Neil put a finger to his lips as they passed the other rooms. He opened the fourth door and ushered her through it, then closed it behind them.

The room was in darkness and she stood very still, listening to her own heartbeat and her shallow breathing. He moved past her, fumbled with the candle, then lit it and held it high, throwing its meager light across the small room. In the center of one wall was a large bed with yellow brocaded bedhangings, a tiny chest of drawers beside it, and under the window, heavy draperies pulled across it, was a table and one chair. Neil gestured at the room.

"Ye deserve better, lass, but this is all I can offer ye now." He put the candle on the chest of drawers, then crossed to the hearth and bent low in front of it, stirring the flames to life. At last he stood and turned to her, his face in shadow. "Do ye want to leave, Eileen? Shall I take ye to the room with the others?"

"No," she whispered.

He flew across the space that separated them, pulling her into his arms. "We dinna ha' to do anything ye dinna want to, lassie. I'll do anything to please ye."

She laughed, and slid her hand around his neck. "I want you to kiss me, Neil MacCurrie, quite thoroughly and without interruption."

He did as she'd asked. He kissed her cheeks, her neck, the hollow of her throat, the tops of her shoulders. How she had longed for this, she thought. How many hours, weeks, months, had she dreamed of this? *I have waited for this man all my life.* His mouth claimed hers again, insistent.

She met him, thrust for thrust, sigh for sigh, their kisses igniting them both. She leaned her head back and smiled at the shadows when he traced a line of kisses from her mouth to the top of her breasts.

"Neil," she whispered. "Tell me you love me."

"I love ye, lass. I ha' always loved ye. *Vous et nul autre.* Tell me."

"Vous et nul autre," she answered. "You and no other."

"Nul autre, Eileen. I ha' never loved any woman but ye, and I never will."

He lifted his head with a startled expression, as though he'd just heard his own words. His grip on her waist loosened and he looked around the room, then stepped away from her to rummage in the leather bag that held his clothing. He pulled out a shirt, then stockings, dumping them on the floor, straightening with a triumphant grin. In his hand was a long scarf, knit of fine wool in a tartan pattern. Neil took both of her hands in one of his, holding them between their bodies.

"Eileen, I'd like ye to handfast wi' me. D'ye ken what that means?"

"No," she whispered.

"We promise to live as man and wife. It's supposed to be for a year, and then, if either of us wants to leave, we dissolve the handfasting. But I am no' giving ye that choice. I'll consider us wed if we do this, nothing less."

"Are you asking me to marry you?"

He nodded. "Well, aye. What did ye think?"

She laughed, suddenly giddy. "Tell me you love me again."

"I love ye, Eileen Ronley. I ha' loved ye since all the seas were one, since men and women desired each other, since . . . always, lass. Ye were born to be wi' me and I wi' ye. Ye are mine, Eileen, and only mine. *Vous et nul autre.*"

"Yes."

"Swear it to me, if ye will."

"You and no other. I swear it," she said, then laughed.

"Then let's do this, lassie." He wrapped the scarf around their joined hands, bringing the last of it with his hand atop hers, then bent to kiss the bundle. He straightened and smiled at her.

"I, Neil MacCurrie, pledge my love and faithfulness, my body and my heart to ye, Eileen Ronley, for all time, for this life and beyond."

"And I, Eileen Ronley, pledge my love and faithfulness, my body and my heart to you, Neil MacCurrie, for all time, for this life and beyond."

He gave a roar of laughter and whirled them in a circle. "It is done. Ye are mine, Eileen! Ye are mine, and I yers."

"And you mine."

She clung to him, her own cry of triumph sounding in her head as he claimed her mouth with a ferocity that left her breathless. He pulled her to stand before the fire, taking the pins from her hair, one by one, and letting them fall unheeded to the hearth. She was never sure afterward how long they were there, together, in that small room, for when his hands began to roam, she lost track of time.

He brushed his lips against hers, then widened his stance and pulled her against him, letting her feel his readiness. She lifted her mouth to his and ran her hands down his neck, into the soft skin at the base of his neck, feeling his heart beat faster at her touch. He moaned and slipped his tongue between her teeth, his hand now caressing the top of her breasts above her bodice, then dipping under the cloth to find one breast, cupping his warm fingers around it.

His breath was ragged, his arousal hard and firm against her. She arched her back, lifting herself to his touch, sighing as his hand tightened on her breast. He leaned away from her then, concentrating on her stays, pulling them from the bodice with impatient movements.

"Let me, love," she said and pushed his hands away.

He watched as she loosened the laces, his eyes growing even darker when she pushed the material back and slid the straps of her chemise from her shoulders, then waited.

"Eileen, ye are so beautiful," he whispered. "Beyond beautiful, lass."

He slipped the last of the cloth from her breasts and bent to kiss them, first one, then the other, then returning to the first to draw her nipple into his mouth. She gasped, closing her eyes, as his tongue darted across her skin.

"I had no idea . . ." she whispered.

He laughed softly. "Just wait. There's much more."

"I'm not sure I can stand it."

"Oh, we'll no' be standing by then."

She laughed and ran her hands through his hair, pulling it free of its bindings, letting the dark shimmer of it spill across his shoulders and her breasts.

He fumbled at the side ties of her skirts and between them they undid all the fastenings of all the layers she wore. He lowered his gaze slowly from her eyes to her feet. "Oh, lassie, ye are very bonnie, and I want ye so."

"And I you," she said.

He gathered her in his arms and crossed to the bed. The brocade coverlet was smooth under her back, the air that slipped across her breasts cool.

"Are ye ready for the rest?" he asked. "Or shall we stop now?"

She raised her arms to him. "Come to me."

He unpinned the brooch from his plaid and let it fall behind him, then tore the blue silk jacket from his shoulders and tossed it aside. He pulled his shirt over his head and grinned at her, his hands on his belt buckle.

"Last chance to tell me no, Eileen."

She tilted her head, pretending to ponder. The candle cast shadows across the muscles of his arms, lighting the dark hair in the center of his chest and the line that went down to his waist and disappeared beneath the leather belt.

"Come to me, Neil," she said.

He unfastened the buckle and let the plaid slide along his hips and down his legs until he stood naked before her. He was as beautiful as she had imagined, his long body lean and hard and taut with desire. He slowly lowered himself atop her, resting his weight on his elbows. His chest was warm against her breasts, his lips soft on her shoulder.

"Neil, you are so splendid. I knew you would be."

He laughed as she wrapped her arms around his shoulders, then slid her hands down his back, feeling the muscles, the smooth skin, under her fingers. She was bolder now, running her hands to his waist and then below, to cup his buttocks and pull him even closer. He shifted his weight with a soft groan as her hand explored the planes of his hip, then slid between them to wrap around him.

He ran his hand up her leg, lifting it against his, skin against skin, the sensations amazing to her. He moved his hand higher, behind her knee, then along her thigh with a gentle but sure touch that made her catch her breath. And then his hand was there, between her legs, and his fingers were pressing against her, searching. He lifted his head and smiled.

"Eileen, I love ye, lass. I kent I would, from the first moment I saw ye. Even then I felt we were connected, as though we'd always kent each other, as though I'd always loved ye."

"It was the same for me."

"I love ye, lassie."

"And I you." She gasped as his fingers slipped inside her, not daring to breathe until he moved them slowly, caressing and soothing her.

"Do ye like that?" he asked.

"Oh, yes." It amazed her. "So this is love."

He laughed, deep in his chest, and moved higher between her legs, his thighs on hers; he withdrew his fingers from her. "No," he said, then slowly entered her. "This is love, Eileen. This." He slid deeper into her. She gasped and called his name. "Are ye a'right, lass?"

She slid her hands along his back. "Show me more now."

"We have forever, lassie. We'll take our time."

They slept, then woke to make love again. And yet again. Somewhere in the village a clock chimed the hours, nine, ten, eleven. The castle, which had been so alive with music and laughter, slowly quieted; the revelers, in small groups now, moved from the hall to the village.

No one came to disturb them, although they occasionally heard voices in the hallway; no one called Eileen's name in horror, or searched for her, crying through the corridors. Probably, she thought, shifting her head on Neil's shoulder, probably no one had even noticed that she was not with the other women. Adara might have, but Adara would be with her husband, or should be, and few others would pay Eileen Ronley any attention.

She did not ask whether Neil and Duncan had planned this, but she doubted Duncan would have been part of it. It was more likely that Duncan had found a willing partner and had not given her or Neil one thought. Or so she hoped.

She did not regret this, not any of it. Nothing had ever felt so right, so natural. She sighed and smoothed a hand across his chest, lingering on the planes there. This magnificent man loved her and she him.

"Eileen?" His voice was quiet, his touch gentle as he brushed the hair from her cheek. "Are ye awake?"

"Yes."

"Lass, we ha' to talk. We need to be in agreement about what's next."

She sat up and pulled the coverlet over her breasts. She'd known this time would end, but she wasn't ready to face other people. Adara would know, the moment she saw Eileen, what had happened, and Phelan might also.

"Yes," she said.

"I'd like to take ye to Torridon and leave ye there while I go to see Seaforth and Fiona. Are ye willing?"

She thought of meeting Neil's mother and grandmother, and James and Ellen. "What will your family say? What will they think of me?"

"They'll love ye, as I do; and if they do not, it doesna matter. It's ye and I who will be together the rest of our lives, no' them, lass. Ha' ye a better idea?"

"Perhaps you should talk to Fiona first, then bring me there."

"And where would ye be?"

"I suppose I could stay here."

"Wi' Phelan? Why would ye want to?"

"I wouldn't. But, Neil, what if Fiona won't release you?"

He sat up to face her, the coverlet bunched around his hips. "It's no' just her decision, ye ken. I'll no' marry her, it's that simple."

She swallowed. "I . . . I would like to meet your family, and I certainly do not want to stay here, but I . . ."

"Are ye afraid they'll think yer a lightskirt?"

"A what?"

"A lightskirt, a lass who's happy to lift her skirt for anyone."

"Oh. Yes, I guess I am."

"Ye're too accustomed to London, lassie. No one would think that of ye."

"How long will it take you to talk to Fiona?"

"An hour. Seaforth's the more difficult one—he's in prison in Inverness and I'll ha' to bribe my way in to see him."

"An hour for Fiona?"

"Aye. It'll take a bit to get to her, but only an hour once I'm there. A month at the most."

"A month."

"Unless the weather prevents traveling; six weeks, then, to be safe."

"I can stand six weeks here."

He sighed. "I can stand six weeks wi'out ye, I guess, but I think ye're mad to worry about what they'll think."

"When we marry, Neil, I want the world to know you were free to do so. Talk to Fiona, then come for me."

He kissed her shoulder. "Keep yer bags packed, Eileen. I'll be here before ye ken it."

Chapter Sixteen

Neil leaned back into the shadows and sighed. This was not the way he'd hoped to spend the wee hours of the morning. Despite his protests, Eileen had insisted that she go back to the room she shared with all the other women; neither Duncan nor Phelan, she'd said, would be pleased to find her in Neil's room. She was probably correct, but their opinions did not concern him much.

He'd made the commitment to her in his mind and body; now he wanted it to be made public. He didn't want Eileen to stay at Glen Mothin while he talked to Fiona and Seaforth, but that's what she wanted, and so that's what they would do. What anyone else thought, including Duncan, did not matter.

They'd be married soon, and another part of the legend would come true; he would, like James, marry a woman from the east. Just as the Seer had predicted. Now he just had to find a way to begin the fifty years of peace. Standing here in the shadows hunting Desmond was an unlikely start, but it had to be done. He'd tried to sleep after she left, but soon abandoned that idea, and came to the village.

It had taken several well-placed coins, but he'd found Desmond, or at least his trail. The MacLeod was in the house opposite now, apparently with an obliging woman. Eventually Desmond would leave, and Neil would confront him. There was no good way to handle this; even an argument with Desmond would spill over into trouble at home. That could not be helped.

The MacCurries had been in conflict with the MacLeods of Gairloch for decades. Two years ago Jamie had killed one of them at Dunfallandy; Neil had had to find a peaceful solution to the uproar, which had led to Calum coming to live with them. Now he was about to confront Desmond, and there would be no good way out of this. If he was fortunate, he'd not let his outrage cloud his judgment. If Desmond was fortunate, he'd already have left Glen Mothin.

He didn't want to be here; he wanted to be up in that room in Phelan's castle with Eileen in his bed, or, failing that, on his way to see Seaforth and Fiona. Neil rubbed his hand across his chin, feeling the stubble there. He was tired; and he was weary of dealing with the likes of Desmond MacLeod and Phelan.

A few minutes later the door to the house opposite opened and Desmond slipped out. With a furtive glance in each direction, he skulked away. In the dark, like a criminal, Neil thought, and stepped forward into the light.

"Desmond!" he called. "Desmond MacLeod!"

Desmond's head snapped up; he looked around, jumping when he saw Neil. He moved his hand to the hilt of his sword. "Torridon!"

"Aye. I saw ye traveling with English soldiers."

"I . . . I ha' left the *Isabel*."

"Who pays ye, Desmond?"

"Ye've been watching me!"

"It's the other way 'round, isn't it? How much did they pay ye to spy on me?"

Desmond drew his sword. "More than ye or Duncan ever paid."

"Did they pay ye a lot?"

"Enough so that I'm no' going back to Torridon. I'm finished working for ye."

"Ye're no loss," Neil said. "It was ye, wasna it, stealing from the men?"

"What if it was?"

"Did ye no' think I'd find ye out? Who pays ye, Desmond?"

"Why should I tell ye anything?"

Neil drew his sword and tried to control his anger. One of his own, a man he'd trusted, had betrayed him. For money. "Why should ye tell me? Because I'll slice ye into small pieces if ye dinna."

"Ye think ye fooled them in London, dinna ye, Torridon? Huguenot! Did ye think they would believe that? I told them who ye were."

"Ye told who? The soldiers?"

"Wouldn't ye like to ken?"

Above Neil a window opened and a man leaned out, talking in Gaelic. "Can ye no' be quiet? Ye're loud enough to wake the dead."

Neil ignored him and took a step toward Desmond. "Tell me who pays ye!"

"Ye're a dead man, Torridon. They ken it was ye in London. Do ye think they'll no' come after ye for stealin' the cousin of the king and queen?"

From the corner came an English voice. "MacLeod, is that you? Are you in your cups again?"

"Over here!" Desmond shouted. "I'm being attacked."

"Are you picking another fight?" asked a second man.

Neil glanced over his shoulder. Four English soldiers, drawing weapons, wary now, as they slowly came forward.

"It's Torridon! He's trying to kill me!"

"He's got reason enough, MacLeod," one of the soldiers said.

Windows were flung wide and lights flickered into the dim street as men asked what was happening. Then one voice cracked through all the others.

"Fight! Fight!"

The cries were loud, and from several directions. Men poured out of the houses surrounding Neil and Desmond, shouting encouragement to one or the other. Someone called Desmond a coward and the MacLeod spat an insult at him, his face scarlet. Neil thought he heard Duncan, and perhaps Beathan, but he concentrated only on Desmond.

He knew the exact instant that Desmond decided to attack, saw the flicker in his eyes before he raised his arm and his voice and lunged forward. Neil braced himself, deflecting Desmond's blow with a twist of his arm, hearing the roar of approval from the watchers. The MacLeod lunged again.

After that it was a blur. Neil and Desmond battled through the dark streets while the watchers followed, shouting and making wagers. In the square, they burst through a crowd of dancing revelers, ignoring the screams and the frightened people who darted out of the way.

Neil heard Duncan behind him, calling encouragement, but he dared not turn. English soldiers were shouting support to Desmond, some, strangely enough, to Neil. They were both tiring; Neil's breathing was ragged in his ears. It was at the foot of the stairs to the castle, with scores watching, that Desmond dropped his guard.

With a feeling of inevitability, Neil plunged his blade deep into Desmond's chest and stepped back, watching him fall to the ground and slowly die. Neil leaned over, hands on knees, and gasped for breath. There would be hell to pay for this.

The noise in the courtyard woke all the women. Eileen rose from her pallet and crowded at the window with the others. Torches lit the courtyard and men surged across the stones, shouting and running toward the gate. One of the women called down in Gaelic and was answered. She faced the others, her eyes wide, saying something in Gaelic. The women turned to stare at Eileen.

"What is it?" Eileen cried. "What has happened?"

"It's Torridon," one of the girls said. "He's killed someone."

The courtyard was mostly empty when Eileen arrived, the few men there standing in groups talking in excited voices. She pushed through the throng to the gates. The castle bridge, over which she'd danced with Adara and Neil such a short time ago, was crowded with people. Many whispered as she passed, but she ignored them and hurried forward.

From behind her came murmurs as Phelan, flanked by his guard and followed by a party of English soldiers, stalked through the people. He paused in front of Eileen, then pulled her with him to the top of the stairs. From here she could see what everyone was staring at, and she put her hand to her throat.

Neil stood in the center of the open space below, the sword in his hand glimmering in the torchlight. His expression was fierce as he stared at the man who lay at his feet, a pool of blood seeping slowly from beneath him. Duncan, who had been hidden before, moved to stand next to Neil.

At a gesture from Phelan, Captain Asher ran down the

steps. He bent over the fallen man, then straightened. "The man is dead," Asher said.

"Explain yerself, Torridon!" Phelan shouted.

Neil's mouth was a thin line as he looked up. He looked from Eileen to Phelan. "It has naught to do wi' ye, Phelan. He's a Torridon man."

"Ye just felt like killing one of yer own?"

"It has naught to do wi' ye."

"This is my home, Torridon, everything here has to do with me."

"He was a translator for us," Asher shouted. "You murdered an innocent man!"

"It was not murder!" Duncan cried. "And he was no translator. He was one of my sailors. It was a fair fight, Grandfather. Desmond was armed and he attacked Neil first. Ask those who saw it."

Many men nodded, agreeing and calling out comments.

Phelan held up his hands for quiet. "Ye always did ha' a temper, Torridon. Now ye've murdered a man because of it. What d'ye have to say in yer defense?"

"I dinna need a defense, Phelan," Neil said. "He attacked me. He's dead."

"He's right," Beathan shouted. "The MacLeod struck first. Ye canna expect Torridon to no' defend himself."

"For God's sake, Torridon," Asher shouted, "can a man not leave your service without you killing him? He was only translating!"

Neil shook his head. "It wasna translating he was doing for ye! Ye were paying him to spy!"

Asher's men started forward, hands on their weapons; Beathan's men did the same. Duncan moved between Neil and Asher.

"Enough!" Phelan roared. "It's simple enough to see what happened. Ye argued wi' the man and killed him. Torridon, ye'll get off my land."

An angry murmur ran through the crowd. Phelan glanced around him with hooded eyes, his surprise at their mood quickly hidden. "Ye'll leave, Torridon. I will no' have my hospitality abused. This is not Glencoe!"

Neil glared at Phelan. "And I murdered no one in his bed."

"Ye'll be off my land before daylight, or I'll ken the reason why."

"No!" Eileen cried. "He was only defending himself!"

Phelan gestured her back. "Ye'll leave, Torridon. Beathan, send a man for his things and his horse. I'll not have him back in my home."

"I'll go, and gladly," Neil said, "but I'll talk to Eileen first."

"Look around ye, Torridon!" Phelan said. "At best ye ha' a handful of men wi' ye. I have my own men and all these soldiers. Ye'll leave, and ye'll leave now. Or ye'll die fighting us. Yer decision."

"Eileen," Neil called. "D'ye wish to leave?"

"She'll stay here!" Phelan shouted.

"That's her decision, no' yers," Neil cried. "Eileen?"

Phelan leaned to whisper to her. "If ye go wi' him, granddaughter, I'll hunt him down and kill him before he leaves my lands. If he leaves alone, he'll live."

"Why are you doing this?" she whispered.

"Tell him to go or I'll bring ye his head with the dawn."

Eileen stared into Phelan's eyes, remembering the story of the man who had hurt her mother. "Our grandfather is a vindictive man," Duncan had said. She had no doubt that he would see his threat through. She called to Neil in French.

"My grandfather says he will have you killed if I go with you!"

"I would risk it gladly," Neil replied in French.

"But I would not," she said. "Go with God, my love, and do what we discussed. I will stay here and await your return."

"Come with me now, Eileen."

"I cannot. Please go!"

Duncan moved forward. "I'll stay with you, Eileen."

"No," she cried, "go with Neil; keep him safe."

"Yes, grandson," Phelan said in French. "Go. You're no longer welcome, Duncan. You cast your lot with Torridon years ago."

Eileen stared at her grandfather in horror. Phelan had understood every word she'd said; how foolish of her to assume otherwise.

"Beathan," Phelan continued, in English now, "ye get yerself gone as well. Ye have until dawn, sirs, and then I'll let Asher's men and mine find ye."

"Phelan MacKenzie!" Neil shouted. "Ye need to be verra careful. Ye ha' threatened my life this night, and by doing so, ye ha' threatened all the MacCurries, all of Torridon! It's no' a thing I take lightly, nor should ye. I give ye a moment to rethink yer words."

"Ye are no' welcome here, Torridon!" Phelan shouted. "Get off my land!"

"So be it, then. But ken that I will come back for Eileen. And ye will welcome me, Phelan, or ye and all of Glen Mothin will pay the price."

"Ye ha' until dawn, Torridon!"

"Eileen?" Neil asked.

"Go, my love! *Vous et nul autre*, Neil!"

Neil nodded. "*Vous et nul autre*, Eileen Ronley. I'll come back for ye!" He disappeared into the crowd.

Phelan gripped her arm. "Torridon is no' for ye, Eileen. Dinna defy me again, or I promise ye ye'll regret it."

"I love him," she said. "And nothing can change that."

"We'll see," Phelan said. "We'll see, lassie."

Neil leaned against the railing of the *Isabel*, not seeing the blue water of Loch Carron; he was remembering the scene at Glen Mothin. No matter what Eileen, or Phelan, had said, he should not have left her there. He still saw her in his mind, her hair around her face like a halo, her eyes dark and fearful, telling him to go. He should have grabbed her and taken her with him and to hell with the consequences.

He knew what had happened; Phelan had immediately recognized her political value, and the incident with Desmond had played right into his hands. He could rid himself of Neil, and then do what Phelan always did, parlay the situation into an advantage for himself. He'd probably try to marry Eileen off to someone immediately, stressing her beauty and her patrimony, crowing that her children would carry the blood of kings. And if it turned out that Adam Ronley had been legitimate, who knew what Phelan would aspire to?

Seaforth was in prison, William and Mary on the throne, and Phelan thought he was invincible. He'd do best, Neil thought, to remember that he was the unpopular leader of a very small clan, which could be destroyed, and few in all the world the sadder for it.

Neil had originally intended to go to Torridon, arm his

men and come back to Glen Mothin for Eileen, and if Phelan resisted, what matter? But as his temper cooled, he reconsidered. Destroying Phelan first, satisfying as it might be, would change little. Neil would go back, well accompanied, but he wouldn't burn down the castle and dance on Phelan's grave. Unless provoked. He smiled wryly.

It would be satisfying, if only to avenge the horror he'd seen on Eileen's face when her grandfather threatened him. And to avenge Phelan's latest rejection of Duncan. His cousin had borne it stoically, but Neil had seen his eyes.

No, much as he'd like to storm Castle Mothin, it made more sense to do what he and Eileen had discussed; he'd see Seaforth, then Fiona. And then he'd go back and get her. And nothing would stop him from taking her away from Glen Mothin forever. He'd set the Highlands aflame if anyone tried to stop him.

James stood on the shingle, watching the *Isabel* land. Duncan's russet hair was visible even in the dim light of the gloaming, Neil's more difficult to see. But his thoughts came through clearly. James would hear the details when they were alone, but he already knew that Neil had left Eileen behind and that it had not been his choice. Neil was angry.

Had she rejected him? Was that possible? What had happened between them since the day James had heard a woman's sigh and the rustle of leaves, and felt Neil's emotions swing between elation and sorrow? He raised his arm in greeting as the *Isabel* reached the dock. They'd sort it out together, he told himself, he and Neil and Duncan, as they had so many times before.

*　　*　　*

James watched his brother twist the glass in his hand and look at their grandmother, but he knew Neil wasn't listening to the story about the new foal. It had been three days since Neil and Duncan had come home, three days they'd waited for this endless late spring storm to end. One didn't need to be a twin to know Neil was thinking of the weather; his continual glances at the windows and out to sea were enough. Neil was ready to go.

They'd spent the time talking about everything that had happened—and everything that might happen. When the wind, which had turned the sea into a carpet of white foam, and the rain, which had hammered at Torridon for days, finally stopped, then Neil and Duncan would sail to Inverness to talk to Seaforth.

Neil had told them that he would not marry Fiona. They knew what that could mean, the contempt in which he would be held, the assumption of his transfer of allegiance. Neil had not asked them what they thought, he'd told them what he was going to do. James supposed he had looked the same way when he'd told them he was in love with Ellen.

How could he, of all people, tell Neil no? Of course, his Ellen had not wanted to be queen. And possibly Eileen did not either. That was the part that confused him, that Neil, normally so rational, had not pinned her down about her future plans. It was an important thing to know, James would have thought, but a sign of just how much in love Neil was. If Eileen wanted the throne, James suspected that Neil would try to give it to her.

While Neil and Duncan were gone, James would ready the Torridon men for battle. If they needed to attack to get Eileen out of Castle Mothin, they'd have help; Beathan MacKenzie had pledged his men to do just that, and James was sure the other western clans would join in. If they were to take on William and Mary, they'd need much more.

Inverness. It had been a long trip; the wind had slowed, but it had cost them time on their voyage north. Everything had taken longer than he'd planned, but at last he and Duncan would be in Inverness. And if all went well, he'd see Seaforth tomorrow. He dreaded it.

He respected Seaforth, liked the man, and knew that his ending the agreement would be a blow. Somehow he'd have to find words to convince Seaforth that this was not a betrayal, simply an end to a marriage agreement. And then Neil had to go to France and do the same with Fiona.

Janet MacKinnon welcomed them warmly at her inn, as full of questions as always. She sat with them as they ate, telling them all the news of the north. The Glencoe massacre had angered many. At first there had been talk of a new uprising, but the talk was fading. Everyone knew that without a king who would join them, and no military leader, the effort was doomed.

When she was finished with her news, Janet laid her chin on her palm. "What's this I hear about ye and an Englishwoman, Neil? It is Neil, right? James is married and I'd like to think he's no' traveling around the country with a woman from London."

He nodded. "It's Neil, Janet."

"I heard ye battled yer way out of Phelan MacKenzie's castle with three hundred men chasing ye. Is that true?"

"No."

"They say ye killed a MacLeod there. Is that true?"

"Aye."

"Would ye ken anything of an Englishwoman named Eileen Ronley?"

He stopped chewing. "Why?"

"King William's men were here, all over Inverness, asking if anyone had seen her. They thought she might be traveling with a Highlander. Big man, they said, black hair. They dinna ken his name. I told them I couldna think of anyone who fit that description, but that they should check in Aberdeen."

"Did ye? Good of ye," Neil said.

"I thought it was. Guard yer back, laddie."

"Dinna have to, Janet; I have ye for that. And I thank ye for it."

"We go back a long way, Neil MacCurrie. I'm no' likely to forget my friends."

"Nor I," he said.

"So who is she, this Eileen Ronley?"

Neil took a bite of fish and chewed while he watched Janet, considering. "How difficult is it to see Seaforth?" he asked at last.

"Depends on how much money ye throw at it," she said. "Several people have visited, but none who dinna pay for the privilege. Why?"

"Thought I'd visit as long as I'm here."

Janet gave a harrumph as she rose to her feet. "Seems to me that that's the whole reason ye're here. Which means that ye're either talking to him about a new uprising, or ye're calling off the match wi' his cousin. So it's her, this Eileen Ronley?"

"Ye look verra bonnie, Janet."

She picked up their empty plates. "I'll see what I can find out about visiting Seaforth. Ye just sit here and drink, aye?"

"We'll do our best," Duncan said.

"I knew I could count on ye, Duncan," she said with a laugh.

It had gone better than he'd expected, Neil thought as he left the prison where Seaforth was held. Kenneth Og MacKenzie told Neil he would consider the agreement voided, but his disappointment had been visible. Neil was not sure he'd been able to convince Seaforth that this had nothing to do with politics, or Seaforth being in prison, but everything to do with Eileen.

If she'd been anyone else's kin but Phelan's it would have been easier for Seaforth to swallow, but for Neil to be rejecting Fiona for the granddaughter of one of Seaforth's worst enemies had been unwelcome news; and that she was also cousin to William and Mary even worse. Any reasonable man would have concluded that Neil was going over to the enemy.

Despite all that, he and Seaforth had parted on cordial terms. Neil had paid the jailers well to take good care of their prisoner, knowing that most of his coin would go to taking good care of the jailers instead. There must be a better way to imprison someone than to make him pay for the basics of life.

And now he had to go to France and tell Fiona. It would be a miserable experience for both of them; Fiona's pride would be hurt. She did not love him, had never pretended that she did—few marriages were based on love and neither of them had expected that. But it would still be a blow to her.

He wandered the streets of Inverness, looking into the shops, trying to lift his cloud of guilt, pausing at a silversmith's. The artisan held his creation up for Neil's approval, a ring with Gaelic words carved into the band, and Neil smiled as the idea came to him. He counted his coins.

He had it the next morning. A band of gold, with four words inscribed on band. In French. *Vous et nul autre.* You and no other.

The days passed so slowly. Eileen was not a prisoner, she told herself. But Phelan would not let her outside the castle walls, and there was little to do within them. Why did Phelan keep her here? Was it that he despised Neil? Was he planning a marriage to someone else for her? Or did it have to do with her father? Phelan had talked of Neil only once since that night. They'd been at dinner and Phelan had patted her hand and smiled into her eyes, his voice kind.

"I ken ye dinna want to believe me, lassie, but I sent him away for yer good. Torridon can be charming, and apparently ye've seen that side of him. But I've kent him most of his life; I've seen him cruel, especially wi' the lasses. If ye'd gone wi' him, what would ha' happened to ye when he married Seaforth's cousin?"

"Perhaps he won't marry her."

"Aye, and perhaps the sun willna set tonight. Ye dinna ken the man as I do. Ye're no' the first he's courted and left at Glen Mothin. Ask Adara. I dinna have courtly manners to convince ye; I am a gruff old man. Forgive me if I sound harsh, but having a man like Torridon prey on ye riled me. He's violent and unpredictable, prone to sudden passions, and even more sudden abandonment of them. I am trying to protect ye. What would I gain by making ye miserable?"

She'd resisted the urge to defend Neil, knowing that no matter what she said, Phelan would never agree with her. "I don't know what you would gain, Grandfather. And I don't know how you could send Duncan away."

Phelan sighed. "My temper got the best of me. I'll regret that always. I've written, asking him to come back and see me, but I've heard nothing in return."

"He's a fine man."

"I never should have let Torridon's father steal him away. Duncan has not been the same since he went to live with the MacCurries." Phelan spread his hands wide. "And that's part of my anger, Eileen. I lost one grandchild to Torridon; I'd rather no' lose another to them. MacCurrie is no' what he seems. He's a willful, violent man who uses people and tosses them aside. He willna come back for ye. He'll ha' forgotten ye within a month."

Eileen had left him then, telling herself that Phelan was lying, that she knew Neil better than that. But his words rang in her head, and as week after week passed with no word from Neil, she began to wonder.

Several days later, Beathan came to visit her, asking to walk in the gardens, one of the few places, he said, where one could talk and not fear being overheard. At the far end of the path Beathan stopped, pointing at the flowers at their feet as though he talked of them. His voice was very quiet.

"Phelan got a letter," he said, "from the king."

Eileen felt a chill creep over her. "From William? Are you sure?"

"My own son delivered it, lass."

"Do you know what was in the letter?"

He smiled. "It just happened to fall open after my wife held it too long over a pot." His expression sobered. "If yer grandda learns I told ye, there will be hell to pay for me."

"If he learns it, it won't be from me. What did it say?"

"The soldiers who were here for the wedding went back to London and told William and Mary where ye are. The king wrote that Phelan needs to send ye back to London, that it would not be wise to keep ye here. Phelan's no' told ye this, has he?"

She put her hand to her throat. "I cannot go back, Beathan!"

"Ye may ha' little choice. Phelan will do as they ask, of course. If ye defy him, it may be too dangerous for ye to stay here. He'll ha' to tell ye soon. No' the truth, of course; he'll say he's fixed it all with the king and queen, that they are grateful to him for backing them when so many in the Highlands dinna."

"My own grandfather will turn me over to them."

"He's been waiting to ha' his loyalty to them repaid; he'll no' put that at risk."

"What can I do?"

"Listen to what he says, verra carefully. If he's no' said anything of it to ye, perhaps he's content to keep ye here. If he mentions going to London and no' the letter he received, then ye'll ken where ye stand. Then get word to me."

She took several deep breaths. "Beathan, why do you tell me this?"

He grinned. "I hate yer grandda, lass. He's a poor leader; he's done horrible things that I'd like to see him pay for. I've escaped most of it, being at the end of the clan lands, but I see what he does. I've been forced to choose between living wi' the man or leaving my home forever; I decided to stay, thinking that he was a'ready an old man and couldna live forever, but he's lasted far longer than I would e'er ha' guessed. Someday he'll be gone at last, and then we'll rebuild the Glen Mothin MacKenzies. Telling ye the truth about him is a kind of revenge for me."

Beathan smiled wistfully. "I kent yer mother; we were friends, nothing more. When ye were dancing with Torridon ye reminded me of her. Ye glowed, lassie, like ye were lit from within, like yer mother always did. I'd like to see Cat's daughter happy, and I can tell ye, ye'll ne'er be happy here, not wi' Phelan."

Neil heard about the gathering at Kilgannon after returning from his latest visit to the MacLeods. The gathering, the messenger said, was not a war council; wives and families were welcome as well. If the invitation had come any earlier, Neil would have had to decline. He'd been trying to repair the fragile peace with the MacLeods. All his years of work had been undone when he'd killed Desmond, and only time would tell if his latest efforts would hold.

It had made no difference to the MacLeods that Desmond had betrayed Neil, nor that he'd attacked first. None of that stopped the whispers of discontent among the MacLeods who lived at Castle Currie, nor those more far afield. Jamie had killed a MacLeod at Dunfallandy, Neil one at Castle Mothin, and that's all they remembered. Don't travel with the MacCurrie brothers if your name is MacLeod, the wits said.

Calum had argued for him, telling all who would listen that they had it wrong. Neil was grateful to Calum, more than grateful, but all of the uproar meant that he'd not been able to leave for France to see Fiona. And now this gathering had been called by Kilgannon and threatened to delay him even more.

He could not bear this separation much longer. He missed

Eileen every moment. There were times he swore he could hear her voice on the wind or smell her scent in the air. At night he dreamed of her touch, of having her beneath him. He would wake then, his body aching, and walk the battlements. He'd written to Eileen, knowing that Phelan would probably stop his letters, but knowing he had to try to explain why he'd been so delayed.

And now this gathering, at the very time Neil was finally ready to leave for France. There must be a damn good reason for the gathering to be called now instead of waiting for the Kilgannon Games held every August. Alexander MacGannon must have heard something he wanted to discuss in person, something too important to wait while he made the rounds of the clans. Which meant Neil needed to be there.

He'd asked Duncan and Jamie to come to his study and discuss it, and when they were both settled into chairs, Neil wasted no time.

"I need to be at Kilgannon for the gathering," he said. "And I need to go to France."

Jamie laughed. "I kent it, could feel this coming. Say it so Duncan kens what we're thinking."

Neil looked at his cousin. "I want Jamie to go to the gathering as me. He did such a fine job at Dunfallandy that I'm asking again." He glanced at his brother. "Unless ye'd rather go to France and talk with Fiona?"

"No, thank ye," Jamie said. "But ye have to explain it to Ellen. She'll no' be pleased that I'm leaving."

"Bring her wi' ye."

"When I'm pretending to be ye? Oh, aye, Neil. That'll fool them."

Neil smiled. "Just dinna kiss her in public."

Chapter Seventeen

A collection of storms battered Castle Mothin that spring, keeping the fields from being tended and travelers at home. Eileen spent her days trying not to wonder when Neil would come for her. If he would come for her at all.

She told herself Phelan had tried to poison her against Neil, had planned for his words to haunt her in just this fashion, that Neil's return had been prevented by the storms. Neil had not forgotten her; had not seduced and then abandoned her. But the days passed and he did not come.

She studied Phelan, trying to decide why he kept her here, watching how he handled the business of the castle. He was a hard man, brooking no arguments, handing out punishments that were designed to penalize, not instruct. His household feared him, rushing to do his bidding. He mistook it for respect.

If she ruled Glen Mothin . . . If she were queen . . .

She caught herself. The thoughts had crept in more often each day. She found herself wondering what was happening in London, why William and Mary wanted her back. Would they welcome her—or were they furious? Were they murderous?

And she wondered whether Phelan would ever talk of the letter he'd received from the king. He had something in mind; she'd seen enough in her short time here to know that he was always plotting.

They rarely talked about anything significant. If she mentioned Neil, he brusquely changed the subject. And when she talked about Duncan, Phelan's comments were bitter. Duncan had defied him, and her grandfather would not forgive that. The list of those who had angered him was lengthy; some days all Phelan did was complain about people who had irritated him. She could see why her mother had leapt at the opportunity to escape this household.

When the storms were at last over and the streams and river had gone down to something close to normal, word of the outside world filtered in. In London, William and Mary were going to rebuild Hampton Court. It would be designed by Christopher Wren, and when finished, would enable William to move from the central London that he hated.

What would you build if you were queen?

Beathan arrived on a cloudy day, with news of crops that had been washed out by the rain, and swollen rivers that had destroyed entire villages as they rampaged to the sea. And of a gathering, called by the Earl of Kilgannon, to discuss the current situation in the Western Highlands. Phelan was not invited, Beathan told her as they walked through the gardens ravaged by all the storms. Neil MacCurrie had sent word he would attend. Beathan watched her face as he told her, then was silent.

Vous et nul autre.

If I were queen . . .

It was sunny the day Phelan finally talked to her, the breeze brisk and cool, sweeping away the mist that had hung over Castle Mothin for almost a week. Eileen was in the courtyard, glorying in the returned warmth, when her grandfather came walking through, commenting to the busy staff. And laughing. She watched in wonder as he approached, thinking how rare this jovial mood was.

"I have news," he said, his tone light. "Come, walk wi' me and I'll tell ye."

Eileen followed him silently, through the tunnel and across the bridge, standing at the top of the stairs that overlooked the village, trying not to remember Neil standing down there.

Phelan looked over the town, hands behind his back. "I wrote to William and Mary on yer behalf."

"Have you?"

"Aye. And they've written back that they are grateful to me for my loyalty. No' many were loyal to them here in the Highlands, and I reminded them of that. "I told them they could not force ye into the marriage with von Hapeman, that ye dinna want it."

"How did you know about that?"

There was a flash of anger in his eyes, quickly suppressed. "Everaone kent about it, Eileen. Duncan told me, but I would ha' learned it from someone. Ye fled to yer family and I was happy to take ye in until the danger was past."

She was silent.

"It's past, now. They say they won't try to force ye to do anything." His eyes narrowed. "Now ye can repay my kindness. I want ye to go to London as my emissary. I need to ken what's happening there, and ye ken all of them; ye can write to me now and then and tell me what's happening."

"What about Neil?"

He looked into her eyes. "Surely ye dinna still hold out hope that he's coming for ye? Tell me ye're no' that foolish."

She took a deep breath.

"Ah," he said, "ye are. Then all the more reason to go to London. And ye owe it to me, Eileen."

"I'll need time to think about this. I'm not sure I want to go back."

"I'll give ye three days to decide."

She sent a message to Beathan, then waited, hardly sleeping that night. By morning she knew what she wanted to do, but not whether Beathan would help her. When he arrived the next morning, she hurried him into the garden and told him what had happened. He listened with a deep frown.

"I'm sorry I was correct about Phelan," he said at last.

"As I am. Beathan, can you get me to Kilgannon? I have some coin, and I have my pearls . . ."

"I would be honored to steal ye away from here, but no' to take yer coin or jewelry, lassie. I'll gladly deliver ye to Torridon."

"He might not accept your delivery."

"I'm willing to bet that he would. There's some good reason he's no' come for ye, Eileen; he's no' forgotten ye. I ha' sons. I've seen the signs before."

"Of?"

"Of a man in love. I'll bet everything I own that he'll accept the delivery."

She smiled then, her heart lighter than it had been in weeks. *A man in love.* "How soon can we leave?"

"How soon can ye be ready?"

Neil walked up the staircase with a heavy heart. They'd been here, at St.-Germain, at King James's court, for two days and he'd still not seen Fiona. She'd not responded to his initial message saying that he needed to see her, nor to his second. This morning he'd sent a third, saying that he was on his way to see her. He went there now.

Had Fiona heard something of his purpose already? Could word have come from Seaforth's camp to her father that Neil was arriving to call off the match? Or was this simply Fiona's usual ennui, nothing more? Would he find her desolated? Furious? Or bored? It no longer mattered. This would be settled, and soon.

And meanwhile Jamie would go to Kilgannon, to discover what the Highlanders thought they should all do. He had already decided against joining any new rebellion, and since he'd been here, knew he was right. What he'd seen of King James's court only confirmed that an uprising would have little chance of success. King James was still ineffectual. And his military leaders did not know one part of their anatomy from another.

At Fiona's door, he paused. Eileen, he thought, I'll be free soon.

A maid answered his knock, saying that her mistress would be another few minutes, and inviting Neil to sit while he waited in the silk-filled room that smelled of lilies and pampering. He tried to tell himself that what he was about to do was not despicable, not completely selfish.

After an hour, his self-loathing was gone. Was Fiona deliberately keeping him waiting, as a way to punish him? Or was she weeping after being told why he was here, trying to gather strength to face him? He paced the room again, weary of his own thoughts.

She arrived long after he'd abandoned hope of seeing her; she paused dramatically in the doorway, a hand on each doorjamb. She was dressed in what must be the latest fashion, her lavender silk skirts very wide and multilayered, her hair piled enormously high on her head, held with a lace cap dripping with ribbons and long loops that draped to her shoulders.

She waved a fan before her face, giving him only glimpses of skin covered with some chalky coating. There was a beauty mark he did not remember at the corner of her mouth. She was pouting.

He thought of Eileen as he'd seen her last, her hair tumbled around her shoulders, her face pale with emotion. He had no idea what she'd been wearing that night at Glen Mothin, but she'd looked beautiful to him.

He bowed. "Fiona."

She flounced to the center of the room, extending her hand for his kiss. "Neil," she said. "You might have given me more notice. I had to hurry through my toilette to accommodate you."

"I'm sorry," he said, wondering when she'd replaced her Scottish burr with this English accent.

"You should be. It was inconsiderate."

"How are ye, Fiona?"

"As well as might be expected, closeted here in this court."

"Ye look well."

She preened. "Do I?"

"That's quite a gown."

She fluffed her skirts. "I love it! I have ever so many new clothes, Neil." She looked at him with narrowed eyes. "Why have you come? Is there to be another war? Have you come to delay our marriage for another war? I thought the last attempt failed."

"It did. But that's no' why I'm here." He took a deep breath. "Fiona, I've come to cancel our agreement to marry. I've talked to Seaforth . . ."

"Cancel the agreement!" She took a step back, her expression horrified. "Are you setting me aside?"

"I wouldna put it that way . . ."

"How would you put it, Neil? Are you refusing to marry me?"

"Aye. I ha' met . . ."

"I don't care who you've met. I don't care who she is! You may have your mistresses, sir, it's no concern of mine." She turned away, her shoulders heaving.

He cursed himself. He was everything despicable. "I'm sorry . . ."

She whirled to face him, her face flushed. "If you think to humiliate me before the entire court, Neil MacCurrie, you need to think again!"

"I'm sorry . . ."

"Sorry! Ye let me think, let us all think, all this time, that ye would marry me, and now ye're reneging on yer promise?"

He'd destroyed her. Neil nodded, miserable.

"Ye scoundrel!" She crossed the space between them in two long strides, slapping his face first with her hand, then with her fan. "Ye bastard!"

"I'm sorry, Fiona. I'll go . . ."

"That's it? 'Sorry'? No, sir, ye canna leave! Get yer hand off the door."

"What would ye ha' me do?"

"Explain this to me!"

"I . . . I met a lass."

"Who is she?"

"Her name is Eileen Ronley."

"Never heard of her."

"Her mother was Catriona MacKenzie. She's Phelan's granddaughter."

Fiona's eyes widened. "Phelan MacKenzie! Ye've gone to William, then."

"No. I dinna ken who she was when I met her. I met her in England." He held his hands out before him. "I dinna intend to do this to ye, Fiona."

She snorted and stood with arms akimbo.

"Her father was one of Charles II's bastards. She's cousin to King William and Mary and Anne."

"Ye have gone over to William."

"No. But I love her, and I intend to marry her if she'll ha' me."

Fiona lifted her chin. "Do ye, Neil?"

"Aye. I'm sorry. I dinna mean to hurt ye."

"Hurt me? I'm not hurt, ye imbecile. I'm angry. Do ye ken how many suitors I've spurned for ye? If ye dinna want to marry me, why did ye wait so long to tell me?"

His mouth dropped open. "I'm sorry . . ."

She waved a hand to silence him. "Fine. We'll not marry." She stomped across the room, then again, at last stopping in front of him.

"Your face is red where I hit you."

"Is it?"

"It is. Rub it, make the red go away."

He did as she said, wondering what was next. Her English accent was back. Did that mean her control was as well?

"It's no loss to me, Neil, not marrying you," she said, her tone matter-of-fact. "You would have left me in that castle and found yourself a mistress while I carried the heir you need. I'm happier here. But I'll be damned if you go out that door and tell everyone at St. Germain that you did not want to marry me."

"I'll tell no one."

She shook her head. "No, you won't. You'll tell everyone I ended the arrangement. And that you're heartsick."

He nodded. "I can do that."

"You will do that. And you have to buy me something. Jewelry." She put a finger to her lips. "Does your Miss Ronley have pearls?"

He nodded. "Aye, but I canna give ye hers."

"I don't want hers, you dolt! Buy me a pearl necklace, Neil. And earrings. Then tell them all that I broke your heart."

"Done. Thank ye, Fiona."

"Imbecile. Why did you not tell me sooner?"

"I thought ye'd be hurt. And angry."

"You overvalue yourself, sir. You are not the prize you think."

"I agree."

"Bring me the gifts before you tell anyone."

He leaned to kiss her cheek. "Thank ye, Fiona."

She pushed him away, then put a hand on his arm. "It is a shame, though. We might have made it work, Neil. If we'd been honest with each other, we might have made it work despite everything."

He nodded, startled by the emotion in her eyes.

She gave him a crooked smile. "Make them nice pearls, Neil."

He shook his head all the way down the stairs and through the palace, bemused. If he lived to be a hundred, he'd never understand women. He found Duncan lounging on a pink silk sofa with a lass on each side, and wondered if he shouldn't warn his cousin of the dangers of their company.

Duncan rose to his feet, ignoring their protests. "Well?"

"It's done."

"She hit ye. Yer face is red."

"Aye."

"How was she?"

"Surprising. I liked her more in the last ten minutes than in the last ten years."

"But it's done?"

"Aye."

"So we'll go."

Neil shook his head, gesturing to the women. "Go back to them, laddie. I have shopping to do before we leave France." At Duncan's raised eyebrow, Neil laughed. "A parting gift. Or two."

Neil watched the shore of France recede into the gloom. He'd bought Fiona the most beautiful pearl necklace and earrings he could find, not hesitating at the cost. She'd refused to see him when he'd returned with them, but her father had had a short discussion with Neil, during which he made it clear that he was angry at Neil for abandoning his daughter, and at Fiona for accepting his gifts.

Bridges burnt, Neil thought. But he had no regrets.

He glanced up at the sails, only half-filled with air, willing the wind to increase and speed him home. By the time they got to Torridon, Jamie would be back from Kilgannon, bringing news of what had happened there. It made no difference. They'd not join any rebellion, even if every other clan in the west did.

And now? Now he'd go home, arm his men, and head for Glen Mothin. He doubted Phelan would actually oppose him, but he'd be ready nonetheless. He was at last free to marry Eileen, and he intended to do just that.

Eileen wrapped her cloak tighter around her throat, and told herself that she would not be sick. If the sea calmed, she might actually enjoy the last of the voyage to Kilgannon. She concentrated on the scenery, tall snow-covered mountains with occasional surprisingly green valleys; to her right the peaks of the Cuillins reached deep blue into the gray clouds.

They'd sailed south, through the Kyle Rhea and into the Sound of Sleat; in those protected waters they'd made good time, but once out from behind the shelter of Skye, they'd had no protection from the raging winds. She gripped the rail again and gave Beathan a weak smile as he joined her.

He'd been very kind, had accompanied her to the MacRaes, with whom he'd made arrangements to travel to the gathering. He'd told them only that she was coming along, leaving them to draw their own conclusions. She knew what they thought, probably, that she was Beathan's mistress. It didn't matter. No one's opinion of her mattered. Except Neil's.

He'd not come to Glen Mothin for her. Would he welcome her at Kilgannon, full of reasons why he'd been delayed—or was this the most foolish thing she'd ever done?

She had told Phelan she would go to London and he'd relaxed his guard on her. The next day she had slipped through the postern gate and gone to find Beathan. They'd left at once, heading for the MacRaes and Kilgannon. And Neil. If Neil was not at Kilgannon, she'd go to Torridon. Beyond that she'd not planned.

She breathed a prayer now that they would arrive safely,

that Neil would be there, that he'd welcome her and tell her he loved her, trying to still the voice in her mind that asked why she should find love when her mother and grand-mother, either grandmother, had not?

Oh, Neil, she thought. I am so afraid.

The mistress of Kilgannon herself welcomed them, the beautiful and elegant Countess Diana MacGannon calling Eileen "Miss MacRae" before she turned to the long line of people waiting to speak to her. Eileen had not bothered to correct her.

The large hall was busy with activity, staff preparing it for the next meal. Some of the clan chiefs, she was told, were meeting in other rooms, some were outside in the courtyard, or down by the docks. Eileen stood alone for a moment, watching as Diana moved among her staff.

What would Torridon be like? Would it have a huge plas-tered hall with a hammered timber ceiling like this one? Or would it be rough-hewn and with little grace, like Castle Mothin? None of the details mattered. It was Neil's home and she would love it.

She wandered out into the courtyard, where Highlanders stood in small clusters, talking. Neil was not here among them, nor was Beathan, and she continued on, walking down the terraces to the dock, standing on the shore while the men climbed all over the newest ship. She spoke to no one.

James was ready for the last discussion of the day to be over. They'd retreated to this small stone room at the rear of Kilgannon Castle, discussing Glencoe and William and Mary and King James for hours. It had been a day full of talk, and most likely an evening of the same was ahead. He was weary of it, and there was still another day of the gathering.

Most of the men sitting here were seasoned warriors; few had any illusions about the future, certainly not about King James, nor after Glencoe about King William. It had quickly become clear that few of them wanted to rise against William. They had spent their time venting their rage at the past and discussing what, if anything, could be done about the future.

They'd had three years of bad crops. Seaforth was in prison. Their goods had been shut out of the English markets. They had to find a way to feed their people and hold off the famine that threatened.

The MacLeod sat a few places down from him, and James was glad peace had been restored between the Mac-Curries and the MacLeods of Gairloch. If it had not, this meeting might have been all about him and Neil. A laugh from the chiefs brought his attention back to the present.

Glengarry, the young leader of the MacDonnells, was energetic as he described his latest exploits in foiling English soldiers. James still remembered his jealousy of the attentions Glengarry had lavished on Ellen Graham. He did not fear that Glengarry would renew those attentions, but just to be sure, he'd kept Ellen far from the lively MacDonnell on their visit here.

His wife laughed at him for that, teasing him with small gestures that only he would recognize, but playing the game, pretending that he was Neil, and that she had come along to visit Kilgannon's wife Diana, leaving James behind to guard Torridon.

The gathering had been productive; the clans would have a united stance on some issues at least. They'd not turn in their weapons despite King William's request; there would be no relinquishing of clan lands for more forts like Fort William. James was pleased; the outcome was just what they'd desired.

He'd let Neil know as soon as he had a quiet moment. The messages he'd gotten from his brother had been intriguing. He'd expected remorse, possibly anger, but Neil had sent light-heartedness—mixed with regret and determination. Something had greatly amused his brother; their reunion would be interesting.

Glengarry finished his story now, and the men rose as Kilgannon bid them to join him for the meal. James lingered to thank Kilgannon for his hospitality.

Kilgannon clapped James on the arm. "Glad ye came. Where's Neil?"

James laughed; he'd wondered if they would fool Mac-Gannon. "Here."

"The two of ye tried this at Dunfallandy; I was there, remember?" Kilgannon said, keeping his voice low. "I'm no' insulted, lad, just wondering."

James shrugged; there was no point in lying. Kilgannon would not betray them. "He went to France. To see Fiona. But how did ye ken?"

Kilgannon pointed at the scar on the back of James's left hand. "Ye got that at Dunfallandy. Neil doesna have one, unless he just got one killing a MacLeod at Glen Mothin."

"Ye hear everything, sir."

"No' everathing. Why was Neil at Glen Mothin? I'm assuming he's no' suddenly enamored of Phelan. Has he changed his politics?"

"It's no' politics; it's a lass. Phelan's granddaughter. Catriona's daughter."

"Ah." Kilgannon rubbed his chin. "And now's he's off to France. Interesting."

"Oh, aye, the last few months ha' been verra interesting."

"This is the lass he asked me about in France—or her father at least. She's King Charles's granddaughter as well, aye?"

"Aye," James said. "So ye see why it's a bit complicated."

Kilgannon laughed. "As soon as ye add a woman, life gets complicated, lad."

Eileen saw Neil at last, framed in the large arched doorway at the rear of the hall, talking to a tall blond man. Kilgannon, Beathan said, following her gaze from their spot at a table with the MacRaes. Neil laughed with the older man, then followed him to a table at the head of the room. He did not look at Eileen as he passed, did not see her smile, nor the hand she held up in greeting. She fought her tears. He'd not expected to see her here. They'd laugh about this later.

Vous et nul autre.

Neil sat with Kilgannon and his countess, three other women, and the man Beathan told her was Glengarry. He seemed comfortable, very much at ease, talking and laughing easily with all of them, but none more than the dark-haired beauty who sat opposite him. Eileen had never seen him like this, light-hearted, relaxed, not at all like a man who was pining for a woman he'd left behind.

He'd not seen her; it was nothing more than that. She could walk up to him now, but she shrank from doing that. She would talk with him alone, not in a room full of listening strangers, not in front of the woman who had claimed so much of his attention. After the meal Neil talked with the

Highlanders or spoke to the dark-haired woman, laughing with her often. When the music began, he stayed where he was; so did Eileen.

The dark-haired woman left, but Neil stayed, still talking with the men. When the music ended, well after midnight, he rose to his feet at last, crossing the room to the stairs. Eileen bolted from her seat and followed, hurrying to keep up with his pace. In the hallway on the second floor she caught him.

"Neil!"

He glanced over his shoulder and paused.

"Neil! Wait!"

He faced her, his brows drawn together.

"I'm here," she cried breathlessly.

"So I see." His tone was polite, puzzled. He glanced at the two men who now stood at the top of the stairs, watching them.

She could feel her heart pounding and swallowed. "What has changed?"

"I dinna understand," he said softly.

"What about destiny?"

"Destiny?"

"Yes! Destiny! Fate! Were they simply words?"

"They are simply words to me, miss. Ye ha' the wrong man."

She stared at him, unable to think. He bowed and left her. The two men brushed past her and joined him, one of them clapping Neil on the shoulder.

"Ye always did ha' a way wi' the lasses, Torridon," he said.

Neil smiled tightly, then glanced at her again before he turned the corner.

Chapter Eighteen

Eileen washed her face and looked at her reflection again. Her eyes were red from crying, her face puffy. She'd cried for hours, then had begun to think. She'd not imagined what had happened between them. Beathan had seen it; a man in love, he'd said. Duncan had seen it; she had read it in his eyes.

And that last night at Glen Mothin—she'd not imagined that. Neil had loved her then, and he'd not been afraid to tell the world. What had changed since? Was it as simple as Phelan would have her believe, that Neil was a cruel man with women? There had to be an explanation and she could only think of one.

James was here, not Neil.

Could they look so much alike that even she could confuse them? Duncan had said that it was easy enough to tell them apart, but what if that was only because he knew them so well? Why would James be here masquerading as Neil? And if Neil was not here, where was he? Still talking with Fiona or Seaforth?

There was only one way to find out, and she'd do just that in the morning. She imagined James's surprised laugh when she confronted him, his explanation, his welcome. Surely that was what would happen. Or would it? What if this was Neil? Was he accustomed to women simply fading away when he tired of them? Had she not only surprised, but shocked him by coming here? Was he even now laughing at her—with that dark-haired woman?

If it had been Neil, then she would face it. In time her dreams would fade, her longing for him would lessen. She'd go back to Glen Mothin and accept Phelan's offer to send her to London, despite what danger may wait there. William and Mary might try to marry her off, but surely they'd not do more. She'd tell Anne everything; Anne would never harm her, nor let her be harmed.

She could not see what other choice she had. She could not go back to Ronley Hall; she would not stay at Castle Mothin.

In a few more hours she'd know.

James looked at the MacRae across the table. He'd seen that woman again, this morning, seated with the MacRaes at breakfast, had retreated before she saw him. Who was she? She'd obviously thought Neil would be glad to see her. He'd asked Kilgannon about her, but learned only that she was a MacRae.

What was Neil doing, toying with a MacRae lass when supposedly his heart belonged to Eileen Ronley? Or had Neil known her before he'd met Eileen? The lass must still care for him. James wanted no part of anything like that; why hadn't Neil warned him? He felt a wave of impatience; the last thing he needed with Ellen here was a lovesick woman mooning over him.

It was time for this gathering to be over. He'd heard everyone's views ten times over. There was nothing left to be said. Tonight the chiefs would eat their last meal together; tomorrow they'd all go home. He would be happy to be in his own bed, with his wife. He'd not play this game again, pretending to be Neil, sleeping alone while Ellen slept with the other women, trying to remember that he wasn't supposed to reach for her hand, or kiss her every time he walked past. Meeting for stolen kisses when no one was looking. It was time to go home.

Eileen ate breakfast with the MacRaes and Beathan, realizing, as the hall emptied, that the chiefs had already gone to their meeting. She'd missed Neil, would have to wait until the midday meal to talk to him.

In the large meadow next to the castle, Kilgannon had set up a series of games to entertain the chief's men and ladies. Eileen watched for a while, then wandered back to the castle. As the hours passed, so did her confidence. Was she simply being stubborn, refusing to face what must be obvious to everyone else?

When Beathan found her, and asked, his eyes kind, if she would be returning to Glen Mothin with him, she'd not been able to stop her tears. He'd patted her shoulder, telling her they'd be leaving this evening instead of tomorrow morning with the crowd, and that she was welcome to travel with them again. Somehow she'd managed to thank him, then retreated to the hall to wait.

The chiefs could be heard before they were seen, the men laughing and talking as they came along the corridor, Neil among them. She gathered her courage and rose to her feet, hurrying to the arched opening just as Neil came into the hall. He saw her, gave her a wary glance, then continued on, obviously with no intention of speaking to her.

"Neil," she said, ignoring the other men who listened. "I need a moment."

He shook his head and stepped forward, as though he'd pass her.

"I insist, sir," she said, finding her anger at last.

He raised one eyebrow, but stopped. "Do ye?" The other men laughed and passed them, leaving them alone.

"Are you Neil or James MacCurrie?" she asked.

"I am Neil, miss."

"Truly?"

"Truly."

"Then how is it you act as if you don't know me?"

"Should I?"

"Don't play games with me! What about destiny?"

"Destiny?"

"Yes, destiny! Fate! Were they simply words? How can you do this to me?"

His expression was pained now. "Lass, I dinna ken what ye think there was between us, but there can be nothing from this point on. D'ye understand?"

She stared at him, speechless, as he left her, striding through the hall and out the door. Eileen stood for a moment, then followed him out to the courtyard. He was gone. She headed for the gate. She would not let him do this to her without an explanation. As she passed the stables, she heard a quiet voice come through a window.

"Come here," he said, Neil's voice low and full of laughter.

Eileen stopped moving. Did he find this amusing?

"Dinna be coy, lassie. Come to me."

He laughed again. How could he see her? She spun around and found the doorway. The stable was a long room, the stalls clean and most filled with Highland ponies. There was no one in sight. He said something too low for her to hear. Where was he?

He wasn't alone. A woman's voice answered him, quickly smothered. Eileen walked slowly past the stalls, hearing her boots on the stone floor, the conversations drifting in from the courtyard, smelling the oats, hay, and horses. A high open window, the one through which she'd heard him, let in a shaft of sunlight, and she stood in it, turning to look into the last stall.

A tall man, his back to her, bent over a dark-haired woman in his embrace. One of her arms was around his waist, the other on his leg, pulling his kilt up, exposing a long lean thigh. His hair was black, pulled back simply and tied with a leather thong. He wore a blue silk jacket, slashed to show the white lining.

Eileen put her hand over her mouth and ran.

Eileen had not cried at first, her shock and anger too overwhelming. She'd run from the stables, from the castle, then had walked for an hour or two, along the shore of the sea loch, reaching the road that disappeared into the trees, heading east. There, in the long shadows cast by the pines, she'd sunk to the ground and wept until she had no more tears, at last turning onto her back and staring into the green canopy above.

When she could think, she faced it. Whatever had been between them was gone. Neil would never have come back to Glen Mothin for her. She would have spent her life wondering what had happened, whether he'd sent letters that somehow had never managed to reach her, whether Phelan had prevented Neil from coming to claim her.

"Ye ha' the wrong man," he'd said. An understatement.

She made her way to the castle and through the hall, praying that he wouldn't see her, relieved when she reached her room. She would not cry again, she told herself as she packed her things. She was neither the first nor the last woman to face the loss of love. Next time she would not give her heart so easily or so completely.

There would be no next time. How many examples did she need? Her grandfather Charles had been promiscuous, her father as bad. Phelan had been proven a liar. And now Neil had betrayed her trust. What more did she need to learn about men?

She waited at the dock for the MacRaes. Beathan found her there, but did not comment as she handed him her bags. She touched her waist, feeling the leather pouch still in place.

She had the blood of kings in her; she would find the strength to see this through. She would go to Glen Mothin and face her grandfather, then to London, to face William and Mary's wrath. She touched the letter again. She still had one more card to play. Now she would see how much it was worth.

Fate, she'd said. Destiny. Odd words to choose. James looked down at his hands, at the signet ring carved with the oak tree and water of the MacCurrie crest. She'd had an English accent. What was a MacRae lass doing with an English accent? She had golden hair, and she was tall.

He swore silently, cursing himself for a fool. Could Eileen Ronley somehow have left Glen Mothin, and despite Phelan's antagonism to the MacRaes have traveled here with them? He rose to his feet, ignoring the curious glances of the clan chiefs.

He'd find the lass and talk with her. If she was Eileen

Ronley, he'd bring her home. If she was not, he'd damned well know what she was to Neil.

"What d'ye mean the MacRaes left?" James cried. "I saw MacRae this morning."

Kilgannon spread his hands wide. "I'm telling ye what I ken. The MacRaes left hours ago; I saw them off myself."

"Did she go with them?"

"She came here wi' them, we canna find her now; I'm thinking she left wi' them. What would ye like me to tell ye?"

"Did ye see her?"

"I dinna notice her, James. She might ha' been there; she might no'. I was no' paying attention to one lass on one ship."

"Aye," James said, controlling his temper. "It's no' yer fault. It's mine. If I'd ha' had half my mind wi' me last night, I would ha' asked her what she meant." He walked across Kilgannon's library. "I think I've let Eileen Ronley slip through my hands."

"That was Neil's lass?"

"I think so. And now she thinks he doesna care about her."

"Ye could try to catch them."

James ran a hand through his hair. Ellen would have some strong words for him. And he could not even imagine what Neil would say. How could he have not realized she could be Eileen Ronley?

"I'm no' sure she'd even speak to me again," James said with a sigh.

"I assume this will be the last time ye play at being each other."

"Aye."

Kilgannon grinned suddenly. "Of course, last time it got ye a wife."

Neil frowned as he felt the emotions that Jamie was sending. Regret. Remorse. Guilt. Why? What had happened at Kilgannon? Short of starting another war, Neil could not imagine what could have Jamie so concerned. Unless . . . if Jamie had killed another MacLeod, there would be hell to pay, and that would explain the messages Neil was receiving. But he didn't think that was it.

Something in Jamie's tone made him think of Eileen. He clenched his hands on the railing. He'd go to Kilgannon and see if Jamie was still there. If the wind held, they'd be there by tomorrow.

What could have happened?

When Neil arrived at Torridon, Jamie was waiting on the shingle. Neil watched him, could see his brother's regret in his stance. It wasn't enough. He couldn't remember being this angry with Jamie, not in all their lives. They'd had times when they did not agree, but now he wasn't even sure he could speak civilly to him. How the hell could this have happened?

He swore loudly, causing Duncan and the others to turn and stare at him. He didn't care; let them think what they wished. He'd talked with Kilgannon, had discovered what had happened, that somehow Eileen had been there. And somehow Jamie had let her leave thinking all was over between them.

Neil stepped off the boat and stopped, reminding himself how he'd felt when Jamie's Ellen had left Torridon, how angry Jamie had been, convinced that Neil had sent her away. Jamie had forgiven him. Could he extend the same understanding now? He wasn't sure. Jamie had not done this purposefully, but the damage was done.

Jamie sent another message of sorrow and regret as Neil crossed the space between them.

"We'll talk about it all later," Neil said. "Now we're going to Glen Mothin."

Jamie nodded.

Eileen found Phelan in the hall at Glen Mothin. He must have been told that she'd arrived, for he sat like a king on a throne, and stared at her, his eyes cold.

"I have returned, Grandfather," she said, coming to stand before him.

His face grew suffused with color, almost purple. "Ye lied to me!"

"Yes."

"Ye lied to *me!*" His voice was louder now. "To *me!* Ye ran off to see yer lover. And now ye're back, tail between yer legs, to beg my forgiveness."

"No. I've returned to say I will go to London."

He was silent, drumming his fingers on the chair. "A woman of easy virtue."

"No."

"Slattern!"

"No, I am not."

He sneered at her. "He wouldna ha' ye, would he? Or, I should say, he had had ye, and tired of ye." He thrust himself from the chair, stalking to lean over her, his eyes gleaming. "Do ye ken what ye almost cost me? Do ye ken what ye almost did?" He grabbed her shoulders and shook her. "Ye stupid woman! I am weary of ye! I dinna ask ye to come here in the first place, but ye came, did ye no', begging for me to take ye in. Grandfather, protect me! And I did, giving ye a home. What did ye give me in return? Lies!"

"You lied to me as well," she said. "You told me you had written to William and Mary on my behalf, that you'd smoothed it all over, when actually William had written demanding me back."

"Who are ye to question me?"

"King Charles's granddaughter, Phelan."

He slapped her across the face, cutting her lip and drawing blood.

She backed away. "What is William promising you, Phelan? Money? A title?"

He threw her to the floor and stood over her, his chest heaving. "I canna think why he wants ye back, but he does, and I will take ye there myself."

Her face had almost healed by the time they reached England, the bruises still visible, but the swelling gone. Phelan had hardly spoken to her on the journey, sitting astride his horse with a sour face and surly manner. He'd brought ten armed men with him, had warned them not to speak to her.

The trip had been without incident, the long days on horseback melding into each other, followed by nights spent in vermin-ridden inns or on the floor of some poor crofter. Phelan would not stay in a decent place, preferring those that catered to guests who spoke little and asked no questions.

In the dark of the night she lay awake, refusing to think of Neil. She'd shed enough tears over him on her way back to Glen Mothin. It was time to think of what she would find in London. A warm welcome? She laughed at herself. Did hope never die? At best she'd be forced to marry Henrick. And at worst? Perhaps another Ronley would drown in the Thames. And it was her own grandfather who was bringing her to her fate, knowing—he had to know—what it might be.

At first she'd watched constantly for an opportunity to escape, but as each day followed the last, she fell into a kind of daze. This must be how prisoners facing their deaths felt, she thought, this mixture of languor and detachment. None of this was real. It couldn't be, for if she thought about it very long, she would panic. And still nothing would change. She was alone in the world, and had been for some time. The difference was that now she understood that.

She glanced at her grandfather now, riding just ahead. Some arrangement had been made, some enticement offered, to make this man leave his lair and make his delivery of her himself. What did she have to compete with that? She fingered her pearls, knowing that they would not be enough. It would take something more, something that would bring Phelan wealth now and for some time to come. Like land.

"Grandfather." She nudged her horse beside him. "Grandfather."

His eyes were cold when he looked at her.

"I have an offer for you."

He looked at her for a moment, then turned away. She waited, biding her time. She'd learned how his mind worked. It might take a few minutes, but his greed and curiosity would get the better of him. She looked at the hills through which they were riding, keeping her expression calm.

They were almost to York. If they changed course and traveled east, they'd reach the lands that should have been hers, that had been her father's, the lands around Whitby that William and Mary had refused to return to her. But Phelan might not know that. She waited.

"What is yer offer?"

She met his gaze, kept her tone as cool as his. "My father left me lands around Whitby, in Yorkshire, on the coast. It has a lovely harbor."

"Aye?"

"Crops have been bad in Scotland for three years. And this year's plantings have been washed out all over Glen Mothin."

"I ken this. What's it to do with Whitby?"

"If one had property in England, say, on the coast, property that brought in income from its tenants no matter what the weather or the success of the crops, perhaps income from fishing. If one had property such as that, one would not care what happened in Scotland. Scots are banned from trading with England, but if one was a property owner in England, he could trade within England, could sell the goods raised on his property."

She could see Phelan considering.

"What is yer offer?"

"I will give you my Whitby lands if you set me free."

He turned away from her. She waited. He turned back.

"How do I ken ye own the property?"

"I'll give you the papers. We can have my father's solicitor witness that I'm signing them to you."

"Where are they?"

"At Ronley Hall."

He considered and she waited. Sometime later he spoke again.

"We'll go to Ronley Hall."

She nodded, then turned away, careful not to let him see her triumph.

Neil stared at Beathan MacKenzie. "What d'ye mean, she's no' here?"

"Phelan took her to London himself. King William wrote and demanded that Phelan send her back. He's delivering her."

"To the king."

"Aye. We couldna stop it, Neil."

At his side, Duncan swore and looked back at the men they'd brought. Two ships, two crews, and fifty additional men to storm Castle Mothin if need be. They'd not expected to need any of them, thinking they'd only be used to help persuade Phelan to be cooperative. They'd left Jamie home, just in case something went wrong, and then had come to get Eileen.

Neil had looked no further than getting here, than talking to her. He'd practiced what he would say to her, sure that if he could explain what had happened, show her the ring he'd bought. He'd tell her what was in his heart and all would be well again. And then he'd take her home.

It had never crossed his mind that Phelan, the spider who rarely left his web, would deliver her into William's hands himself. Was it possible that Phelan did not know that his daughter had been murdered, that Eileen could face the same? What had he been promised to deliver his own grand-daughter?

Neil vaulted into the saddle.

Eileen told herself not to let her spirits rise as they ap-proached Ronley Hall, but she could not help it. There were people here who might be able to help her. If all went well, she would elude Phelan and could hide until he left.

But there was something else, and she should have thought of it months ago. If a marriage license had ever existed that proved Charles married her grandmother, Father Jessop would know.

Milford gave them a guarded welcome, Jack a warmer one, his whole face brightening when he saw her. She explained who Phelan was, but not why they were here. She wouldn't ask Milford, who had profited, at least, from her parents' deaths, and might even have been responsible for them, for help. He'd not be likely to extend it in any case.

Milford led them into the hall, introducing his wife, who greeted Phelan pleasantly and looked through Eileen, then left them. Eileen tamped her anger, telling herself she needed the energy to think. If she was to escape, it would be on her own, or perhaps with Jack's help. She had no other allies here. She did have one advantage: she knew about the tunnel from the potting shed to the priest hole. Somehow she had to find a way to get into Milford's office alone.

But first she needed to talk to the priest. She told Phelan and Milford that she wanted to visit her parents' grave. Neither objected, but when Phelan sent two men with her, telling them to watch her closely, Milford looked at him with narrowed eyes and a speculative expression. It would not be long before Phelan would discover that Milford was no ally of hers, and would tell him some story that twisted the facts in his favor.

She would have to be very quick. The only real danger was from the two guards, who walked only a few steps behind her. The small Norman chapel had stood at Ronley Hall for centuries; its small graveyard now in the shade of the stone church. All the earlier generations of the Ronleys of Warwickshire, three hundred years of her line, were buried here; she was the last. She stood over her parents' graves for a few moments, then told the guards she wanted to visit the priest. They nodded, bored.

Father Jessop was in the small church office, hunched over his desk, reading aloud from one of the pages strewn over the surface. He did not hear her enter over his own quiet muttering, and she watched him for a moment. The cleric had always been good to her, and she had no desire to startle the aged man. She cleared her throat.

"Father," she said.

He looked around at her, then smiled. "Goodness, child! You're home! How delightful! I'd not heard you were coming."

"I'm only here for one day, Father."

"One day! How can you stay for only one day? Wait while I put these pages away. I was just trying to determine if I'd already written this sermon once before; it seems quite familiar to me. Never mind. It doesn't matter; no one listens to what I say anyway."

She waited while he shuffled the pages into order, then turned in the chair, looking at her with a puzzled expression.

"Why are you here, Eileen?" he asked softly. "Is it unsafe in London? We heard there is unrest there, that King William is receiving a lot of criticism."

"Yes, he is. But I . . . Father, I'm in trouble. I ran away from London, to Scotland, and now my grandfather is bringing me back to London. I do not know what I face there. There are two men outside who are guarding me. Not protecting me, but making sure I do not escape. I have only a few minutes. I . . . I have to know the truth."

He stared at her for a moment, then nodded. "Very well," he said, not pretending to misunderstand. "I'll send for Jack. We'll tell you together."

"It were a lovely June day," Jack said. "Your grandmother were all dressed in yellow. Your grandfather told her she were more beautiful than all the flowers in the world."

Jack had come at once. The guards were sitting against a tree outside. One was sleeping, Jack said, but they'd still better be quick. He groaned as he tried to lift the square stone from the floor before the altar, and Father Jessop bent to help.

"We were all very young," the priest said. "This stone seemed light then."

The two men were silent as they pulled the paving stone from its resting place and slid it atop its neighbor with a ringing clunk. Eileen watched them, thinking of how many times she'd stood at this very spot, never once suspecting what lay hidden beneath the floor.

Jack pulled a leather bag from its hiding place. It was oiled and ancient, the twin of the bag that held her grandmother's letter. He handed it to Father Jessop.

"My Emmy and me were the witnesses," Jack said. "There weren't anyone else there, just the five of us."

"Her father would have forbidden the match if he'd known," Father Jessop said. "Charles was very wild in those days and the times were troubled. I thought I was doing the right thing by making sure he married her."

"None of us knew she were already with child," Jack said. "Well, leastways, Emmy and me didn't. Emmy cried. She thought it were so nice, them falling in love like we had, even as young as they were. They was children, really."

The priest drew the folded paper from the bag gingerly, holding it in both hands out to her. Eileen took it with trembling fingers.

"I wish they could have been happy together," Jack said. "My Emmy and me didn't know it that day, but we were the lucky ones. We've had a lifetime together."

Father Jessop nodded. "They only had a week together before your grandfather left; she never saw him again. Your grandmother gave birth to your father and died three days later, of a fever."

"She died of a broken heart," Jack said. "The fever just helped."

"Charles was in Jersey when your father was born," Father Jessop said, "but he'd left instructions to name his son Adam, because your father was the first." He paused, then looked into her eyes. "Open it, child."

The paper crackled as she unfolded it, the writing spidery and faded. It was a marriage license, dated June 5, 1646, which stated that Charles Stuart, Prince of Wales, son of King Charles I of England, Scotland and Ireland, had married Miss Jane Ronley in the chapel at Ronley Hall.

Charles had signed it with the flourish she'd come to know. Underneath was her grandmother's signature, then the priest's, and lastly the "x's" that signified that Jack and Emmy Hanford of Ronley Hall had witnessed the ceremony.

Her father had been born six months later. He was not a bastard.

There were three licenses created that day, Father Jessop said, all identical. Charles had taken one with him; Jane had kept one; and the third had been sealed in the floor after Jane's death. Neither man knew what had become of the other two. Eileen refolded the license carefully, then stared at it.

Her father had told her, had told the world, but Charles had denied it. Oh, yes, he'd acknowledged Adam as his son, but never his legitimate son. She felt a wave of rage, then one of sadness. How different her father's life would have been if Charles had acknowledged the marriage, how different her own life would have been. She sat down on the oak pew, trying to still her pounding heart, as the truth of it hit her. Her father had been the firstborn of a king.

She was the true queen of Britain.

God help her. Nothing would be the same now that she knew for certain all her father's stories were true. She might not be the only one of her family who knew; the other licenses might have been kept. Her grandmother's might be in Ronley Hall.

And her grandfather's might be in London. It all made sense now, the plan to leave her at Ronley Hall, to marry her off to Henrick. She dashed her tears away. She should be happy, should be crowing that she could vindicate her father. She should be queen. And her cousins hated and feared her for it.

"You should keep the license, child," Father Jessop said gently.

Eileen nodded and slipped it into the leather pouch he handed her, watching as the two men struggled to replace the stone. It took several minutes, but at last it was back in its berth. Father Jessop stepped on it to tamp it down, then looked over her shoulder, his face blanching. She turned slowly, expecting Milford. But no one was there, only the door slowly closing.

"Run, Eileen," Father Jessop said. "They'll have gone to get Milford."

"Head for Warwick, miss," Jack said. "We'll find you."

She nodded, and clutched the bag to her chest, then turned and slipped it into her bodice. At the door, she turned. "Thank you both. Thank you."

"Go with God," the priest said. "Now run, child."

She took two steps outside in the sun. The guards were gone. She turned to the trees, planning to hide in their shadows. Hands grabbed her arms and she turned to look into the faces of Phelan's men.

Chapter Nineteen

At the door to the hall, Phelan's guard released her arms. She checked that the leather bags were still there, hidden against her waist, then took a deep breath and entered. Phelan and Milford, sitting at the long table, both turned. One of the guards from the church whispered to Phelan while Milford watched. Phelan looked at her, then nodded. She stiffened, expecting him to ask what she'd been doing, what they'd uncovered.

Instead, Phelan's tone was mild. "That took a long time."

"I was talking with Father Jessop."

"So I heard." Phelan rose to his feet. "Let's get the Whitby papers."

"I don't know where they are," Milford said.

"They're in your office," Eileen said.

Milford shook his head. "No they're not. I've gone through everything."

"I'll show you."

She led the way to Milford's office, took the key from its hiding place behind the desk drawer, and handed it to her grandfather. "It fits in the lock of the chest behind you."

"You don't need a key," Milford said. "I broke the lock when I searched it. There's nothing in it but her father's old books."

"The papers are in one of my father's books. It was hollowed out and the covers glued together."

"Which book?" Phelan asked.

"A copy of the King James Bible."

Milford grunted and stared at her. Phelan gave a snort of laughter and threw open the chest. He rummaged through the books, tossing them aside as he dug to the bottom, finding the bible and breaking it open. He unfolded the papers on the desk and studied them while Milford read them over his shoulder.

Phelan looked up, his expression triumphant. "These are legal documents, signed by Charles II," he crowed.

She nodded. "He gave my father the Whitby lands just after my parents married, when he gave my father the title. I inherited them."

Phelan thrust them across the desk. "Sign them over to me."

She signed each page of the document, writing at the end that she had given Phelan MacKenzie all her rights of ownership, then looked up at him. "I have kept my part of the bargain."

"So ye have," Phelan said, nodding. "So ye have."

Milford's eyes narrowed. "What bargain?"

"Just a wee exchange," Phelan said. "She thinks I will give her her freedom for these papers."

"No," Milford said. He crossed to the door and slammed it. "You're not the only one under orders to return her to London. I'm not letting her go."

"It's no' yer decision, laddie," Phelan said.

"You're in my house, Phelan, surrounded by my men. It is my decision. I'm taking her to London."

Phelan laughed. "I've no intention of releasing her. I just told her I would."

At Eileen's cry, Phelan turned to her.

"D'ye think I'd be fool enough to defy the king?" He folded the Whitby documents and put them in his shirt. "This was a boon, nothing more. William will pay me well, I trust. What did he promise ye, Milford? This house?"

"I already earned this house."

"How did you do that?" Phelan asked.

"He killed my parents," Eileen said. "Your daughter, Phelan. He killed her."

Milford looked away, then back at her, his eyes defiant. There was no remorse, no protest, just displeasure.

"Enough!" Phelan said. "Where is the license?"

Her heart lurched. She opened her mouth, then closed it.

"Speak up, lassie. I dinna hear ye."

"What license?" she whispered.

Phelan slapped her. "My man saw the priest digging up a stone and talking about a wedding, about a son being born. There's only one wedding that matters to us all. Where is the license, Eileen?"

She backed away from him, throwing a look at the tapestry. Could she manage to cross the room, open the door, and get down the stairs before they could catch her? Phelan stepped forward, his hand raised to strike her again.

"Where is it?" he asked.

Milford put out a hand to stop him. "She won't tell you. Don't hit her again, Phelan; the king and queen will see the bruises. There's a smarter way." He moved to stand over Eileen, lifting her chin so that she looked into his eyes. "All this time with you under my roof at my expense, keeping you on the king's orders, making sure you stayed out of London. All this time, and the damned third copy of the license was here? In the church?" He whirled away from her to stride to the door, speaking to Phelan. "We'll talk to Father Jessop."

Phelan nodded. "Aye, good idea. Come, Eileen."

"No," Milford said. "Leave her here. He'll talk if he thinks we'll hurt her. Lock her in; put two of your men at the door."

When the door closed, Eileen stood for a moment, trying to control her trembling. She'd succeeded in getting into Milford's office alone, but the wolves were about to descend upon Father Jessop, and she must stop them. She grabbed the candle from the mantel.

The stairs were steeper than she'd remembered. Eileen held the candle higher, careful of her footing. She'd made sure that the tapestry was back in place before she'd closed the door it concealed, but they would know as soon as they found her gone that there must be another entrance to Milford's office. And Milford would remember that Neil had somehow escaped from the priest hole. He would tear the room apart, but would he find the tunnel?

She could go through it now, find someone, send him for the sheriff, or to the village, for help. She hoped Father Jessop would tell her grandfather quickly that she had taken the license, so that they wouldn't hurt him. The priest's age would be no protection from Phelan's greed or Milford's determination.

If she was very lucky, Father Jessop would have already told them, and she could hurry him back here, to hide with her in the tunnel until help came. She would not think further than that, would not think of what Milford might say to the sheriff, what story they'd invent to justify bringing her to London.

If she had been valuable to Phelan as the daughter of an

illegitimate son of a king; what value would she have as the rightful queen? She'd be in prison on some trumped-up charge within a week. Or dead. William knew. Mary knew. Milford had been told to keep her here, far from London, probably had been given orders to marry her off to someone who would keep her in the countryside forever. He'd been searching for the third marriage license; he'd probably given them her grandmother's copy. They must have had Charles's copy already.

This was why Mary had never shown any affection when Eileen returned to London. She'd no doubt been horrified to have the problem arrive on her doorstep. If Eileen had married Henrick, would some unfortunate accident have befallen her in Holland? Had Anne known as well?

Had her invitation to Eileen been in defiance of William and Mary's wish to keep her hidden away? Had it been completely unconnected, innocent? Or had Anne's invitation been with the compliance of William and Mary—was it easier to kill Eileen in London than in Warwickshire? She thought of the man who had followed her. Would that have been the day she disappeared?

Eileen put the candle down and fumbled at the stones that would release the door to the tunnel, then found it and breathed a prayer of thanks as the door swung open. She reached for the candle, looking down the rest of the stairs, remembering Neil tied to the bed in the priest hole, Milford holding the sword above him, Neil leaning to kiss her, here at this very spot. She shook her head and wiped her sudden tears aside. She would not think of Neil, not now. Maybe never.

She looked at the dark tunnel ahead, imagining the spiders and rats waiting for her. She could not let Father Jessop pay the price of her cowardice. She stepped into the dark, running as quickly as she dared. She pushed at the trapdoor with both hands, sobbing as it refused to budge, then stepped back and ran at it, shoving with all her strength. It shot up into the air, freed from whatever had held it, flying across the potting shed to slam against the wall, raising clouds of dust that shimmered in the rays of sunlight coming through the dirty windows.

She tiptoed to the glass, peering through, trying to see if the noise had done more than startle her, if people were now coming to see what had happened in what was supposed to be an old abandoned shed. When she saw no one, she reached inside her bodice, putting the leather bags on the first step below the trapdoor opening, then dragged the trapdoor back across the shed and back in its slot, covering it with the broken pots that lay next to it.

She opened the door a crack, then she began to run. The shouts began as she ducked behind the stables. At first she thought they were shouting at her, then realized it was Milford shouting, somewhere near the church.

"Tell me! Does she have it?" Milford roared.

"May God have mercy on your soul," Father Jessop said.

"I will give you one last chance to tell me where it is!"

"You have killed before, Milford; I expect no mercy from you now."

"Then you choose your fate, priest," Milford said grimly.

"Father," the priest said, "into your hands I commend my soul."

"No!"

Eileen's screams were lost in the roar of the pistol's discharge. Smoke filled the air as she ran toward the knot of men gathered on the lawns. Father Jessop lay on his back.

Milford stood over him, pistol in hand. Phelan and the other men stared at Father Jessop. She threw herself down on her knees next to the priest. She was too late, Father Jessop was dead.

She whirled on Milford's men. "How could you let him do this to an old man? To a priest? What kind of men are you?"

Milford's men looked at her impassively.

"Where is it, Eileen?" Phelan asked.

"You did not stop this!" she screamed at him.

Phelan called over his shoulder. "Bring the other one."

She cried out as Phelan's men dragged Jack from the porch of the church, holding him between them, throwing him roughly to the ground at Phelan's feet. She stepped between Jack and Milford.

"You will not do this!"

Milford took the gun one of his men handed to him, checked the loading, then aimed it at Jack's head. "Where is the license? Tell me or Jack dies as well."

Eileen looked into Milford's eyes, then at Jack. "In the potting shed, under the trapdoor. The license is on the top step with a letter from my grandmother. She wrote two letters to Charles; she sent one. The other is here."

"Ye dug that up as well?" Phelan asked.

"I've had it for years."

Milford tucked the pistol in his belt and strode away, Phelan at his heels. She sank to the ground, laying her cheek on the grass. Jack put a hand on her head.

She could smell London. Even with the leather window coverings drawn tightly shut in the carriage Phelan had hired, she could smell London. She knew this mixture of coal dust and sewage and horses. They must be near the river, for she could smell that too, could hear the sound of boatmen calling to each other. It must be foggy.

Her hands were bound before her, but Phelan had removed the coverings from her eyes and taken out the wad of cloth he'd stuffed in her mouth for much of their trip here. He sat opposite her, watching her now.

She could hear Milford's voice, asking how to get to the palace. Ask anyone, she thought. Just tell them that you're bringing the king and queen's cousin to her death. The carriage started to move again.

It was almost over, this endless trip, the entire disaster that had been her life. William and Mary would have her killed quietly. They would not bother with the charade of a trial. They wouldn't want the world to know that Adam Ronley's daughter was about to die. It would raise too many questions about Adam's death, would remind everyone of Glencoe.

She'd been such a trusting fool. She'd believed Milford had mourned her parents with her, that he'd let her stay at Ronley Hall because he was generous, that he was trying to find her a husband. And she'd been grateful. He would deliver her to William and Mary. And receive what in return this time? Her Whitby lands?

Or would they go to Phelan after all? She'd been a fool there as well, with Phelan, although less of one. She'd never believed him, had never trusted him, thanks to all the warnings Neil and Duncan had given her, but she'd underestimated him, had not realized how potent the mixture of greed and ruthlessness could be. Father Jessop was dead because of her underestimation, Jack might have been.

She'd heard the stories, of the man cut into ten pieces and

her mother made to watch. She'd thought then that Phelan had been so vicious because his precious daughter had been harmed; now she knew that he had been vicious because he enjoyed it. She'd seen his face when Milford shot Father Jessop. He had taken cruel pleasure in it, in seeing her shocked realization of what was happening. If Milford hadn't pulled the trigger, Phelan would have.

She'd been such a fool, so many times.

But never more than with Neil MacCurrie. She'd believed him, trusted him, had given him her heart. A tear rolled down her cheek and she hurried to wipe it away before Phelan saw it. The only one she had been right to trust was Duncan. He was a good man. Would he ever think of her? Would Neil?

She had to stop remembering him, had to stop remembering the feel of his lips on hers, of his skin beneath her hands. She loved him. Dear God, even after all that had happened, she loved him. Her tears ran down her face now, unstoppable. Phelan watched her cry, then handed her a handkerchief.

"Dry yer tears," he said. "Yer about to see yer cousins."

"How can you do this?"

"What? Bring ye to them?" He laughed quietly. "There's no tie between us, Eileen. Ye may carry my blood, but ye mean nothing to me. Yer mother meant nothing, just a bothersome lass who defied me. It was ye who found me, remember? I kent ye lived. I could ha' sought ye out anytime."

"How can you be so heartless?"

He shrugged. "It's no' heartless, lass. Life is cruel. Ye ha' to find a way to survive. In years to come ye may thank me."

"Thank you in years to come! Oh, please, sir! They'll kill

me. You will soon have yet another death on your head. I'll be dead within a week."

"No' if my plan works."

The door of the carriage opened and Milford leaned in. "We're here."

James stopped in front of the breastplate he'd worn to war. Neil and Duncan had taken their own, had left this one, and him, behind. He unwrapped it, fingering the dent from Killiecrankie. Duncan had told him how Neil had worried and prayed when James had been injured, how distraught Neil had been, how helpless he'd felt.

That was how James felt now. He'd heard nothing from Neil in days.

He and Neil had not argued when Neil came home from Kilgannon, although James almost wished they had. He'd seen the battle raging in his brother's eyes, felt the waves of emotion, but Neil had controlled them. In the days that followed, Neil had been like a man possessed, with only one thought. Bring her home.

He'd told James to stay behind. Neil had not meant it to be a punishment or a rejection, he explained. He meant it as a sign of trust. He needed James here at Torridon to keep their family safe. "I need ye to be me if I canna," Neil had said. "If aught happens at Glen Mothin to me, ye'll be here to guide the MacCurries to the fifty years of peace."

When he'd left for London, Neil had sent some of his men home, and a letter for James, saying the same again, but more forcefully. And he'd told his brother he loved him, and was proud to have had all these years together. James had read the letter, felt his brother's resolve, and was grateful, but struck by how final a farewell it seemed. Had Neil had some sense that he would not be returning?

James would protect this land and its people until Neil came home to lead them himself. He would go to the chapel and pray for Neil, for Duncan, for Calum and all the Torridon men who had gone with them.

And for Eileen. Destiny, she'd said, fate. She was right; her fate was tied to Neil's, his to hers. However, why ever, James did not know, did not understand. But they were linked, had been, long before they'd met.

Fifty years of peace was what the Seer had predicted, that both brothers would rule, but never at the same time. He spent an hour in the chapel, then roamed the parapets, looking over the water below.

And at last a message came from Neil, the emotion coming in huge waves, one crashing atop the last, the pounding continuing, increasing. The pounding of horses' hooves, of water on a shingled shore.

Rage.

Anne's house. Eileen climbed from the carriage, staring up at the familiar building. Why were they here? And why were Milford's men now streaming up the stairs and inside, mixed with Phelan's?

"Go on," Phelan said, pushing her forward.

She took two steps in the sunlight, then stopped. Milford's and Phelan's men were not alone; at least a dozen of William and Mary's palace guard were here with them, in livery, armed, and watching her.

"Why are we here?" she asked Phelan.

"This is where William told us to take ye."

Milford grabbed her arm now and ushered her up the

stairs, through the door, and into the small sitting room where Anne stood waiting, her face pale.

"I don't understand," Anne said. "Why are you here? Eileen, why are they bringing you here like this? What has happened?"

Milford thrust Eileen at her, then turned to his men. "Get them all. Bring them to one room, then call me."

"We await the king and queen," Phelan said as he entered the room.

"Here?" Anne asked. "They don't come to see me at the best of times. We've been arguing for months, my sister and I. They will not come here. You have been misinformed."

Phelan walked to stand before her, leaning very close to her face. Anne backed away. "D'ye see yer cousin, there, next to ye?"

Anne nodded.

"They come to see her, not ye."

Anne shook her head. "They won't come here, they'd have you come to them."

Phelan pushed the window covering aside. "Look outside, Princess Anne. Those are William's guard. Would they ha' come wi' us without her permission?"

Anne looked through the window, then at Eileen.

"Do what they say, Anne," Eileen said.

"Eileen," Anne asked, her voice high with fear. "What has happened?"

"Do what they say," Eileen said again.

Milford's men watched as he paced Anne's receiving chamber. They'd run through the house and had brought everyone here. Bess and Celia stood with the weeping maids and the pale-faced footmen who were lined up against the wall. Anne had few staff left, and they had been easily cowed by the emotionless men who stood guard over them with drawn weapons. She sat with Eileen at the end of the room, her son in her lap, as Milford explained what would happen.

"You will all remain in this room," he said, turning to look at each of them in turn. "You will be guarded. Do not think to escape. Those you see here are only a fraction of the force I have outside. If you attempt to leave, you will die. After the king and queen have left, you will be released. Do you have any questions?"

The staff stared at him, silent.

"Why are William and Mary coming here?" Anne asked.

Milford turned to look at her. "Not to see you. This has nothing to do with you." He looked at Anne's son, then back at her. "I would keep it that way." He spun on his heel, nodded to his men, and left the room.

Anne turned to Eileen with a shake of her head. "I don't understand."

"I will explain," Eileen told her.

They had hours to talk. The afternoon passed slowly while they waited, the hours tolled by London's churches. Two, three, four o'clock. The bells' music came through the open windows, but Eileen hardly heard them.

She told Anne everything that had happened since she'd left London. She'd been strangely unemotional through most of it, but cried when she spoke of Neil, and again as she described Father Jessop's death, her grief welling up once more. Anne had cried as well. And now there was nothing more to say.

"What will we do?" Anne had asked.

"What can we do?" Eileen had answered. "Your husband

is in Denmark. Sarah has gone to the country. There is no one else to help us. We'll wait. When William and Mary come, we'll talk to them."

"I cannot believe this," Anne whispered.

Eileen smiled sadly. Somehow it all fit, the pattern of her life. Charles and Jane had unwittingly begun the process; her parents had been unwilling participants. But it would end with her. Three hundred years of Ronleys would die with her. Milford's sons would inherit Ronley Hall.

And William and Mary's children would rule. Or, if they had none, Anne's son. Not Eileen, not her children.

If Charles had told the truth about her father's birth . . . She glanced at Phelan, dozing near the door. If either of her grandfathers had been otherwise . . . If any of the men in her life had been otherwise . . . She would never know what might have been. Birth, death. Greed, power. The pattern had not started with her; the process would go on long after she was gone.

The church clocks struck eight, then nine, then ten. There was silence in the house now except for the movement of Milford's and Phelan's men. Eileen closed her eyes. Let them kill her. It did not matter. Nothing mattered.

She must have slept, for she woke with a start. Anne stood near her, facing Phelan, talking quietly.

"You're her grandfather!" Anne said. "How can you do this?"

Phelan tilted his head. "I am a practical man. I bear her no malice. But she'd ne'er be queen. Even if England and Scotland were ready to put her on the throne, could she win a war against William and Mary? I dinna think so. If ye had the throne, would ye give it up?"

"Do you expect me to be party to this?"

"We dinna care if ye are or not."

"What will they do to her?"

"D'ye think they will let her live, to tell the tale of what happened to her parents? To tell the world about her father? She dinna ken before, but she does now. She has only one hope."

"Which is?" Anne asked, her tone expectant.

"Me."

"You! Surely you cannot be serious!"

"Aye, lassie, I am. If word were to get out that the king and queen had their cousin, the rightful queen, killed, how long d'ye think William and Mary would stay on the throne?"

"Who would tell them?"

"Me."

"What's to keep them from killing you?"

"I left letters at Glen Mothin, with my granddaughter Adara. She'll send them to King James if I dinna return. I think he will find them interesting."

"How does this help Eileen?"

"I hope to convince them to let me take her to Scotland. I'll keep her close at Glen Mothin. She'll tell no one what happened."

"Why would you do that?"

Phelan laughed. "For money, Princess Anne. They'll pay and I'll stay silent."

"You don't think that will work, do you?"

"We'll see. We'll see."

"What about Milford?"

"Milford has his own plan. He doesn't care if she lives or dies. He just wants his reward. If he disappears, he has someone here in London who will spread the seeds, tell the rumors, or so he says."

"Who is it?" Anne asked.

"Ye dinna think I would tell ye, did ye?"

"Phelan probably doesn't know," Eileen said, rising to her feet. "But I do. His name is Howard Templeton."

"Templeton," Anne said, her eyes widening. "He came here to see you before, didn't he?"

"Yes. He was once a friend of my father's, but I think he helped kill him. He was well paid." She turned to Phelan. "I'm sure you will be as well."

Everyone turned as the door opened. "They're here," Milford said. "The king and queen are here."

Chapter Twenty

Milford led them to the long, narrow room where Eileen had once received Neil, gesturing them inside. The window coverings were drawn; candles burned brightly. Anne walked across the floor, clasping and unclasping her hands.

Eileen paused just inside the door, hearing the tramping of boots on the wooden floor of the corridor. There was the bench on which she'd sat with Neil while he'd explained his ring and the MacCurrie crest. Land and sea. And a legend about an oak tree. Neil.

Milford opened the door, holding it wide for William and Mary, who hurried into the room, Phelan right behind them. Milford spoke quietly to someone in the corridor, then closed the door and leaned against it. Eileen looked at her cousins.

They met her gaze—William with calm assurance, Mary with a sidelong glance quickly removed. It was William who had made these decisions, Eileen realized. And Mary acquiesced. It was no solace to know that Mary was uncomfortable with what had been done.

"How can you think to harm her?" Anne hissed. "How can you?"

"Leave us," William said to Anne.

Anne shook her head. "No. Whatever happens here tonight concerns me as well. I will stay."

William shook his head. "I strongly advise that you leave

us, Anne. Please remember that your son is in another room."

"You would not dare harm him!" Anne cried.

William made a sharp gesture. "You forget that I am the king!"

"Only because I helped you to be!" Anne shouted. "Only because I put my own claim aside! If you touch my son, the world will know what has happened."

"Anne," Mary said quietly. "Go. We will not harm her."

"You had Adam killed," Anne said.

"I never told them to do that," William said.

"But you paid them well for it," Eileen said. "You paid both Templeton and Milford well, didn't you?"

William glared at her.

"You wanted her to marry von Hapeman's son," Anne said.

"It's neither the first nor the last time a king has arranged a marriage for his cousin to a wealthy man," William said. "No one will believe you, Anne. No one will leap to help."

"He's right, Anne," Eileen said. "There is no one to help. Go and be with your son and your staff. That way no one will ever be able to place blame for what happens here tonight on you." Anne shook her head, her mouth trembling; Eileen smiled at her, speaking more gently now. "Thank you, dear cousin, for all your kindnesses. Now go. Please go."

"God will judge you," Anne said to Mary.

"God will judge us all," Mary said.

Anne ran toward the door. Milford opened it, letting her through, then closed it firmly behind her. He gestured to Eileen.

"You'll be paid," William told Milford. "Eileen, I am truly sorry."

Eileen gave a short laugh. "I'm sure you are, William."

William looked at her for just a moment before he turned to Phelan and Milford. "Gentlemen, thank you for your services. Miss Ronley will leave with us. You may gather your payment downstairs."

"Will the money be what we agreed?" Phelan asked.

William shrugged, his expression scornful. "Count it yourself."

"I'll see it before she leaves," Milford said.

William looked at Milford blandly. "Will you?"

"What will ye do wi' her?" Phelan asked.

"That is not your concern," William said.

"She is my granddaughter."

"A bit late to be remembering that."

"There is another way, Yer Majesty," Phelan said, stepping forward. "Let the lass come home with me. I will keep her silent. That way no one can accuse ye of another murder."

William sneered at him. "No one will accuse me now. No, Phelan, I will not continue to pay for your silence. Take the coin I've offered and do not look for more. And should you think to mention this after you get home, should it cross your mind, know that I will burn your home and sentence you to a traitor's death for your part in my cousin Eileen's unfortunate death. Who will they believe, a Scot? Or the king? Will the Highlands rise to avenge you? Will the English give a damn? Do not tempt my displeasure or you will share her fate."

"I have left letters."

"The ravings of an old man who lost a beloved granddaughter. You will not be believed. Take your money, sir, and do not look for more!"

"I have the marriage license."

"I have my own copy." William sneered. "It matters not if she is unable to rule. I grow weary of this discussion!"

"Then I thank ye, Yer Majesty," Phelan said, bowing.

At the door Phelan turned to look at Eileen. She held his gaze for a moment, silent. She had nothing to say to him, to this man who had failed both her and her mother. She turned her back on him and a moment later heard the door close.

"Shall we go?" William said.

Eileen turned to face him. Before she could speak, there was the sound of running feet. The door burst open. Phelan threw himself inside.

"They're here!"

"Who's here?" William demanded.

Milford drew his sword and faced the door. Mary gasped and moved behind William. Phelan ran to the end of the room.

"Who, Phelan?" Milford shouted.

Phelan turned to stare at the door. They could all hear it now, the war cries, the screams from Anne's receiving chamber, the sounds of battle from the street below, gunshots fired there and somewhere within the house itself. Men shouted and ran along the corridor, shouting again.

There was the sudden ringing of metal, of sword on sword, several shots, then a long shrill scream. Eileen began to pray as the door flew open.

Neil burst into the room with his sword drawn. Milford stood before him, sword ready; there was at least one man here who would fight. The king was behind Milford, his expression dazed. The queen screamed and clutched at

William's sleeve, drawing him backward. Phelan huddled against the cabinets at the end of the room.

And Eileen stared at him in astonishment.

"I ha' come for ye, Eileen," he said. "Are ye a'right?"

"Neil!" she cried.

"Lassie, are ye a'right?"

"Yes, yes! How did you find me?"

"We discovered that ye'd come to London. Dinna think of it, Milford," Neil said as Milford shifted his weight. "I'd love to take ye on, ye bastard."

Milford glared at him.

"Ye werena here yet," Neil continued. "So we went to Ronley Hall."

"Milford killed Father Jessop!"

"Aye, lass, I ken. I heard all about it, about everything that happened there. I ken what ye found, Eileen. I ken ye are the rightful queen." He looked at Milford. "Jack missed ye so much he came wi' us, wanted to give ye a special greeting. He's waiting for ye downstairs. And sorry to tell ye, Yer Majesties, but all yer men are dead."

"That's impossible!" William cried.

"Is it?" Neil asked.

"I have a hundred men on the way!" William shouted.

Neil shifted his gaze from Milford to William. "No, ye don't, ye fool."

"You may not speak to me this way! Who are you, sir?"

"Ah," Neil said. "Forgive me, Yer Majesty. I dinna introduce myself. Neil MacCurrie, the Earl of Torridon. And if ye canna tell by my accent and my clothes, a Scot. Who fought for King James, not for ye."

"Belmond!" Mary shrieked. "You're Belmond!"

Neil bent his head. *"Mais oui, madam."*

"A spy!" Mary cried. "William, he's been in our court. He's a French spy!"

"No, madam. I came to yer court to find Eileen." He grinned and turned to look at her. "I love ye, lassie. It was Jamie at Kilgannon, lass, no' me. *Vous et nul autre*."

"I love you, Neil!" she cried, then screamed a warning as Milford lunged at Neil, throwing his full weight into the charge.

Neil spun around, deflecting Milford's thrust. "I'm armed this time, Milford."

Milford lunged again; Neil parried. They fought down the length of the room, Phelan scurrying to get out of their way, Mary screaming. The men battled into the center of the room, Milford's face twisted, Neil's intent.

Milford kicked, trying to wrap his leg around the back of Neil's knees. Neil gave a low growl and leapt forward, smashing his sword from side to side, backing Milford to the benches. With a hoarse cry, Milford struck at Neil's neck.

Neil thrust his sword under Milford's raised arm, running it far into Milford's chest. He stared into Milford's eyes, then heaved himself back, bringing his sword with him, watching as Milford staggered and fell to his knees, clutching his chest.

"Ye brought Eileen here to London to die!" Neil shouted at him. "Why? So that ye could be paid by this villain ye call king? Ye killed her parents and ye were willing to let her die so that the truth wasna kent? Ye killed an unarmed man, a man of God who never did ye harm! I came to avenge all of them, Milford, to kill ye! And I'm glad I ha'."

Milford opened his mouth in convulsive spasms, then fell forward to the floor. William gasped, Mary screamed again.

Neil, chest heaving, watched Milford. When Milford took his last breath, Neil closed his eyes.

Phelan darted for the door, screaming with rage as Duncan stepped into the opening. "Get out of my way!"

Duncan shook his head.

"I've no' dealt wi' ye yet, Phelan," Neil said.

Phelan pulled his pistol from its holster and aimed it at Duncan's chest.

"No!" Eileen screamed and started forward. "No!"

"Phelan!" Neil shouted, drawing his pistol from his belt.

Duncan looked into Phelan's eyes, then shoved his grandfather away from him, knocking him to the floor. Phelan, on his side, lifted his pistol and aimed it at Duncan.

Neil shot Phelan.

Phelan's gun fell to the floor, clattering against the wood with a hollow sound. Neil bent over Phelan, then looked up at her.

"He's dead," Neil said. "I'm sorry, lass. Duncan, I'm sorry."

"There's no sorrow in his death, Neil," she said.

"Ye shouldna feel sorry for saving my life," Duncan said. He added something in Gaelic that made Neil smile, then another that caused Neil to find the marriage license and Whitby deed in Phelan's pockets. Neil handed both to Eileen.

"How is it out there?" he asked Duncan.

"All's quiet. Princess Anne and her household are gathered and secure. Calum's comforting Miss Lockwood." He nodded at William and Mary. "What will we do wi' them?"

The king watched them with a hostile expression. Mary wept into her hands. Neil walked slowly to stand before

William, looking into the king's eyes as he slid his sword against William's neck.

"Eileen is the rightful queen," Neil told William and Mary. "If I were to draw my sword closer, I could put her on the throne. With one stroke she could be queen. Ye thought to deprive her of her birthright, William, but if she chooses, I will restore it. And avenge all those poor souls at Glencoe. I should kill ye just for that."

Eileen could hear her heart beat in the silence that followed.

"Lass, what d'ye want me to do?"

"Neil," she said. "I love you."

"And I ye, Eileen. If ye wish to be queen, ye'll ha' my sword. Ye already ha' my heart. I can give ye his head."

"I need nothing more than you, Neil. Take me home, love."

"Are ye sure, lass? Is this what ye want?"

"*Vous et nul autre*, Neil MacCurrie. Take me to Torridon."

"Ye dinna wish to be queen?"

"I want no part of it."

"So be it," Neil said, stepping away from William and lowering his sword. "But understand this, William. Ye made a grave mistake by allowing Glencoe; there are many who would avenge it with great delight, especially if they thought they could put the daughter of a Scot on the throne. And ye ha' made enemies in France by declaring war. D'ye no' think I'd find aid to topple ye? Let us live in peace, and I will not reveal the truth."

"Eileen?" William asked. "You agree to this?"

"Yes," she said. "Let us go, William, let us live in peace, and no one will know about my father. Make one move to harm us, and I'll trumpet it to the world."

William nodded.

"Good," Neil said. "If ye try to come after us, if ye think to come to Torridon, think again. I will raise the Highlands against ye; the last uprising will be nothing to what will come. And I'll come here myself, to kill ye. Do ye understand?"

William nodded.

"Say it!" Neil roared.

"I will leave you in peace."

"Good," Neil said. "Now, come. Ye're going for a boat ride."

"You cannot be serious!" William said.

Neil smiled slowly. "Ye canna think I'll just walk away and leave ye to raise the guard. Ye'll behave, aye, William?"

Neil stole one quick kiss from her, then led Eileen through the house, telling her not to look. He'd been right; all of William's men were dead. But he'd not told her that so were Phelan's and Milford's, the stairs and corridors littered with them.

She'd asked for a moment with Anne, and had received it, embracing her cousin and Celia, and even Bess, while Duncan stood with her and Neil brought William and Mary to the hired carriage that she'd arrived in with Phelan just hours—or was it years—before.

Eileen thanked Anne for all her many kindnesses, wished her well, and embraced her cousin yet again, while both women cried. Anne told Eileen she'd not known, had not imagined, all that William had condoned in his name.

"You could be queen," Anne whispered. "Do you truly not want the throne?"

"Truly, I do not." Eileen smiled. "My destiny is elsewhere."

"And you're happy?"

"I will be. I intend to be very happy."

"Then go with my blessing."

"I will. Be safe, Anne. I'm leaving you with William and Mary and their memories. Take care."

"Be happy." Anne put a hand on her cheek. "I do believe, Eileen, that you may be the wisest of us all."

Eileen shook her head. "Not wisest, Anne. Most fortunate."

She hurried through the building at Duncan's heels then, wondering where Celia had gone. He guided her outside, to where the carriage waited. Torridon men guarded the stairs and road, dark silhouettes in the dim light. Jack bounced forward to embrace her. Neil wrapped an arm around her, was about to hand her into the coach when Celia and Calum burst from the door, running down the stairs.

"Take me with you, sir!" Celia said to Neil. "Do not leave me here!"

Calum turned to Neil. "Please, sir!"

Neil shook his head. "Laddie, we canna. The lass stays here. We canna ha' her father raising the cry and William using her abduction to come after us."

"My father won't even notice I'm gone," Celia cried, and held up her satchel. "I'm ready to go to Scotland. Please!"

Neil turned to Eileen. "Lass?"

"Yes!" she said, and bundled Celia into the carriage.

Neil handed her in, and followed, taking her hand in his as he sat next to her. Calum and Duncan jumped up with the coachman. Eileen leaned back in the seat as they raced through the empty streets. She could hear the Torridon men on horseback all around her. There must be many men. They sounded like an army as they rushed through London. William, opposite her with Mary, glared.

"I cannot believe this of you, Eileen," he said.

Eileen laughed softly. "Of me, William. Oh, isn't that rich! You would have had me killed, cousin."

"Which is precisely what you will allow Torridon to do to us. He will show no mercy to an unarmed man."

Neil leaned forward then, to stare into William's eyes. "No, William, I'm no' going to kill ye. Although I do ha' to admit that when I had my sword to yer throat it did cross my mind to avenge all yer insults to Eileen. And Glencoe. And Dundee and all the men lost fighting yer armies. And I could ha', with one wee swipe of my blade, made the woman I love queen." He sat back. "Ye'll ha' years to wonder if I'll come back for ye. I promise ye this, William, if ye harass my people—and by that I mean all of Scotland, no' just Torridon—I will slit yer throat myself."

"You'd never get to me again."

Neil laughed. "Think on it, William. I'm going to let ye live, both of ye, though God kens ye dinna deserve it. I'll put ye ashore at Greenwich. Ye can find yer way home from there. In return for my mercy, ye'll do several things."

"Such as?"

"Leave Scotland alone. I want fifty years of peace. No more armies in the Highlands, no more English frigates running along my coastline. I want ye to restore Eileen's Whitby lands to her. And Ronley Hall as well. Milford's dead. Give it back to Eileen. I want the papers brought to Glen Mothin within a month. If ye dinna agree now, I'll toss ye in the Thames myself and see if ye can swim. And if ye consider going back on any of this later, think on me standing over yer bed, sword in hand, aiming at yer neck. Next time we'll come get ye, William. We willna fight yer army; we'll fight ye. And, laddie, I wouldna mind having yer blood on my hands. I want ye to remember all this, and ken that I ha' the rightful queen wi' me. If Eileen ever changes her mind about being queen, I'll see to it that she gets the throne. Think of me standing next to yer bed, then tell me I will have all I ask."

William nodded. "You will have all you ask."

Mary, weeping, called out to Eileen now. "How can you be so unfeeling?"

"Unfeeling?" Eileen asked. "Hardly the word I would use, Mary. We're letting you live, which is more than you would have done with me."

"We would never have killed you!"

"No, not yourself. But you'd suggest it, and look the other way when it happened. And then Templeton, or someone like him, would suddenly have a new home and expensive clothing. No, you would not kill me, Mary, but I wouldn't have lived long and we all know that."

They were all silent then as the carriage bumped over the rough streets. At the dock William and Mary were led onto the *Isabel*. Neil stood with Eileen at the railing as Duncan quietly gave the order to sail and the ship glided into the middle of the quiet river. In a few hours this water would teem with activity, with boats hurrying to and fro, ferries and boatmen bringing workers and merchants across.

She would never see this again, Eileen thought. She would never return to London, to this city she loved so much. She'd never smell that mixture that was uniquely London, would never see this proud city. She turned to look at Neil, who watched the lights of the city fade as they headed east.

"If ye wish, lass," Neil said, "I'll drop ye at Greenwich with them." He looked into her eyes. "Tell me what ye want."

She put her arms around his neck. "I want a kiss from the man I love. Then I want to see Torridon. I was promised a visit there, remember?"

He smiled and reached into his sporran, holding his hand out, showing her the ring on his palm. "I bought it in Inverness," he said.

She held the ring to the light. *"Vous et nul autre,"* she read, then kissed him.

He wrapped his arms around her, laughing, then pulled her to his chest and kissed her. "Will ye marry me, Eileen? Will ye spend yer life with me in Torridon?"

"Tell me you love me."

"I love ye, lassie, with all my heart. Forever."

"I'll take the next fifty years," she said and pulled his mouth to hers.

Eileen sighed contentedly and watched the light play off the roof of the cabin. She was in Neil's arms, on her way to Scotland. They'd left William and Mary at Greenwich, standing in the dim summer dawn. Before they were out of the Thames William would have raised the cry, she knew. Or would he? Would William listen to all that Neil had said? Would he leave them in peace?

"I wonder what we've done by letting William live," she said.

"Aye. So do I, lass."

"But I don't want to be queen."

"No?"

"No." She showed him her ring. *Vous et nul autre.* "This is what I want."

Neil ran a hand along her naked arm and kissed her shoulder. She turned to meet his kisses, insistent now.

They'd handfasted again, promised themselves to each other, with Duncan, Calum and Celia, and all of the Torridon men as witnesses.

And when they'd reached the open sea, he'd led her below, to the small cabin she'd had before, to make love. She'd become a woman, had given herself to this splendid man without fear. His hand moved lower now, to cup her breast. She spread her hands across his chest, then slid them down to his waist. He was ready for her and she laughed.

"Come to me, love," she said.

Neil moved on top of her, then inside her, and Eileen sighed.

"If I were queen, I'd order you to make love to me constantly."

He laughed, his lips against her neck. "I just might put ye on the throne then, lassie. That would be quite a fate."

"No," she whispered. "Torridon is our destiny."

Kathleen Givens loves to travel, read, and study history, which makes writing historical novels a perfect career. She lives in Southern California with her husband and a neurotic cat. She loves to hear from readers and can be reached at www.kathleengivens.com.

THE EDITOR'S DIARY

Dear Reader,

Discover romance at its sexiest and history at its grandest with our two Warner Forever titles this month. Find a cozy spot, put your feet up, and escape—to Regency England and seventeenth-century Scotland.

When Amanda Quick says that *SEDUCED* by **Pamela Britton** is "everything a historical romance reader could ever want," it's time to pay attention. When she adds that **Pamela Britton** "writes the kind of wonderfully romantic, sexy, witty historical romance that readers dream of discovering," it's time to read the book already! Here's what you'll find in this Regency-set tale: Lucien St. Aubyn and Elizabeth Monclair loathe each other. Elizabeth sees Lucien for the scoundrel that he is. Lucien finds Elizabeth too straitlaced, if only because she's the one woman who has ever resisted his charms. When he devises a plan to seduce her and the two are caught alone, their worst fears come true—they must marry each other!

If a spectacular drama set in seventeenth-century Scotland is your fantasy, then get ready to be swept away by **Kathleen Givens'** *THE DESTINY*. This story involving an ancient prophecy about twin brothers began with *THE LEGEND* and continues with the tale of Neil MacCurrie, Highland chieftain and enemy of the Crown. When Neil is captured in the home of a foe, the owner's royal-blooded daughter, Eileen Rowley, has her passion awakened by the handsome stranger and helps him escape. Fate brings them together again in London's gilded court, where their star-crossed destiny is tested by Neil's duties to his clan, the lure of the crown and the desires of Eileen's heart.

To find out more about Warner Forever, these April titles, and the authors, visit us at www.warnerforever.com.

With warmest wishes,

Karen Kosztolnyik, Senior Editor

P.S. Mother's Day is coming up, so be on the lookout for these perfect gifts: **Leanne Banks** offers some not-so-traditional mother's advice in the hilarious romantic comedy **SOME GIRLS DO**; and in **LAST BREATH** romantic suspense writer **Rachel Lee** offers a chilly reminder of things our mothers warned us about.

DISCOVER THE PASSION AND DRAMA
OF SCOTLAND WITH THESE TALES
OF HIGHLAND WARRIORS AND
STRONG-WILLED MAIDENS

᭱

DEVIL IN A KILT
by Sue-Ellen Welfonder

Bartered as a bride to her father's sworn enemy,
Linnet MacDonnell has no choice but to marry
nobly born Highlander Duncan MacKenzie, a man
with a forbidding past.

KNIGHT IN MY BED
by Sue-Ellen Welfonder

As chieftain of the clan MacInnes, Lady Isolde will
do anything, to protect her people—even seduce
her adversary, Donall the Bold.

THE SECRET CLAN: ABDUCTED HEIRESS
by Amanda Scott

Sir Finlay MacKenzie takes possession of Molly
Gordon for her hidden fortune. But he soon realizes
what he truly wants is her heart.

DISCOVER MORE OF THE PASSIONATE,
BREATHTAKING WORLD OF
MEDIEVAL SCOTLAND!

MASTER OF THE HIGHLANDS
By Sue-Ellen Welfonder

Hot-tempered Iain MacLean meets his match in Lady Madeline Drummond, a fiery noble-woman seeking revenge against those who destroyed her family.

Coming to your local bookstore
in August 2003 from
Warner Forever